SWEET POSSESSION

Brander touched Kelda's face. She tensed and drew away from him. His facial features hardened before his hand reached behind her neck to draw her close.

"Fight me if you must, Kelda of the Vikings, but know in the end I will possess you."

"You may take my body, because you are physically stronger than I am, but you will never possess me."

He lowered his head, his face moving to hers. At first his eyes captured her reflection, then her. Caught in their velvet depths, she was willingly drowning in this wild, mysterious world that was Brander of the Iroquois. With no struggle at all, she was giving herself to this barbarian.

Angered by the thought of his taking her so easily, she stiffened. But his mouth clamped down on hers, in a hot and demanding kiss, the like of which Kelda had never before known.

Finally, he raised his head and laughed harshly. "You are not unaffected by my touch, Viking. I hear your response in your breathing. I feel it in your heartbeat."

"Aye, my body is affected," she admitted, "but not my heart."

"Given time, I will possess that also."

VIKING CAPTIVE

EMMA MERRITT

ZEBRA BOOKS
KENSINGTON PUBLISHING CORP.

ZEBRA BOOKS

are published by

Kensington Publishing Corp.
475 Park Avenue South
New York, NY 10016

First printing: January, 1992

Printed in the United States of America

Chapter One

The new world was wild and untamed; so was the barbarian.

His muscular legs were covered with brown leggings of soft, worked leather and knee-high boots, their cuffs decorated with colorful beadwork and a tawny fringe. The shirt, the same shade and fabric as the fringe, accented the bronzed column of his throat and stone-hewn face.

Unlike the countless warriors who had swarmed ashore from the long, slender birch-bark boats with him to surround Kelda and her Vikings, he was taller, his shoulders broader. Also in contrast to them, his black hair was cut short to brush against the collar of his shirt.

"We of the Iroquois have long awaited your return, Viking." The barbarian spoke Norse, his words underscored with disdain.

Kelda's heart skipped a beat to hear him speak her language. Surely she and her Vikings were in the right place; these were the people whom they sought.

"Your waiting has not been for me," she said. "This is my first visit to your land."

Perhaps already she had found the Skrelling seed. This man, this barbarian could be Jarl Thoruald's son, the one he had sired thirty winters ago when he and a band of Vikings had visited these shores. Her brother by the law.

She raised her white shield a little higher. "I am Kelda, leader of these Vikings and adopted daughter to Jarl Thoruald. My Vikings and I come in peace. Are you the chief of these warriors?"

"I am a war chief, but not the high chief."

"I demand to see your high chief."

In answer, his gaze contemptuously swept over her, quickly dismissing the shield, lingering on her hair.

She was not surprised that he was fascinated by it. Of all her attributes, it was her most beautiful, her most striking. When she was a child her mother often held her on her lap, brushing her hair and telling her how fortunate she was that it was thick and curly and golden yellow like the sun. Truly, she had been blessed by Sol, the sun goddess. Because of this Kelda claimed the sun as her talisman.

She touched the gold brooch—a likeness of the sun—that fastened her mantle about her neck.

Throughout Kelda's entire twenty-one years she had been complimented on her blond tresses. The young women had envied it; the young men had admired it. It had been her husband's pride and glory . . . before he died.

She felt the barbarian's gaze as it slowly, carefully moved over her clothing: the big-sleeved white shirt, the yellow leather jerkin, the tight-fitting brown trousers, the soft knee-high leather boots she wore.

He smiled, but the gesture touched only his lips. "You call yourself a warrior. I trust you can wield the sword you wear strapped over your shoulder and the dagger hanging about your waist."

"I can."

"Yet you and your men made no effort to defend yourselves when we surrounded you?"

"We come in peace." Again she held up the white shield. "My men and I have sailed close to the shores during these past few weeks in hopes you would see us and in hopes we could draw you out."

That was the easy part of their mission, she thought.

6

The hardest part was going to be convincing the Skrellings they came in peace—especially after the devastating raid the Vikings from their village had launched against them two winters past.

"If that was your plan, it was successful." Clearly he doubted what she said.

"It was my plan," Kelda said, regretting immediately that she quickly leaped to a defensive position.

"Then, Viking, that is your weakness."

Summarily dismissing her, he turned his head to issue an order in his native language. She saw several of the Skrellings board her ship. Checking to see that no Vikings hid there, Kelda surmised. Other Skrellings surrounded her warriors and bunched them into a tight circle.

"Turn them loose," she ordered.

Impervious to her, Brander barked another command. His warriors disarmed the Vikings and moved them away from Kelda.

"Return their weapons!" she shouted and started toward them. The barbarian nodded his head, and one of his men caught her. She twisted but could not break out of the grip.

Protesting their own treatment, the Vikings shouted oaths against the Skrellings and jabbed their fists in the air. Kelda felt the heat of their accusatory gazes; they blamed her for the predicament in which they found themselves.

"We landed under the white shield of peace," Kelda grunted, still twisting, but her captor held her firmly. His fingers bit into the flesh of her arms. "Return their weapons to them immediately," she repeated.

No Viking wanted to lose his weapon, especially his sword. He wanted to die with it in his hand in order to carry it to Valhalla with him. To lose his weapons in battle was a situation a warrior could handle because he could still die gloriously; to have them taken from him without a fight was a dishonor.

"War chief!" Kelda shouted.

7

The barbarian turned his head in her direction, his eyes flicking over her. The early morning breeze blew strands of hair across his forehead, and behind him a ray of sunlight splintered through the haze of dawn to set his hair on fire with a deep reddish hue.

"In case you did not hear me—".

"I heard," he answered softly. "You shouted loudly enough for all the inhabitants of the forest to hear. In case you do not understand, I am the one who gives orders around here, not you."

Although she looked directly into his eyes, she was not aware of their color, only their darkness, only the intense loathing they openly projected toward her.

"What are you called?" she asked. "How did you learn my language?"

"What I am called and how I learned your language are not your concern, Viking."

His gaze shifted from her to fasten on a distant point, his attention already directed elsewhere. He motioned to one of his warriors.

"You are wrong," Kelda said. "My Vikings and I have come to Skrellingland to—"

The black eyes bored into her. She had his full attention. With another nod, his warrior turned her loose and stepped away.

"Skrellingland! Land of the barbarians!" The war chief's voice was low and controlled, but his visage was darkly angry. "We are not barbarians. We are the Ongwanonsionni—the People of the Extended Lodge. We are a tribe of the Iroquois—the most powerful confederation of the Forestland people."

Kelda had seen many magnificent Vikings, but had never witnessed such an overpowering presence as that of the barbarian. Standing inches in front of her, he was even taller and more muscular than she had first imagined. He made her feel small and fragile, and she was a tall woman.

"Your people with their white shields and words of peace are the barbarians. When you came two years

8

ago, you claimed to come in peace, but you lied and deceived us."

"I did not come two years ago. I do not lie to you, nor do I deceive you. Perhaps others did, but not I."

Their gazes locked. As before, his irises were black and unreadable; then they were hard, an emotion akin to hatred swimming in their depths. The intensity of his gaze startled her. Beyond that she saw no color. She saw strength and power and arrogance.

She felt emanating from him the same characteristics she had seen in his eyes. At this moment he was the mountains that spanned her country, unyielding and indomitable. He was the wind-swept shores of the sea. Always there. He was the long, sleek dragonship, the proud and arrogant conqueror of the sea.

Like the mountains, the wind-swept shore, and the dragonship, he was a dangerous force to be reckoned with.

He would not be easily convinced of their peaceful mission. He wanted to believe the worst of them.

"I, Kelda of the Vikings, speak the truth. I give you my word."

"I have little regard for any words spoken by the Vikings, especially their promises, Viking woman. You will not have the opportunity to take advantage of us a second time," he vowed. "I, Brander, War Chief of the Iroquois, promise you that."

Brander! His name was Norse. Was this a confirmation that he was the offspring she sought?

"Help me find the answers to my question," Kelda said, "and my Vikings and I will be gone from your shores to cause you no more trouble."

He laughed, the sound derisive and mocking. "Your going and coming are no longer at your command, Viking woman. Until the village elders decide differently, you and your men are our . . . guests."

"Prisoners, you mean," Kelda said. "After that, what? Slavery or death?"

His gaze raked hotly and suggestively over her body,

lingering on her breasts, then finally coming back to her face, to rest on her lips.

"Slavery is a good guess," he said. "But not death. You have too much life in your body. You are not as young as one would hope, but you are young enough and you are yet good to look upon. I will take many moons of pleasure from you."

"Although you place little regard in the words of a Viking," Kelda said, "you can be sure to regard my words, barbarian. I promise I will never *give* you my body or any pleasure from it."

"I wait not to be given, Viking. I take what I want."

The breeze blew harder, whipping hair from her headband and wrapping the long strands around her face and neck. To remove them she raised her right hand; he did, too; their fingertips touched. As if burned, she jerked away from him. Yet she did not lower her hand. Her gaze never faltered from his.

His expression never changing, he moved her hand aside. She lowered it so that it hovered above the hilt of the stiletto that hung at her waist. The breeze picked up momentum, more hair blew across her face, tickling her cheeks and the skin beneath her nose.

He wanted to touch her hair, she knew. He wanted to remove the strands from her face. She sucked air into her lungs. She tensed and laid her hand loosely on her weapon. She would kill this man before she let him put his pagan hands on her, before she let him touch her. She curled her fingers around the dagger.

No sooner had she made her resolve, than Brander's hand covered hers. He moved closer to her and squeezed until she felt the bite of tears.

"Nay, Viking. That will be a grave mistake. If I do not wound or kill you, my men will. I allowed you to keep your weapons because I wanted to see what game you would play with me. Be aware, I have told my warriors to watch and to make sure you do nothing foolish."

Refusing to let this man see any show of weakness in

her, Kelda blinked the tears back and stiffened. Out of the corner of her eyes she saw those Skrelling warriors closest to her, standing with their arrows nocked. Her gaze strayed to the ones who guarded her men.

She had no one to protect her. Her men had only her to protect them. She — and they, because of her — found themselves in a dire situation.

"I'm the only one among my braves who wants you alive," Brander said. "They would prefer to take their revenge on you and your Vikings. They would like to torture your men slowly, dismembering their bodies part by part. They would eventually do the same to you, but first they would rape you. Not one of them, but all of them, one at a time, each following the other. They would repay in kind what your people did to ours."

He twisted her fingers, prying them from the dagger. He clasped her hand tightly. She thought he would break her fingers and render her weapon hand useless.

"That kind of torture leads to a slow, painful death. Even if you should live, you would be filled with self-disgust and hatred."

The pain was so intense his words hardly registered.

"All you would have to look forward to is the same punishment over and over." His grasp slackened.

Kelda let out the breath she was holding, and she looked from the countenance of one Skrelling to another. She did not doubt a word the barbarian told her. All of his warriors wore the same expression as he: hatred and contempt.

Keeping the one hand imprisoned, Brander lifted his other to clasp strands of her hair. His fingers brushed against her skin. Though light, almost no touch at all, she felt it throughout her entire body. It angered and unsettled her. His facial features which appeared to be carved out of stone never changed.

"Your hair is much to be admired."

He released her hand, which she flexed.

"Gold like the sun. And your eyes — they are blue like

11

the sky." Though the words were spoken like a compliment, they seemed to be grudgingly given. "Aye, you are good to look upon, Kelda of the Vikings, even in your warrior's attire."

He held his hand out, palm upward and looked at the strands of hair. He rubbed them between his fingers and spoke to his braves. Those closest to him nodded. He hooked the curl behind her ear, then laid his palm against her cheek. Startled, Kelda did not move. Fire—pure fire—rushed through her veins.

"Your coloring is also pretty, Viking woman. You are so white compared to my darkness."

His words insinuated intimacy; it was like a caress between lovers. But there was no love between Kelda and this man. She tensed, then pulled back from him. His hand moved quicker than she to catch her hair in his fist. He pulled. Her scalp stung.

"That was unwise."

He tugged the hair harder, bringing her closer. So close she could feel the warmth of his breath against her skin. So close she could see the texture of his skin. So close she could see the image of her face in the hard, ebony eyes.

"Turn my hair loose." She gritted the words between clenched teeth.

"You no longer give the orders. I do," Brander said. "Do not fight me, and you will not hurt yourself."

He spoke to his warriors who laughed. He smiled. The smile softened the color of his eyes so that they reminded Kelda of the midnight—that brief second of time when night and morning merge to become one, when blue and black become the same color. A mysterious and evocative color, their true color.

"If I did not need you, Skrelling," Kelda swore softly, "I would kill you this very minute. But I will wait. When I do kill you, I will take great pleasure in the doing."

He laughed, the sardonic sound mocking her. "If you kill me, Viking, it will be from pure pleasure. The pleasure a woman gives to a man when she makes love to him."

"Never!" Kelda spat the words at him.

"Never?"

He released her hair to draw the tips of his fingers over her face. Sensation spilled through her body, sensation she had never experienced before, that seemed as wild and unpredictable as this wilderness, as this man.

When he removed his hand, when the sensation ceased, she felt empty and alone. As if he read her thoughts, as if he sensed her emotions, he laughed. It served as the impetus she needed to move away from him.

"I am not chattel; I am no man's property," Kelda exclaimed. "I am Kelda, leader of these Vikings."

"You are mine!"

Yes, this woman was his!

She was the instrument of his revenge. She would pay for what the Vikings had done to him, for what they had taken away from him, for what they had denied him. His heart was hardened to the Norse, and unlike those women in his village thirty winters ago, he would not allow a Norse to enter the private chambers of his heart.

The Viking was spirited, and he liked that in a woman. Spirit. Vigor. Strength. Defiance. All of these seemed to be essential elements of the woman standing so tall and proud in front of him. Elements that attracted him to her, that made his revenge more pleasant.

"I am the daughter of a jarl," she said. "You would do well to treat me with the honor due a chief."

Brander heard the throb of anger, the venom that underscored her words.

"Had you behaved like a chief, I would honor you. But you surrendered your men without a fight. You led them into captivity without letting them lift their weapons. I hold you in contempt for professing to be their

13

leader. I hold them in contempt for following one like you."

"I am a skilled warrior and a good leader," Kelda told him. "I am following the orders of my jarl. Now, I demand you take me to your high chief. I will squander no more of my time with you."

Brander gazed into outraged blue eyes. Sunlight glistened on the long, dark lashes that framed them. He saw the flush of anger that tinged her cheeks. He lifted his hand and reached out to touch the creamy flesh again, but she dodged away from him. Again he imprisoned her with his hand and pulled her to him.

In his native language, he murmured, "Before I am through with you, Viking woman, you will not back away from me and you will not consider time spent with me squandered. You will beg for my touch, for my possession. Fate has sent you to these shores so that I may avenge the deaths of my family."

His gaze slowly traveled from her lips, to her cheeks, finally to her blond hair. His hand touched it, the strands smooth like the feel of crystal, clear water between his fingers, delicate like the velvet petals of a newly opened flower blossom.

Again he spoke in Iroquois. "I will have touched more than your golden hair and the white flesh of your cheeks. I will have touched and possessed every inch of your body. I will have touched and possessed you in ways you never dreamed possible."

Although the Viking did not understand what he said, she glared at him, hatred and defiance swirling in the depths of those big blue eyes.

"Take me to your high chief!"

"Aye," Brander said in Norse, a mocking smile lazing across his mouth, "I will take you, Viking. Be assured of that."

Chapter Two

"What are we going to do with the Vikings?" an Iroquois warrior asked Brander.

"Take them to the village as we planned," he answered.

"There we will take our revenge."

"Aye, Black Bear." Brander again looked at Kelda, his gaze traveling once again from the top of her head to the bottom of her booted feet.

"The Viking woman is yours." Black Bear asked no question. He made a statement.

Brander nodded.

"You will put your brand on her?"

"Aye."

The warrior laughed, and his gaze drifted from the large sword across her back to the stiletto at her waist. "I have no doubt you will brand her, my chief, but beware, this Viking woman would enjoy leaving her mark on you."

"Nay," Brander returned softly, "no woman has the power. I touch, my brother. I take and I give at my pleasure, but I am never touched. Never."

He turned and called, "Flat Tail Beaver, you and your braves take the prisoners and return to the village by canoe. The woman will ride with me."

With economy of motion and in silence, the Iroquois carried out Brander's command.

Kelda caught his arm and said, "I must return to the *langskip*. I have something I must get."

He said nothing.

"The token of friendship," she explained. "The gift that our high chief, Jarl Thoruald, sends to your high chief."

"You have said the right words, Viking," he answered. "Your gift would be no more than a token of friendship. We seek friendship, not the token."

"I would have the gift," she said firmly. "I would let your high chief know we respect him. This is done by the bringing of a gift of peace."

Brander's gaze swept to the anchored ship. With the red and yellow shields lined along the sides, it was majestic. Although the sail was lowered and rested on a support beam, it boasted the same brilliant colors as the shields. He looked even higher to see the yellow banner waving in the breeze. Embroidered on it was a large red sun.

"May I get the gift?" she asked.

He nodded. "So be it."

He and several of his braves accompanied her to the *langskip*. First, she lowered her banner, then she searched through her trunk for her leather pouch that contained the gift.

Leaving a small party to guard the ship, the Skrellings launched their long, slender birch bark canoes loaded with passengers. Brander, traveling with two other braves, was in the lead, his only captive Kelda. They navigated through the inlet, finally turning into a smaller body of water—a river, Kelda guessed from her knowledge of the sea.

When they landed, Brander quietly issued orders, his braves obeying. Several warriors hoisted each canoe, bottom up, to carry it ashore. Others guarded the Vikings, keeping them separated and away from Kelda.

Sending scouts ahead, Brander led the party single-file through the forest. He was followed immediately by Kelda and three braves. Next came those who bore the canoes, then the Vikings who were hobbled together and closely guarded.

Kelda and her men were accustomed to walking, but the Skrellings traveled at a trot. Hardly an hour had passed before she was winded. In the distance she heard the grumbling and curses of the Vikings and knew that some — if not most — of the discontent was directed toward her. Brander spared not a backward glance as he led the way down the narrow pathway.

After an hour of traveling — in circles to keep Kelda and her men from finding their way back to the *langskip* if they managed to escape, she figured — the barbarian raised his hand and signaled they would rest. He motioned the guards to march her warriors further down the stream so that she and they were still separated and could not talk; he kept Kelda close to him.

She drew in a deep breath and dropped to the ground, landing on a soft, leafy plant that grew thickly and covered a large flat area. She leaned back to enjoy the cool foliage and the breeze against her body.

One of the Skrellings lightly prodded her with the point of his spear and pointed to the stream. With his hand he motioned that she should get herself a drink of water. She shook her head. Tired, she wanted to rest. The man moved away from her.

Laying the shield down, she spread her mantle and sat on it. She gazed at the tall, stately trees, their boughs covered in thick, green foliage. All around her was the sound of the forest, the gurgling of water in the close distance, the chirrup of birds, the scurry of small furry animals as they darted about.

This bountiful new land was full of the resources her people needed. Water for commuting; trees for

17

ships and homes; *mosur* trees for their burls out of which they would carve their eating utensils; game for food. She picked up a handful of the dark earth — and rich soil for their crops.

Kelda closed her eyes and laid her head back, resting it on the thickness of her cape that cowled in the back. This was the most peaceful place she had been in a long time. She breathed in deeply several times, the babbling of the water growing louder and more enticing. She loved water, and this was a fresh water inlet, one where she could bathe and wash her hair without having a salt residue.

The sounds of the forest abruptly quieted, and Kelda felt *his* presence. He walked silently upon the leaves so that she heard no sound to indicate he had moved to where she was, but she knew without opening her eyes *the barbarian* was here. Slowly she lifted her lids and saw his feet, one planted on each side of her. Her gaze slid up beyond his hips, his torso, finally to his face.

It seemed to Kelda that he never moved, but the next thing she knew, his hand balled around the mantle at her neck and he jerked her to her feet. She stared into eyes that were deep, black caverns of hatred and contempt.

He was like the other Skrellings, yet he was different. She remembered the play of sunlight in his hair, the reddish hue that highlighted the black, and his height and breadth of shoulders when compared to his fellow warriors.

She had studied the group even more at a closer distance as they rested and had noticed another difference between the leader and his companions. His face was clean shaven, but she could see the shadow of close-cut beard stubble. The faces of the other Skrellings were smooth; they grew no facial hair.

"Why are you not drinking the water?" he demanded.

18

"I wanted to rest first."

"You obey my orders first!" Cold, black eyes bored into hers. "It is the custom of my people to beat disobedient prisoners and slaves in public. Unless you want that to happen to you, you are advised to obey me. Drink. You need sustenance for the journey ahead of us."

Although he spoke harshly, although she resented his mistreatment of her, she was held captive by his enigmatic eyes. She would have liked to remove her gaze from his, but by some inexplicable force she was drawn to him.

Equal parts of anger and frustration rushed through her. It was humiliating enough to be physically captured by this man, but to be visually and sensually bound to him was degrading. He led her to the river.

"Drink."

She glared at him. With his ordering her to drink, a part of her—the obstinate part—wanted to refuse, no matter what her body wanted or needed. But the wiser part knew she must keep up her strength.

"Turn me loose, and I will."

He withdrew his hand from her neck. In an act of defiance she reached up and brushed the wrinkles from the material he had released, as if to brush away his touch. She straightened the cowl of her cape before she knelt by the bank of the brook to scoop water to her mouth by hand. When she finished, she rose. Face to face with him, she again returned his glare.

"Do you wish to drag me back?" she asked sarcastically.

She saw his facial muscles tense.

He opened his mouth as if to say something; then he closed it again. He tensed and immediately directed his attention elsewhere. Something was wrong. Although his body never moved, his head never turned, his eyes darted about. Kelda glanced at those around her. Routine in the camp continued as before, but she sensed an alertness that had not been present only seconds ago.

The Iroquois warriors, attuned to the sights, sounds, and smells of their forest, were aware of change. They tightly bunched the Vikings together and hid them in the shelter of the forest. Uncertain about what was happening, Kelda worried about the safety of her men. Brander whistled softly — the sound reminiscent of that made by the birds Kelda had heard earlier.

She heard more bird calls, and he relaxed. Within seconds the scouts he had dispatched when they began their overland journey trotted into the camp, not stopping until they reached him. In hushed tones they conversed. He nodded and waved his hand, his men bringing her warriors into the clearing again. The scouts went to the river for a drink of water, and Brander, bending, plucked a twig from a bush and chewed on it. He turned to her.

"We are going to be joined by others from my village." He spat out the leaf. "They have been out for several days hunting."

As much as he loathed the Vikings, Kelda wondered why he bothered to explain to her.

A sardonic smile played at the corners of his lips. "We have already begun preparing for the feast to celebrate our capture of the Norsemen. The women are also ready. According to our custom, they receive the prisoners, meting out punishment as they deem fit. Some they torture to death slowly, painfully. Others they keep as slaves. The last, the bravest, are adopted into the tribe."

"I would rather be killed or kept as a slave than be adopted into your tribe." Kelda hurled the words at him. She might have known his purpose was spiteful; she presumed spite was his primary motivation.

"I wager your chances of having your wish granted are great, Viking."

A rustling of leaves caught Kelda's attention, and she turned to see four Iroquois warriors emerging from the forest into the clearing where she and Brander were standing. A long pole rested on the shoulders of two of them who walked single file. On it hung varieties of animals of the forest. The leader of the hunters moved to Brander and spoke to him.

When Kelda had first met Brander, heard him speak her language, and learned that his name was also Norse, she was excited. She thought perhaps she had found the jarl's son. Now, she wondered how many more among the Iroquois were possibly half-Norse.

This man *had* to be, Kelda thought. His hair, hanging in braids, was a deep auburn as was the shadow of beard on his face. Perhaps he was the son of the jarl whom she sought.

The conversation was getting heated when the hunter's gaze slid past Brander to light on Kelda. He raised a brow. The conversation continued. Finally the hunter laughed and clapped the chieftain on the back.

He walked to where Kelda stood. "I am Rauthell of the Iroquois."

"I am Kelda," she said.

Her gaze ran over Rauthell. His name was well-chosen. He was the man of the red well.

Still speaking Norse, Rauthell said over his shoulder, "You believe the Master of Life has blessed my hunt, my brother. I think he has blessed you more greatly. My trophy is three dead deer, a bear, and several squirrels, all of which will be gone by the going down of the next sun. Yours is a lovely woman who will fill your lonely nights for many moons."

Rauthell's dark eyes flickered over her hair, as did Brander's. "A lovely Viking woman with hair the

21

color of gold, War Chief. Would you consider making a trade? My bed is empty."

Brander's sardonic smile widened. "Since my bed is also empty, my friend, you would have to have something of great value to barter."

"I am not property to be bartered about!" Kelda shouted, not caring about her display of temper.

She jerked her head away from Brander and winced when his fist balled in her hair and he tugged forcibly.

"The two of you are not going to discuss me as if I were not present."

Once men had bandied over Kelda. Not again. Not *ever again!*

"Quiet!"

Brander spoke the one word softly, but Kelda felt the full impact of his fury. He pulled her to him by the hair until their faces almost touched. The force with which he pulled caused her head to ache. His warm breath, smelling clean from the herb he had chewed, blew against her skin to make her more aware of him, somehow to diminish the pain he inflicted on her.

"You belong to me. Never ever address me in that tone again. I do not believe in beating prisoners until their usefulness is spent, but if you defy me in public, you leave me no choice. No woman—especially a Viking woman—will humiliate me in front of my men."

Kelda stared at the man who claimed her as his prisoner, who held her prisoner by a fistful of her hair. There had been many men during her twenty-one winters whom she had despised, but she had never despised one as she did this . . . this barbarian.

Gravely Rauthell added, "He means what he says, Viking. It would be in your best interest to obey him." He smiled reassuringly. "You will find the Firebrand is not such a hard master when you please him."

"Firebrand. Pooh!"

She spat on the ground, the spittle barely missing the tip of Brander's moccasin. She spoke to him.

"If you are related to the fire at all, chief of the Skrellings, you are the tiniest of embers, easily carried away by the wind or in the beak of the most inconsequential bird."

He studied her momentarily. Finally his lips twitched and his eyes actually lost some of their anger. Releasing her hair, his lips moved into a slight smile.

"I am well named, and you will do well to remember."

"I, too, am well named, Skrelling. I am Kelda, named after the spring water." She stared fully into his face. "I am the one who can put out the fire. You will do well to remember that."

Finally he said, "Aye, I will remember that, Viking woman."

His voice softened. "I promise, you will be the one to douse the fire of the Firebrand. Even if the elders should decide to let your warriors return to their land, I will keep you with me. You will provide me with great sport."

"Aye." Kelda stared fearlessly into his eyes. "I promise great sport. I will kill you."

Brander mocked her. "So you said earlier, Viking. But I doubt you can. It will take more than a mere woman to kill the Firebrand."

"If you are around me long enough, Skrelling, you will learn that I am more rather than mere."

Brander's smile turned into laughter, rich, warm, and mellow. He truly laughed. Kelda could see it on his face and in his eyes.

"Are you proposing to douse the flames of the firebrand with the little toy you have banded around your waist?"

His hand slid between their bodies. The thickness of her clothes was inadequate to protect her skin from the searing heat of his touch. He pulled the stiletto from the sheath and pressed the tip against her chin.

"With this?"

"By Thor!" Kelda breathed, her victory snatched away quicker than she had gained it. "At this very minute I wish I had never sworn my oath to Thoruald to find his son. I would show you what I can do with that little toy—as you put it—Skrelling."

"Let me show you what I can do with it." His voice was low, dangerously low.

He released the pressure of the knife and drew it along the outline of her chin, down the column of her throat. It was ice cold against her skin; it was deadly.

"One cut from here to here—" he drew the knife beneath her chin from ear to ear "—and you will bleed to death."

Her argument forgotten, she breathed in deeply. His eyes, blacker than the tar with which they painted the bow of their ships, were merciless daggers as they bored into hers.

"Do not call me Skrelling again." He shifted the blade to trace the outline of her mouth. "From now on, I am Chief Brander of the Iroquois."

"I may be compelled to call you Chief Brander," she said, forcing a calmness into her voice that she no longer possessed, "but that does not make you a chief and does not mean that I respect you as one. No matter what I call you, you know I think of you as a barbarian. You will always be a barbarian to me."

Brander glared at her for endless seconds before he pushed her away and ran his other thumb down the

24

blade. A thin line of blood dotted his finger.

"Your toy is sharp enough to silence a defiant tongue."

"You may cut out the tongue, *Chief Brander*, but you will not cut out the defiance. As long as there is breath in this body, I will fight to be what I am — a free Viking and a free woman. I will never be any man's chattel, especially yours."

"Chattel is not the word I would use for the services I envision you performing, Kelda of the Vikings."

As he had done before, he allowed his gaze to run the full length of her body, lingering on her breasts first, then on her hips. He lightly drew the tip of the dagger across the fullness of her breasts.

Kelda was afraid of the man, yet he excited her. Her nipples hardened and peaked against the softness of her shirt. She sucked in her breath. Brander chuckled, softly and sardonically.

"Let me make one thing clear, Viking. You *are* mine!"

He spoke so softly she had to lean forward to hear him, but not for once did she doubt the threat — or promise — in his words.

"Perhaps I should take you now to prove it."

Her breasts rose and fell. He touched her cheeks with his knuckles, and she twisted her head violently. His fingers trailed over her throat and cupped over her breast, caressing the soft mound. His thumb moved in a rhythmic circle over the crest.

She inhaled sharply.

Quelling the quaking in her body, she looked at the man who stood in front of her. She had been told about the feelings that exist between a man and a woman, but this was the closest she had been to experiencing these sensations. She definitely had not felt this with Ragnar. He had been her friend not her lover, and he had died before they physically became husband and wife.

"For now I only own your body," Brander said, easing the knife into the scabbard, "but soon I will also possess your soul."

Chapter Three

"You have captured the Vikings."

An old woman, her hair liberally streaked with white, stepped forward. Behind her stood a large group of women and children, war clubs and sundry weapons in hand. She looked first at Kelda, then at the Viking men who were being guarded near the entrance into the village. She motioned, directing part of the hostile group to them. She returned her gaze to Brander.

"You have not beaten the prisoners," she charged. "If we do not discipline them, how shall they know their place in our tribe? To be good slaves they must be conquered."

Gray Dawn walked around Kelda several times, then reached out to touch her. Glaring at the woman, Kelda edged closer to Brander. Amused at her reaction, he wondered if she was aware she was seeking protection from him, the hated barbarian. He saw one of the Vikings scowl and lurch as if to come to Kelda's rescue. The guard hit the warrior across the forehead with the shaft of his spear, the blow drawing blood that ran down to mat in the blond beard. Kelda started as if to run to him, but Brander clasped her arm and kept her by his side. She glared at him, hatred spitting out of her eyes.

"They must run the gauntlet," Gray Dawn declared.

Brander held the white shield up for all the villagers to see. "They came with this."

"I care not that they came with the white shield," Gray Dawn exclaimed. "They are our prisoners, and we will follow our custom in dealing with them."

"*Ho!*" A younger woman stepped forward. "I, Woman of the Planting, demand a man to replace my husband who was killed by the Vikings two winters ago. I will take one of the Vikings as my slave."

Kelda glanced at her men, her anxious gaze seeking out the one who was wounded. Concern shadowed her face.

"And I make my demands, too," another one shouted. "I will have two slaves. Another I will choose to adopt into my family as my son."

"We will take the Vikings to the Council of Elders," Brander said. "It is the elders' authority to decide the fate of the Vikings. If they declare them to be prisoners, so be it."

"We already have a custom," Gray Dawn said. "The prisoners belong to us—to the women."

"I, Brander, War Chief of the Iroquois, have spoken. Make your argument to the Council after I have spoken to them and given my report."

Gray Dawn stepped aside, but her face was yet lined with anger and contempt. She reached out and caught a handful of Kelda's hair, holding the blade of her dagger to it as if to cut. Immediately Kelda tensed.

"Stand still, or your hair will be shorn," Brander commanded softly in Norse, his gaze never leaving the Iroquois woman's face.

"If she cuts one strand of my hair—" Kelda curled her fingers around the hilt of her stiletto "—I will deal with her personally and will not be merciful."

"I will take the woman's hair," Gray Dawn shouted.

The women and children shouted.

"Turn her loose." When Brander knocked Gray Dawn's hand and the dagger from Kelda's hair, the Iroquois woman pinned a venomous gaze to him.

Circling his arm around Kelda's waist, Brander pulled her close to him. The Viking woman was his. No one, not even the village women, would take her from him. He would not let them touch her.

Gray Dawn sulked.

"I am going to speak to the Council of the Elders," Brander repeated, this time with the force of anger behind his words. "If you have an argument, present it to them. They make the final decisions for the People of the Forestland."

The women and children, muttering their anger, backed away. They relented for the moment. The Vikings cursed the Iroquois.

"Come with me and put up no resistance," Brander instructed in Norse to Kelda as he began to walk up the main street. To a group of his warriors whom he passed, he yelled another order in his native language. Kelda glanced over to see the Vikings being marched in the opposite direction from her.

Hauk, her mentor and advisor, her second in command, dug his heels in the ground. The cut on his forehead still bled, yet one of the Iroquois slapped him across the shoulder with a short leather whip. Hauk winced. Still he did not move. The brave shouted angrily; he lashed him harder, blow after blow.

"Stop!" Catching Brander's arm, Kelda shouted, "Order them to stop!"

Brander turned to stare at her in surprised shock. He pried her fingers loose and clasped them tightly in his hand. "You take much liberty, Viking woman," he said. "You have pushed me too far. The women are correct when they say you need to be aware of your status in our village."

"How is that done, Chief Brander?" Kelda demanded sarcastically.

Brander caught a handful of her hair with one hand and whipped her stiletto out of the sheath with the other. "One way is by shearing your hair, Viking."

Not my hair! Kelda wanted to scream.

"Or by beating you. And by branding you."

Kelda flinched from the last words and grasped her right wrist. She rubbed her thumb over the small scar.

"Possibly all three."

Holding onto her knife, Brander released her hair and caught her wrist. Long strides carried him down one of the dirt streets, Kelda stumbling along behind him, her satchel swinging back and forth, brushing against her hip.

Over her shoulder she saw the Skrellings march her men to the other side of the village from her. Beside her ran the women and children, laughing and taunting. They swung their clubs, the sharpened edges of the tomahawks barely missing her.

Kelda had a strong desire to turn on her tormentors. She knew they far outnumbered her, but she despised herself for being in a position to have to suffer this. She knew, as did the barbarian, that her weapons were useless to her. Her purpose was one of peace not of war. She was to find Jarl Thoruald's son.

"Where are you taking me?" she demanded.

Brander continued to drag her up the street.

Kelda dug her heels into the ground and yanked her arm. Her resistance did not faze him. He never broke stride.

"I want to know where you are taking me."

He pulled her all the harder, and she stumbled, almost falling. Because he never slackened his pace, she had to run to keep up with him. The women and children cheered him. Kelda cursed him for ever having been born, but he paid her scant attention. Finally they arrived at a lodge.

"I will take care of the Viking woman," he told the spectators.

"We would see how you torture her," Gray Dawn said. "We would know she has been subdued."

"You will know," Brander replied.

"How?" the old woman asked.

"You will hear, and you will see a subdued woman when I bring her out," Brander answered and turned to look at Kelda. "I promise you, Gray Dawn, I hate the Vikings as much, if not more so than any of you."

"Ho!" the old woman cried and nodded her head. "They brought you much grief, my son the Firebrand."

"I will mete them out more grief than they have given me, old woman."

She nodded and turned, waving the crowd some distance from the house.

Brander picked Kelda up and moved inside, dropping her unceremoniously on the bench built against the wall of the entry room. He stood over her, his arms crossed over his chest. His eyes and visage were furiously dark.

"The one thing you can count on, Viking woman, is that no one in this village is sympathetic to the Norse, not after their raid two winters past. Everyone here lost someone or something to them,

31

and they are hungry — greedy — for revenge."

He reached for a leather strap that hung on a peg on the wall. *To beat me with!* Kelda wondered, fighting back panic at such a thought.

"The women in particular will hate you because you are different, and the men of the village will be attracted to you."

He drew his arm back. He did intend to beat her! The strap lashed against the wall next to Kelda, the slap cracking through the air. She jumped and immediately regretted having reacted to the threat. She regretted even more than he had the pleasure of seeing her react.

Kelda lowered her lashes so that he could not see the fear in her eyes. The leather sliced by her again cracking against the wall. This time she held herself still and stifled her cry of fright. Even if the barbarian struck her, she would not cry aloud. She would never show fear in front of him or his people.

"They will lust after your body and your long golden hair."

Shaking inwardly but hoping to give the appearance of nonchalance, Kelda made a study of her clothes. She pushed up on the bench, straightening first her shirt, then the mantle about her shoulders. She straightened the strap of the satchel and brushed the dirt from her trousers.

In quick, successive movements, Brander struck the wall on either side of Kelda, the slap of leather ringing in her ears, echoing throughout the room. Again she did not flinch.

His hand flew out, his fingers gripping painfully into her chin and cheeks. "Pay attention to me when I speak to you."

"When you spoke, I listened," she answered quietly, aware of his closeness, aware of the leather strap that brushed against her cheeks. The odor of

32

worked leather filled her nostrils. "For the most part, you are slinging the leather strap around, trying to instill fear in me. That I refuse to let you do, barbarian."

"Have you no regard for your life?"

"Yes," Kelda replied, "I do. I hope you do also."

He relaxed his grip, but did not remove his hand or move his body. Still she felt the graze of the strap on her face. All she could see was the broad expanse of his shoulders covered in the soft leather jacket.

"You appear to be so innocent," he murmured. "Yet I know you are not."

"I know what you think—" Kelda began.

"Nay!" He spat the word at her. "You have no idea what I think. You have no idea what havoc your people wreaked on my village when they raided us two winters past."

His hand moved from her face to the band around her arm. He pulled her to her feet, and again she was made aware of his towering strength. Her mantle dragged the floor, and her boot caught in it, unbalancing her and causing her to fall against him. To catch herself she threw her palms against his chest.

She felt the heat of his body through the leather shirt. She felt his hardness against her entire length. Knowing absolute fear, she pushed away from him.

"Because of me, Viking, your golden hair has not been cut and you have not been beaten," Brander said. "The women wanted to do so, but I forbade them. I promised them that you would be an obedient slave, and if you wish to keep your golden locks, if you wish to avoid a beating, you will be. I promised them I would beat you. So be it."

Awaiting the blows, Kelda tensed. He swung the leather strap and lightly tapped her buttocks through the thick material of the mantle.

"This is a fair warning."

"You do not frighten me," Kelda said.

"Then you are foolish. I am going to take you to the village elders now, but I promise you, Kelda of the Vikings, I will not protect you from the women who wish to shear your hair and torture you."

Holding out one hand, he slapped the leather strap against his palm time and again. A warning, she knew.

"One more word from you, one more instance where you defy my authority in public, and you will be given to them as an example to the rest of your people of what happens to disobedient prisoners."

Kelda backed up a step to further the distance between them. Her hair was her pride and joy, and while she did not wish to have it sheared, it would be only a momentary shame. It would soon grow long again. Her fear was not Brander's threats. They meant nothing to her; she would welcome a fight with the women. Her fear was her own treacherous body, her response to the barbarian.

He moved to the door, and Kelda called. "Wait!"

"Have I not made my instructions about your behavior clear to you?"

"Please."

He nodded.

"Hauk is my second in command," she said. "I would like for him to be with me. It is necessary for him to learn all things with me in case . . . something should happen to me. Then he will have to lead my men. Also he can help keep my men calm."

"For our protection?" he mocked.

"For theirs at present," she answered. "For your protection should they ever get their weapons back."

Brander contemplated for a second before he said, "I will give your request thought."

Once they were outside the lodge, he said, "Walk a few paces behind me as is befitting a slave. This way the women and children will know that you have been properly punished."

Kelda gritted her teeth, but determined she would obey until she had accomplished her mission. As they walked, Brander slapped the leather strap against his leg. The villagers pointed at it, laughing and cheering. Kelda thought about confessing that he did not punish her but as quickly as the thought came, she dismissed it. She, too, stared at the strap. To confess and to humiliate him would be foolish indeed.

When they reached the intersection with the main street, Brander called out to a group of braves in his native language. One of the braves disappeared to return shortly with Hauk. As the Viking warrior drew near, Kelda was relieved to see that his face had been cleaned. His wound was a superficial cut and a bruised forehead.

Speaking in Norse, Brander said, "The woman has asked that you be allowed to stay with her."

"I would go with her," Hauk answered.

"I, too, shall remain with Kelda." A slight man pushed through the guards and ran to Kelda's side. His gray hair was thinning as was his beard. "I am Canby, reader of the law, and enjoy high rank among my people. Kelda might have need of my services."

A derisive smile curled Brander's mouth. "Only one of you may go with her."

"Then I shall be the one," Canby decided, craning his head forward as he rubbed his hands down his shirt and mantle to straighten them, as if he were preparing for a meeting of the Herred-thing—the

Norse District Assembly, their legal assembly. "I am the one Thoruald sent to—"

"Nay, old man," Brander said. "If she has need of either one of you, it will be the warrior not a reader of the law. You are in our land, governed by *our* laws. You will do well to remember this. You will stay with the others."

"Kelda," Canby shouted, "reason with this man. Tell him I should be the one—"

Brander waved a silencing hand at Kelda who opened her mouth to speak.

"I have spoken," he said. "So be it."

"I will be safe, Canby," Kelda assured him. "Please do not worry. Assure the men that all is well."

If Canby heard her, he gave no indication. He glared at Brander. "Thoruald will kill you, Skrelling, if you harm his adopted daughter."

Brander laughed. "I look forward to his trying."

Brander motioned to one of the guards to come get the Viking and return him to the rest of the prisoners. Then he said, "Hauk, you go with us."

As they continued their walk up the main street, women and children, war clubs in their hands, again ran beside them, glaring contemptuously and tauntingly. But they made no attempt to hurt them. Brander and the two prisoners passed several old men who sat on the side of the street chipping arrowheads. They gazed curiously but never ceased their work.

Positioned at the end of the street was a longhouse. Sitting in front of it were two women and two men. One was an Iroquois; the other boasted faded red hair and a bushy beard the same color. Surely he was Delling, the thrall Thoruald had left behind, Kelda thought with a lightening of heart. Surely this man would help them. After all, he was

Norse. He was one of them.

When they neared, Brander held up his hand in greeting.

"*Ho,* Tall Tree, Peace Chief of the Iroquois," he said.

"*Ho,* Brander, War Chief of the Iroquois. You return the victorious champion of the Iroquois."

"I return with Viking prisoners." He held out Kelda's shield. "I also bring their sign of peace."

The Iroquois nodded. "Sit and tell us of your exploits."

When Brander took his seat with the elders, Hauk and Kelda were left standing. Kelda gazed at the people who crowded around to stare at her and Hauk. They hated the Vikings. She saw the hatred on their countenances; hatred permeated the entire camp.

To calm herself she ran her fingers over her mother's brooch. With what she hoped passed as idle curiosity, she studied the group before her who sat on brightly colored mats of straw. She gazed in interest at the articles and appliances that lay beside them, most of which she could not identify.

Brander spoke, his voice loud and clear. He pointed at Kelda first, then to the white shield. Another answered. The conversation grew heated. Brander shook his head. The oldest man, the one whom Brander addressed when he approached the elders, the one whom Kelda figured was the high chief, spoke quietly.

As the discussion lost its intensity, Kelda's attention wandered. She again surveyed her surroundings.

On a rack in front of the elder who sat in the center of the group was the most curious article Kelda had seen. It was a long reedlike instrument with a small cup attached to the end. Because it was beaded, feathered, ribboned, and sculptured in such a lavish fashion Kelda figured it was a musical instrument of some kind. Beside it lay a pouch and a long kindling stick.

When she spotted and recognized the game board beside the bearded man, she did not have to worry about what it was. She knew. She had spent many a winter evening playing *hnefatafl* with any one of the three, Thoruald, Ragnar, or Hauk.

"Although this is a war game between two jarls," Thoruald contended when he had first begun instructing her, "playing it will teach you to think and to have patience. Never rush the game, child. It is a game of strategy to be won only by those who think best. Only one jarl can win. Not the strongest but the smartest."

Not the strongest but the smartest. Ever since that night Thoruald's words had rung in her heart, and she had practiced the game until she mastered it.

Finally Brander turned to Kelda and Hauk to say in Norse, "Come sit beside me. Kelda on my right, Hauk on the left. Peace Chief Tall Tree of the Iroquois has spoken for the Council of Elders of the Iroquois. We will decide the fate of you and your warriors on the rising sun. Until then you are to be our prisoners."

Kelda and Hauk took their respective places.

"*You* do not believe my words of peace?" said she.

"I am cautious. I remember too well what the Vikings did to me," Brander said coldly. "The Council of Elders is more lenient than I am, but they should be. And I should not be. I am the war chief."

"You persuaded them to make us prisoners?"

"I did. I spoke eloquently," he admitted. "My words were wise, and they listened. As long as none of you do anything to excite or irritate the villagers

38

you will be safe."

He continued, "Your warriors have been placed in a longhouse where they will be served the morning meal and where they will stay until they are given permission to move around the village. At all times they will be kept under guard."

"What about Hauk and me?" Kelda asked.

Brander paused, then said, "Since you are their leaders, you will take your meals with the Council of Elders."

Rauthell looked at Brander as if he expected him to say more. When Brander did not, Rauthell frowned. Was the war chief keeping information from them? Kelda wondered. If so, what?

Tall Tree opened the pouch and poured a brown, leafy substance into the bowl of the reedlike instrument. Chanting, he pushed the kindling stick into the fire and placed the end of the instrument into his mouth. Spellbound, Kelda and Hauk watched as he held the flame over the bowl and sucked through it. A sweet odor from the burning leaves drifted to Kelda. She inhaled deeply and watched Tall Tree blow smoke out of his mouth.

"The pipe," Brander explained, "is our earnest of peace and a token of brotherhood. We are pledging to honor our word that you and your men are not to be harmed until after tomorrow's meeting when the elders render judgment."

Tall Tree blew short puffs of smoke into different directions, chanting as he did so and holding the pipe aloft with each puff.

"We are making our promise to the Master of Life, to the Sun who gives us light, and to the Earth and Water by which we are nourished. We also send a puff to each of the four winds. We will not break our word, Viking."

Tall Tree sat down to take his last puff on the

pipe before he handed it to Kelda. Puzzled, she stared at Brander.

"You are to smoke it," he instructed, "to let the Iroquois know you understand the wisdom of their words, to assure them you and your men will abide by our laws while you are in our land."

Kelda lifted the long thin reed to her mouth and drew the smoke into her mouth. Not really sure what to do with it, she swallowed. Her eyes and chest burned and she coughed. The elders laughed.

"This time," Brander said, "hold it in your mouth, so you may blow it out as a sacrifice to the Spirits."

Reaching up to brush the tears from her cheeks, Kelda glared at him. But she was pleased with herself when the second time, she succeeded in blowing out a mouthful of smoke without doing herself injury.

"Now pass it on," Brander said. "Each of us will smoke to acknowledge our promise to the Spirits of Life."

When Tall Tree was once more in possession of the pipe, Kelda rose. She unfastened the leather thong that bound her satchel and pulled out a red mantle which she handed to Tall Tree.

"I present this to you, Great Chief. It is a token of friendship from my great chief, Jarl Thoruald of the Vikings."

The elders murmured their appreciation, several of them reaching out to rub the material between their fingers.

"I accept the gift," Tall Tree said, throwing the mantle around his shoulders as Brander interpreted. "Red is a magical color among the Iroquois. This will indeed bring me great magic as well as warmth when Grandfather North Wind visits us. We honor this gift as a token of your chief's friendship. We hope his warriors prove trustworthy."

40

He held the pipe above his head and chanted to conclude the ceremony. After emptying the ashes, he rose to disappear into the longhouse. The others remained seated.

"Who is going to take us to our longhouse?" Kelda asked.

"Rauthell will take Hauk to your other men. You will come with me."

"Why?" she demanded.

"You belong to me," Brander said quietly.

Chapter Four

"I belong to you!"

Kelda reeled from the blow. She had known there was the possibility of torture and imprisonment, but the actuality of it was devastating. Belonging to the barbarian was unthinkable! Intolerable!

"I would rather belong to the women!" She would not restrain her anger.

"I am sure you would."

"Why you?"

"As the victorious chief, I have the right to make a demand of the elders and to have it granted. I have sworn revenge on the Vikings for what they did to me during their last raid; therefore, I demanded that you be given to me as my slave. For them to refuse would be to break our laws."

"Does this mean I will not be returning to my homeland?"

"Yes," he answered. Dismissing her, he turned to Hauk and said, "Tonight is the last night of our Spring Festival. We begin each night's feast and festivities with afternoon games. Our Council of Elders has ordered your men to compete against us."

Raising her voice, Kelda said, "According to your law, I may be your slave, but according to mine, I am still the leader of my men. I speak for them."

Brander turned his head, his gaze again encompassing the sword and the stiletto. "No answer is required, Viking. We, the Council of the Elders, have already decided."

He picked up a twig and stuck it in the ground. "You and your men will be given time to rest and to bathe. When the shadow of the sun reaches here," he said, drawing a mark in the sand, "you will be taken to a place to practice for the games. Our villagers will be allowed to watch, so they will know how to place their wagers."

"Will we be told what games we are going to compete in," Kelda asked, "or has the Council of Elders already *decided* that is to be kept secret from us?"

"You will be told. Since Rauthell speaks your language, he will coach the Vikings. We will give you and your warriors every opportunity to win. Only with worthy opponents can one enjoy victory."

Followed by Rauthell and an Iroquois woman, whom Kelda judged to have seen fewer than fifty winters, Tall Tree exited from the longhouse to rejoin the elders.

"We will talk about the games later," Brander said. "Now it is time for the morning meal."

When all were seated, Tall Tree raised his arms to the heavens and offered a prayer of thanksgiving. He concluded by clapping his hands.

Several small girls moved out of the longhouse. One lay woven mats of straw on the ground in front of the elders and guests; a second handed each his bark bowl and spoon. Kelda and Hauk received a different kind of spoon, one carved from a horn similar to the ones the Vikings used at home.

"These are special," Rauthell told her.

Unlike Brander he did not seem to harbor deep-seated resentment and hatred for the Vikings; he was friendly.

43

"We traded for them long ago. They are carved from the horns of the bison."

Kelda listened in fascination as he described the huge beasts called bison that roamed freely on the tribal grounds of the people of the Plainsland. Rauthell had seen them only once, he told her, when as a small child he had been allowed to go on a trading expedition with his uncle.

During the telling of his story, several women carried large dishes of steaming food and began to serve, the aroma of stew tantalizing Kelda's nostrils and reminding her how long it had been since she last ate. Rauthell lifted his dish beneath his nose and inhaled deeply, but did not eat.

"The high chief always begins the meal," he explained. "Following him are the men."

Tall Tree dipped his spoon into his dish first and ate several spoonfuls. Looking at his wife, he said, "It is good, my wife. Thank you for preparing this for me and our guests."

All the men sampled the food, nodded their heads and murmured their satisfaction and thanks.

Tall Tree then picked up one of the sticks on which venison had been broiled. Throwing a piece of the meat into the fire, he said, "Grandfather Fire, I give this to you in appreciation of the fire with which we prepare our food."

Then he bit into a morsel yet remaining on the stick, chewed and swallowed. He smiled at the women who knelt behind him.

"It is tender, my wife. You have honored our guests and me with your hospitality. Thank you."

He spoke to the villagers. "Let us eat. Today we enjoy a tournament. Tonight we conclude the celebration of the Spring Festival."

Rauthell held a spoonful of the rich broth and

dark meat to his mouth. "Ah, food," he said. "We have been without for two days. Venison seasoned with bear fat is my favorite."

Having taken several bites, Hauk agreed. "Aye, this is good food. Reminds me of the thick stews we cook at home, mistress. Eat up. No telling what this day or the morrow may bring, and you are going to be needing your strength."

"Aye, mistress," Brander mimicked softly for her ears only while Hauk and Rauthell talked between themselves. "Eat up. You surely need your strength."

As Kelda stirred her spoon in the rich broth, he leaned his head close to her ear and whispered, "The games we Iroquois play are exciting and strenuous."

Like the waves of the ocean steadily lapping away at the coastline of her beloved home, Brander's tauntings were beginning to wear Kelda down. On the one hand, she had known when she volunteered to come to this land, that being killed or taken prisoner were among the consequences.

Death was an option most Vikings welcomed; being taken prisoner was one to be hated. She had been a thrall once; she had no desire to be one again. Certainly in the back of Kelda's mind had been the concern that she could and would be sexually abused, but she had not reckoned on its being at the hands of one who was half-Norse.

When the meal was over, Tall Tree spoke; Brander translated. "Kelda, leader of the Vikings, the Iroquois want to hear why you are here."

As if she were home in Thoruald's *stofa*, the building filled with revelling Vikings who clamored for a good story, Kelda rose. Although her people might have heard the tale many times, they would want to be spared none of the details. In fact, the *skald* would embellish the story with each retelling. Kelda would not elaborate, but she would spare none of the details for the Iroquois.

She described the Wendes, the pirates who had attacked their village, killing their chief's son and wounding the chief. Grief-stricken over the death of his son, Jarl Thoruald was left without a direct heir by blood.

"If the chief dies," Kelda declared, Brander's voice echoing the translation, "leadership, symbolized by the sword Talon of the Falcon, will go to Asgaut, Thoruald's nephew by marriage. Although Asgaut is a brave warrior who took his warriors and went in search of the Wendes, Thoruald does not think Asgaut will be a good leader for our people. Thoruald does not believe in Asgaut's dream for the people because it is not a strong dream, blessed by the gods."

The Iroquois nodded their heads and murmured. Dreams they understood and believed in.

"Before Asgaut left on his mission," Kelda continued, "he presented the household of Thoruald with a gift: an Iroquois thrall—a child who has seen about twelve winters—whom he had recently acquired on a raid along the coast of the Iroquois forestland."

"*Ho!*" one of the elders shouted and clapped his hands.

Kelda ceased talking, and Tall Tree asked through interpretation, "Your Viking Asgaut returned to the land of the Norse with tales of his raid on the Iroquois?"

Kelda nodded.

"The Vikings who travel with you, did any of them come with Asgaut?"

"Nay."

"How did you know on which shores to land to find our village?"

"From Asgaut's *skald*," she replied. "Asgaut's bard told the story to us describing the landmarks we should search for."

"You have this storyteller with you?"

"Nay, but I have my *skald* with me. He is called Ulmer."

Satisfied, Tall Tree nodded. "That is good. We will hear your storyteller while you are with us."

The elders nodded their agreement. The woman sitting closest to Tall Tree whispered to him. He spoke.

"Thoruald, your jarl, was chief of your village when the Viking Asgaut and his men raided our village?"

"Yes," Kelda answered.

"Thoruald is as guilty of raiding our village and killing our women, children, and old people as Asgaut!" Rauthell exclaimed.

"Yes. Yes." The elders murmured in unison, their heads bobbing.

"It is true, Thoruald is the village chief," Kelda said, disturbed that they would blame Thoruald for Asgaut's attack, "but he has no control over the strong Viking leaders who gather their own warriors about them. That is why he needs a strong heir. If Jarl Thoruald has no blood heirs, Asgaut—this same man who led the attack on your village—will become the next jarl of the Vikings."

No comment was made as the elders leaned back to ponder this. Finally Tall Tree spoke, Brander again translating for him.

"I would hear the remainder of your story. I would learn why Thoruald thinks he has a blood

47

heir among the Iroquois."

Kelda spoke. "One day the ailing chief noticed the arm band which the Iroquois slave child wore and immediately recognized it as being his. He questioned the boy who said it was in his leather pouch when he regained consciousness in the ship.

"Further questions," Kelda explained, "revealed the thrall knew not how he came to have it because he remembered nothing prior to his capture."

She unfastened the cloth purse that hung from her belt, extracted the arm band and held it up for everyone to see.

"This belonged to my chief. Thirty and two winters past, he had it and a matching collar crafted, his name worked in subtly among the runes and designs. Soon after Thoruald purchased the jewelry, he sailed to these distant shores where he fell in love with and married an Iroquois maiden. When time came for him to leave, she chose to remain with her people."

Kelda paused and looked from one of the elders to the next. Still their expressions remained impassive with no hint of curiosity.

"Thoruald gave the arm band and collar to his wife and left behind a thrall by the name of Delling to take care of her. Jarl Thoruald, my father through adoption, wondered if this Iroquois captive whom he has is indeed his grandson."

She received no response.

"He also wondered if perhaps he has a son or daughter."

Still there was no response.

"Is his wife among you?"

Kelda's gaze slowly moved from one to the other of the elders. She waited. For someone to answer. For someone to speak. For something to happen.

Eventually Tall Tree spoke, the words translated. "Why have you been chosen to lead these men to our land?"

"I owed my father a blood debt. After my family died in the plague, Jarl Thoruald took me into his home and made me his ward. After the pirates attacked, he was wounded, near death, and grieving the loss of his son, and I—" she hesitated, deciding to leave out many of the details, especially that concerning the adoption and her sacred oath "—I agreed to come to this land to find his family, if he has one."

Tall Tree motioned for Kelda to sit down. She did so; then Tall Tree gave Brander permission to address the elders. That he was an eloquent and persuasive speaker, Kelda did not doubt. When he spoke all the elders listened to him; they acknowledged his words with nods and shakes of their heads. When he was through, the council talked among themselves; then the high chief, looking at Kelda, spoke.

"Tall Tree would like to see the arm band," Brander said.

Kelda handed it to Brander who held it a long time, studying it, tracing the designs with his fingertip; then he turned it over several times as if loath to part with it. Once his hand strayed to the neckline of his shirt. Looking up to see Kelda staring at him, he quickly passed the arm band to the elder sitting next to him.

Kelda thought in that brief second that their gazes caught and held she had seen grief and sorrow in his eyes. Before she could be sure, he turned his head and stared straight ahead.

One by one the elders studied the jewelry, each taking as long to examine it as Brander had. While they talked among themselves, the arm band began its journey back to her. She waited for a reaction, a sign that the boy was Brander's or Rauthell's son or that either was Thoruald's son. None came. She looked expectantly from the bearded man to Rauthell to Brander. No one spoke.

The woman who had been the last to join the circle of elders spoke. When Brander translated, he said, "Our shaman, the Woman of Dreams, wants to know what the child is called?"

"He does not remember his Iroquois name," Kelda explained. "We call him Kolby which in our language means from the black or dark settlement."

"Were there any distinguishing marks on the child who was found wearing the arm band?" the woman asked.

"Yes, he has a small tattoo of a falcon on his upper arm."

Kelda remembered how excited Thoruald had become when they discovered the falcon. The tattoo had assured the jarl that the child was indeed his grandchild and that Odin in all his wisdom had brought him to their village.

"When he wears the arm band, you cannot see the falcon."

Tall Tree spoke, Brander interpreted. "The Council of Elders will consider what you have said. On tomorrow's sun after the final games of the Spring Festival, we will meet again and give you an answer."

Tall Tree clapped his hands and spoke to Rauthell. "It has already been decided the Vikings will compete against the Iroquois. You will instruct the Iroquois captain to choose for his team his most skilled warriors."

Rauthell translated the high chief's words. "Your

men, Viking, will compete with ours on one to one. Each team has a champion who is its captain. In case of a tie, the points of the champions will be tallied. Their scores determine the winner of the game. Our first game will be played when the Sun is directly overhead and will last no longer than nightfall. That is when we gather at the Big House for the last night of our Spring Ceremony when the women tell their dreams and visions."

While the idea of competing against the Iroquois interested Kelda, she was more interested in fulfilling her mission. Because she wanted to press the matter of the Iroquois child and the arm band, she resented squandering precious time with the playing of games. But if these people were anything like hers, there would be no hurrying them.

She would get nothing more from them until after the tournament. Certainly she did not want to irritate them with her impatience. As long as they were favorably disposed toward her, she might learn the information she sought.

Vaguely she heard Rauthell as he outlined the rules of the games.

"The champions of each team will be presented to the Council of Elders of the Iroquois before the competition begins. According to our custom these champions will receive a gift of great value from the elders in gratitude for their skill, and also according to our custom the losing champion will present a valuable gift to the winner before the competition is closed by the elders."

When the Iroquois ceased speaking, Tall Tree clapped his hands and rose. The elders also rose, each going in a different direction.

"Come," Brander said. "I will take you to your quarters. Hauk, you will stay with the other Vikings so that you may prepare for the tournament."

"Are your tribesmen allowed to wager with our warriors?" the Viking asked.

Brander nodded. "Each team will give an exhibition of skills this afternoon, so that the villagers can see all the contenders. Then prior to the game, each of you will be able to wager."

"Good." Hauk rubbed his hands together as he and Brander fell into step together. "It has been a long time since we have had some sporting fun."

Walking to the side and about a step behind them, Kelda asked, "Am I not to be prepared for the competition?"

Never slacking his gait, Brander said, "You may join any competition you wish. I will see that you have a coach to tutor you. Rauthell," he ordered, "escort Hauk to his longhouse."

Irritated by Brander's curt behavior toward her, Kelda said, "I will have the same coach as my warriors, and I will practice with them."

Brander gazed at her contemptuously. Finally he murmured, "So be it." Then he said, "Come, now. It is time for me to take you to your quarters."

To his home, Kelda wondered apprehensively, as they parted way with Rauthell and Hauk.

"Until we conclude the celebration of the Spring Festival," Brander said, as if he had read her thoughts, "I cannot be with a woman; therefore, you will stay in a small wigwam close to mine."

"So you can watch over me," Kelda charged.

"Yes. I will leave you in the care of Wild Flower, the woman who spoke up at the meeting today. She will assign a slave to see to your needs."

"I can take care of myself."

"You will do as I say."

The remainder of the walk was in silence. He led

her into a small lodge that was situated on the outer periphery of the village and close to the river that ran through.

"This is where you will stay," he informed her, "until I bring you into my lodge."

"When will that be?" Kelda asked.

"After the ceremony."

"Tonight after the women tell their dreams or tomorrow after the games?" Kelda persisted.

"Be patient, my slave," Brander said, a small smile touching his mouth. He reached out to run the tip of his fingers down the bridge of her nose. "Have you been so long without a man?"

"Even if you take me," Kelda said, dodging away from his hand, "I will find myself without a man."

"You are speaking from inexperience," he said quietly, but his eyes narrowed angrily. "We will see what tale you carry once I have made you mine."

He walked from one opening in the wall to the other, rolling up and securing the flaps, so that sunshine streamed into the room.

"Do you have clean clothing for the celebration?"

"In my trunk," she answered.

"I will send one of my braves after it," he said. "Describe it for me, so he will know which one to get."

"Take some of my men," Kelda suggested. "They will know my trunk from the others, and probably will want an opportunity to get theirs so they can change clothes also." She added sarcastically, "If it is not against your customs."

Brander walked to where she stood and touched her face again. Kelda tensed and drew away from him. His facial features hardened. He curled his hand around her neck, his fingers biting into the delicate flesh as he drew her close to him.

"Fight me if you must, Kelda of the Vikings, but know in the end I will possess you."

Her eyes never wavering from his, her voice calm, Kelda said, "You may take my body, Skrelling, because you are physically stronger than I am, but you will never possess me. You may enter my body, but you will never enter my soul. That belongs to me and always shall."

He lowered his head, his face moving to hers. At first his eyes captured her reflection, then her. Caught in the velvet depths, she was willingly drowning in this wild, mysterious world that was Brander of the Iroquois.

Denials so hotly proclaimed only seconds ago were quickly reduced to ashes—ashes like those Tall Tree had knocked so effortless out of the peace pipe, ashes that had been scattered by the tiniest of breezes. With no struggle at all, she was giving herself to this barbarian.

Angered by the thought of his taking her so easily, she stiffened. As his lips brushed hers, she turned her head. His hand moved to her cheeks, his fingers biting into the softness of her flesh. His mouth clamped down on hers, hot, heavy, and demanding.

Whereas Ragnar's kisses had been sweet and gentle, this man's were fiery and exacting. Ragnar loved the innocent maiden; this man lusted for the woman.

She pushed her hands between them, her palms flat against his chest. Effortlessly he caught her in the circle of his arms, making her his prisoner, binding her arms and rendering them a useless weapon for her. He pressed his body against the length of hers; she felt the hardness of his arousal. She quivered.

She squirmed in the iron-tight embrace. She twisted her head, but he held her tight. He refused to give up her lips. Despite her effort to resist, her resolve was melting beneath the heated assault.

His lips coaxed hers into response. His tongue teased the closed indentation of her mouth. She despised this man, but he was causing strange things to happen to her body, to her emotions.

She raised her leg, but he quickly discerned her intention. He wrapped one of his legs around hers. Both of them toppled to the ground. He cushioned the fall, quickly turning so that she was beneath him.

Her breath came deeply, and she felt a heat stirring in her loins that she had only heard women in her village talk about. Was this the heat of a woman who wants a man?

It must be! It must be the feelings that a man and a woman shared between them, the feelings her mother had explained to her when she came of age. Whether a man or woman cared for each other, they could be attracted on a base level.

The man could arouse a woman to respond to him although she did not love or want him. A woman could do the same to a man. She had been afraid when Brander taunted her with the knife; yet its slight stroke on her skin evoked a response from her body. Since this was true, how could she maintain her distance?

Why had she ever convinced Thoruald that she should be the one to come to this strange land to find out if he had a family, to seek out his only possible living heir?

His hand slid down Kelda's body. A shiver followed. The gods help her. She despised this man; yet he was arousing her. He was stimulating her.

She felt a quickening in her nether parts that had nothing to do with love.

She did not want Brander. Aye, she did want him. At the moment she despised herself for being weak where this man was concerned. She was tempted to open to him, but in doing so she would be opening her body and eventually her soul to him. Then he would truly possess her.

Fighting him was futile; the more she had fought, the more aroused he had seemed to become. Her resistance was only fueling the fires of his desires. Clamping her teeth together, she ceased all struggle.

She could not stop her irregular breathing when his mouth moved from hers to scatter feather-light kisses along her cheeks and her temples. When his lips touched her eyes, she held herself rigid in his arms.

His embrace slackened; she felt him pull away from her. She opened her eyes and looked up into the dark, rugged face.

He laughed harshly. "You are not unaffected by my touch, Viking. I hear your response in your breathing. I feel it in your heartbeat. I taste it on your lips."

"Aye, my body is affected," she admitted, glad her voice did not quaver, "but not my heart."

"Given time I will possess that also."

"Why would you want it?" she asked.

"To hurt you as your people have hurt us."

"You will never touch my heart, Skrelling. Whatever else you get, you will have to take from me."

"It will be much more pleasurable for you, Viking, if you submit to me willingly." His warm breath against her skin added to the feelings that now ran rampant through her. "I can take you anytime I wish, but it will be much better for both of us—you in particular—if you cooperate."

"*Never* shall I submit willingly."

"You will," Brander promised, his eyes black as the stones that dotted the shore of the river that ran behind his lodge. "The time will come when you will beg for my touch."

"You will have counted all the leaves on all the trees of this great forest before that day arrives."

He laughed. "With the coming of the winter, I will make you repeat your words to me. Grandfather North Wind shall blow all the foliage from the trees, leaving them bare. The leaves are easy to count then."

Chapter Five

After Brander left Kelda, he returned to his lodge. Unable to dismiss thoughts of her, he remembered the feel of her body in his arms, her mouth beneath his. Although he had not planned to kiss her, had not contemplated their ending up on the floor, their bodies tangled together, he could not erase the feel of her softness against himself. He wanted that woman, and he would have her.

But in having her was he destroying himself? he wondered. Revenge was a part of the Iroquois tradition and custom; law demanded a man revenge himself and his family for wrongdoings. But Brander recognized that revenge also exacted a high price from the one who sought it.

Taking his revenge on the Norse did not bother him; in fact, he was exhilarated by the thought. But the burning desire he had for the woman, this need he was feeling to have her submit to him filled him with self-disgust.

No woman—not even his wife—had aroused such depth of feeling in him.

He was standing in the center of the large room, pondering his relationship with the Viking woman, when he heard a soft knock.

"Enter," he called.

The door opened, and Wild Flower walked in.

"Black Bear sends word that he will meet you on the playing field."

Brander nodded. "I will meet him, after I send someone to get the Viking woman's trunk."

Wild Flower raised an eyebrow.

Brander shrugged. "She would like to change clothing for the ceremony this night."

Wild Flower continued to stare at him dubiously.

"I would also have her change clothes."

"Are you attracted to her?"

"She is beautiful," he admitted grudgingly.

He was by no means ready to admit that he had fallen under the spell of the golden-haired Viking. Nor was he willing to confess that he had kissed her and would have taken more had he not gone through the purification rites for the games prior to the last night of the Spring Festival.

"But she means nothing to me."

"You were so determined to have her you fought the Council of Elders."

"I want her," he agreed, "but she is merely a means through which I will exact my revenge."

"So you told the elders."

Brander's voice hardened. "Unlike my mother, I have no fondness for the Norsemen."

"We are not discussing a Norseman, my son," the woman said softly. "We are talking about a Norse-woman."

Brander walked across the room and slipped his longbow off the hook. He tested the tautness of the cord and the strength and resilience of the wood; next he picked up his quiver and examined his arrows, running his fingertips lightly over the fletching.

"The child is Eirik," Wild Flower said.

His back to her, Brander laid the bow down.

"When we were unable to locate his body after the massacre, I hoped he was alive. I prayed that he was," she said. "He is the issue of your body, my son."

"After hearing the woman's story today," Brander said, clutching the shaft of the arrow so tightly it broke, "I pray that he is not alive. If he has no memory, he is better dead." He tossed the useless arrow to the floor.

"He is alive, Brander. I have always known that, and he is not disgraced with a weak mind. I told you about my dream. Eirik will grow up to be an outstanding warrior like his father and his grandfather before him."

"You heard the woman speak today. You were at the meeting. The boy has no memory of his previous life — his life as an Iroquois. All he remembers is his life as a Norse slave."

The last words tasted bitter in Brander's mouth. His entire life he had felt nothing but contempt for the Norse, in particular for the one who had sailed to their land thirty winters ago, met and mated his mother, and left her when she was with child. His only legacy had been a few pieces of jewelry.

He unfastened the thongs that bound the opening of his shirt, pulled the buckskin aside, and touched the collar he had worn since he became a man, since he earned his right to be called a warrior of the Iroquois Nation. He had worn it with pride, not because of his father, but because it meant so much to his mother and because his people revered it.

Two years ago the resentment and contempt he felt for the Norsemen had turned into burning fury that only fermented with time. The Vikings had come under the pretense of peace and had attacked the village when the men were away hunting. On their arrival home, the Iroquois found devastation and destruction. Dead were Brander's two daughters and his wife who was big with child; gone was his son—his only son and heir.

"It is time for you to go to Norwegia, the land of the Norse, my son."

Brander turned to gaze at the woman standing in front of him. She was one of the most beautiful and courageous women he had ever known. A woman of dreams, she was highly respected by the Iroquois Nation. Many tribes scattered through the Forest-land came to her for healing and a translation of their dreams.

"You still love him, do you not?" Brander asked, unable to keep the resentment and bitterness out of his voice. "After the passing of thirty winters, you still love him?"

"Yes," said she, "I do. That is why I never took another mate, my son. I found mine in Thoruald. I could love no other man, and I would not live with one for less."

"My Mother, I am not going to Norwegia, no matter what your dreams say, no matter what you decide fate has decreed," Brander answered as softly as she had spoken.

"I know why you insisted that Delling teach me the Norse language, alphabet, and traditions, but I am Iroquois. Not Norse. I am not the son of Thoruald the Viking. I am Brander, son of Wild Flower of the Iroquois."

Wild Flower walked to her son and laid a hand on his shoulder. "I am proud of you, Brander, but your walk with the Iroquois will soon be ended. Now it is time for you to go the way of the Viking."

"Never."

Brander pulled away from her and moved to the other side of the room, as if he could escape her words of prophesy. He did not wish to hear them because he knew they would come true. His mother had the gift. He had witnessed it too often to disbelieve. He might not believe in the spirits, but he believed in his mother.

"I could have gone with your father," she continued. "He asked me to return to his land with him, but I was too young to understand that my future was with him wherever he may go."

Wild Flower fingered the medicine pouch that hung about her neck.

"I was frightened of the unknown," she said. "The Iroquois are a brave people; we love heights that bring us nearer to the Maker of Life. We love the land and the sea, but we have never wanted to stray from our beloved land. We have all we need or want here."

Brander pegged his longbow on the wall.

"The Vikings are different," Wild Flower said. "Their land does not produce their needs. Thus, they sail to many strange lands, returning with booty and becoming a part of them all. Not admitting you are Norse does not make it fact."

He grasped his tomahawk, flexing his fingers around the handle.

"In your heart you have that yearning to travel beyond the horizon," she said, "to see what lies beyond the Great Water. I have prepared you for your life among them."

He neither acknowledged or dismissed his mother's words. Instead, he said, "We do not know that this child is Eirik. During the massacre anyone could have gotten the arm band."

"It is Eirik," Wild Flower insisted. "She described

the tattoo on his arm. You cannot deny that. I saw him last night in a dream. He was calling for you, Brander. He wants you to come to him."

"He has no memory, my mother. How can he call to me?"

"The child without the memory is only a small part of Eirik. Your son is the whole—the physical and the spiritual. It is he who calls his father."

She held her hands out to Brander, appealing to him to hear her, to understand her words.

"The child's destiny is not sealed, my son. He will regain his memory and prove to be a powerful warrior, like his father. At this moment, he needs his father's strength. Without you, he will not recover his mind."

Brander gripped the handle of the tomahawk tightly. Then he shook his head. "No, I will not be sailing to Norwegia."

"Because you deny your Norse blood does not keep it from flowing through your veins. One day, my son, you and fate will meet head on."

Brander laughed. "And I will win, my mother. You have taught your son well. Of all the Iroquois warriors, he is best."

Laughing with him, Wild Flower walked to where he stood and motherlike tousled his hair. "A little arrogant at times, but always honest. Still fate is stronger than any mortal. She always prevails. Remember that, my son."

Kelda opened the door and stared into the face of the Iroquois woman. The Woman of Dreams, Brander had called her. Her hair, thick and black, was parted in the middle and hung in two long braids, one over each shoulder. Her buckskin dress was white with yellow and green designs. Out of the almond-colored face, large ebony eyes stared solemnly at Kelda.

"I am Wild Flower," she said in faltering Norse. "I am to give you a slave to help you prepare for the competition."

Kelda was no longer surprised that many of the Iroquois spoke Norse. She was reconciled that finding Thoruald's offspring—if indeed he had one over here—would be difficult, perhaps futile. The Norse were a lusty lot of men who did not deny themselves the pleasure of women. Those who traveled with Thoruald evidently mated freely with the Indian maidens.

Kelda swung open the door and invited the Iroquois woman into the lodge. "Brander said I am to attend the ceremony tonight."

"Yes," Wild Flower agreed. "You will enjoy it. The Spring Festival is one of great importance for us."

On entering the room, she set a large leather pouch on the bench that ran along the side of one wall, serving as a seat during the day and a bed by night.

"Winter is gone, and new life has begun. We have this feast for four risings and settings of the sun so that we may thank the Master of Life for life, the Sun for the light he provides, and the Earth and Water for their nourishment. We then offer prayers and sacrifices and ask them for their blessing during the coming year."

"We have a spring ceremony that we celebrate about this time of the year also," Kelda said. "It is called the *Sirgblot* or the success sacrifice and sounds as though it is quite similar to yours. We make sacrifices to the gods and pray for good crops in the coming season and for victory during our summer raids."

Kelda felt the heat rush into her face when she realized what she had said.

"Since yours is quite similar to ours," Wild Flower said, taking no umbrage at Kelda's words, "you will not find our celebration strange. This night—the last night—is the night for the women. They will be allowed to tell their dreams and to give their interpretations if they know them or to ask for their interpretation."

"You are the Woman of Dreams," Kelda murmured, wondering what role Wild Flower played in the ceremony.

"Yes, I am the shaman, blessed by the Master of Life to see my own dreams and to understand others' dreams. Because I possess this power, I live alone," she explained. "I spend most of my time communing with the Master of Life and learning about this world he has created for us, learning which herbs will give life and health."

"Yet you speak Norse fluently," Kelda said.

"Delling insists I speak with him so he will not forget his native language."

"So the bearded man is Delling, the thrall Thoruald left behind," Kelda murmured.

"He is," Wild Flower said.

"Do you know the wife Thoruald left behind?" Kelda asked.

"Yes."

Excited, Kelda said, "Please tell me who she is. I have a gift for her from Thoruald."

"You never mentioned this when you told your tale to the elders," Wild Flower said, breaking into Kelda's thoughts.

"No, it is for her alone."

65

"That is as it should be," Wild Flower answered. "However, since the Council of Elders has spoken, I cannot speak about her. You will receive your answers tomorrow."

Kelda sighed.

As if the conversation had not digressed to Thoruald's wife, Wild Flower said, "Delling spends a great deal of time with me as I gather herbs. We have become close friends."

"Is he a shaman also?"

Wild Flower nodded. "A wise man with much knowledge of the world beyond the Great Water, he is also one of our teachers."

"Has he never wanted to return to his homeland?"

"Not that I know of," Wild Flower answered. "But that is a question you will have to ask him. Over there he was a thrall. Here he is an honored man in our village. One of the Elders. But enough talk of Delling. Look what I brought you."

She sat on the bench and unfastened the leather satchel she had brought in. Kelda moved closer to her, fascinated by the variety of pottery jars and small, tightly woven baskets Wild Flower took from the leather case.

"Herbs and salves of color that we use on our faces. I thought perhaps you would want to look beautiful for the celebration."

"Aye, we use face and eye colors also," Kelda said.

Wild Flower lined up the containers, opening one. Reaching into her satchel, she held up small brushes and a long fluffy plant.

"Brushes made from sweet gum twigs and a cattail to be used as a face puff," she explained. She dipped the cattail head into an opened container and tapped it against Kelda's nose. "Powder takes the shine off your face."

66

"Why am I attending?" Kelda asked.

"Brander wants you to." She smiled.

Brander wants you . . . as long as she belonged to him this would be the only logic behind any decision made in her life. The words churned like an angry sea in Kelda's mind. She could not forget his kiss; she could not erase his touch from her skin. Most of all, she could not forgive herself for wanting him in return, for wanting more than the kisses of this barbarian.

"Come," Wild Flower said. "It is time for you to bathe. When you are through, my slave, Quiet Woman, will apply color to your face so you will be beautiful for Brander today."

"I do not understand why he, or anyone of you, would expect me to want to look beautiful for him."

Kelda followed Wild Flower out of the lodge.

"I, alone of the Vikings, belong to someone. I am Brander's captive."

"You should be grateful. Feel honored that Brander fought the Council of Elders for you."

"Would you be honored that a man fought for you to be his slave?"

Wild Flower said, "One thing you should learn about the Iroquois, Kelda, is that they speak and act from the heart. Do not always believe what the eye sees or the ear hears."

They walked on the narrow path through the wooded section of the village behind Brander's lodge.

"Brander treats his captives well," the shaman said. "That is why you should please him. If you are pleasing to him, he will be gentler with you."

Saying nothing, Kelda thought of the inequality of the situation. In order to make her servitude more tolerable, she had to be pleasing to him.

"If you present him with a son, he would be grateful and possibly give you your freedom," Wild Flower said. "Yes, Kelda of the Vikings, I would like for you to present the war chief of the Iroquois with a child."

"I would find absolutely no pleasure in that," Kelda said.

Wild Flower laughed softly as if she enjoyed a secret.

"He is not the easiest person to like," she confessed, "but you will be happy with him. He is a strong man who needs a strong woman. As a war chief, he has a position in the village that will make you the envy of many a maiden."

"I will not be happy with anyone as long as I am considered a captive."

"Then, Kelda of the Vikings," Wild Flower said, "it is up to you to make certain that Brander does not consider you a captive."

Kelda dwelled on Wild Flower's words as they continued their walk to the sweat-lodge. Although she was curious about Brander, she was also curious about Thoruald's wife.

In her mind's eye Kelda saw Thoruald's trunk in the corner of his sleeping chamber. It had been locked all the winters she had been living in his household. The house slaves dusted it, but they never opened it; they never moved it from the foot of his bed.

Often she had wondered what it held, but the content had remained a secret. Her husband, Ragnar, had once told her it contained mementoes of her father's first voyage to a faraway land. Mementoes of his Iroquois wife? Kelda wondered.

Since the Iroquois child had entered their lives, Thoruald had become more pensive. When she and

68

he had played the game of the jarls, he had lost more frequently, and Kelda had known he was distracted. Often he would pick up the falcon piece and stare at it, a faraway gleam in his eye.

To find his Skrelling family had become an obsession with him.

Only when she was ready to board the *langskip* had he given her the gift for his wife.

Arriving in front of the sweat-lodge, the two women halted. Along the outside of the building were piles of uniform, rounded stones, and water jugs. A woman—evidently Wild Flower's slave—scurried around.

"Are you familiar with our steam-baths?" Wild Flower asked.

"Not yours," Kelda answered. "But we have them in our land. I know what to do."

"Then I will leave you with Quiet Water, my slave. When you are through bathing and have dressed, she will take you to meet your Vikings."

Wild Flower turned, took several steps, then stopped. She returned to Kelda.

"I am glad you arrived in our land."

"For that you can thank Jarl Thoruald," Kelda said.

"No."

Wild Flower searched Kelda's face as if she sought answers to unasked questions.

"I thank fate. She is the one who brought you, my child."

As soon she uttered the words, the Iroquois shaman walked away.

"Will fate help me to find Thoruald's family?" Kelda called after her.

"I cannot answer for her," Wild Flower answered, her stride never slowing.

Kelda walked into the room and undressed. Glad she left her mantle at the lodge, she handed her clothes to the woman, then lay down on the bench and closed her eyes. Water, poured over heated stones, spit and sizzled to fill the room with steam.

It grew hotter, and Kelda was soon covered in a sheen of perspiration. Beginning to relax, her concerns in abeyance and Wild Flower's words temporarily pushed aside, she inhaled the fragrance of the resinous boughs and flowers the slave strew about.

Time passed; the woman entered several more times with water; the heat was almost suffocating. Kelda's hair stuck to her body. When she thought she could endure no more, Quiet Woman opened the doors and raised the flaps over the windows to allow the room to cool.

When all the steam had evaporated, Quiet Woman, carrying large water jugs, entered the lodge. She motioned to Kelda that it was time to wash her hair. When they were through, Quiet Woman doused Kelda's entire body in cool water and bound her hair in a large drying cloth. Afterwards Kelda stood, and the slave slipped a flowing robe over her head and soft leather shoes on her feet.

It was then that Kelda noticed the tattoo on her forehead. Unable to stop herself, she reached out and touched the flower that had been colored into the woman's skin. Wild Flower's totem.

Kelda removed her hand, and the slave smiled. She pulled up the sleeve of her dress and proudly showed Kelda two more designs. She acted as if they were marks of beauty rather than servitude.

Walking out of the lodge, still thinking about the tattoos, Kelda picked up her clothing, checking to see that she had her sword and stiletto. Then she followed the slave to her quarters.

Because the day was cool and the forest beautiful, Kelda left the door to the lodge open when she returned. She enjoyed listening to the wind sighing through the trees and to the birds singing. Quiet Woman motioned her to sit on the shelf.

For the next few minutes Kelda sat in fascination as the slave showed her the ways she could deepen the color of her eyes by outlining them, lengthen her lashes, and color her lips with different salves made from vegetable, root, and bark dies; berries pressed against her cheeks and lips gave them soft color, and powder, pulverized bark of a tree, took the sheen from her face.

When Quiet Woman was gone, Kelda was alone. She stretched out on the shelf and closed her eyes. Again Wild Flower's words returned. *I thank fate. She is the one who brought you.*

Kelda wanted to deny the assertion but could not. From the minute she learned the story of the gold arm band and collar and saw the falcon tattoo on the Iroquois child, she knew fate had intervened in her and Thoruald's life. Had she wanted to refuse to come to this new land to discover the boy's past, she could not. Inexplicably, something drew her, and to be honest it was not the sacred oath.

Shortly an Iroquois brave entered the room with her trunk on his shoulder. Without a word he set it in the center of the room, turned, and departed. Earlier today when Brander had led them to the village, Kelda had suspected him of leading them in circles in order to make it more difficult for them to find their way back to the *langskip* in case they escaped. Now she was sure of it. Otherwise, there was no way they could have gotten her trunk so quickly.

71

She picked up her mantle and removed the brooch by which she fastened it about her neck. Then she moved to the center of the room and knelt beside the trunk, opening it and picking up her jewelry casket. Unlocking the lid, she dropped the brooch in with her other jewelry. The Golden Sol. This was her talisman. Her mother had given it to her on the coming of her tenth winter, and she never went anywhere without it. Finally she shut the casket lid and returned it to the trunk.

She searched until she found her favorite dress, one Ragnar had given to her before he was killed. She held the soft blue material against her face and remembered the last time she had worn it. The banquet at which her engagement to Ragnar had been announced.

Scooped low with tiny straps rather than sleeves, it revealed her arms and shoulders and the fullness of her breasts. The gold collar and long dangling earrings Ragnar had given her as his betrothal gift looked beautiful with it.

But even as she held the material against her face, she knew she could not wear this dress in front of Brander. She would feel vulnerable beneath his hot gaze. Ragnar had never made her feel the way Brander did. Brander made her feel hot and cold at the same time. Beneath his gaze, fear and excitement joined together to course through her body and to cause her to forget reason.

She imagined that life with Brander would be like the feeling she had experienced as a child when she walked the narrow precipice of the cliff and looked down at the jagged and rocky shores of the fjord. One false step and she would have been over the side. Yet no matter how precarious the position, she always returned to the cliff; she always balanced on the edge. She hoped she was not the woman to share this fate with Brander of the Iroquois. Yet a small voice whispered to her that her fate did lie with this dark Iroquois.

"You have finished your bath?"

Brander spoke from behind her. Kelda quickly dropped the dress and rose to face him. She felt warmth seep into her face and hoped her color did not heighten so that he would notice. His voice, his presence, all robbed her of her senses.

"You have painted your face," he murmured. "That is good. It pleases me."

His attentive gaze moved from her head to the bottom of her feet back up to her face. Although she was fully clothed, she felt as if he had completely disrobed her and she stood before him naked. So caressing was his gaze, she felt her breasts tighten, her nipples press against the soft leather.

"When you are dressed, Quiet Water will take you to the field where your warriors are meeting."

Kelda nodded. She knew he felt the tension between them as greatly as she did. She believed he deliberately created this tension as if he took pleasure in knowing that he could manipulate her emotions.

"Tonight you are to be my guest at the ceremony."

Again she nodded. He stared at her long and hard, his gaze slowly moving over her face before it lowered to linger on her breasts. Abruptly Brander turned and walked to the door.

His back to her, he said in a slightly husky voice, "May you have strong magic, Kelda of the Vikings. You are going to need it because my magic is extremely strong. It has never failed me."

"I will need strong magic," Kelda agreed, "but you will need more, Brander of the Iroquois."

73

Without another word, he left the lodge. After he was gone, Kelda shut the door; she would have locked it, but it had no bolt. Her palms and cheek on the cool wood, she leaned against the door for several seconds, breathing in deeply.

When strength had returned to her limbs, she moved back to the trunk and dug through the clothes until she found a shirt, a pair of trousers, and a mantle. She shut the trunk, then quickly re-opened it and lifted out her jewelry casket.

Indeed, she needed strong magic, and she had it. She held her mother's brooch in her palm, the golden disc glinting in the sunlight that spilled into the room. She moved to the door to look up at the sun, to revel in its warmth. At that moment a mass of dark clouds passed in front of it, obscuring the brilliance of its rays and dimming the glint of the gold.

An omen? Kelda wondered. Foreboding, like the clouds, enshrouded her. She had a premonition she had no magic strong enough to protect her from this man; she would forever be his, branded by him. She closed her hand, squeezing so tightly the brooch pin pricked the soft skin of her palm.

Today she was a Viking warrior.

Tonight . . . quickly Kelda returned to the trunk and shoved the blue gown along with her fantasies to the bottom. She slammed the lid down and fastened it tightly. Tonight she would be a Viking warrior, also.

Chapter Six

Tonight the Viking woman would be his.

Lying on the bench in the sweat-house, his eyes closed, Brander reached up and wiped the perspiration from his forehead. He heard the splash of water as it hit the hot rocks; he felt the spurt of steam, warm and caressing, as it enveloped his body.

Purification rites for body, mind, and soul! he thought skeptically. It would take more than steamed heat to cleanse his body and mind of the Viking woman. He was quickly becoming obsessed with her.

He remembered the softness of her hair, the way it hung to her waist like strands of pure gold glistening in the sunlight. He could imagine her naked, her skin creamy white against the brownness of his; how warm and smooth her flesh would be beneath his searching hands.

Again he tasted the sweetness of her lips, of her body. In his imagination he felt her tremble and convulse in his arms as he brought her to fulfillment. Sheer pleasure inundated him when he imagined the proud woman tamed by passion, repeatedly begging him to make love to her.

But his pleasure should not be derived by her fulfillment, he thought. His pleasure should be the fulfillment of his revenge.

It had been two years since Brander had touched a woman sexually. Two years since he had wanted one. Now he felt an urgency in his body, a heaviness in his loins that would be relieved only when he took the golden-haired woman, when he released his seed inside her. He was glad that tonight was the final night of the ceremony.

He would take her!

He rolled over, drew in a deep breath of the sweetened bough that was suspended from the ceiling, and pressed his palm against the wall of the lodge. How could he have so little willpower where this particular woman was concerned?

During the twenty-nine winters the Master of Life had granted to him, he had suffered many tragedies, but always he had proved himself stronger than they. He had triumphed.

All his life he had proved himself, proved that he, a half-Norse, was as good as a full-blooded Iroquois. Not one warrior could boast of being better than he. No matter whether hunter, runner, navigator, or warrior, he was the champion.

He had no fear of man or of beast, but this woman unsettled him. Despite his hatred for the Norse, despite his resolve to avenge the deaths of his family, he was attracted to the woman and had been since he first saw her long golden hair.

This attraction he considered to be a weakness — one generated by his hated Norse blood. Her ability to touch chords of awareness in him that had never been touched, angered him.

Black Bear had taunted him, saying if he left his brand on the woman, she would leave hers on him. But that would not be so. Brander was not weak like his mother; he would take the golden-haired Viking, but would not allow her to take him. She

76

would not mark his heart. That he promised himself.

Today, Kelda of the Vikings was a warrior.

Tonight, she would be his woman.

Brander and Black Bear walked to the women's field and joined the villagers who observed and studied the Vikings. When Brander could not locate Kelda, he watched the Vikings who competed against one another by throwing their knives into targets and into the ground so that the hilts stood upright.

They also practiced using the broadaxes. The weapons were larger than those used by the Iroquois, the heads of their tomahawks being made out of metal rather than stone. Then Rauthell brought them several tomahawks.

Brander laughed at their first clumsy attempts to hit the target, but they were a determined and skillful lot. Before long they had the feel of the weapon and were hitting the target's eye.

"They are skillful," Black Bear muttered. "We are going to need strong magic, my friend. Strong magic indeed."

"Yes," Brander murmured, but his mind was not on the Vikings' skill or their magic. His thoughts were centered on the Viking woman who walked onto the practice field.

She unfastened the brooch that held the mantle about her shoulders and furled the red material through the air before she laid it on the ground. Her long hair, banded at the forehead, was tucked into the belt that secured her stiletto around her waist.

"The Viking woman is beautiful," Black Bear

77

said. "Truly she is a slave to be desired."

"You may look at her," Brander warned his friend, "but do not touch her."

Black Bear laughed. "I am older than you, my friend. I have not the patience or the spirit to tame a woman as wild as the golden-haired Viking. I will leave that to you. I am content with looking."

Kelda's brightly colored shirt went well with the black trousers that fit her tightly and showed her woman's body to an advantage. Although Brander had held her in his arms, pressing her softness against himself, he had not realized until now how tall she was, or how slender. Her buttocks were gently rounded, tapering into long legs, the lower part of them clad in leather boots.

When she looked over and saw him, she called, "Are you spying out the competition, Chief Brander?"

"No," Black Bear murmured for Brander's ears only, "Chief Brander is keeping his eagle eyes on his property, Viking woman."

Slightly irritated with his friend, Brander ignored his teasing. Walking away from Black Bear toward Kelda, Brander said, "I wanted to see how skilled you were."

"We will be worthy opponents," she promised.

"Have you chosen the games you and your men will compete in?" Brander asked.

"Tomahawk and knife throwing and bows and arrows," she answered. "We are more familiar with the battle-ax, but your tomahawk is similar to our short-handled ax. We think we can handle it well enough."

"I think you can, too," Brander said dryly. "I saw your men practicing with it."

Kelda gave him a slight smile, but quickly returned her attention to the Vikings.

"Nay, Einar," she shouted and moved onto the field. "The tomahawk is much smaller than our broadax. Treat it like a calf rather than a full-grown cow."

As she walked, Brander watched with pleasure the gentle sway of her hips. When he had kissed her, he was sure he had aroused her. At other times he could tell she was very much aware of the tension between them—the tension that is created when a man and woman want each other sexually. Now, she seemed oblivious to him.

Why should it bother him? He did not like to be rebuffed in any way. He did not want a lifeless woman in his bed, submitting to his lovemaking. He wanted a woman full of spirit, one capable of giving love as well as receiving it.

Since he had become a warrior, he had been a favorite among the women. After his wife died, he could have his pick of the maidens. In fact, the elders were pressuring him to marry again. According to them, he was getting too old not to have any sons or daughters.

His hand clenched into a fist. He would have had sons and daughters and a wife had it not been for the Norse. In one swipe they took his entire family from him. And now they had the audacity to send for him.

The same man who was responsible for the death of his family, now crooked his finger at Brander and promised to make him a chieftain of the Vikings if he would come to his land.

If Brander were to go, he would kill Thoruald for what he had done to his family. Afterwards he would get his son and bring him home and pray that his mother's dreams were true and Eirik would be whole in mind once again.

Brander breathed deeply. The Viking woman caused him to have many heavy and troubled thoughts.

Kelda returned to where he stood. "Soon it will be time for the games to begin."

Brander nodded. "Since you are a woman," he said, "our referee has decided that you will have different marks from the other warriors. You are not as strong as a man."

Kelda rounded on him. "I will use the same marks. If I lose, I lose. But you will not give me special favors because I am a woman."

"You do not like womanhood?"

"I like it," she answered, "but I'm not here as a woman. I'm a Viking warrior."

Brander looked up and down her entire height, at the alluring curves and softness that were definitely feminine.

"You may want to separate the two," he said dryly, "but you cannot. You are both warrior and woman. The one you must be because the Master of Life decreed you be. The other you have chosen."

"Then I choose to be treated no differently than any other warrior."

"So shall it be," Brander said, moving toward his friend. "I will instruct Black Bear that you will compete, following the same rules as the men."

From the other end of the field, Rauthell shouted, "Vikings, it is time for the competition."

The Norsemen shouted their pleasure, gathered their weapons, and followed Rauthell. Their exuberance showed they were ready.

"Kelda!" A young man scarcely old enough to have a beard came running.

"Aye, Ulmer?"

"Egil may have had stories to tell about the Skrellings, but none of his will compare to the ones I will recite when we return to the jarl's *stofa*." Gray eyes glittered in a face that was framed with a mop of unruly red hair.

"True," she replied. "Asgaut's *skald* will rue the day he said you could not get your tales straight, will he not?"

Ulmer bobbed his head. "I may have seen only ten and six winters, but I will be the better *skald*. Egil will be jealous when we return. I must go now. I want to be with the warriors when they take their places at the field of competition."

Returning to Kelda, Brander asked, "Who is the boy?"

"Ulmer," she answered, "my storyteller."

"A warrior also?"

"Nay. His weapon is his ability to memorize our history and to pass it down to our children so they will know, understand, and be proud of their heritage."

"It is the same with us," Brander said.

Lapsing into silence, they walked side-by-side toward the field where the competition would take place. With each step she took, their arms brushing together every so often, Kelda was made aware of him. She was sure that his walking close to her, that this occasional physical contact was deliberate.

On the one level she was oblivious to his advances; on the other she was not. Her body continually responded to the primitive overtures. In fact, at times she seemed to encourage them. But not at the moment. She needed a clear head if she was going to present any contest to him at all.

"I suppose we will see how skillful your warriors

are with their weapons," she said to break the silence.

Brander laughed, the sound low and raspy coming from deep within his chest. It sent pleasure singing through her body.

"We are good. You will do well to wager on us."

"Not I," she answered. "Most Vikings love to wager and take it seriously, but I do not."

"Do not what?" Brander asked. "Wager or take it seriously?"

"Wager," she replied.

Dark and painful memories returned to haunt Kelda as she thought about the slave auction. Drunk Vikings wagering each other they would be the one to get her as they raised their bids. As they raised their wagers. As they sloshed mead, beer, and ale on her. As their greasy hands ripped off her clothing until she stood naked before them.

Because she was a virgin and they were assured of this, the price kept rising higher and higher. Then Ragnar and Hauk had appeared to rescue her. Ragnar outbid all others, wrapped her tenderly in his mantle, and took her to his father Jarl Thoruald.

Every day of her life, Kelda thanked Odin that Ragnar had rescued her and that Thoruald had adopted her, removing her from the status of thrall to that of beloved daughter.

"I must leave you now," Brander said. "I hope your magic is strong, Viking woman."

"It is."

She bent and picked up her mantle, hooking the material through her mother's brooch. Her hand brushed over the aged piece of jewelry, and she traced its radial symmetry with the tip of a finger. It instilled her with a confidence that seemed to lag

82

when she was around the Iroquois chieftain.

When Kelda arrived at the playing field, villagers had already gathered and were sitting on bright yellow, green, and red blankets, made from opossum skins, Rauthell explained. The villagers laughed and talked boisterously as they made their wagers. At one end, sitting on a elevated wooden platform were the elders.

Wild Flower appeared, sprinkling powder across the length and breadth of the field. Then she walked to stand in front of the elders, lifting her hands to the sky. After the prayer, the musicians, dancers, and singers moved to the field and began to entertain the spectators.

"When the dancers and singers form an aisle toward you," Rauthell instructed Kelda, "your champion is to walk through to the center of the field."

Kelda turned to her old friend and mentor. "Hauk, you are rightly the champion of the Vikings."

He and Rauthell shook their heads at the same time. Kelda looked from one to the other in surprise.

"It must be their chieftain," Rauthell said.

Kelda swallowed the knot that formed in her throat. She had not intended to be cast as the Vikings' champion. There was no way she could win against the Iroquois, and she would disappoint her men.

"Brander knew this when he allowed me to compete," she accused. "By his silence he has deliberately misled me."

"I would not think so," Rauthell said. "That is not Brander's way."

"Perhaps I know a different Brander from you," Kelda said.

The dancing and singing continued, but Kelda heard little of it. She was deep in thought, wondering how she would avenge herself, wondering how she would salvage her warriors from the situation she had put them in. If only she had thought before she insisted. If only she had thought.

She paced back and forth, searching for an answer. There had to be one.

Canby, his hands clasped behind his back, walked to her side. "Have you devised a way by which we can win this game?" he asked.

Kelda shook her head.

"I told Thoruald this trip was doomed before it ever began," he muttered. "How could a man claim one of these barbarians as his son?"

Kelda's gaze went to Brander.

"Why would he wish to do so?" Canby insisted. "Have you learned anything about this offspring?"

Knowing that Hauk had recounted to the Vikings all that had transpired at the council meeting, Kelda resented Canby's questioning her further, but she would not antagonize him by pointing this out. She wanted and needed his full cooperation in order to keep the men conciliatory. Succinctly she repeated all that had taken place in regards to their mission to Skrellingland, the gold collar, and the identity of Thoruald's spawn.

Canby worried with his beard. "Do you think the Skrellings will release us on the morrow, Kelda?"

"I cannot outguess them," she answered. "We will have to wait to see."

They may release you and the others, she thought, *but it is doubtful Brander will let me go.* She had sworn Hauk to secrecy about her being Brander's slave. She did not want Canby any more upset than he already was and knew he would be unable to han-

84

dle the idea of her being a slave or of her being unable to return home.

Hauk approached her with a grim smile on his weathered face. Gingerly he touched the bruised swelling on his forehead. "Our men have performed well, mistress, but not well enough for us to win the tournament."

She laid a hand on her friend's shoulder. "I will think of something."

"Aye," he answered. "I have confidence in you."

He nodded his head and returned to the sidelines. Canby, grumbling and complaining, followed him.

Think, Kelda! Think! The Iroquois is more powerful than you, but surely you can think better than he. If you can outwit him, you will be a champion. Something nagged at her, but she could not remember. Something she should remember.

Two lines of dancers and singers who faced each other and formed a corridor, moved toward her. She allowed them to escort her to the field so that she was standing in front of the elders.

Tall Tree nodded, and the villagers clapped and shouted. Standing erect, Kelda turned several times so that all could see her. Her gaze caught Hauk's. He smiled and winked at her.

Heavy beating on the drums began, and the dancers and singers, moving in rhythm to the beat, crossed the field to the sidelines of the Iroquois. Kelda saw someone briefly. Brander? she wondered, as they surrounded him and led him to the field. Singing and waving their feathered sticks in the air, they began to move back away from him. Still she could not see the person.

Was it Brander?

Chapter Seven

It was Brander!

Kelda's heartbeat quickened. She had thought him awesome, almost overpowering when she first saw him. Now she thought him august in appearance. He wore no shirt, and the sun glistened on the bronze, muscled biceps and on the fire-dark chest hair that thickly swirled into the waistband of his tight-fitting, buff-colored breeches that were tucked into high-top moccasins.

Already she knew he was graced with extraordinary power in his muscles, in the breadth of his shoulders, in the width of his chest, and in the strength of his thighs. Today she saw that his belly was whipcord lean and taut muscle also.

Her face lifted. He was smiling broadly and waving to the villagers. Indeed, Brander, War Chief of the Iroquois, was a champion. She would recognize the stance, the smile, and the pride anywhere. She had seen it often enough in her own village. Evidently it was common to all males.

Then he turned so that he was facing her; their gazes locked. All thoughts, all others faded into nothingness. Her anger, her thoughts of revenge temporarily forgotten, she stared into the depths of those mysterious eyes, as if to read his mind or perhaps his soul.

Wild Flower stood and walked to Kelda. Speaking

in Iroquois, she handed her a basket.

"Take it," Brander instructed, then translated, "This is the gift from the Council of the Elders. Do not open it until the gift has been presented to the second captain."

As he talked, Delling rose and, from the other direction, approached him.

"The person who represents the Council of the Elders," Brander continued, "is the one who bestows the gift."

Wild Flower slipped the lid off the container to pull out a gold collar. For a moment the world seemed to spin around Kelda, and she thought her heart would stop beating. The collar that matched the arm band. Wild Flower held it out to her, and Tall Tree spoke. Delling translated.

"You came in search of the gold collar that belonged to Thoruald the Viking. We, the Iroquois of the Forestland, make you a gift of the collar."

I came not after the collar, Kelda wanted to scream. *I came after the offspring. I want Thoruald's son* . . . and there was no doubt in her mind that his child was a son and Brander was the son.

Kelda shook her head. "I cannot accept the collar."

"Yes, you can," Canby called from the sidelines.

Hauk, holding him by the shoulders, kept Canby from running onto the field.

"We can take that back to Thoruald and prove to him that he has no son over here," Canby continued to yell. "Our mission will be completed. Take the collar, Kelda."

Hauk clamped his hand over Canby's mouth and pulled him behind the lines.

"You must take it," Brander said. "It is our custom. To refuse is to defy the wishes of the Council

87

of Elders of the Iroquois; it is to defy the Spirits who guide our life on earth and in the afterlife."

"You defy them."

He paused only fractionally before he said softly, "For you to do so, Viking, is sure death."

Still Kelda did not reach for the collar.

"Take the collar," Brander commanded in a harsh tone. Grasping her wrist, he held out her hand.

Reluctantly Kelda accepted the gift.

Delling opened the basket he carried to withdraw a small ivory statue. "This is yours, Brander of the Iroquois. The Council of Elders of the Iroquois wants you to have a strong talisman, one that will be your symbol, your totem. I present you with this carving. It is the head of the hawk."

Brander reached for it, and Kelda, fascinated by the play of muscles in his body, glanced at his upper arm. He wore a wide arm band. Beneath it, she wondered if perhaps he had a hawk tattooed on him—like the Iroquois thrall. Then she glanced at the small ivory statue lying on his palm.

His hand closed; he gripped it tightly in his fist. Black fury on his face, Brander looked at his mother. Because he spoke his native language, Kelda did not understand what he was saying, but his voice was smooth and void of emotion, in direct contrast to his expression.

Speaking to Brander, Wild Flower moved closer to him. She shook her rattle, a fine powder spraying on his shoulders. Softly she chanted, then moved to where Kelda stood.

After she had sprinkled her, Wild Flower said in Norse, "Kelda of the Vikings, we are glad the Master of Life brought you to our shores and that your mission is one of peace. May you receive the answer to your questions, and know that nothing in

88

life simply happens. There is a reason for all things."

"Thank you," Kelda said, her words sounding hollow.

"The gold collar has been entrusted to you," Wild Flower said. "Give it to the one to whom it belongs."

Kelda glanced at Brander. "I will," she answered and returned it to the basket. "Will you take care of it for me until the games are over?"

"I will. Now I will lead you to your warriors, so the games can begin."

"One moment, Kelda of the Vikings," Brander said, "I would also give you a gift."

Wild Flower started as did Delling; nonplussed, both stared at the Iroquois chieftain as did Kelda.

Brander held out his open hand, and Kelda looked down to see the tiny statue. He had gripped it so tightly, it left a red indentation in his palm. Having seen another similar to it, she recognized it as a game piece.

Thoruald's falcon! Only Thoruald had the audacity to have a falcon rather than the elephant of the Arabians or the counselor of the Europeans for his game set. He had chosen his own totem. The falcon was far the wiser, he argued. Could this, like the gold collar and armband, belong to Thoruald?

"Although it is not customary for one champion to give another a totem, I would like to give one to you," Brander continued.

"No, Kelda," Wild Flower said, speaking in Norse, "you must not accept the gift. Brander does not have the right to give it away. It is his, blessed by the Master of Life, the Sun, the Earth, and the Water. It is breathed upon by the four winds. If he is to have magic, he must keep it."

89

"You knew, when Delling presented me with the game piece, my mother, that I would not gladly receive it. I want nothing to do with the Norse." He spat on the ground. "This is what I do to them. This belongs to the Viking. He is her jarl, her father."

Brander caught Kelda's hand in his, planted the carving in her palm, and closed her fingers around it. "I have given the head of the hawk to the Viking woman. It is done."

Wild Flower gasped and fell back; Delling caught her in his arms. The crowd quieted—it was an ominous quiet. Their gazes fastened on the activity in the field.

Tall Tree stood and called out. Delling moved to the high chief and spoke to him. Out of the corner of her eye, Kelda saw Rauthell as he spoke to the Vikings.

His voice clear and strong, Brander said, "Kelda of the Vikings, may the Master of Life bless you and give you great magic. As the hawk swoops to her prey, so may you. May her victory be yours, adopted daughter of the Falcon. It is right that this belongs to you."

Not fully apprehending the impact of what had happened, Kelda's head spun. She was unsure if the game piece had ever belonged to her jarl or not, but she knew that Brander, in rejecting it, had rejected Thoruald and the Norse. Not only had he rejected Thoruald, but he had defied Iroquois custom.

He defied all gods!

She dropped the carving into the pocket of her mantle.

"Come, Kelda." Wild Flower clutched the basket close to her side. Color was gone from her face, and her voice was low and pained. "I will take you to your warriors now. The games will begin."

When Kelda reached the sidelines, her warriors were busy talking among themselves. So were the villagers.

"They are changing their wagers," Rauthell explained. "They think Brander's magic is evil now that he has defied custom. They believe you have the good magic."

At that moment Brander's voice rose above the commotion. The crowd hushed; they settled down to hear their champion speak. The Vikings crowded around Rauthell, who was their translator.

"My people, my magic is strong," Brander said and grasped the talon necklace about his neck.

He had always been different from the other tribesmen. Having always believed more in himself than in external or spiritual forces, he had no deep-seated religious beliefs. He had little patience with dogmas.

If the gold collar had had any magic, that had been weakened when Eirik was taken prisoner by the Vikings and the arm band had been separated from the collar. With the coming of the Vikings and with their request — nay with their demands — that Thoruald's son return to Norwegia with them, the power of the totem was completely broken.

"My magic is strong," he repeated. He lifted the necklace over his head and held it out, moving around the field, so that all the spectators could view it. "I wear a new totem, one made especially for Brander the Iroquois. It is a necklace fashioned and crafted by the Woman of Dreams. It carries her magic, my brothers."

"Hear! Hear!" The crowd cheered him on.

"No matter what my talisman, I refuse to wear

the totem of the Norse. It has no magic for the Iroquois. Remember the evil they have brought to our shores and our village."

"Hear! Hear!" the people chanted again and clapped their sticks together.

"First, they came, took our women to wife, and when they sailed away in their dragonships, they left behind women big with their children, children whom they did not want, children in whom the Norse blood flows with the Iroquois."

"Hear! Hear!"

"Then they came two winters ago to raid and take captive our children — perhaps their own children — for their slaves. My people, Brander of the Iroquois, declares that his blood is Iroquois. He wears the totem of the Firebrand of the Iroquois. Today we will be victorious over the Norsemen."

He was so confident, his speech so fiery, that the villagers clapped and hurrahed for him. Quickly they forgot his defiance. They beat their sticks together and chanted his name. He had convinced them of his magic. They believed in the Firebrand of the Iroquois.

The games began. Excitement buzzed through the air. Each took his turn, both a Viking and an Iroquois keeping score. When Kelda was not competing, she was searching her mind for the illusive piece of information she sought. She knew she had it, if only she could remember.

Standing behind the shooting line, longbow in hand and a leather bracer on her left arm, Kelda nocked an arrow and aimed at a target drawn on a large sheet of bark. Although the distance was far greater than she had suspected, she knew she had the strength to hit the center of the target at least three out of the six tries she had. She let her first arrow go; it flew through the air straight to the center of the target. Arrow after arrow she shot, her arms getting tired with the release of each. She managed to hit the center of the circle four out of six tries. When her quiver was empty, she stepped back, unfastened the bracer, and smiled at the villagers who applauded and cheered her.

Brander walked to where she stood. "You handle your weapons with skill, Viking."

"All Viking women are taught to use them. When the men go off a-viking in the spring and summer, we women have to run the houses and the village. We must be able to protect ourselves."

As well as teaching her how to use the bow and arrow, dagger, sword, and the broadax, Ragnar and Hauk had taught her to play games of skill and thought. Both knew that she as a woman did not have the physical prowess of a man; therefore, she needed an edge if she were to be able to protect herself.

Brander, taking his place behind the lines, shot six arrows, each of them splitting the ones Kelda had shot. When he lowered his longbow, amidst the cheering and adulation, he gave Kelda a superior smile.

Next came the tomahawk throwing. At the distance marked, Kelda had no chance. The weapon was too unfamiliar, and she lacked the physical strength.

The Iroquois, whose physiques were more wiry than the Vikings, were skillful. They could throw accurately from great distances; seldom did one hit outside the center circle on the target. Of them all, Brander was the best. His boasting had not been in vain.

Unable to take her eyes off him, Kelda watched

as he drew his arm back and threw the tomahawk, the handle slipping easily out of his opened hand. As if it were an extension of him, certainly an extension of the skilled warrior, the tomahawk sliced cleanly through the air, whining in the wind until it thwacked to a halt in the center of the innermost circle of the target.

Six times he had thrown; six times he had hit the same spot. Proudly, he smiled at her as he walked off the field. Although he was arrogant in his victory, she returned the smile. He deserved it; he had performed well.

Viking and Iroquois were put to the test as they pitted their martial skills against one another until one game remained, the knife throwing. Only Kelda and Brander were left to compete. He was first to throw. Kelda followed immediately. Both their knives hit the center of the circle, hilt up.

Their scores were even until the sixth throw. Now it was time for Kelda to show the war chief of the Iroquois how skilled she was with the knife. Certainly her overall tally would be lower than his, but she would win this event.

She ran her fingers over her mother's brooch for good luck.

The tip of the blade balanced between her fingers, she threw the knife. It twinged through the air, sliced into the earth, the hilt vibrating seconds before it stood upright. She threw her knife so close to Brander's that it knocked his over.

When the scores were tallied, the Vikings and the Iroquois had tied. The scorekeepers had to do no tally for Kelda to know who had won. Her scores did not begin to compare with Brander's. Her warriors mumbled their disappointment, but she could do nothing about their loss.

94

The Iroquois, proud of their warriors, were whooping and hollering their victory. They busily rushed around the field, collecting their wagers. Kelda walked into the center of the field to meet Brander.

"You are the champion," she said, aware that her men felt as if she were the one who had given them the decided disadvantage. And she was. "Your magic was strong."

Remembering that the loser was to present the winner with a gift, she pulled her dagger from the sheath and handed it to him hilt first.

"I would give you my sword, my bow, or my short-handled ax," she said, "but they are smaller than those used by the men. I give you my dagger, my favorite weapon, the one with which I am most proficient and one you will find useful."

His eyes shining, Brander took the weapon, running his thumb carefully over the flat side of the blade. "Thank you, Kelda of the Vikings."

Brander held the dagger in the air to let the villagers see his gift. While they clapped and cheered, Kelda made her way back to where her gloomy warriors stood. She plunged her hands into the pockets of her mantle and felt the tiny statue, the game piece.

The game piece! *Hnefatafl!* Why had she not thought of it sooner?

She turned to Canby and Hauk. "I have the answer!" she exclaimed and moved back to the center of the field. Raising her voice, she said, "Brander of the Iroquois, grant me one request."

She returned to where he stood.

"I accepted your challenge and played your games. Now, I would like to issue a challenge of my own."

Surprised, Brander stared at her. Quickly the word spread among the Iroquois; their activities ceased. They crept closer to the field. Curiously, they watched Kelda and Brander. They listened for the interpretations of their conversation; they waited to see if they would have the opportunity to place more wagers.

"What is your challenge?" he asked.

She held up the game piece. "I would like to challenge you to a game of *hnefatafl*."

Brander said nothing. The crowd urged him on.

"You do play, do you not?"

"I do," he replied.

"Are you afraid that I will win this one? Can it be that a woman fought you on your terms, but you cannot fight her on her terms? Surely the Firebrand of the Iroquois is not afraid of a *mere* woman."

"As I get to know you better, Viking, I find you more than mere."

Kelda laughed. "I assured you that I keep my promises, Skrelling. Does this mean that you have accepted my challenge?"

He nodded. "What are your terms?"

"I will win my dagger from you and be champion of the day; I will also win my freedom."

"You will be granted your first two stipulations, not the third. You, Viking woman, are a prize of war and belong to me. I will not give you up." The words were final.

"Hear! Hear!" The Iroquois shouted in unison, hitting their sticks together.

Kelda wanted to press for all three of her terms, but that was not to be. She could push Brander no further. Being champion of the day would please her warriors, and she would have her beloved dagger back. She would have to think of another way to win her freedom, but win it she would.

"I accept," she said loudly enough that her voice carried to the spectators.

Their murmur of approval reached her ears.

She added softly for Brander's ears only, "Know that between you and me the war has only begun. Know also, Brander of the Iroquois, that my magic is stronger."

"It is strong," Brander agreed, "but not as strong as that I create for myself."

Kelda held out her hand, the ivory carving resting in her palm. "As long as the hawk is in my hand, I control him."

She closed her fingers around the game piece and smiled.

"Now he cannot fly."

Chapter Eight

"You had no right to reject the game piece."

Wild Flower walked back and forth in the entry room of Brander's lodge. She was so upset her hands shook as she fingered the medicine pouch that hung about her neck.

"You, my son, a mortal, have flaunted the laws of the Spirits before them. They will be angry at you. They will turn against you."

"Have you ever wondered, my mother, if perhaps they would be proud of me for my actions? For my having stood up for myself and creating the world I wish to have?"

"Be silent, Brander!" Wild Flower hissed. "Do not anger them anymore. Have you no respect for our customs?"

"Which are my customs? The Iroquois or the Norse? I am so filled with both of them, they begin to run together and it is hard to distinguish."

His back to his mother, Brander stood in front of one of the wall openings, the mat covering rolled up so that the late afternoon sun spilled warmly into the room. He heard the revelling in the distance as the villagers laid wagers and prepared for the game of the jarls between him and the Viking.

Wild Flower's hand closed over his upper arm, and she tugged him around so they were looking into each other's faces. "What is happening to you,

Brander? Why are you doing this to yourself?"

Brander removed his mother's hand and stepped away from her. "You, my mother, the Wild Flower, have always been blessed to know who and what you are. Only Iroquois blood runs through your veins."

"I have been torn also," Wild Flower protested. "I am the shaman, one of the Iroquois yet one who is set aside."

"Yes," Brander agreed. "You are the Woman of Dreams. You chose to be that. But you have never been torn in two because you belong to two peoples, and you were never really sure which one to whom you belong."

"I knew this would be," Wild Flower said, "that is why—"

"That is why you reared me to be both Norse and Iroquois," Brander exclaimed. "My being an Iroquois was not enough for you, my mother."

"Brander—"

But he would not be stopped. "Because of your dreams I had to be Norse also. When I was too small to make my own decisions, when I was yet guided by your wisdom, you had Delling teach me Norse customs."

He tugged the bracelet off, tossed it across the room, and pointed to the tattoo on his upper arm.

"The brand you gave to me is not even my own. It is Thoruald's falcon, not my hawk. Everything I am—all my symbols belong to Thoruald. My son carries the same talisman, and he, too, has become a part of Thoruald."

Brander slid Kelda's dagger from his waistband and held it to his wrist.

"I would cut myself and drain all the Norse blood from my veins if I could, but in doing that I would

99

also drain out my Iroquois blood. To kill the Norse, I must also kill the Iroquois."

Tears ran down Wild Flower's cheeks. "It is an odd thing, my son, but blood knows no color. It honors no races. Indiscriminately it gives life to all. I am sorry you have caused yourself suffering because you cannot accept you are different."

She wiped the tears from her face. "I have always thought this difference set you apart from others, proving that you were the superior. I had Delling teach you the way of the Norse, my son, because I knew your destiny would lie over the Great Water."

"Perhaps your dreams were true in part," Brander said. "My son, Eirik, whom the Vikings call Kolby, is living with them. He has already been taken into the household of Jarl Thoruald—his Norse grandfather."

He moved to where his arm band lay, bent, and picked it up. He ran his fingers over the engravings.

"Perhaps the Master of Life was being kind to him when he erased all memory of the Iroquois from Eirik-Kolby. Now my son can become one of the Norse without feeling as if he has betrayed his own people. He will not be divided between two peoples as I have been. He will not hate the one blood and love the other."

"I am sorry that you are causing yourself such grief, my son," Wild Flower said, "but I cannot be sorry for the decisions I made about your education when you were a child. Knowing what I know at this moment, I would not go back and change one thing."

"Not even to giving me an Iroquois father?"

Wild Flower shook her head. "Most of all, not that, my son. No Iroquois, no other Norse warrior

100

could have produced Brander, the Firebrand. You are what you are because of Thoruald and me. I would have none other than you for my son. Some day you will realize that you would have none other than Thoruald and me for your parents."

Some of Brander's anger evaporated. He softened his voice. "I am blessed to have you for my mother. I would have none other but you."

"Thank you, my son." Wild Flower walked to the door. "Now, I go. I will meet you at the marking of the sun for the game."

"I will meet you there," he said.

At her words Brander's eyes went to the time stick that stood upright in the clearing in front of the lodge. The shadow was surely moving to the mark, the time when he and Kelda would play the war game of the jarls, when they would pit themselves against one another in yet another game — this one of strategy.

He had clearly won the games played by the Iroquois, but that had been no contest. Surely his prowess was greater than that of the women.

He had to admit — albeit grudgingly — the Viking woman was a clever one. She demanded they compete against each other in a mind-skill game of the Norse — a game that reflected the way they lived and fought their battles. It reflected nothing about Brander's Iroquois heritage; it called for him to compete as a Norse.

Wild Flower slowly made her way to her lodge that was set far apart from the village. Even had village custom not dictated, she would have chosen to be by herself. She had time to think as she prepared her medicines.

She stopped by one of the trees and knelt to ex-

101

amine a plant. She ran her fingers gently over the leaves, inspecting it to determine if it was ready to be plucked. Deciding that it was too young, her gaze moved to one of the potherbs, a dandelion that grew around the base of the tree. Her favorite flower.

She picked the yellow bloom and held it to her nose, smelling the fragrance and remembering a time when Thoruald had picked her a bouquet of such flowers and had given them to her. Tears again rushed down her cheeks and blurred her vision.

Thoruald had not been thinking of his Iroquois bride when he sent his Vikings to the land of the Iroquois. He was searching for his offspring.

Still holding the blossom, Wild Flower began her walk to her lodge. She had known what the consequences were when she refused to accompany Thoruald to his homeland. He was a virile man, and it would not be long before he found female companionship.

His having other women in his life did not perturb Wild Flower. She accepted and understood this was a necessary part of life, but she had often wondered if he had truly loved again.

She would have enjoyed talking to Kelda about Thoruald. She wanted to know what he looked like in the winter of his life. Had his golden red hair and beard now turned white? Was he still a robust warrior, his height and breadth a measurement in muscles? What had he sent to his wife of so many winters past?

"Here you are." Delling's voice broke into her reverie.

"Welcome, Delling," Wild Flower said.

"You are sad." He scrutinized her face.

"Aye," she replied. "I am thinking that it was this

102

time thirty springs ago that I parted with Thoruald. Now it is time for me to part with my son."

"You believe he will journey to Norwegia?" Delling asked.

"Yes," Wild Flower replied, and the two of them fell into step as they walked the pathway to her lodge. "I have seen it in a dream, Delling. He will go, but he will be unhappy about going. He will fight it and the Viking woman. Much unhappiness lies ahead for my son before he finds his destiny."

"Have you seen anything else in your dreams that has saddened you?" Delling asked.

As always, Wild Flower was astonished by Delling's perceptiveness. Once again inundated with memories, she gazed at the dandelion.

"I do not know if it is an omen or not," she finally answered, "but tonight I will recount my dream for all the Iroquois to hear."

They walked several more paces before she again spoke.

"I confess, Delling, for the first time since I received the gift, I am unsure of its meaning. The Master of Life told me that another would interpret it for me."

She stopped walking and turned to her friend; she clasped his forearm.

"Perhaps I should not have given Brander the game piece. Delling, I have seen forty and eight winters. Never have I been frightened of the future. I am now."

He caught her hands in his and squeezed them tightly.

"Please do not worry, my friend. The Master of Life has not abandoned you. Whatever the future is, wherever it may take you, the Master of Life will be with you."

"Thank you, Delling," Wild Flower said. "I do not know what I would have done without you all these winters. You have been an able student. Your medicine grows stronger each day."

"Because you taught me well," he said and smiled. "I will leave you now. I will see you at the game."

"Yes, I am to escort Kelda as you will Brander."

Delling laughed softly. "Truly, he is the son of Thoruald."

"Yes, he is the son of the Falcon."

"Brander is the son of the Falcon," Kelda declared. "I know it, Canby."

Beneath the shade of a large tree, Kelda stood outside the longhouse where her Vikings were housed.

"This is a feeling you have," Canby argued. "It would be unkind of us to take this news to Thoruald when you cannot prove it."

"True." Kelda sighed. "And no one is willing to discuss it with me. Brander has even said that I may not learn any more tomorrow than I know right now."

Canby paced back and forth agitatedly. "Thoruald and I have known each other since we were lads, I cannot understand why he has become obsessed with the idea that he has a son over here."

"Can you not?" Kelda scoffed softly. "Would you wish Asgaut to inherit leadership if you were Thoruald?"

Canby ran his hand through his thinning hair. "Nay, I suppose not," he answered. "But, there is far worse to inherit than Asgaut. Can you imagine what our lives will be like if one of these Skrellings should return to claim Talon of the Falcon?"

"He would have to prove himself," Kelda reminded the old man. "Neither Thoruald nor the villagers would accept him without a testing."

Through watery eyes, Canby peered at her. "He has not touched you, has he?"

"He has tried to frighten me," Kelda admitted, "but he has done me no bodily harm."

"Remember you belong to Asgaut. You are his betrothed."

"Aye." She deliberately pushed her betrothal to Asgaut from mind, but she would not forget her sacred oath to Thoruald.

"Asgaut is a good man, mistress. He will give you fine sons to rule the House of the Falcon."

"Asgaut is not a man," Kelda said. "He is a warrior only."

Canby lowered his head and again plucked at his beard. "I am pleased you thought to challenge the Skrelling to a game of the jarls. You are skillful, and I believe you can win."

"I must win," Kelda said.

The game board sat on the ground between Kelda and Brander; both stared at it. In a circle around them sat the villagers and the Vikings, quietly watching. They had been watching for a long time. To one side of them sat Wild Flower and Delling. To the other were Hauk, Canby, and Ulmer.

Wild Flower studied her son and the woman who had challenged him. Their heads were bent low over the board; one was dark, the other was fair. The way it had been so many winters ago when her love was here. Both she and her love had contemplated the game pieces — game pieces that Thoruald had

105

had crafted for himself in one of the major towns in Norwegia.

Losing herself in thoughts of Thoruald, Wild Flower gazed into the forest. Afternoon sunlight slid through a crack in the thick foliage of the trees. Rays danced from the sky to the ground creating a mystical, golden corridor. At the end of the corridor Wild Flower saw someone moving toward her.

Grandfather Time walked backward.

She saw a warrior. Her Viking warrior! His red hair and beard gleamed like golden fire as he made his way to her. He was a tall man with broad shoulders. The biceps on his arms were well developed by exercise with the sword and battle-ax. But today he carried only a huge bouquet of dandelions. They were so at odds with her warrior lover.

"Thoruald," Wild Flower whispered in broken Norse, the language he had taught her to speak, "is that you?"

"Aye, mistress, 'tis I," he answered, his blue eyes moving over her entire body before they came back to rest on her face. He held out the flowers. "I brought you these."

Wild Flower took them and lowered her face to bury it in the scent and beauty of the flowers. He had not yet spoken of his purpose in coming but she knew. And her heart was heavy.

"It is with sadness that I come."

"I know," she whispered.

Still she did not lift her face from the flowers. Still she did not look into those eyes that were the color of the Great Water.

"You and your people are leaving our shores. You are returning to your land."

"Aye," he answered.

His callused hand, so accustomed to violence and war, tenderly touched her chin and lifted her face so that she was looking at him.

"How did you know?"

"I saw it in a dream last night," she said.

She had seen more, but she could not tell Thoruald. She was not willing to go to his land, and if he knew she was carrying his child, he would insist on her going with him. He would abduct her if necessary.

"I want you to return with me as my lady-wife," he said. "I know the land and the customs will be different, but you will love my country and my people."

Wild Flower reached up and touched the craggy face she loved more than any other, the face she must commit to memory as that would be all she had of him when he was gone. With his golden red beard and hair, he reminded her of the majesty of the sun.

"I cannot leave my people, Thoruald. I am their Woman of Dreams. I am their shaman. I cannot desert them."

"So you will desert me?" he asked.

His hand closed over hers. The calluses on his palm were an abrasive caress to her flesh.

"The Master of Life gave me this gift for them," she murmured, as desire flamed through her entire body.

No man had ever excited her before Thoruald; no man had ever touched her heart and soul but Thoruald. She knew as she stood here, looking at him for perhaps the last time, that no other man would ever excite or touch her. No other! Thoruald was the love of her life.

"I cannot leave them."

"And I cannot stay because of my people," Thoruald said sadly.

He unfastened the brooch that held his mantle about his neck and furled the rich cloth through the air. Laying it on the ground, he made a pallet on which both gladly sat. He slipped off the gold collar and arm band and laid them in her lap.

"These are yours," he said.

"A token of your love?" Wild Flower said.

"Nay, mistress," Thoruald said, his eyes troubled. "The token of my love is the broad expanse of the ocean, the height and depth of the sky. It is as eternal as the sun and the moon. But I cannot give you what belongs to the gods. I can only give you what belongs to me. My heart and soul you already have. All that is left is jewelry. Of all my jewelry, these two pieces are the most important and valuable to me. I would that you have them."

"Thank you, my love. I will have them."

Thoruald leaned forward, his lips taking hers. At first the kiss was tentative and soft, but when she moved against him, his mouth forced hers open.

Wild Flower arched her back to the gentle pressure of his big hand, a warmth spreading across her breasts to sink into her belly. A tingling sensation moved downward all the way to her toes before it rose again to throb at the joining of her legs.

Finally Thoruald broke the kiss, and his lips, warm and firm, nipped hers, moving around her mouth, butterflying across her cheeks back to her mouth. The thick beard and moustache brushed against her skin. His hands cupped the fullness of her breasts.

Wild Flower gasped and lifted her hand to catch him and to still his movements. Her stomach quivered, then drew taut with her desires. She was overwhelmed by those feelings that only Thoruald had the ability to arouse in her. As always they were startling and intensely passionate.

She placed light, feathery kisses against his neck and snuggled against his sturdy frame. When her hand slid through the opening of his shirt to touch his hairy chest, she felt the pounding of his heart.

His hand moved in agonizing sweetness up Wild Flower's arms, over her shoulders, and down her back. He placed hot, searing kisses along the hollow of her neck, along the opening of her buckskin dress.

His touch filled Wild Flower with an undeniable desire. As his caresses roamed boldly over her body, she moaned softly, surrendering to the passionate spell this man could always weave about her. Gladly she surrendered to the heady pleasure that possessed her flesh.

They pulled apart only long enough to undress, then they came together again. Wild Flower gazed at the bronzed, muscle-rich chest and trim waist; she let her gaze settle on his erection.

"Of all men, Thoruald," she said, "you are indeed the most magnificent."

"And you, my wildflower, are the most beautiful of all women."

Wild Flower's hands moved across his chest until they touched his nipples. With a groan of unleashed desire, Thoruald lowered his mouth to capture hers with tender abandon. Finally he raised his lips and lowered her to the mantle.

When both were lying down, his lips captured hers in a hot, moist kiss. His hand moved slowly, surely down her body until he spread her legs. He lifted himself over her, murmuring words of endearment between kisses. His hands prepared her for entry; her pleasure was his.

Wild Flower arched to receive him. She gasped as the bigness and warmth settled smoothly inside her. His lips captured hers in a long deep kiss, and he began to stroke her gently.

Wild Flower moved with him. She felt his hands slip beneath her buttocks, his fingers digging into the sensitive flesh. They kneaded and pulled her tighter against him.

He kissed her lips, her neck, her breasts; he thrust deeply, more rapidly, more fiercely. As she moved in rhythm with him, Wild Flower's body burst into an uncontrollable blaze of passion.

Her blood turned into fiery passion, burning through her veins. Her heart pounded. Her breath came in short, ragged gasps. Every nerve in her body tensed. She reached her climax.

Only then did Thoruald bury his face in her shoulder as he buried himself deeply within her, releasing himself. He rolled over, and quietly they lay together.

Wild Flower pressed her head and palm against Thoruald's chest. She felt his heartbeat and breathing regulate.

"I never knew being with a man could be so fulfilling," she said.

"No other woman has ever satisfied me so," he confessed.

Combing her fingers through his beard, she looked at the gold arm band and collar lying on the edge of the pallet. Thoruald's good-bye gift.

In the warmth of the sunshine, secluded from the village, they lay together, embracing each other. They did not talk, but they needed not. Their togetherness itself was all that was necessary.

Each knew this would be the last time they made love; neither admitted it aloud.

Later that afternoon, they played the game of the jarls Thoruald had taught her, the game he loved so much. So far she had not won, but she was getting better at it. She gazed at the game board.

"The jarl," he said and pointed to a carving. "That is me." Another carving. He smiled. "The jarl's lady. That is you."

Even as he said the words, she knew she would not be the jarl's wife. She would remain here to be the shaman, the Woman of Dreams—a woman destined to spend her life alone and in meditation with nature and the Spirits of life.

"And the falcon," she joined in, picking up the third tiny carving. "That is you also."

"Aye, my lady-love," he said softly. "The falcon and I are the same. According to the Arabians and the people of India, who fashioned the game after their military strategy, this should have been an elephant piece to symbolize their choice elephant corps."

Thoruald picked up the falcon and turned it over in his fingers as he stared at it.

"According to the Europeans, it should be a count or a counselor. For me, Thoruald Eiriksson, heir of the Talon of the Falcon and one day to be jarl, the falcon is the wisest of all creatures, the best strategist of the predators; therefore, I chose to have him fashioned as one of my game pieces."

Thoruald placed the game piece in Wild Flower's palm and closed her hand around it. He closed his hand around hers.

"I leave this falcon game piece with you, my love, in hopes that the falcon shall one day bring you home to me."

"Your set will be incomplete without it," Wild Flower said.

"Aye, as will be my heart without you. Ever I will keep it, my love, to remind me of my Iroquois bride."

Tears stung Wild Flower's lids. She had lost her jarl!

"You are about to lose your jarl," Brander said, jarring Wild Flower from her reverie and bringing her back to the present.

Blinking her eyes, she looked around. The sun had already journeyed by two of the markings of the time stick. Fire torches, to be lit if the game continued into the night, had been erected on high poles situated around Kelda and Brander.

Although the wood-carved pieces were not like the one Wild Flower and the Council of the Elders had given earlier in the day to Brander, the counselor was a falcon on this one also. Delling had created the game board and had carved the pieces himself.

Brander possessed Thoruald's skill in playing *hne-fatafl*, Wild Flower thought. Brander had never known his father and had not been trained by him to play the game, yet he used Thoruald's favorite opening formations and the same tactics in the middle game. That, too, Wild Flower credited to Delling. He had taught Brander to play the game of the jarls, and he had learned from Thoruald himself.

Now Kelda and Brander were nearing the end. His fingers curled around one of the pieces.

"Only one jarl can win," Brander said and moved the piece.

"Aye." Kelda reached up to brush a strand of hair out of her eyes.

Brander had successfully stopped her progress and cut her forces out from under her. She had only a

112

few warriors to protect her jarl. She was close to the outer edge of the board but was far from winning.

"You are hemmed in, my lady, with no way to escape," he said softly, mockingly, as he picked up her jarl. "Do you surrender?" Surrender? Wild Flower repeated silently. No, neither Brander nor Kelda could surrender. Both were too proud, too arrogant. Neither would give.

Of course, Wild Flower understood. It was the same with her and Thoruald. She rose and walked into the shadows. She needed time to be alone. Time to think about her warrior. Time to ponder her dream.

"Perhaps you did not hear me," Brander said.

"I did," Kelda replied. "You wanted me to surrender."

She lifted her head and gazed at the warrior sitting across the game board from her. His lashes were long and thick. Half closed, they shielded his eyes from her. He spoke not only of the game, but of her. She watched as he played with the game piece, twining it through his fingers.

"Well?"

"You must know, Chief Brander, that I cannot."

"I know you think you cannot."

"The battle is not yet lost. Give me some time to study the situation."

"Warriors without their jarl seldom win," he taunted.

"These will," Kelda promised.

Brander leaned back on his elbow and gazed at her, a sardonic smile playing on his lips. Kelda forced her thoughts from the man back to the board and her remaining game pieces. Her jarl was gone, and the few men she had left were surrounded and greatly outnumbered by Brander's

113

men. Still there had to be a way of escape.

Her counselor—the hawk in this instance—would have to become the leader of her men. If she were to save her forces, reach the outer edge and win the game, she must sacrifice one of her warriors.

She was tired, her back and neck stiff from having sat so long. She was frightened. So far Brander had outmaneuvered her. Her next move was vitally important; it was the game point.

She studied the board, marked the positions of Brander's men. She contemplated her pieces, wondering which she could afford to use, which would give her the win. In her mind she moved them all; she studied the consequences; she contemplated more.

The torches were lit while she pondered, the flames flickering light across the huge board. Lifting her hand, she rubbed her mother's brooch. She decided and finally moved her warrior.

Brander laughed softly. Without disturbing himself from his lazing position, he reached out and slid one of his men to take her sacrificial piece. He caught it securely in his fist and grinned at her.

Ulmer groaned his disappointment; Hauk compressed his mouth in a straight line. Canby's attention had not once strayed from the game board; now he looked at Kelda and smiled.

Savoring the moment, savoring her triumph, Kelda grinned at Canby, then at Brander. She then caught her hawk, swept him across the board to take Brander's jarl and to rest on the outer edge of the board. Excited, Ulmer bobbed up and down; Canby and Hauk each flashed her a big grin.

"I am sorry, Chief Brander—" she flaunted her victory by holding up high his jarl so that all could see "—but only one can win. And I have won."

114

Brander gazed at the game piece she held in the air. He looked back at the board and gazed at her hawk piece sitting on the designated spot.

Wild Flower ran into the lighted area. She smiled when she saw Kelda holding the jarl piece in the air.

Aye, she thought, *the falcon has won!*

Chapter Nine

"The Viking wins," Brander finally announced. He rose and slipped her dagger from the belt at his waist. "In accordance with the terms of her challenge, I return her dagger to her and proclaim her the champion of the day."

Amidst the cheering of the Vikings, and the grumbling of the Iroquois, Kelda rose. "I accept my dagger and the honor of being champion."

After Tall Tree spoke, ending the tournament, the villagers broke up, the guards returning the Vikings to their longhouse. Wild Flower approached Kelda.

"You played the game with great skill," the older woman said. "You deserve to be a champion."

Kelda watched Brander's back as he walked with the elders into the longhouse. "Is he angry?"

Wild Flower smiled. "I would think so. It is seldom my son the Firebrand is defeated in any competition. Certainly it is his first defeat by a woman."

"Your son," Kelda murmured. "I should have known. He has the strength of your character."

"Thank you. His father's blood also flows through his veins to color his personality and character."

If Kelda's suspicions were correct, Brander was Thoruald's son, Wild Flower his wife!

Kelda smiled. "Is it time for us to attend the final night of the Spring Festival?"

"It is," Wild Flower answered. "Come with me."

While they walked toward the largest building in the village, Wild Flower said, "This is the Big House. We use it twice a year when we celebrate our Spring and Harvest Festivals."

As they entered through the eastern door, Kelda's gaze swept around the entire building, coming to rest on a raised platform on the north side. The village elders were already assembled and seated. Tall Tree wore his red mantle, and Brander was yet bare-chested, wearing the leather breeches and high-cuffed moccasins he had worn during the competition. Their gazes collided and held briefly. Without giving any indication of having seen her, he looked straight ahead.

"Those are the seats of honor for the elders and village guests." Wild Flower pointed, and Kelda followed the imaginary line to where Brander sat.

How arrogant and indomitable he was. At the moment Kelda could find no trace of gentleness or kindness in his face.

"You will sit here on this bench below Brander," Wild Flower said.

Kelda dragged her gaze from Brander to look at the log benches below the platform. *Below Brander,* she thought. *Always in a subservient position. Always reminded that I am his slave, his property. To be branded like Quiet Woman.*

The earth floor was lined with dry grass and lying near the walls were logs on which the gathering people had begun to sit. Swallowing her nasty thoughts, Kelda sat down and continued to look around.

The building was large, about forty feet long and twenty-five feet wide, with a sloping roof; it was as high as a man at the eaves and twice as high at the center. Its walls and roof were covered with large squares of bark. There were two openings in the roof through which the smoke from two ceremonial fires could escape. The only decorations were two center posts which supported the roof. On these posts Iroquois men had carefully carved two masks.

"These are called the Solid Faces," Wild Flower said, "representing the two faces of the Master of Life—birth and death and good and evil. The Iroquois believe all men are born to die and that they are a mixture of good and evil."

She opened her medicine pouch and took out a small rattle which she shook around the bench where she and Kelda were sitting. A cloud of powder settled around them causing Kelda to sneeze several times.

"At the Spring Festival we celebrate the return of Grandmother South Wind. The forest turns green and our gardens are planted. We throw away old clothes, and put on the new ones we made when Grandfather North Wind forced us to stay inside our lodges."

Along two walls were more carved posts that represented the different levels of heaven and supported the framework of the roof.

Kelda felt a movement on the platform behind her, and for a moment her heartbeat quickened, her pulse fluttered. She thought Brander had moved to her side; however, it was Delling.

"You may take your place with the elders," he told Wild Flower in Norse without looking at Kelda.

"Thank you," Wild Flower said. "You will direct her in all that she is to do. I have not yet had time to instruct her."

"What I am to do!" Kelda exclaimed. "I was not told that I would have a role in tonight's ceremony."

"Brander only just requested it," said Wild Flower.

Kelda glanced up to where he sat. "Then he can withdraw his request. I will not make a fool of myself because he is angry that I won the game of the jarls."

118

The sole indication of Brander's anger was the ticking of the muscle in his jaw. He slid down to the bench where she sat. When Kelda flinched away from him, he capped her head with his hand and drew her to him. Her cheek rested against his chest.

His mouth close to her ear, he said, "I am not angry because you won the game of the jarls. I care not whether you make a fool of yourself, but you will not make a fool of me. You will carry out your duties as my slave. You are my woman — my bed slave — and you will behave as one."

"Even when I have not been instructed as to what those duties are?" Kelda countered.

"Delling will instruct you," Brander replied. "They are not so difficult you cannot perform them."

"Why did you not tell me before?"

He still held her tightly, but Kelda lifted her head to gaze into his face. At times she was afraid of him, but even in her fear she refused to quail before him. She may be his slave, but she would never willingly submit to doing any service for him.

"Answer her, my son."

Smiling, Wild Flower moved up to the higher platform to sit beside Tall Tree.

When Brander did not answer, Kelda said, "If I make a fool of myself in front of your people, then I make you look foolish also. Like you, Chief Brander, I care not whether you are humiliated or not, but I will not humiliate myself."

Brander's grip slackened, and Kelda wiggled away from him.

Still speaking softly for her ears only, he said, "Tall Tree and the Council of the Elders have spoken. In order to keep you, I must openly claim you as my woman. If I do not do that in this ceremony, the women can rightfully demand you as their prisoner."

"Perhaps I would be better off being theirs."

119

Brander caught a strand of hair and ran it through his fingers. "They could not kill you without the permission of the elders, but they will surely shear your hair. That I will not permit, Viking woman. I like your long, golden hair."

"What about the woman who wears the hair?"

Brander laughed softly, his warm breath blowing against her flushed skin. It smelled clean and fresh and she wondered if he had been chewing an herb as he had done in the forest earlier in the day.

"If you wish me to like the woman also, you must behave like one," he said. "As far as the warrior—"

"If I do not obey you tonight at this ceremony—" Kelda cut him short. She did want to hear what he thought about her as a woman or a warrior "—then I will be given to the women?"

Brander contemplated her before he finally nodded his head.

Kelda smiled. "Chief Brander, sit on your elevated platform in your seat of honor and wonder what your slave is going to do. Wonder who she prefers to be her master."

Brander tucked a fist beneath her chin and rubbed the sensitive skin. "The decision is yours to make, Viking, but you will suffer a more pleasurable lot with me. If you become the property of the women, you will be given to any and sundry men. You will be the village harlot by night and the personal slave of the women by day."

"Is there more honor in being your harlot than in being the village harlot?" Kelda said. "As I see it, a harlot is a harlot."

Brander's expression grew thunderous. "Think carefully before you make your decision, Viking. If you choose to go with the women, I can do nothing to protect you."

He dropped his hand and returned to his seat.

120

Once more he stared straight ahead of himself as if the conversation had never occurred, as if he cared not a jot what decision she made. Kelda drew in a deep breath of air.

"You will do well to listen to Brander," Delling said. "Your future will be much brighter with him than with the women."

"Will the women brand me also?"

"Aye. You will have a much better chance on leaving with your men if you belong to Brander," Delling answered. "The women would never give you your freedom."

"What must I do?" she asked.

"After the ceremony is finished, we will dance. You will be expected to dance with Brander since you belong to him."

"I know nothing of your music or your dance patterns."

"They are easy to learn. Watch the people when they dance and follow their examples."

The musicians took their places close to the fire by the west door, the drummers lightly tapping the buckskin drums. Tall Tree stood and walked to one of the ceremonial fires in the center of the building, lit his pipe and offered a sacrifice of smoke to the Spirits of Life.

"Oh, great Orenda—Spirits of Life," he prayed and Delling softly interpreted for Kelda, "I ask your blessings on the crops that have been planted. Grant us a bountiful harvest."

The drum began to beat, and all the people chanted, *"Ho-o-o-o!"*

Tall Tree took his rattle—made of a turtle's shell, Delling explained—and began to dance. From different places around the fires, men and boys got up, shaking their rattles, too. A woman stood and danced to the center of the lodge; the other women, forming a separate line from the men, followed her.

"Look closely at the woman in the lead," Delling said. "That is Earth Woman, Tall Tree's wife. See how she uses her heel and her toes. Heel. Toe. Rock. Back. Forward. Sway. Watch her hands."

Kelda studied the woman's movements, her feet, her hands, her head. Continuing to watch, she tapped her feet to the rhythm of the drums and memorized the dance pattern.

After the Iroquois danced several times around the fires, the men and Council of the Elders returned to their places; all other women filed out of the building.

When all were seated but Tall Tree, he again spoke. "Tall Tree of the Forest welcomes all of you to this the fourth and final night of the Spring Festival. The Spirits of Life have blessed this day."

He recounted Brander's exploits during the day, the capturing of the Vikings and the games that followed. He told them of Kelda's winning the game of the jarls.

"Her magic is strong," he concluded and raised his rattle above his head.

"*Ho-o-o!* Her magic is strong," the people chanted and shook their rattles.

"On this last night of the Spring Festival," Tall Tree said, "it is the women's turn to tell their visions."

Holding large baskets, Wild Flower and Tall Tree arose, each moving to one of the fires into which they threw green cedar leaves.

"This is the last part of the purification rites," Delling said.

The building filled with the odiferous smoke. Kelda's eyes watered, and she coughed.

When her body convulsed, Delling said, "Come, you have been purified. It is time for you to go outside."

He caught Kelda's hand and led her out of the building. She yet coughed when Tall Tree's wife handed her a small pottery dish and guided her to the front of the line. Wiping the tears from her eyes, she gazed at the red and black salves.

"What am I to do with this?" she asked Delling.

"You are to paint Brander's face. Watch Earth Woman and do as she does."

"What if I am unable to do this correctly?" Kelda asked.

"You will or Brander will be shamed."

The Iroquois woman caught her by the shoulders and pushed her into line. When the rhythm of the drums changed, the women began to chant and slowly filed into the Big House. Earth Woman led the procession; Kelda was second behind her. The older woman stopped when she stood in front of her husband. The other women scattered throughout the assembly moving toward theirs. Kelda stopped in front of Brander.

Murmuring in Iroquois, Earth Woman dipped her fingers into the red paste and began to color one half of Tall Tree's face. The other women did the same.

Over her shoulder, Kelda saw two men, one of them Delling, as they painted the two Solid Faces, one half of each face red, the other half black.

Kelda felt the iron bands of Brander's hand clamp around her wrist. In Norse he said, "You forget who you are and what you are supposed to be doing, slave."

Kelda slowly turned her head and stared at him. "Nay, master, I am learning from the other women."

She twisted her arm from his grip and dipped her fingers into the grease and lifted them. Her first inclination was to paint her own design on Brander's face, one that was different from that on the Solid Faces, but as her eyes met his, all such thoughts fled.

123

She inhaled the herbal scent of him, reminiscent of the resinous boughs in the sweat-lodge. Did the women bathe separately? she wondered. Possibly he had lain on the same bench as she. The thought of being in the sweat-lodge with him, naked with him, seduced her senses as surely as his touch.

Slightly trembling fingers touched him. He was warm, his face rough from beard stubble. She felt his breath on her hands. He closed his eyes, and she saw his lashes form a thick, dark crescent on his sun-bronzed skin.

So dark, she thought, and ruggedly handsome. So different from the Vikings among whom she had always lived.

She smoothed the red salve around the eye, over the cheek and temple. Dipping out more, she colored one half of his forehead, then ran the grease down his nose to color in his chin and lower face.

"Red signifies good magic," Brander told her, his voice low, "one of the two faces of life."

Unable to help herself, she ran the tip of her index finger over one half of his lips, the outer line, the indentation where they met. He opened his lips and captured one of her fingers lightly between his teeth.

Her heartbeat quickened as the ebony eyes pierced hers, as his breath softly blew over her hand. A weakness assailed her, and she began to tremble. He laughed and she withdrew her hand.

"Black," Brander said, "symbolizes black magic."

"And the dark side of life," Kelda whispered.

She transferred the pottery dish to the other hand and dipped clean fingers into the black grease to begin the coloring.

"Aye, the dark side. The side of life with which we are most curious and most interested. The one we are drawn to."

"The fearful side," Kelda said.

124

"The exciting," Brander countered. "It is the black clouds before the storm; it is the lightning and the thunder."

"All deadly," Kelda said.

"Only if one fears them. Exciting and exhilarating if one does not."

When she was finished—and she was unsure how she managed when she was a trembling mass—she stood back and gazed at him, at the eerie and fearful mask that covered his face. This man, who was part good, part evil, claimed her as his. She was unsure which part of his nature appealed to her most; she feared it was the dark side.

The ebony eyes stared at her, as if they read her inner thoughts. Like an iron bar heated in the forge, the end red hot, she felt as if his gaze branded her. She felt the pain, the pleasure of belonging to him.

Never taking her eyes from Brander's face, Kelda accepted the bundle of moss one of the Iroquois women pressed into her hands and wiped the paint from them. Earth Woman caught Kelda's right hand, another Iroquois woman caught her left.

They moved to the center of the room and danced in a circle around the poles. Still Kelda continued to gaze at the man who claimed her for his own—the man whom she now claimed as her master by way of her actions. All that was lacking was the brand.

Not knowing the steps, Kelda felt awkward at first, but soon the rhythm of the drums took over, and she began to imitate the heel-to-toe movements. Eventually the women stopped. Still holding hands, their backs to the pole, they faced the congregation.

The drumbeats softened, the frenzy of their rhythm diminished. Caught up in the music, Kelda's gaze fastened with Brander's. At this moment she knew destiny had brought her here, that destiny was binding her to this darkly handsome barbarian.

The women released each other's hands and moved through the Big House, each searching out her mate. When she located him, each woman handed him a small gift. Still staring at Brander, at the eerie shadows the torchlight played on his face, Kelda remained where she was standing. She had no gift for him. No one told her about the gift.

The drums began to gain in momentum as the men joined their wives in the center of the building.

Kelda was humiliated. He was angry. His hand clenched into a fist; otherwise, he did not move. She should be glad, but was not. She understood humiliation. Slowly moving toward the bench where Brander sat, she reached up and unfastened her mantle. Taking it off, she held it out to him. A murmur of appreciation rippled through the crowd. The red material, rich in color and texture, gleamed in the torchlight.

"For you," she murmured. "Red signifies good magic."

He touched it, his eyes never leaving her face.

She swirled it over his shoulder, then knelt in front of him to fasten it with her mother's brooch. Her fingers brushed over the thick chest hair.

He stood now, the mantle falling over one shoulder to emphasize the breadth of his chest. His hand touched the brooch.

"This has been worn many winters," he said. "Although the design is getting smooth, it still reflects the radiant beauty of the sun."

"Aye," she whispered, near tears, "the golden *sol*."

"I have seen you touching it many times today during the competition. Is it your talisman?"

"Yes, it belonged to my mother. She gave it to me for my tenth winter."

"I am honored to accept it."

Brander caught her hand in his, the clasp was

126

warm and gentle; it revealed another facet of this primitive man to her. Looking at her, his eyes sparkling, he led her to the center of the building, where they joined the other dancers.

"Does your mother not care that you are traveling with Viking warriors and sailing to lands beyond the Great Water?"

"She is dead," Kelda answered. "A plague hit our village, and my entire family died."

"That is when Thoruald took you into his house as his ward?"

"No, we belonged to another household at the time. It was later that Thoruald opened his home and his heart to me. Ragnar and Hauk took me to him."

"You trust this man called Hauk?"

"Yes."

Kelda smiled as she thought of the crusty old warrior. He had been her mentor and protector; now he was her second in command. He never left her side willingly. When he had learned of the mission to Skrellingland, he had begged her not to go, but he also understood Kelda's sacred oath to the jarl, solemnized before the Herred-thing when Thoruald had adopted her as his own daughter. Hauk agreed to come with her, swearing by Odin that he would protect her life with his own if necessary. He stood by her ready to prove his vow of loyalty.

"Now that you belong to me you have no need of a champion."

"You are my champion?" she asked.

"A good master always takes care of his property."

Once again Brander smoothly put Kelda into her place. The smile left her countenance. The music continued; the spectators clapped their hands and chanted, but the pleasure of the dance ended for

Kelda. She turned as if to walk away, but Brander caught her.

"What are you doing?"

"I am leaving," she replied.

"You will remain here to finish what you began."

"What you began," she corrected, "and I was a fool to agree to."

"What is wrong?" he asked kindly, his eyes searching her face.

"Everything you do for me is done because I am your slave."

"Aye," he replied, "that is as it should be. I am a good master. That should please you."

"You do not understand," Kelda said. "No matter how good or thoughtful the master, he is still the master, the slave his property."

"You will stay, Kelda, and finish the dance." The words were spoken softly, but they were a command nonetheless.

Kelda and he stared at each other for a second before she took her place in the inner circle, her back to the two poles of the Solid Faces. The men, facing the women, stood in the outer circle. The spectators chanted to the rhythm of the buckskin drum.

The women held out their hands palm up; their mates laid theirs palm down. Kelda wanted to move away from Brander, but at the same time, she felt a flow of energy between them that drew her to him, that bound them together. Her anger slowly dissipated. She forgot their argument.

As they moved to the slow beat of the drum, she felt the sensuous brush of Brander's palm against hers; then the electrifying sensation stopped as quickly as it began. The men circled the women who remained standing.

Kelda watched the huge warrior as he deftly moved around the circle to return to her. The torchlight

128

gleamed on his hair, casting it in that all too familiar reddish hue. When he stood in front of her again, her gaze locked on the thick swirl of hair down his chest beyond the waistband of his breeches.

He caught her hands, the only parts of their bodies to touch, but she felt him from the top of her head to the bottom of her feet. Although no other woman did so, Kelda reached out her hand and touched the dark side of his face.

"You are a maelstrom of turbulence, Chief Brander of the Iroquois."

"Aye," he answered gravely, laying his hand over hers. "I should turn you loose, Viking."

"You should."

"I cannot."

"I will escape."

"Nay, Viking, you will not."

"Keeping one by force is no challenge."

"I will not have to use force. You will stay because of what you feel between us, Viking. Both of us are drawn to each other. We were from the beginning."

Aye, we were drawn together from the beginning!

They faced each other and danced around the poles of the Solid Faces. Surrounded by people, they were alone; they were one. As if they were in their sleeping chambers, Brander made love to her. He possessed her.

When the drums were silent, the dancing ceased. Kelda and Brander stood looking at each other. She ran her tongue over her dry lips. Brander reached out and touched the tip of his finger to them. His mildest touch caused desire to pulse through her body.

"You have pleased me, Viking."

"I have a name," she said. "Viking is the name of many. My name is the name of one. It makes me an individual."

"Aye." A pause. "You have pleased me . . . Kelda."

He pressed a soft kiss to her lips, a kiss Kelda wanted to deepen, one she wanted to last forever, before he straightened and returned to his seat. Her hand going to her mouth as if she could save the caress, Kelda stood for a moment in bemusement. Then, following the example of the other people, she returned to her seat beside Delling. All sat quietly on the benches. Eventually Tall Tree rose.

"Now we will pass the turtle around for anyone who wants to speak of his visions," he said, and handed his turtle-shell rattler to his wife.

Earth Woman shook the rattle slowly. The drummer picked up the beat, and the woman danced around the circle, chanting a simple song. Everyone listened.

Delling interpreted for Kelda, but she did not listen. She could not rid her mind of thoughts of Brander.

For the first time in her twenty-one winters, she felt desire for a man.

When Earth Woman finally finished her dream, she said, *"Ho-o-o-o"* and stopped shaking Tall Tree's rattle.

The audience echoed *"Ho-o-o"* while the musician continued to beat the drum. Returning the rattle to Tall Tree, Earth Woman sat down.

Men and women got up and moved about the two fires, lifting their pipes for a few puffs of tobacco.

Brander slid down the bench until he sat beside Kelda. "The Iroquois believe tobacco smoke pleases all the spirits," he told her.

"Yet you carry no pipe."

Out of the corner of her eye, she saw the black half of his face. It looked sinister and evil, so at odds with the soft tone of his voice.

"No."

Kelda did not understand anything about this man whom she thought to be Thoruald's son. Vikings were known to be the most fierce of all warriors, yet even they did not defy the gods.

"You have no fear of the gods," she murmured.

"I know no gods of whom to be afraid," he said. "The Iroquois have their gods, the Norse have theirs. Each claims theirs are the true ones. Which am I to believe?"

"What do you believe?"

Kelda turned to look at him, studying the shadows that flickered across his painted features, that gave him an even more grotesque visage.

"I believe in me." After a long pause, he said, "Thank you for the mantle and the brooch. They please me."

"I did not do it to please you," Kelda answered. "I was thinking only of what is best for me."

"That was wise of you."

He said no more to her, but continued to sit by her throughout the remainder of the ceremony.

One by one, the women shook their rattles slowly and told of their vision. Frequently Wild Flower was called upon to give the meaning of the vision. After a long interval, Wild Flower took the rattle.

"Last night as I lay upon my sleeping platform, I had a vision." Wild Flower paused. When she spoke, her voice was husky with emotion. "I saw a falcon flying over the Great Waters, and in her mouth she carried her prey."

Brander began the interpretation, but stopped. His countenance hardened.

"What is she saying?" Kelda asked.

Softly Delling began to translate for her.

"I could not see what it was," Wild Flower said. "Then the falcon disappeared into the sun. Next I saw a huge serpent rise out of the Great Water. It

131

mastered both the sun and the falcon, carrying them off to a distant land. I awakened without knowing the meaning of my dream."

Delling rose, picked up the rattle and began to speak. Wild Flower sat next to Kelda. Her face drained of color.

"What is he saying?" Kelda asked. "What is wrong, Wild Flower?"

"You!" Brander exclaimed angrily. "You and your Vikings and your search for Thoruald's seed."

"What did he say?" Kelda demanded.

Finally Wild Flower answered. "The Falcon flying over the Great Waters is Jarl Thoruald from the land of the Norse. He, the Falcon, has sent his messenger in her dragonship. She is now in our assembly. The Falcon carries not prey in its mouth, but its family. The Falcon carries a yellow flower to symbolize his Iroquois wife, a yellow bud to symbolize his seed."

Brander rose and moved to the center of the building.

"The Falcon is a bird of prey," he said strongly, "and if it does symbolize Jarl Thoruald from the land of the Norse, he has come to prey on our land and our people. He left his Iroquois wife thirty winters past. He has no seed here among the people whom he calls the Skrellings."

In the same tone, Wild Flower again interpreted for Kelda. What Wild Flower's voice lacked in inflection as she translated, Brander made up for. Kelda could feel the anger in his voice; she saw it in his stance.

"For thirty winters the jarl never sent anyone to search out his wife or to find out if he had an offspring here among the Iroquois. He remarried and had another family. It was only after that son was killed and the jarl saw the thrall child with the gold arm band that he remembered about his wife among

132

the Skrellings. Now that he is too old to produce more sons, he wants to find out if he has an offspring among us."

Brander paused and turned, his eyes making contact with each person who sat in the assembly.

"I say we must wait and meditate on this dream of the Woman of Dreams. We cannot be sure Delling's interpretation is the correct one. He has been adopted by the Iroquois and does not speak with a forked tongue, but he may be deceived by the evil spirits of the Vikings. These spirits may have given him an incorrect interpretation."

"Hear! Hear!" the majority of the people called out, clapping their hands.

Tall Tree rose. "Delling and Brander have spoken wisely. It is time for us to meditate on Wild Flower's dream. We must pray for the correct interpretation so that her life will be blessed."

"Hear! Hear!" the people called out, nodding their heads in agreement.

Kelda opened her purse and withdrew two combs Thoruald had sent with her. She handed them to Wild Flower. "These are for you," she said. "Thoruald sent them to you for you to wear in your hair."

"Did he not send them to his Iroquois bride?" Wild Flower questioned.

Kelda nodded.

Wild Flower took the combs, and both women gazed at the etching of a falcon holding in its beak a fully opened yellow flower and a small yellow bud.

"Perhaps I am not the woman whom you seek," Wild Flower said, yet she traced the outline of the flower.

"You are." Kelda was confident.

She turned to look at Brander who sat further down the log bench below the elders. "He is the son Thoruald seeks."

Wild Flower also looked at Brander. "Thoruald seeks a son," she repeated, then added pensively, "but he will not find one. Too many years, too many memories separate father and son."

Brander looked from Kelda to his mother and back to Kelda. Even through the red and black paint Kelda could see the anger on his face. She could feel it in his body. He was displeased with the dream and with the gift of the combs. He motioned for Kelda to move closer to him.

A master had that right, she thought bitterly. She slowly slid down the bench to sit closer to him. He ignored her.

That, too, a master had the right to do!

Tall Tree rose. He passed wampum around, and each person received a few beads. Then he announced in a loud voice, "I end the meeting with the telling of the dreams. It has been going on for four days and nights. Now we will feast, dance, and visit."

The eastern door was closed and barred; the people filed out the western one. When they were the only ones remaining in the building, Brander rose.

"Come," he said, "it is time."

"Time for what?" Kelda asked.

"Time to make you mine."

Chapter Ten

"How do you make me yours?" Kelda asked.

Smiling curiously, he stopped walking and turned to face her. "Are you jesting?"

Kelda shook her head. "What went on in here tonight," she said. "Is that all of the ceremony? Now do we simply—do we—"

His smile turned into soft laughter. Finally he said, "I never do anything *simply*." He paused, then asked curiously, "Were you not married?"

"I have been, but my husband—"

"So you understand what goes on between a man and a woman?"

"Yes, but I am not asking about that. Are you going to brand me?" She thought of Quiet Woman and her facial tattoos.

She thought he looked disappointed, but the paint distorted his features so much she was not certain.

"That is the way we show our ownership," he said.

"Is it not enough that I will be your harlot? Must you also physically mark me?"

"Aye."

"How? With a red, hot iron?"

"No, I will be gentle with you. The shaman will tattoo my mark on you here." He touched her forehead. "For all to see and know that you are mine."

Kelda had not felt such bitter anger or such helplessness since her mother had died. She was confused, unable to understand the feelings that ran through her body. Ever since she met this barbarian—and although it had been mere hours, it felt as if it had been a lifetime—she had suffered terrible inner conflict. She was drawn to him, yet she despised him. She felt an urgency in her body for his touch, but she abhorred the idea of his taking her.

"Tattooing is not such a bad ordeal," he told her, his voice softening. "You will be given an herb to chew before Wild Flower begins the pricking. It will alleviate much of the pain you will feel. You can even take enough that you will sleep through the ceremony."

Thinking only of her disfigurement, Kelda touched her forehead. Vikings marked their slaves, but her marking had been a white uniform and a small band that had been soldered around her arm. Her hand dropped to her wrist and she began to rub the sensitive inner side. This barbarian was talking about marking her skin—a mark that could never be taken off, that would be there for all to see, for all time.

"Is the marking so bad for you?"

"Yes."

His placed his hand beneath her chin and lifted her head so that she was looking into his eyes. "It is for your protection. As long as you wear my mark, no one can harm you."

"Have you ever belonged to another person?" Kelda asked, unmindful that her eyes filled with tears.

Brander shook his head.

"I have, and I hated it. Just like my owner I had a life and an identity. I had dreams and goals. But I was denied all. Because another owned me, my life and identity became theirs; my dreams and goals meant nothing."

He caught her hand and led her out of the building. But they did not walk toward the huge bonfire in the middle of the competition field around which the villagers had gathered and were now revelling.

"How did you come to be a thrall?" Brander asked. "You are not a Viking by birth?"

"I am," she answered, glad he was allowing her to talk, glad they were walking in the dark away from the villagers. "My parents were karls. We worked for Jarl Harould."

"Karls—"

"Free people of trade," Kelda explained. "My father was a maker of swords. We had our own longhouse, although it was not so grand as Jarl Harould's *stofa*. During my twelfth winter, my parents were killed by a plague. I alone survived. I was sent to live with the family of my father's sister."

They walked farther before Kelda again spoke. The memories were painful, and she had never confessed them to anyone. For the past nine years she had kept them locked in her heart. Ironically the person to whom she was confessing was one who also enslaved her.

Eventually she said, "I was considered good to be looked upon, and my uncle-by-law many times tried to force his affections on me, but I successfully fought them off. Because of his interest in me my aunt came to despise me."

Drawing in a deep breath, Kelda walked farther before she said, "One night at the *stofa* my uncle-by-law, Oscar, was celebrating with the warriors who had recently returned from a highly successful summer raid. They were drinking, playing games and wagering. Oscar lost all my possessions, the house, the animals, and most of my mother's jewelry."

"Except your mother's brooch," Brander said.

"That and several other pieces I hid from him," Kelda said. "I was determined they would be

137

mine. It was all I had left of my mother."

"Oscar later tried to force his affections on me. When I resisted, he beat me almost senseless. He was going to rape me, but I grabbed a cooking knife and stabbed him."

"You have always been handy with daggers."

"It was the only weapon I could find," she explained. "I would have killed him, but I was too weak from the beating, and he was too big and powerful for me." She breathed deeply. "When he recovered from his wound, he carried me before the Herred-thing, our district legal assembly, and claimed I was forcing my attention on him. Because he rebuffed my advances I grew angry and attacked him. He further claimed that I stole valuable goods and a horse so that I could run away."

By now they had reached the river that ran in the back of Brander's lodge. The moonlight cast the water in silver. Throwing his mantle over his shoulder out of the way, he knelt on the bank, scooped water into his hands, and washed the paint from his face.

"The penalty for stealing a man's horse is death," Kelda continued. "But Oscar argued to the Herred-thing that I was running away out of guilt and fear. He did not ask for the death penalty because I was his wife's niece. I was a virgin and good to look upon, and he would sell me into bondage as a bed-thrall. The money he received for me would pay for the things I had stolen and the personal injury I had done to him."

His face dripping water, Brander straightened and walked to her. Each droplet glistened like a silver tear in the moonlight. His features were hard.

"Did you become a bed-thrall?" Brander asked.

"Oscar put me up for auction," Kelda answered, wrapping her arms around her breasts as if to protect herself from the flailing hands of the men who had

138

fawned over her. "He made me stand on a table, and the men began to bid. They even laid wagers on which one of them would get me. The more they drank, the less content they were to bid; they wanted to view the goods. They tore my clothes from me until I stood before them naked."

"Aye," Brander said softly, "when one is buying goods, he demands the right to view them."

"A human should never be considered goods," Kelda said. "Never."

Brander took her into his arms and crushed her to his chest. Against her cheek she felt the crisp chest hair, damp from the water that ran down his face.

"Yet Delling tells me that the Norse are infamous for their slave-trading."

"Aye." Kelda sighed. "Because Thoruald treats his slaves kind, most of them do not want their freedom. Those who do, earn it within a few years. Still I do not believe in slavery and will do all I can to abolish the custom among my people."

Brander rubbed his hands across her back in soothing motion. "You never answered my question. Did you become a bed-thrall?"

"No," Kelda whispered, content to stand in his embrace. "Ragnar and Hauk arrived in time to save me. Ragnar bought me and took me to his father's village. Thoruald accepted me into his household, and for several winters I was their thrall. Thoruald came to love me as a daughter. Eventually he gave me my freedom and—and after Ragnar died he adopted me as his daughter."

"This Ragnar is Thoruald's son?" Brander said.

"Yes, and he also became my husband."

"You have an innocence about you that makes it seem as if you have never been with a man before."

She raised her head to look at him. "Would it make any difference to you?"

139

"No," Brander said. "I would make you mine either way."

"That is barbaric, is it not?"

"It is a way of life here."

Kelda closed her eyes when his hands caught her face and then slid through her temples to tangle in her hair. He drew his fingers through her hair time and again. His touch was as gentle as the wind on her face when she stood on the cliff above the fjord; it was as hot as glowing coals in the fire pit in the early morning.

Kelda was so mesmerized by this man, she was so captivated by the magic of his spell that she blatantly disregarded the warnings of her conscience. She conveniently forgot she was his slave, his property to do with as he wished.

At the moment she accepted the side of the face he wanted to present to her, the kind one, the comforting one. At the moment she accepted his way of life as hers.

Yet she knew she was walking the edge of the precipice; one false step and she would fall to destruction on the jagged rocks below. She did not care.

"Barbaric. Barbarian," Brander murmured. "These are terms that you continually associate with me, Viking. Is this what fascinates you about me?"

His fingers lightly brushed against her scalp to send erotic tingles down her spine.

"You defy me when I hold the knife to your throat. You disobey me in order to have your champion by your side," he murmured. "Yet you tremble when I hold you, when I push my fingers through your hair."

"You are different from any other man I have ever met," Kelda confessed. She cupped his face with her hand. "As you saw when you captured my warriors, they all wore beards. Your face is the first clean-shaven one I have seen."

He laughed. "Ah, sweet Kelda, your fascination is not for a clean-shaven face only. Your trembling signifies that you desire me the man."

"Nay," she murmured. "How could I desire you? I hate you."

"Love and hate are like the two sides of the Solid Faces. It is hard to distinguish where one ends, the other begins. Without the paint they merge to become one; that is why we use the paint, to remind us that they really are two separate emotions."

She rubbed his face with her hands, moving the tips of her fingers through the damp black hair. He moved his hands to her shoulders and drew her into his embrace, his arms pressing her hips close to him. With a groan, he lowered his head, his lips touching hers at the same time that she thrust her breasts against his chest. His lips opened hers with the driving force of his tongue, and his hands moved over her back.

They glided to her waist where his fingers slipped beneath the band of her breeches. As his warm fingertips kneaded the soft roundness of her buttocks, as the callused palms gently rubbed them, Kelda shivered and wrapped her arms about him.

He was right, she thought. She was fascinated with his primitiveness, and she wanted to be possessed by him. Her lips moved against his, and she welcomed the exploration of his tongue in her mouth. His fingers played havoc with the sensitive skin of her buttocks causing her to wiggle closer to him, to feel the impression of his erection against her pelvis.

She asked for her own seduction and cared not.

Brander lifted his lips from her and pulled his hands from her breeches. "It is time for us to go in and know each other fully," he said softly.

He swept her into his arms. With her face pressed against the soft hair on his chest, Kelda listened to

141

his heartbeat. She felt the rise and fall of his breathing. She smelled the herbs of fragrance, the blending of hers and his. Hers from the mantle he wore; his from the bath.

He carried her into the sleeping chamber. The flaps over the wall openings had been rolled up and secured so that moonlight brightened the room. A spring breeze cooled it. The bed had already been prepared, and he laid her on the soft bearskin blankets that covered the thick corn-husk mattress.

He sat on the edge of the platform, his dark eyes smoldering. His hand, so big and strong, was also kind as it stroked the tangled hair from her face. He trailed his index finger over the delicate contour of her lips, brushing the fullness.

"You were the most beautiful woman at the celebration tonight," he said. "I was proud that you belonged to me. All the men in the room were jealous of you."

He moved his hand from her lips, around her nose up to her eyebrows. He unfastened the shirt and drew it aside. The night air touched her flushed skin. Then his hands caught her breasts, and he massaged the tips with his thumbs.

It seemed to her that lightning ran the length of her body, burning and searing her insides. Each stroke heightened her excitement, it whetted her yearning to know the intimate secrets shared between a woman and a man during their lovemaking.

"When you were dancing, I wanted to take you then. I wanted to make you fully mine," he confessed in a husky voice, his hands still touching her body in a wonderful, magical way.

"I could feel the envious eyes of the other warriors on my slave, and no one, *no one*, is going to have my property. Once you belonged to Ragnar and

142

Thoruald, but now you belong to me, Viking. You are mine."

The meaning of the words were harsh, but they were softly spoken; they were tempered with desire. Rather than their destroying the intimacy Brander had created, they enhanced it.

"As your slave," Kelda whispered, "it is my duty to please you?"

"Aye, in all ways."

"By warming your bed and your body?"

Brander laughed quietly. "An old man may seek warmth, my beautiful Kelda. A young man seeks more — much more."

Kelda fought to keep from succumbing to the maelstrom of emotions that threatened her sanity and reason. "I have been told by the sages, that one does not always find what one seeks."

His cool lips touched her breasts, ironically to set her on fire anew with desire. She felt sensations in places she had never dreamed possible. She tingled with awareness; she throbbed with wanting.

"Perhaps our sages are wiser than those to whom you have been listening. Ours claim that if one seeks long and diligently enough, he will find."

Breathing deeply, surfacing the delicious emotions, Kelda said, "I shall never be yours willingly. Does it not bother you to take me against my will?"

His soft lips finally captured the tip of her breast; he caressed it with his tongue. Without moving his mouth, he spoke. "It would bother me more not to take you." His warm breath spread across her already flushed flesh.

"Are you not concerned at all with what I desire?" she asked.

"Aye, that is why I am taking you with tenderness. Any man can take a woman forcibly. The test of his sexual prowess is to take her gently, to build up the same desire in her that he has flowing in him."

Kelda pushed her hand through his hair, loving the feel of the coarse strands between her fingers. "You are arrogant," she accused softly.

"Nay," his hand cupped her breast and shoved the nipple further into his mouth; his tongue ceased its forays. "I am but a man . . . a man confident he can remove all your resistance, my slave."

He sucked on her breast, and Kelda gasped; she closed her eyes as wanting shot through her body. She felt the prick of tears behind her lids. Her lips trembled.

In her mind she was not willing to give herself to him. She hated him. But her body wanted him. She craved his touch. She wanted to know the full possession of a man. She desired him!

But she could not.

Chapter Eleven

"Why do you want me?" Kelda asked. "Because I am different from your women? Because I have fairer skin and golden hair?"

"Because you are beautiful. Because your body begs to be loved. Mostly because my body needs release."

"There must be other reasons?" Kelda insisted.

His gaze raked her face before he finally said, "Perhaps, but we will not discuss them." He smiled. "Now, no more questions, no more putting off the inevitable."

He stood to slip out of the mantle and laid it across a clothing rod that was suspended from the ceiling; then he took off the arm band and necklace to hang them on a wall peg. Sitting down on the bench across the room, he removed his moccasins.

His gaze flicked to hers. Intently she watched him undress. He stood, untied the belt as his waist and slipped out of his breeches.

Kelda pushed up on an elbow. She should not be watching, but she would not take her eyes off him. She had never seen a man totally naked and probably should have been embarrassed but was not. She was captivated by the man who stood in front of her.

Muscles rippling from his chest to his feet, his body gleamed in the moonlight. Visually she traced the hard line of his stomach to his erection.

He never moved, but she knew his purpose. Although the moonlight softened and beautified all that it touched, it did nothing to soften the resolve on his countenance.

"You said you would take me with tenderness," she reminded him.

"Aye."

"How can you promise that? Tenderness only comes from caring, and you do not care for me, for Kelda of the Vikings. Please do not do this. Give me my freedom."

"It is too late for that."

"Let me return to my people."

"I am your people now."

"Neither of us wants it this way," she argued.

"Will you undress for me, or shall I do it for you?"

Shaking her head, Kelda pushed into the corner of the sleeping platform as if she could escape him.

"It will be more pleasurable," Brander said, "if you do not resist me. I will be gentle with you."

"I do not want you, the pleasure you claim you can give, or your gentleness," Kelda swore.

"If you value your clothes, you will disrobe," he said quietly. "If not, I shall take them off the easiest way possible." He reached over to the nearby shelf and picked up a knife.

Her eyes widened. "My dagger!" she exclaimed, suddenly afraid of him. "Why do you have it? I left it in my lodge."

"I had all your possessions moved to my house," he said. "Now, if you are not willing to undress, I shall cut the offending material from your body."

"Perhaps cutting the body in the process," Kelda goaded.

"It is not my desire," he told her.

They stared at each other through the moon-silvered shadows. Kelda was the one to relent. She finally sat up and took off her boots. She unfastened her trousers and let them slide down her legs and pool at her feet. Next came her undergarments.

She stood in front of him naked, her body trembling as he slowly lowered his gaze.

"You are indeed beautiful," he murmured. "As I thought you would be."

He dropped the knife to the floor and walked to her. Bending his head ever so much, his mouth circled a nipple. He sucked it gently, and Kelda felt the excruciating pain of desire pierce her body afresh, taking residence in the lower part of her stomach.

She tried to resist the passion his caress generated, but her body ruled sovereign at the moment, rendering her no more than a woman who desired a man's most complete, most possessive touch.

"You say you do not want me, Viking," he mocked, his lips moving against her breasts, his warm breath blowing against her stomach.

"Aye."

He brushed his mouth to her other breast, his tongue exploring the areola.

"You say you do not want the pleasure I can give you." His mouth moistly laved the fullness of her breast.

"Aye." She closed her eyes and ran her fingers in his hair, massaging his scalp with the tips of her fingers.

He lay her down; he lay down beside her, stretching his lean body along the length of hers. His lips closed over hers, and his hands joined his mouth to caress her.

He moved his hand to her thighs, to the warmth between them. His fingers had no sooner touched the sensitive area, than Kelda responded.

She balled her hands and crammed them between

147

their bodies, pushing against him, fighting. She wiggled beneath him, but Brander would not be stopped.

He wanted her and would take her.

His leg covered both of hers, and he stopped the flailing. He heaved his body up and over, his chest touching her breasts. He pulled her hands above her head, clamping her wrists together in an iron-banded fist.

"Although you do not want my gentleness or the pleasure I promise," he murmured, "I shall give both to you."

He brushed his lips down her throat, across the collarbone, back and forth in whisper-soft motions that he knew teased and tormented. His mouth reclaimed the creamy whiteness of her breasts. His tongue sought the strutted tip.

His other hand brushed over her breasts, down her stomach, around her navel. Then his fingers touched the soft triangle of hair. He looked down her stomach to behold the golden beauty that beckoned to him like ripe fruit hanging on the boughs ready to be plucked.

He touched her secret spot; Kelda groaned and convulsed.

"How can this be?" she murmured. "I despise you, Skrelling. I hate what you are doing to me, yet I feel on fire."

"It is life, my beautiful Viking," he murmured. "The blending of the good and the evil, so that one is not a vice, the other a virtue. Together they make a whole."

Sensing her surrender, Brander released her hands, and she slipped them into his hair. She arched, and he flattened his body against hers, his chest rubbing against her breasts.

When he pressed his erection into the golden trian-

148

gle, she arched to receive him; she moved her hips around the pressing tip of manhood. Still he withdrew.

"I would have you ready," he whispered. His fingers slid between to touch her again and again to prepare her.

Kelda whimpered her pleasure, lifting herself to him when he removed his hand. "Do not leave me," she cried.

"I am not," he promised.

He lowered the weight of his body over hers, his knee spreading her legs apart, his hand continuing to stroke the inner line of her thigh. He placed his manhood where his hand had been.

She tensed.

"I will be gentle," he promised.

His hands moved reassuringly before he tenderly sheathed himself in her warm femininity. He felt the tightness, the barrier.

The barrier!

She was a maiden!

He was surrounded by the moist warmth; it pulsed around him. He could not—he would not stop, no matter that she was a maiden. This made his possession of her all the more pleasurable.

The Viking woman was his . . . his alone.

Kelda gasped when she felt the strange bigness in her. Tears ran down the sides of her face.

"Nay," he said, catching her chin and pulling her face up. "I will have no tears. This is a moment of joy, not sorrow."

"For you," she murmured, "not for me."

He kissed her at the same time that he gently moved in her, at the same time that his hand gently caressed her breasts.

Kelda found that he brought her too much pleasure for her to deny. She closed her arms about him, her fingers digging into his back. She clung to him, and he began to move faster and deeper. She received him.

His hand, his lips, they spoke to her of his needs and wants. They told her of his pleasure in touching and in loving her.

She felt the sensation building up so that she thought she would explode into fire like a dry piece of wood hit by lightning. She tore her lips from his; she rolled her head to the side; her body drew taut.

He tensed. She cried out. He groaned. She felt the warmth of his seed as it spilled inside her.

She shuddered and tightened her arms about Brander. She turned her face to his shoulders, her teeth softly nipping into his burning flesh, her fingers digging into his shoulders. She felt the small beads of perspiration on his hot skin; she rubbed her cheek against the dampness on his chest.

"This is the way it is with a man and a woman?" she whispered.

He pushed himself off of her and brushed the hair from her face. "Aye. Now you are a woman."

Kelda laughed softly. "How arrogant you are, barbarian, to think because you took my maidenhood that you have made a woman out of me." Even as she mocked him, Kelda knew that he had not only taken her maidenhood but he had captured her heart.

Brander gazed down at her in bemusement.

"Do you honestly believe that a small barrier a man can penetrate with his body can be considered the whole of a woman?"

"The penetration of such a barrier awakens a woman to adulthood."

Kelda pondered his words, then asked, "Is it the act itself or the attitude of the man who does it to her that is responsible for the awakening."

"What are you asking?" He was clearly puzzled.

150

"If the man loves her," she answered, cautiously making her way through her thoughts, "she blossoms into womanhood because she desires it; she wants to take what womanhood has to offer her."

Brander smiled. "Have you an equally ponderous explanation of her feeling toward carnal pleasure?"

"Aye," Kelda returned seriously. "If the man is lusting after her, she becomes a woman in self-defense to make sure that nothing like this happens to her again or in order to cope with what has happened and will continue to happen to her."

"How do you feel about my making love to you?"

"I truly enjoyed it," she confessed. "I am glad you were tender with me, but I found much lacking in it."

He bolted away and stared at her.

"Surely there must be more to womanhood than this! The way the women talked about it, I thought it was something special."

As his hand started another exploration of her body, Brander laughed, the husky sound filling the room where they lay. "Ah, my Viking wench, you are begging for more, are you not? That is fine with me. We have the entire night before us for me to prove to you that what we share is indeed special. On the morrow I must take you to Wild Flower so she can place the tattoo on you."

"Is that necessary?" Kelda murmured. "As surely as you have touched a heated iron to my body, you have already branded me yours. You have taken my maidenhood."

"My taking that will not protect you," he answered. "You must wear my mark to let all know you belong to Brander, War Chief of the Iroquois."

"I already wear one mark of bondage," Kelda said. "Is it not enough?"

"What mark?" Brander demanded, his voice harsh.

151

"Light a torch," Kelda said. "I will show you."

Brander slid off the bed, detached a torch from its holder on the wall, and walked into the darkened center room of the lodge where embers glowed in the fire pit. When he returned to the bedroom, he touched the tip of the torch to others positioned on the wall, then returned the first to its holder.

When he sat down on the edge of the bed, Kelda held out her right arm, palm up.

"Here." She pointed to her wrist.

He caught her hand and brought it closer to him.

"They burned me," she told him, "when they soldered the band around my wrist. It could not heal because the metal band kept rubbing against it."

Brander rubbed his thumb gently over the scar. "I would kill the men who did this to you," he said.

Kelda stared at him in astonishment. "Yet you would do the same thing to me."

"Nay." He pressed a kiss to her wrist. "I would give you a mark of beauty, one to be worn with pride. Tattoos are not ugly like the scars of a burn. They are artistic."

"I do not wear this scar with pride," Kelda replied. "It will always serve to remind me that I once belonged to someone, that I was not a free woman. I will view your mark the same, Iroquois."

"The scar is beautiful," Brander told her, gently pulling her into the bed with him, "because it is a part of you."

"Whether it is or not," she said, "I do not want another. Can you not mark me in another way? Perhaps you have a piece of jewelry I could wear that would signify I belonged to you."

"You could lose that, or it could be taken from you. The tattoo is better."

Kelda opened her mouth to protest, but he laid his hand over it. "No more argument. My mind is fixed."

He moved from the bed and tugged her up; then he removed the soiled top blanket, folded, and laid it in a basket close to the entrance door.

"The mating blanket of a maiden must be cleaned," he told her. "You can do so tomorrow. I will have Wild Flower instruct you on your duties."

Returning to the room, he reached for a pouch on the upper wall shelf. That in hand, he lifted Kelda into his arms.

"When a man takes a woman's maidenhood, there is blood. I will take you to the river, so we can clean ourselves."

Kelda did not fight him. She faced the inevitable and wondered how she was going to free herself of this man. Even if he were to say she was no longer his slave, she would yet be bound to him. If she were to escape him, she would still be his.

Aye, as she had admitted before, when he had made love to her, he had taken more than her maidenhood. He had taken her heart. She lay in the shelter of his towering strength, feeling his body as he moved. She closed her eyes, snuggling her face against his chest.

He carried her into the river, standing her in the shallows. Opening the pouch, he thumped some herbs into the palm of his hand. He rubbed them together to create a fragrant lotion. Then he began to wash gently the area between her legs.

"This is soothing," he told her, "and it will take most of the soreness away."

He washed himself, then led her into the deep water so they could rinse off. He again picked her up in his arms and carried her out of the water.

He returned her to the sleeping room. Using a deerskin, he dried her off and placed her on the bed. After he had dried himself, he doused the torches and joined her.

153

As they lay there together, Brander thought about Kelda's being a maiden. He thought about her insisting there was yet another reason for his taking her.

There had been. Revenge. And it tasted even sweeter knowing that his half-brother had been Kelda's first husband, and it was he, Brander, who had taken her maidenhood and had spilled his seed deep within her.

When she had confessed she was Thoruald's adopted daughter, Brander had seen the irony in his making her his slave, in his impregnating her and keeping her and the child here with him. The child would be Iroquois and would be far away from Thoruald's influence. As soon as it was weaned, Brander would take it from the slave and give it to a woman of his choice—an Iroquois woman whom he would marry. His wife would adopt the baby, and it would share her clan.

"Tell me, Kelda, if you were married, why were you yet a maiden?"

"The pirates attacked our village the same day that Ragnar and I exchanged the vows of marriage. He was killed before he made love to me."

"Had Ragnar made love to you and had you conceived his child," Brander mused, "you probably would not have journeyed to this land."

"No," Kelda answered, "I would have presented Thoruald with an heir for the Talon of the Falcon."

Abruptly a thought popped into Kelda's mind, one that erased many of the bad memories of her being held captive by Brander. He had spilled his seed inside her; she could conceive his child. Perhaps Freya was smiling on her. If she could not take Thoruald's son back to him, she would carry his grandchild, his second grandchild. He would be assured an heir. He would release her from the portion of the sacred oath

154

that required she marry Asgaut.

"Talon of the Falcon," Brander repeated. "That is Thoruald's sword?"

"The sword that has been handed down for several generations in Thoruald's family," Kelda replied. "It is the sword of leadership of the clan of the Falcon." She paused. "Are you the son of the Falcon?"

"I am the Falcon," he answered, then asked, "Do these pirates who killed your husband attack your villages frequently?"

"No," Kelda said, "we have never been attacked before. That is why we did not defend ourselves any better. We were caught by surprise."

After a moment of thoughtful silence, she said, "It was obvious they were acquainted with Viking warfare."

"They used your own tactics against you?"

Kelda nodded. "One minute Ragnar was alive and sitting next to me. The next he was slumped in my lap, his blood staining my wedding gown. I thought for sure when I saw Thoruald go down that he, too, was dead."

"You are fortunate you were not captured," he mused.

"No women or children were taken," Kelda said. "But they robbed Thoruald of much of his personal booty."

Brander laughed. "He should take more care with his possessions and hide them in a secret place. Thoruald is getting too old and soft to lead Vikings. Perhaps it is time for this Asgaut to take over the leadership."

"Never," Kelda said. "Asgaut is a weak man with no vision for the people of the village. All he can think about is fighting and raiding."

"You criticize him for doing what all Vikings do,"

155

Brander charged. "How can this be when you are a warrior yourself, always wearing your sword and dagger?"

"Hauk and Ragnar insisted that I learn to use them. Ragnar had these specially crafted for me."

That phase of her life seemed so far away to her, so long ago as not to be real anymore. How different the future was going to be. So different from what she had planned when she suggested she be the one to search for Thoruald's Skrelling offspring.

Now she was a slave, less than a captive, less than a concubine.

Nothing was to be solved with worry. She was tired and sleepy. She turned on her side. Lying beside her, Brander curved his large frame around hers. He draped an arm over her, locking her in his embrace, leaving her in no doubt of his ownership.

Chained to him the rest of my life, she thought. *Or until I escape.* Kelda consoled herself with thoughts of running away. But where would she go? Once the Vikings had returned to their homeland, this would be the only safe place for her.

No matter how far you run, a small inner voice assured her, *you will never run far enough.*

Tears slipped from beneath closed lids. Brander wanted to mark her so that everyone would recognize that she was his slave. There was no need. By making love to her, he had marked her for life.

Her only joy was the thought that perhaps she had already or would conceive Brander's child.

Their child.

Chapter Twelve

Wanting to wash the barbarian's touch from her body, Kelda stood beneath the water fall the next morning, her face lifted to the peppering spray. Her only consolation was that she might be with child.

She felt Brander's presence and opened her eyes to see him standing naked on the shore, the morning sun to his back. The breeze riffled his black hair.

The effect she had on him was evident.

He stepped into the water and walked to where she stood. "Why did you not awaken me?"

"I wanted to be by myself," she answered.

"I want to be with you."

He reached for her, but she stepped backwards. Brander stepped forward and caught her in the circle of his arms, not roughly but possessively.

"Never forget that you belong to me."

His hands tangled in her hair; he lowered his head to lick the water droplets from each of her breasts. Then his mouth closed around one of the hardened tips, and he sucked.

Kelda gasped. "Did you not get enough last night?" she cried, wanting to deny him, at the same time wanting to know his possession again.

"Never!"

He released her breasts and slid to his knees, his mouth trailing hot caresses down her stomach to her navel. She quivered beneath his love strokes.

She hated him for being able to arouse her to such an intensity. She hated herself for responding to him like a bitch in heat.

Weak with desire she slid into the water with him, moaning when she felt his hand stroking her inner thigh. Those fingers went higher and higher, tantalizing her, whetting her desires to fever pitch.

She shuddered and her fingers clenched in his hair. He moved above her, his lips claiming hers in a long kiss. They sank beneath the water, the cool water that did little to cool their ardor.

When she could hold her breath no longer, when she could bear the sweet torment between her legs no longer, she pushed her way to the surface and gasped air.

She felt Brander's erection against her pelvis; she arched to receive him. As easily as the two of them slid into the water, he slid into her. His thrusts built her passion until she felt as if she had burst into tiny particles that were floating in the air above her, until she felt as if she were one with the sky.

Later when they lay together on the sleeping platform, Kelda propped herself up on an elbow and leaned over Brander. She ran her hand through the thick swirl of chest hair. She ran her finger down his arm, stopping when she saw the tattoo.

She had forgotten about it.

"You wear the falcon," she murmured.

"Aye," he answered. "It is my talisman."

"You are Thoruald's son," she said.

"So you say," Brander parried.

"Why will you not admit you are half-Norse?"

He smiled lazily and reached up to smooth the furrow between her brows. "Why should I?"

"Why have you not claimed the Iroquois thrall as

your son? He wears a tattoo of your talisman on his upper arm."

Brander pushed Kelda's hand aside and rose. He moved to the clothesline that hung from the ceiling and removed a pair of breeches. After putting them and his high-topped moccasins on, he reached for his arm band and talon necklace.

Kelda slipped out of the bed and walked to him. She pressed her naked body against his, her pleasure increasing when he caught her in a tight embrace.

"Please return to Norwegia with me," she begged.

"You are not returning." He spoke as softly. "You are going to remain here with me."

"Brander, think about Thoruald. He's old and wounded; he has no heir. Please consider going to him."

"He never considered coming to find his family until he had none left in Norwegia, until he was too old to sire any more children."

Brander's hands moved up and down her back in caressing motion.

"Nay, Kelda, I will not consider. I have no loyalty for the man who claims to have sired me. I have no father."

"You have a son."

Brander guided Kelda back to the sleeping platform and sat her down.

"I have no son or daughters. I have no wife. Asgaut saw to that when he raided our village." His face darkened; his eyes smoldered. "I had taken the men hunting for game so that we could feast with the Vikings. When we returned after the second day, we found our village destroyed. The food was stolen, our lodges burned. Young and old had been killed. Among the dead were my wife who was big with

159

child and my two daughters. My son, Eirik, could not be found."

"He is the child whom Thoruald has," Kelda told him. "He bears the same tattoo as you, Brander. He had the golden arm band in his possession. He *must* surely be your son."

"Nay," Brander replied sadly, "you have an Iroquois child whom you call Kolby, and that is who he should remain. Eirik, my son, is gone."

"How can you say that? Have you no feelings for your own child?" Kelda exclaimed.

"You said the Iroquois child has no memory of his life before his capture."

Kelda nodded.

"According to Iroquois belief, a person who does not have his memory is insane. He is considered to be weak of the mind. If I were to bring him back here, he would be treated with pity and compassion, but he would be an outcast. He would not be allowed to marry or to take part in any village functions."

"Then join him in Norwegia," Kelda suggested. "Both of you will be accepted by our people, and eventually each of you will be jarl."

Brander chuckled. "I observed how well accepted we are by your Vikings, especially the one called Canby."

"He is the reader of the law, one of Thoruald's closest friends and advisers," Kelda explained. "He thinks perhaps the fevers Thoruald has suffered since he was wounded in the raid has touched his mind. Canby fears Thoruald would accept any of you as his son in order to have an heir other than Asgaut."

"Cannot Thoruald appoint another Viking to be chief in his stead?"

Kelda shook her head. "The leadership would go to the most distinguished warrior. In this case, it would be Asgaut who also has another claim. Having married a distant niece of Thoruald's, Asgaut is related to him by marriage. The Herred-thing would give the Talon of the Falcon to him without question."

A knock at the entrance interrupted the conversation. While Kelda scurried about the room for her clothes, Brander moved into the entry room.

"Enter," he called.

Wild Flower, followed by Quiet Woman, walked through the corridor into the central room. When she saw the blanket folded in a basket near the door, she raised a brow.

"A maiden's blanket," he explained. "I want you to instruct my slave what to do with it."

"I shall be happy to, my son. It is a great honor to teach her how to please and do service for you."

His mother wanted to ask questions, but Brander did not encourage them. He had no intention of assuaging her curiosity. She handed him a small leather pouch.

"Give these roots to Kelda to chew about an hour before she is to be tattooed. Make sure she swallows the juice. Otherwise, her pain will be greater. Bring her to my lodge when you are ready to have her marked. I will be waiting," Wild Flower said.

After Wild Flower departed, Brander returned to the sleeping chamber where Kelda paced the floor. She wore her boots, trousers, and shirt. Her jerkin hung across the clothes bar next to the red mantle she had given to Brander last night. She gazed at her mother's brooch which she held in her hand. "I have some herbs for you to chew before the marking," he said and held out his hand, the pouch twirling around the thong that hung suspended. "They will make the pain easier to bear."

"What will they do to me?"

161

"If you swallow enough of the juice, it will put you to sleep. When you awaken, the marking will be over."

"Do the Iroquois take herbs when they are marked?"

"It is no disgrace to use them," Brander explained without answering her question. "My people are taught from childhood not to show emotion to outsiders or to give in to pain."

"My people are, too," Kelda replied. "I will not take the herbs. I would be fully awake and aware of all that is being done to my body."

He moved to take her into his arms, but Kelda moved away from him.

"When will this be done?"

"Now. Would you like to take your mother's brooch with you?"

Kelda shook her head and thrust the pin of the brooch through the red material of the mantle. "I gave it to you last night. A slave has no talisman; her mark is that of her master."

When she reached for her sword, Brander caught the strap. Shaking his head, he returned the weapon to the shelf. Defiantly she reached for her dagger and thrust it into her sheath.

"A slave has no weapons," Brander mocked softly. "Her defense is her master."

"You are my enemy!" She marched out of the room.

"Kelda!"

When she reached the corridor, Brander caught her. "I will not let them disfigure you."

"Any mark made on my body without my permission is disfigurement," she said coldly. She snatched her arm from his grip and opened the door.

Again she felt the bite of his fingers in her flesh as

162

he whirled her around to face him.

"In this lodge you may speak to me about your likes and dislikes, but once you walk out into public, you will be the obedient slave. A slave does not lead; she follows."

He stepped out of the lodge ahead of Kelda. Furious, she waited a moment before she followed him out. They walked the path by the sweat-house into a wooded section. To reach Wild Flower's lodge they had to cross the log bridge.

Brander moved across it quickly, but Kelda stopped to admire the fish. Although the outermost sides of the bridge were thick with green mold, Kelda ignored it. She moved closer to the edge so she could see better.

Her right foot hit the mold and slipped out from under her. Flailing her arms in the air, she yelled. Her left foot slid. She fell on her bottom and bounced into the river going down, down into the cold water.

When she surfaced, she gasped and wiped hair and trash out of her eyes. Brander, standing on the shore, laughed at her. Not soft sympathetic laughter, but loud mocking laughter.

Kelda swam to the shallows where she stood to wring water out of her hair. Her clothes clung to her body. Still laughing, Brander walked to her and held out his hand.

Glaring angrily at him, Kelda slapped it away. She had taken several steps up the steep incline when she began to slide. To stop her fall she grabbed at the low-hanging tree limbs but missed them. She caught several small bushes but they were too weak. Her weight pulled them out by the roots.

She rolled down the incline, a large rock finally breaking her fall. She gasped when she felt the sharp

163

edge tear her shirt. Brushing her wet, dirty, and straggly hair out of her face, she sat there a moment catching her breath.

"The next time accept my help, and you will not do yourself harm."

A foot planted on either side of her, his hand extended to her, Brander glared down.

Refusing his aid, Kelda slowly pulled herself up. "Of course, the master would not want to see anything happen to his goods."

"The man does not want to see the woman harmed," he said. He moved closer, his hands lightly examining her body. "Are you hurt?"

"My pride," she answered. Water dripped out of her clothing to splatter into the dirt at her feet.

"Did you do this on purpose to delay the branding?" Brander asked.

"Had I planned it," Kelda retorted, "I would have done something with more dignity."

"Nothing you planned could have been this effective," he said, his voice going husky.

His eyes seemed to touch every inch of her body; only then did Kelda realize to what extent the wet clothing revealed her body. She recoiled from the intimacy.

He reached out to touch the breast that peeked out of the tear in her shirt.

"Stop!"

She insinuated her hands between their bodies. At the same time that she shoved with her hands, she bent her leg and hit him hard in the crotch with her knee.

Brander groaned. Thrown off balance, he slipped down the bank to land in the shallows. Spewing water out of his mouth, his black hair plastered to his face, he looked at her in surprise. Kelda laughed.

"You want to play games." Brander snarled the words. His face was dark.

Grabbing the nearest tree limb, Kelda pulled herself up. Despite her wet clothing and her hair that slapped her face with stinging blows, she ran through the forest.

She heard him . . . no, she felt him behind her.

She ran until her heart hammered, her legs ached, and her lungs were in agony. She tore more and more deeply into the forest, farther and farther away from the clustering of longhouses.

At last, having entered fully into the green darkness of the forest, she stopped to get her breath. Her hands braced on bent legs, she looked about her. She could see him nowhere, but she felt him. She knew he was close by.

Frightened, she once more glanced all around her, then began to run again. She hit something solid and hard. Something immovable.

Hands, like manacles, clamped about her upper arms. She felt the sheer power of his touch, the vibrancy of his barbarously muscled form. He was towering fury, and she was frightened for her life.

She raised her head. His face was hard and chilling and strikingly still. His eyes were fire and ice; they seared and burned into her; they froze her.

Both were breathing raggedly; both were soaking wet.

"I have been kind to you, Viking," he said between breaths. "But you have refused to listen to me. It is time I taught you a lesson."

Cautiously, Kelda moved her hand to touch the hilt of her dagger. According to Iroquois custom this man might claim to own her, but she would make his ownership of her onerous.

165

"It is time I gave you the beating the women demanded."

Kelda whipped the weapon from the sheath and pressed the point into his abdomen.

"It may be a custom among the Iroquois to beat their women, but I will not tolerate a man beating me."

"It is the custom to beat the slaves, not the women," Brander corrected. "And I advise you, mistress, to think carefully about pointing a knife into a war chief's belly."

"I have. I will see you dead before I let you degrade me," Kelda said, putting a little more pressure to the dagger. "Know that I can handle the weapon, and I can sink it into you quicker than you can move."

"You only wounded Oscar," Brander taunted. "What makes you think you can do better with me?"

"I have learned much since I stabbed Oscar. I now know where to sink the blade of the knife so that I control what kind of wound I inflict. I promised myself that after Oscar no man would press unwanted attention on me."

Brander laughed softly. "Are you telling me, Vik—Kelda, that you allowed me to make love to you?"

"Aye," she replied, "I did. I wanted to know what it was like to lie with a man."

His hand moved; she gouged the knife deeper into his flesh. He brushed a strand of wet hair out of her face.

"Already I have created a wanting in you," he said. "I will also make you love me."

"Nay the wanting between a man and a woman is natural. It is part of survival. This kind of wanting is like that of animals. Loving is different. My mother and my father shared it. Oscar and my aunt did not."

166

"You want loving?" Brander asked.

"Aye, I want to receive and to give it."

"It can be that way between us," Brander said. He removed the knife from her hand and slipped it into her scabbard.

Kelda shook her head. "Not as long as you are the master and I am the slave."

Unable to stop them, tears slid down Kelda's cheeks. She had been through an emotional battle the past day and night; never had she fought a battle that demoralized her as this inner conflict had.

Brander lifted a hand and gently grazed his knuckles across her cheeks and the bridge of her nose. He lowered his head and tenderly kissed the tear track.

He sighed. "Return to my lodge where you may wash your hair and change into dry clothes."

"What about the tattooing?" she asked.

"We will discuss it later," he said.

"You are wet also," she said.

She and Brander stared at each for endless time, before he turned and disappeared into the forest. Slowly Kelda retraced her steps to the river where she rinsed the dirt and trash from her body and clothing. Then she returned to his lodge to brush her hair dry and to change clothes.

This time for Brander she put on a dress, the blue one — Ragnar's favorite. For Brander she painted her face.

When she heard him enter the center room, her heart quickened.

"Are we going to the games today?" she asked.

He entered the sleeping chamber. "Yes."

His back to her, he rummaged through a basket until he extracted another pair of breeches and new moccasins.

"Are you competing?"

"No."

As if she were not present, Brander slipped out of his wet clothes and redressed. Without a word he walked out of the room.

"Brander!" Kelda ran after him.

He continued to walk down the street toward the game field, Kelda running behind.

"Brander, speak to me. What about the tattoo?"

He stopped and turned. "Quiet, Kelda. I am weary. We will talk later."

Without waiting for any response from her, he walked again. She stared at the back of his broad shoulders until they reached the elevated platform of the elders. She took her place on the colored mat below him.

The Vikings, closely guarded by several Iroquois warriors, sat in a small cluster a long way down the field from Kelda. She watched the ballgame, but she was so preoccupied with the change in Brander's disposition that she was hardly aware of what was going on.

After the ceremonies in which the champions were presented with their gifts, Tall Tree called the final council meeting of the celebration. Rauthell was sent to get Hauk. When the two of them returned, Hauk sat next to Kelda.

In no hurry, Tall Tree went through the rituals of prayer and sacrifice before the meeting began. For several hours the Iroquois talked among themselves, the conversation getting heated and adamant at times. Several of the members rose, making their point with loud voices and dramatic gestures.

Finally they quieted, and Tall Tree spoke. Delling interpreted.

"You and your warriors came to our shores to discover if your father by adoption has a son among our people," Tall Tree said. "He does. He is Brander the Firebrand, the one who wears the Falcon as his talisman. The wife Thoruald left behind those thirty winters past is Wild Flower. Brander has considered your request to travel to the land of the Norse with you; he refuses."

Kelda's gaze swung over to Brander. Only once during the meeting had his expression changed. That was when he spoke, and again his speech was eloquent and sweeping, if Kelda was to judge by the reaction of the elders.

"What about his son?" Kelda asked. "Is he going to leave him in Norwegia with Thoruald?"

She could not believe Brander would! She had listened when he explained how the Iroquois looked upon Eirik's memory loss, but she could not believe Brander would abandon his son.

She turned to Brander. "Surely the hatred you feel for your father cannot be so great as to separate you from your son. Are you going to let Thoruald steal your own child from you without a fight?"

Speaking, Tall Tree clapped his hands.

"You must be quiet," Delling told Kelda. "You do not have a voice at the council meeting unless you are recognized by Tall Tree."

Angry at Brander, at the circumstances that had created the present situation, Kelda fumed.

"On the rising of the sun," Delling interpreted for Kelda and Hauk, "your longship is to be burned."

"No!" Kelda exclaimed. *Not my ship!*

Brander motioned and warriors immediately came to stand behind her and Hauk.

"Neither you nor your men will return to Norwegia."

"You cannot do this!" Kelda looked at Brander.

Delling clamped his hand over her mouth. As

quickly she pried his fingers off.

"You can keep me as your slave, Brander, but you cannot keep my men. Do not let them burn my ship!"

"We can do what we please in our land, Viking," Brander responded. "We live by our laws."

"I brought the Vikings here under the white shield," she said. "I did not allow them to fight."

"As I told you before, that is your weakness," Brander said.

"Let them go. Let them return to Thoruald with the gold collar and with news that the grandchild is his."

Brander shook his head. "If they were to return to homeland without you, Thoruald, Asgaut, or both would send another expedition in search of you. If not this summer, then the next, or the next."

"Your keeping us here will not stop them from coming," Kelda argued. "I know Thoruald will not rest until I have returned. He will send another and another ship until he gets his answer. My men will not tolerate this kind of treatment."

As if she had not spoken, Brander said, "Your men will be granted their freedom once the long boat has been burned. If they choose, they can become members of the tribe. Or they can fight us and become slaves. The choice is theirs."

Tall Tree spoke again.

"The meeting is over," Brander announced. He turned to Hauk. "You can give the news to the other warriors."

The old Viking nodded his head. "Will we be able to get all our possessions off the ship before you burn it?"

"I will send my men before the sun sets," Brander replied. "You may go with them." He turned to

Kelda. "It is time for us to return to our lodge."

"I want to go to the ship with Hauk and your men," Kelda said, her heart heavy.

"So be it," Brander replied.

They walked toward his lodge in silence. Kelda was deep in thought about the decision of the Council of the Elders and the burning of the ship. Her banner she had with her, but she wanted to save the sail as well as the personal items she had brought along with her.

"I wager Asgaut will sail over here," Brander said.

"You stated that once before, but I cannot imagine why he would come again. He is looking for riches as well as slaves. While we really need natural riches like the forest and rivers and fertile soil for our gardens, his eyes are still on gold and silver and ivory. Those items are to be found in Europe and Arabia, not here."

"As long as he knows there is the possibility that one of Thoruald's children is alive, he will come. His leadership will not be confirmed as long as there is a shadow of a doubt. He will have to find out for himself if indeed Thoruald has issue here."

Kelda thought for a second, then said, "I would make a wager with you."

Brander raised a brow. "The Viking who does not wager wants to wager."

Kelda stopped in front of him. "Yes, for my freedom. If I can persuade you to return to Norwegia before my ship is burned, you will grant me my freedom. Otherwise, I shall be your docile and obedient slave for the remainder of my life, and I shall do the best of my ability to make my men accept their lot peacefully."

Brander laughed softly and reached out to run his hand through her hair. "Kelda, why do I wonder if

171

there is a hidden meaning in this wager?"

Shrugging, she laughed with him. "It is all in the open for you to view. It is up to you if you wager."

"There is no way you can win," he pointed out, "and already you are my slave."

"Not a willing one," she told him. "Unless I choose to stay in bondage, I shall escape you."

"You will die in the forest."

"I will take my chances."

"You prefer death to the security of my protection and my home . . . and to the pleasure of my loving."

"The loving is a bittersweet pleasure at best when one is a slave. Only when both are freely giving and receiving can it really be loving; only then can it indeed be a pleasure."

He caught her hands in his and tugged her closer so that she was standing inches in front of him. "How do you expect to persuade me to sail to Norwegia with you?"

She traced the line of his lips with the tip of her finger, then leaned over to brush her mouth lightly over his. "It is not fair for you to ask what tactics I shall use," she murmured. "Surely it will be more pleasant to be surprised."

Brander's gaze lowered to her dagger. "Pleasant surprise!" he murmured, and both laughed. "Sometimes, Kelda, your surprises are more painful than pleasant."

"That, Brander, War Chief of the Iroquois, is the two facets of the Solid Faces."

"Now you are quoting me."

Her lips, stained red with berry juice as Quiet Woman had taught her, were curled into a provocative smile; her blue eyes sparkled.

Brander found himself totally intrigued with this woman. True, she was an instrument of his revenge,

172

but he enjoyed her. After two long years of darkness she had brought him the light of laughter.

She spun away from him, her hair and her skirt swirling around her body. "You did not notice my dress."

"I did," he said. "It is beautiful as are you."

Her cheeks colored. "Thank you," she murmured. "I wanted you to be pleased with me."

"I am," he answered. "So much so that I am not going to have you marked."

"You are not!" she exclaimed.

"Nay, I think everyone will recognize the golden-haired woman as belonging to me."

"My hair. I do not know that I like to think of it as my mark of slavery."

"You can always have the tattoo."

"No," she murmured, "this is much better than that."

The sun to her back shined through the thin material of the dress. Her hips and legs silhouetted through the material were evocative; they reminded Brander of the pleasure of her body. He felt a tightening in his groin. He had made love to her last night and today, yet he wanted her again with the intensity of a man who had long been denied a woman. This surprised him.

"This evening I shall prepare a meal for you," she said. "Do you have any food in your lodge?"

"Nay, I take my meals with the elders."

"Where may I barter for some?"

"Wild Flower will help you," Brander answered. "We shall go to the ship first and get your belongings."

"Nay," Kelda whispered, "we will go to the lodge and seal our bargain. We do not have to go to the ship tonight at all. We can get our possessions off in

173

the morning before you set it afire."

She drew the tips of her fingers down his chest, slipping them beneath the waistband of his breeches. She caught his manhood and felt it grow in her hand.

"I would set you afire first, War Chief."

Chapter Thirteen

"I would have you set me afire," Brander murmured, his eyes smoldering with desire. He removed her hands from his trousers, took her into his arms, and bent to capture her lips.

Giving herself to the kiss, Kelda moved her hands restlessly over his chest, pausing to tease the flat male nipples. She moved onto his back, probing the line of his spine between the ridges of muscle, stroking him, again enjoying the feel of a man's arms about her, the taste of his lips upon hers.

Closing her eyes, sighing, she kneaded the long heavy muscles of Brander's back, openly savoring the heat and power of his body.

And then Brander's arms withdrew from her; his hands curled around her shoulders and he put her away from him.

"I must help my warriors ready the canoes for the burning of the *langskip* on the morrow," he said, his voice husky with passion.

"I would have more of you," Kelda whispered.

"I would give you more," he answered.

Her hand slid between their bodies and through the material of his breeches she felt his hard, eager flesh. She measured his arousal with a slow pressure of her palm, and Brander let out a hiss of breath. He caught her hands and eased them up his body, kissed her fingertips and palms and held them hard against his chest.

"I am the war chief, and I must be a leader to my warriors, else they will turn to another."

"Aye," Kelda whispered, fully understanding the role of leadership among warriors. "I shall get Wild Flower to help me with the evening meal." She lowered her hands and kissed him quickly on the lips. "I will be eagerly awaiting your return, my chief."

Brander walked away from her—reluctantly, she could tell, and she smiled. She moved into the lodge to begin preparations for the evening meal. She examined the contents of each of the baskets that was located beneath the wall benches in the central room. A thorough search revealed one bark plate and a spoon, no pots or cooking baskets.

Not only was she going to barter for food but also for utensils. She moved into the sleeping chamber and searched through her trunk for goods to use for barter. As soon as she had a leather satchel full of them, she walked through the woods to Wild Flower's lodge.

"I would barter for food and cooking pots," she told the shaman as soon as she was sitting cross-legged in the central room. "I want to prepare the evening meal for Brander."

Not looking up from the colored corn-husks she was hand pressing, sorting, and putting into different baskets, Wild Flower murmured, "Has the spirited slave been so easily subdued?"

"The Council of Elders made their decision," Kelda answered. "I cannot change it. If I am to live here, I want to be as happy as I can. My happiness comes from pleasing my master."

Wild Flower laid her work aside and looked up to study Kelda before she smiled. "So you say."

176

Kelda admired and respected the older woman and regretted that she must be the one to separate mother and son. She wanted to lower her gaze. She had the feeling that if Wild Flower continued to stare into her eyes she would know all Kelda planned to do. Still she could not break eye contact.

Eventually Wild Flower did it herself. Sighing, she picked up another corn-husk and worked it with her hands, flattening and softening it, before she dropped it into a basket.

"I shall help you, Kelda. I would like to see my son happy."

Would this bring him happiness? Kelda wondered, but whether it did or not, her course was set. It had been ever since she walked aboard her *langskip* and set sail for Skrellingland. She could not — nay, she would not — change it now. She reasoned that if Brander was determined to return to Skrellingland after he had met Thoruald, a ship would be provided. Always there would be adventure-loving Vikings who without the promise of booty and out of their sheer love of the sea would volunteer for the trip.

"May I help with whatever you are doing?" Kelda asked.

Wild Flower nodded. "These are the coverings on the maize we grow. We have many purposes for them. These that I have already dyed —" she pointed to the separated stacks of yellow, red, blue, and green husks "— are to be used to weave mats for eating and sitting. The undyed ones in the basket by the entrance are to be used to stuff mattresses."

Kelda drew a batch of the corn-husks near her and following Wild Flower's example, she sorted them into piles by color, then pressed them flat before putting them into their individual baskets.

As she worked, she glanced at the bent head of

177

Wild Flower. Her hair, parted in the middle and combed smooth to hang in braids, had not one white hair among the thick black ones. Holding it from her face were the two combs Thoruald had sent her. Kelda studied the etching on them and remembered Wild Flower's dream. The Falcon returning to Norwegia with the yellow blossom and the small yellow bud. Thoruald, Wild Flower, and Brander? she wondered. Or could it be Thoruald, Wild Flower, and Eirik?

"The combs Thoruald sent you look beautiful in your hair," she said.

Wild Flower ran her fingers over one of them. "Thoruald always knew how to please me."

"You loved him," Kelda said.

"Yes."

"But you would not go with him when he returned to Norwegia?"

"No," Wild Flower answered, "the Spirits of Life had bestowed a great gift upon me, and I had to use it for my people. I felt I could not leave them." After a brief pause, she added, "Nor would he stay with me. His gods had spoken to him, and he knew his destiny lay over the Great Water."

Holding one of the husks in her hand, Kelda rubbed her finger over the ribbed fiber. "Do you ever regret your decision?"

Wild Flower completed her sorting before she said, "Aye. More times than not, I wish Thoruald and I were together. I wish he could have seen his son growing into manhood. He would have enjoyed seeing him earn his feathers." She smiled. "While we barter, Kelda, I will tell you about the Thoruald I knew, and you can tell me about the Thoruald you know."

Wild Flower pushed the baskets of corn-husks into

the storage area beneath the wall benches and pulled out others from which she extracted several cooking pots and long-handled wooden spoons.

"Will you also tell me of the Brander you know?" Kelda asked.

"I will tell you what I know, but I sometimes think perhaps I know Thoruald better than I do Brander. Brander is a man caught between two peoples and their customs. He has not come to accept that he is both. He cannot be the one without being the other."

"And thus far he has rejected being Norse?"

"Yes."

Wild Flower rose and lifted her leather satchel from the wall peg. "Come, we will go bartering."

An hour later, the two women, their baskets bulging with foodstuffs—grains, vegetables, herbs, and freshly killed, skinned and cleaned rabbit—walked into Brander's lodge. Wild Flower built the fire in the central room, while Kelda laid out the cooking dishes and the baskets and jars of food. Picking up the large pottery water jar, she raced to the river.

Downstream she saw Brander working with several braves to fasten torches to their canoes. Working without a shirt, he had his back to her. As he hoisted a canoe by himself to move it to another location, she saw the muscles of his back, shoulders, and biceps flex and ripple.

He was a study in contradiction. How strong he was! How gentle he could be with her!

As if he felt her gaze on him, he set the canoe down and turned. His hair caught from his face by a headband, glistened brilliant and shiny black like the raven in the afternoon sun; a sheen of perspiration covered his face and chest. They stared at each other, and though physically a distance apart, they were together. They were one.

179

He smiled; so did she. She waved; so did he.

A brave called to him. Brander continued to stare at her. The brave shouted something else, and the others joined in loud, teasing laughter. Brander even grinned with them, spoke and returned to his work. The jar full of water, Kelda made her way back to the lodge. Wild Flower pointed out that rabbit was one of their favorite foods, and Brander would be extremely pleased that she had prepared it for him. She also told Kelda the names of the various foods she had bartered for and instructed her on how to prepare them so that they would be tender, well-flavored, and would compliment the meat she was preparing.

"Do you think you can win this wager against Brander?" Wild Flower asked as she watched Kelda cut the rabbit and drop it into the pot of water.

"Aye, I must. I have pitted my freedom against my being able to persuade him to go to Norwegia with me."

"Brander is a wily man," Wild Flower answered. "I hope you can persuade him to go with you, but I am afraid, my child, it is a futile task, certainly a thankless one."

"Sometimes persuasion must be forceful; other times it can be gentle," Kelda replied.

Wild Flower dropped the thin slices of cornmeal dough into a basket, placing corn-husks between the layers so they would not stick together before time to put them into the broth.

When she covered the basket, she stood and walked to one of the openings in the wall and stared at the men who worked on the canoes at the river.

Kelda opened some of the smaller baskets and peered in them. Much of this food was new to her, and she was unsure how to prepare it. Those she put

180

into one of the cool storage pits in the floor. Leaving the lids off the containers of food she planned to use in preparation of the meal, she set them in a row.

"While passion is new," Wild Flower said, "you can use it to your advantage, but it is not wise to abuse your desires like that. If abused they cease to become a pleasure and become a weapon of control. One, perhaps, both will be hurt. You need to build a foundation of trust for your life with Brander."

"Your son is quite content with passion at the moment," Kelda said. "The only foundation he wants is the sleeping platform beneath us."

Wild Flower laughed. "He is very much like his father. Thoruald was a virile man."

"He still is," Kelda said. "I always suspected that he had a secret love in his life. When I learned about his family over here, I was sure of it. I think Thoruald still loves you."

"Nay." Wild Flower sighed. "Thoruald and I are much like you and Brander. He desired me; I loved him."

Kelda stopped her work to gaze at Wild Flower. "You are saying I love Brander."

"Yes," Wild Flower answered. "He desires you, and you love him. It is your love for him that I am depending on. I only hope you succeed with whatever scheme you have in mind."

"I may not have one," Kelda countered.

Wild Flower smiled. "You have one, Kelda, else you would not have wagered with Brander. But you must also beware of him. He is an astute man. He also knows that you are up to something."

"Then it is up to me to be wilier than the Firebrand." Kelda remembered the bearskin blanket by the door. "Brander said you would show me how to clean the blanket," she said.

181

Wild Flower nodded. "Later I will go to my lodge to get some cleansing herbs."

"Would you share the evening meal with us?" Kelda invited.

"No," Wild Flower said. "After I have completed instructing you for the day, I will leave the two of you alone. I shall meditate upon my dream tonight."

It had been a long while since Kelda had cooked, and she enjoyed the experience. Soon the aroma of the rabbit stew filled the lodge and she had other dishes cooking also. Wild Flower then left to get the cleansing herbs for the blanket. Kelda chopped herbs; she diced flavoring roots; she measured different grains; she scooped bear fat. She chopped more herbs.

Wild Flower returned, and the two of them cleaned the blanket, hanging it to dry on a frame outside the lodge. They walked through the forest gathering fragrant plants—Wild Flower naming each and describing its function—to hang throughout the lodge to freshen it. The sun was dipping low when they finished and Wild Flower left for her lodge.

After checking on her cooking, Kelda went into the sleeping chamber and reapplied the paints and powders to her face; she brushed her hair. Returning to the central room, she awaited Brander.

Her head was bowed and she was stirring the stew when he came in. He walked so lightly she did not hear him, but she felt his presence; she knew he was there. She looked up as he entered the central room. Again she was captured by his gaze, by the wondrous gentling of his expression—a gentling that she felt was for her alone.

"You remind me of a wife," he said.

"I feel like one." *But I am not!*

"The evening meal smells good."

"Thank you." Kelda smiled shyly. "I hope it tastes as good. Your mother helped me prepare it. I asked her to share it with us, but she declined."

"My mother is a wise woman."

Brander sat down beside Kelda to take the bark plate she offered. He tasted the vegetables first; then he ate a bite of the rabbit.

"Thank you for cooking for me," he said. "You honor me and my lodge with your presence and work."

Brander's compliment seemed to melt Kelda's heart and to run warmly through her body.

"I am glad you came to our shores," he said. "You have made me a happy man."

For the first time since she had met him, Kelda sensed a vulnerability in Brander, one that was because of and for her. At that moment she sensed her power over the man, and she recalled Wild Flower's warning. She must not abuse this glorious emotion that existed between them for dishonorable purposes.

"Thank you," she murmured, lowering her eyes and looking at her bowl of food. Her appetite was abruptly gone. "In many ways you have made me a happy woman."

Brander laughed quietly and tucked a hand beneath her chin to lift her face. "Is my valiant Viking going shy on me?"

She shook her head unable to look at the emotion in his eyes. Such gentleness, such caring would be her undoing. At the moment he was treating her like a wife, not a slave.

"I shall be good to you, Kelda. You will have no regrets."

"Aye, no regrets," she replied sadly.

Quietly they ate, Kelda sparingly, but Brander seemed not to notice. She cleaned up the dishes, returning them to the baskets which she slid beneath the wall benches. Sitting on the floor, Brander watched her. When she was through, she smiled at him.

"Shall we play a game or go into the sleeping chamber?" she asked.

He clasped her hand and held it between him, the clasp, the warmth of his flesh a caress in itself.

"I believe, Viking, that you are already playing a game with me."

Chapter Fourteen

"Aye, my lord," Kelda whispered, " 'tis the age-old game that men and women have played through the ages."

Yet clasping his hand, she rose and tugged him to his feet.

"The competition was exhilarating; the game of the jarls tense and exciting. For each of those there could only be one winner. For the game I propose, each of us can win."

He stood and gazed down into her face. "I think, Kelda, I would enjoy playing this game with you. It promises much."

"I promise much, my lord," she murmured.

"Aye."

"I give as much and more."

Together they went into the other room. When Brander doused the last torch, he remained standing by the wall. Kelda stood in front of the sleeping platform across the room. They stared at each other in the dim shadows.

Divesting herself of the dress, she walked to where he stood. He glanced down at her. Moonlight spilled across her face and shoulder, giving her breasts a beautiful silver sheen, silhouetting the nipples.

"Is it true that a woman can arouse a man as easily as he can her?"

She slid her palms up his chest, around his neck to

tangle her fingers in his hair.

"It is."

It was also true that he was afraid of the Viking woman. When he had spotted her getting out of the *langskip*, he had known she would bring disruption to his way of living. Because she was Norse, because she was sent by Thoruald, she represented everything Brander had fought against his entire life. The changes she demanded were those he had always feared and dreaded.

She pressed herself against him. She rubbed him with her breasts. Her hand slid lower to flatten against his stomach.

"I am new at this," she whispered, placing her mouth over one of his nipples, "but I am a quick learner. You did this to me, and it brought me pleasure. I would see if it does the same to you."

She circled her tongue around the hard nubbin and whispered, "I may be your slave, but I shall also make you mine."

"Never." Brander forced himself to laugh; he tightened his stomach muscles. He would not give this woman, this Viking, control of the situation.

"Never?" she questioned, repeating his question from the morning.

Brander caught her by the shoulders and put her away from him. Her skin was warm and smooth to his touch. She had claimed to be different from the Vikings who raided their village two winters ago, but she was not. As surely as the others came to raid the village, so did she. She was determined to take Thoruald's offspring back to Norwegia with her.

He must remember this was a game to her. She had not surrendered.

Kelda laughed. "Perhaps the warrior is not so brave as he thought."

"Perhaps the slave is not so wise as she thinks."

Brander knew that the Viking woman would not give up her purpose so easily. He recognized a kindred spirit when he met one.

"She is not thinking," Kelda responded. "She is reacting to the request of her master. Is she not pleasing him? Is she not pleasing to him?"

"Aye," he murmured, his gaze running over the beauty of her body that was softened by the silver glaze of the moon. "You are both, Viking, and more."

It was the more that disturbed him. She was the vital connection between his world and a land, culture, and father he wanted to forget. According to the Norse way of thinking he was the missing link in the family chain, and the man who had sired him wanted to return him to Norwegia.

"I am more," she admitted. "Otherwise, you would not be interested in me. Otherwise, you would not have fought the elders for ownership of me."

"How do you know I fought for you?"

"Wild Flower told me."

He watched as she walked back to the bed. The silver light outlined the soft curve of her buttocks, and the slender length of her legs. The moonlight cast her in mystic beauty. She paused a moment to stand by the sleeping platform. Her back to him, she drew in a breath and her back arched. He could only imagine the thrust of her breasts, the taste of their sweetness.

"Indeed I am prey for the Falcon. I was your brother's wife."

Brander had to fight through desire to think coherently. He gazed in hunger at her breasts. "I have no brother."

As if he had not spoken, she continued, "I am

187

Thoruald's adopted daughter. Now I am your slave . . . your woman."

She was his slave, but she was not his woman.

She belonged to Thoruald. He had sent her to get him because he wanted him to take the position of his son; Thoruald wanted him now that he no longer had any other living sons — now that he no longer had any full-blooded Norse sons. This made Brander hate his father even more deeply.

This mattered not to the Viking. She was determined to present him to Thoruald as the repayment of her blood debt.

Brander turned and looked at Kelda; she was now standing beside the sleeping platform. Her breasts were large and round, succulent to taste, wonderful to fondle. His gaze lowered, and he ached to possess her, to know her fully.

"You may have married another," he told her, "but you were not a wife. You were not a woman."

"Are you going to teach me to be these things?"

"The wife, no," he replied. "The woman, yes."

He would teach Thoruald to send a woman to do a man's job. He would remain in the Forestland, and he would keep the jarl's daughter with him. He would keep his brother's widow as his slave.

Aye, he would burn the ship. That was her only means of escape and return to her homeland.

Kelda turned, held out her hand and beckoned him to her. "Then it is time for our lessons to begin. Shall we go to bed, my lord?"

He smiled and obeyed. One arm went around his neck and she pressed her body close to him.

"I would touch you as you touched me to give you pleasure."

She felt the warm moistness of his skin. She raised her face and her lips gently touched his as her other hand slowly moved down, circling his nipple, arousing it to a hard point. She move down the line of crisp hair to his navel. She felt his hard, masculine body tremble from her caresses.

"You made me undress for you," she whispered, "but your slave will undress you."

Her fingers deftly unfastened his breeches, and she pulled them apart, knowing the soft leather would slither down his legs to pool around his feet.

He touched her.

"Nay," she whispered.

Now her hand touched the mat of thick black hair that pillowed his manhood. She tantalized him with her touch, so close to his growing arousal, yet not close enough.

"I cannot keep my hands off you, my beautiful slave." Brander circled her waist with his arms, locking her against his strength. Yet her fingers would not be stilled. When the pressure of his mouth pushed her head back, when his lips opened hers, and his tongue invaded her mouth, her hand curled around his masculinity.

Drawing her mouth from his, she murmured, "Does this please you?"

Brander's moans turned into a groan of mixed pleasure and pain. He slid to his knees pulling Kelda with him. She lowered her face and circled his nipple with her mouth. She swung her head so that her hair brushed against his torso. She began to caress his other nipple with her tongue. One hand spread through the thick hair of his head, the other gently touched his most intimate parts.

As Brander breathed more heavily, Kelda lowered her head, her hair and her lips brushing caresses down his stomach. Her tongue flicked against the taught stomach muscle.

189

"Kelda," Brander whispered, his voice thick with desire, "I am weak with wanting you. You think I have had much loving since I met you, but it has been two years since I have taken a woman. You are the first since my — since —"

Kelda's heart received and locked his confession within its secret chambers. She sank fully into the floor with him.

"I am giving to you." She lifted her face and gazed at him. "Whatever you are willing to give me, I will gladly receive. Tonight I want to give to you. I do not know what the morrow may hold for us."

His hands dug into her shoulders and he swung her into his arms. She lowered her head to plant kisses across his stomach and to trail her fingers up and down his thighs. She pushed him down so that he was lying on the floor again. She stood. Swathed in moonlight, she let Brander look at her.

"Come to me," Brander commanded.

Kelda straddled him, standing a little longer before she slowly knelt and lowered herself on him.

"Kelda. Kelda." Brander's voice was thick. "You are indeed setting me afire with wanting."

She sheathed his erection with her moist warmth. When she leaned over him, balancing herself on the palms, she ran the soles of her feet down his legs, stretching her length with his.

Brander captured one of her nipples in his mouth, and as he began to tug gently, he caught her buttocks with both hands. He settled her on top of him and began to arch and thrust.

Wanting to please him and to be pleased, Kelda worked with him, their bodies moving in matched rhythm.

Finally Kelda murmured, "Kiss me, Brander."

He released her breast to catch her face in both his

hands, bringing her lips down on his. She gasped and arched when her tongue darted into his mouth. Then in the duel of love, of aggression, his tongue pushed into her mouth. Filled with her man, Kelda groaned her pleasure, moving faster with longer strokes.

As they neared their climax, Kelda gasped for breath, but she did not release Brander's mouth. Rather she cupped his buttocks with her hands as he cupped hers, and they made the last arch and thrust together.

Spent, Kelda collapsed on him, breathing heavily, hoping to replace the passion in her body with air. She closed her eyes and reveled in the sweet aftermath. She enjoyed Brander pushing dampened tendrils from her face. She enjoyed his tracing the outline of her ears and of her breasts. She enjoyed his tickling her buttocks.

Later they moved to the sleeping platform and she lay there with her head on his chest.

"Good night," she whispered.

"Was this your attempt at persuasion?" Brander asked sleepily.

Kelda chuckled. "If it was, was it successful?"

"Nay," he replied softly, "it would take more than a lifetime of this to convince me, Kelda of the Vikings."

"Then I shall have to think of something else before the sun rises, shall I not, master?"

Her only answer was the rhythmic rise and fall of his chest as he slept soundly.

Kelda did not move for a long while. She wanted to take no chance on awaking him. Eventually she slid off the bed and slipped into a pair of trousers, shirt, and her boots. She moved to the opening in the wall and stared into the shadowed forest.

A part of her wanted to stay in Skrellingland and

to accept what Brander was offering her. Another encouraged her to remember her purpose in being here. It reminded her that although Brander could be gentle and giving at times, she was still his slave. She was his property to do with as he chose. At any moment his feelings toward her could change. On a whim he could do with her as he wished — beat her or sell her.

Nay, she dared not take such a risk.

Turning from the opening and walking to the wall shelf, she strapped her sword over her shoulder, her dagger about her waist.

She knelt beside the bed and whispered, "I am leaving for a short while, Chief Brander. I shall return and see if my persuasion is working at all."

Lowering her face, she kissed him lightly on the cheeks and pushed strands of hair from his forehead. She listened to his rhythmic breathing. She wished his going to Norwegia could be different, could be easier, but he had forced her take drastic measures. She had not been around the Firebrand long, but she knew she would pay the consequences for her actions.

"If all goes well, tomorrow we will be on our way to Norwegia," she whispered.

Chapter Fifteen

All must go well. The words her prayer, her hope, Kelda repeated them silently as she made her way to the longhouse where her warriors were imprisoned.

Keeping out of sight of the guards, she darted to the side. With her dagger, she cut a hole along one wall and squirmed into the building.

She heard someone turn over. She pressed herself into the shadows, hardly daring to breathe. In the moonlight it would be hard to identify Hauk, but he was the one whom she must awaken first. She could make no mistake. Too much was at stake.

"Halt! Who goes there?" a low voice asked.

"Kelda," she answered.

"Kelda!" Hauk exclaimed, still keeping his voice down. He bolted up, his feet thumping to the floor. "What are you doing here, mistress?"

"I have drugged Brander." Kelda, too, spoke quietly. "He is in a deep sleep in his lodge. We need to plan our escape."

"Thanks be to Thor!" he exclaimed. "I thought the gods had abandoned us and our future was here in this land with these people."

"Not if I can help it," Kelda replied.

"Who is talking?" another voice called from deeper within the longhouse. "Hauk, is someone with you?"

"Canby," Hauk whispered and moved to where he slept. He clamped a hand over the lawreader's mouth. "It is Kelda," he murmured. "She is come to rescue us.

Come help us. We need to devise a plan whereby we can move this Iroquois to our ship before the sun rises."

Canby clawed Hauk's hand from his mouth. "By Odin, we should plan our escape and forget this savage." He pushed off his platform and moved to where Kelda and Hauk sat. "We should never have come to this pagan land to begin with."

"It matters not what we should have or should not have done. We are here," Hauk said, "and we must devise a way of leaving."

"Make no mistake, Canby, we are *going* to take Brander back with us," Kelda vowed.

"How did you get the sleeping herbs?" Hauk asked.

"Today he was going to mark me as his slave," she explained. "He had the shaman give them to me. Tonight when I prepared his evening meal, I chopped the herbs up in his food. Now he is sleeping like a baby in the lodge, but I do not know for how long. We must find some way to transport him to the ship, and we must be on our way before dawn."

"One of these sleeping platforms," Hauk said. "We could disconnect it from the wall and tie him to it. Two to four men could easily carry him."

"It would slow us down," Canby pointed out. "Let us not worry about the Iroquois. We have the gold collar. Thoruald has his grandson. We have proof that the child is Brander's. That is enough. Let us save ourselves while we have the chance. By the gods, if we abduct this man, he is going to be nothing but trouble for us."

"I promised Thoruald I would bring his spawn back if he had one," Kelda said. "I must keep my word, Canby. That is the law."

"Aye," he grudgingly agreed. "This way you will have repaid your blood debt." He smiled kindly at her. "I would not have it different, child. All that has transpired recently—the raid on the village, Ragnar's death, Thoruald's wound, this voyage to Skrellingland and the search for Thoruald's offspring—all of this is getting to me."

"To all of us," Kelda responded softly. "Soon it will be as it used to be. We are going home."

"We are going home," Canby repeated, "but it will not be as it used to be."

"What about provisions?" Hauk asked, cutting off their conversation. "If the Skrellings have not taken ours from the ship, we will have enough for the return. But if they have . . ." His words echoed into silence.

"If they have taken ours," Kelda said, "we shall have to take from theirs."

"What about our weapons?" Hauk asked.

"I do not know where they are," she replied, "but we will find them."

"We must," Hauk said, pacing in front of the sleeping platform. "We will have to have them."

Canby walked from them to the entrance of the lodge and glanced about. When he returned to the platform where Kelda sat, in front of which Hauk still paced, he asked, "Are there more guards than the ones posted at the entrance?"

Kelda shook her head. "I will take care of them. I will bring them some of the drugged food, and within an hour they will be sleeping. If all goes well, we shall be on our way home in a few hours."

"Aye," Canby lamented, "if all goes well."

"You get the men up and dressed," Kelda ordered, "while Hauk and I get the weapons and take care of the guards. Make no noise. Make no effort to free yourself. Wait for me!"

Canby nodded, dragging his hand through his beard.

Kelda slipped her sword over her head and handed it to Hauk. Smiling, she said, "I know it is much too

195

small for you, but it is better than no weapon at all, and I am much more skillful with the dagger than the sword."

Hauk brushed his hand through thick red hair and grinned. "Ah, mistress, it feels good to hold a sword again, no matter that it is smaller than my sword The Vindicator."

"Cease the talking," Canby muttered, "and be gone. I would like to be away from this place as quickly as possible."

Kelda and Hauk slipped out the hole she had cut in the lodge, quickly replacing the bark. Soon they were lost in the darkness of the forest. Hauk followed closely behind Kelda as she led the way.

"Since Brander is asleep in his lodge," she whispered, "we will make a carrier out of the sleeping platform there."

"I am not worried about that," Hauk said. "I am wondering how we are going to get our weapons since none of us know where they are being kept."

"Wild Flower," Kelda said.

"Do you think she will help us kidnap her son?"

"She will have no choice in the matter," Kelda said, regretful that she would have to use the woman like this. "I promised Th016uald I would bring his offspring back to him, and I shall."

The two of them lapsed into silence as they drew near the cluster of longhouses. They sneaked around them to the wooded section to the rear. Warning Hauk about the lichen, they carefully crossed the bridge that spanned the river and eased up to Wild Flower's lodge.

Because dim torchlight glowed through the entrance, Kelda figured she was still awake. She reached down to make sure her stiletto was in the sheath.

She called softly, "Wild Flower."

"Enter, Kelda."

Motioning to Hauk to remain outside, Kelda moved

through the entrance corridor into the center room. Wild Flower was weaving the colored corn-husks into mats. She glanced up, smiled and returned her attention to her weaving.

"How was the evening meal?"

"Brander enjoyed it," Kelda replied. "He is asleep now."

Still smiling, Wild Flower looked at her again. "Aye, I would imagine."

Finishing the mat on which she worked, Wild Flower tied off and snipped the end with a small bone knife. Laying the knife down, she placed the mat on top of a stack she had already completed.

"Those are pretty," Kelda said. "Did you weave all of them?"

"Aye, when I am thinking, I work on them, and I work fast. I always have plenty of gifts to bestow on my friends. I shall instruct you how to weave them. You and Brander will be needing them for your lodge."

"I would enjoy knowing how," Kelda said, unable to bring herself to tell Wild Flower of her purpose in visiting with her.

Wild Flower reached into the different baskets of corn-husks, selecting the colors she wanted for her next mat. Without looking up, she said, "I see you have changed clothes."

"Yes," Kelda murmured, her task proving more difficult than she had imagined. She had come to like and respect Wild Flower greatly.

"You are no longer the seducer but the warrior," the shaman commented.

"Aye." Kelda moved swiftly, economically so that she was behind Wild Flower, her knife against her back, an arm around her so that she held her hand tightly over her mouth. "One sound," she warned, "and you will be mortally wounded. My men and I are leaving tonight to return to our home."

197

"With or without Brander?" Wild Flower asked, her voice muffled.

Surprised by the question, Kelda's clasp loosened. "With."

"Is he aware he is going?"

"No, he is fast asleep. I fed him the herbs you gave to me for the tattooing ceremony." She paused. "I need you to help us find our weapons."

"You are asking me to help you kidnap my son and to find your weapons which you and your warriors can use on my people?"

"Nay," Kelda said. "If you help us, we will hurt no one. If you do not help us, I fear Brander will be one of the ones surely hurt, possibly killed."

"Move your hand from my mouth and your dagger from my back," Wild Flower said. "I will help you. Not because you forced me to, but because the Spirits of Life have shown me in dreams and visions that Brander must go to the land of the Norse. Eirik calls to him, and Brander is the only one to save him."

"What about Thoruald?"

"Like me, Thoruald knew the consequences of his actions when he sailed from these shores thirty winters ago. I know not what will happen between father and son, but it will not be what either of them expect. I do want Brander to get his son. Because of Thoruald's never claiming him, Brander has been — was — unduly close to his own children."

"Wild Flower, I wish it could be different."

"But it cannot," the woman answered sadly. "Brander must find his own destiny. Put your dagger away."

"I can trust you not to raise an alarm?"

"I give my word."

They exited from the lodge and when Kelda signaled, Hauk joined them.

"Have you any more of the food you fed to Brander?" Wild Flower asked. When Kelda nodded, she said, "First, I will show you and Hauk where your weapons are stored. Then I will get the food and give it to the guards. They will accept it from me without question. We will need an hour for it to take its effect on them. Remember, you promised that you would do no harm to my people."

"I have given my word," Kelda said. "You can trust me as I trust you."

Wild Flower led them around the village to a small lodge built close to the entrance corridor.

"It is not guarded," she said, "so you will be able to get your weapons easily. Pray that your capture of Brander will be as easy. "

They returned to Brander's lodge where he was still asleep. While Wild Flower prepared the food for the guards, Kelda and Hauk disconnected one of the sleeping platforms from the wall and secured Brander to it.

"Do you trust the woman?" Hauk asked.

"Yes," Kelda answered. "She is the Woman of Dreams, a woman of *sight*. She believes in dreams and visions."

"Aye," Hauk murmured, "she is set apart by the gods."

Securing a knot, Kelda nodded. "She believes the Spirits of Life are responsible for Brander's going to Norwegia. She wants him to be with his son."

Hauk cinched the last thong around Brander, then tested the others to make sure they were tight and would not give.

"He is ready."

"Nay," Kelda said, "he is not, Hauk, but he is going nevertheless."

The Viking pushed up and moved about the room, slipping Brander's longbow and quiver full of arrows over his shoulder. He gripped the tomahawk, flexing his hand around the handle a time or two to get the feel of it. Then he tucked it into the waistband of his trousers.

"The men must not do harm to one Skrelling," Kelda warned. "Our mission is to get Brander back to Norwegia, not to take our revenge on the Skrellings."

"As angry as our men are, that will be a hard task for them," Hauk said. "It would do well if we had some booty for them."

"They knew when they sailed with me the only booty we were looking for was that which Thoruald paid them when we returned with either news of or his offspring. They volunteered for the expedition under those conditions. They will keep their word."

Even as she spoke, Kelda knew Hauk spoke the truth. Immediate booty would help, since Canby was one to stir up the men. In order for them to escape, in order for her to take Brander to Norwegia, she had to have her warriors' cooperation. She snapped her fingers and laughed softly.

"We must convince them that when Thoruald hears of the ordeal they have gone through, he will give them an even greater reward. He will pay each of them handsomely for the return of his son and for the promise of no trouble in the doing."

Wild Flower walked into the room and stood looking down at her sleeping son. She knelt to brush the hair from his forehead and murmured to him in Iroquois.

"Please forgive me, my son, for having become a part of this plan to take you to the land of the Norse—a land you have hated from childhood—to a man whom you think you also hate. I am filled with grief and pain that you will be leaving me, but I have seen the dreams. I have heard the voices. When the Spirits of Life speak to me, I must obey their words. One day perhaps you will understand and forgive me."

She kissed his forehead; then she opened her pouch and withdrew some powdered herbs which she strew about him. Standing, she announced, "I will return shortly. I am going to feed the guards."

Kelda nodded. "Hauk and I will slip inside and give orders to the men."

"I will alert you when the guards are asleep," Wild Flower said.

Several hours later, Kelda and her men — sea-chests hoisted on their shoulders, four of them carrying Brander on the platform — quietly moved through the forest following Wild Flower, who led them to their ship.

"What about the Skrellings who are guarding it?" Canby asked.

"I will take care of them," Wild Flower said. Over one shoulder she carried a large leather case; over the other a basket. "There is no need for violence."

The leather case she left with Kelda. The basket containing the food and eating utensils she carried with her as she advanced to the ship. Brander groaned in his sleep, and Kelda looked around. Unsure how long the drug would keep him sedated, she was nervous and would be until they had him secured aboard the *langskip* and were well on their way.

Lowering the stretcher, the men sat down. Kelda and Hauk paced. Canby grumbled. Impatiently they awaited Wild Flower's return. More murmurs. More pacing. More grumbling from Canby. Finally they heard a rustle in the bushes. Instantly alert, all grabbed their weapons.

"They are asleep," Wild Flower announced. "It is safe to board your ship."

Apprehension turned into anticipation. Worried frowns reversed into smiles and soft laughter. They picked up their burdens with renewed courage and rushed to the harbor.

Never had a *langskip* looked so beautiful to Kelda. Her ship! She and her men paused for a brief second before they began to trot. She envisioned their victorious return to their village; the cries of praise; the reward from the jarl for having brought his son home.

Once they were boarded and Brander secured to the breastbeam, Kelda ordered a torch to be lit. Opening her trunk, she withdrew her banner. As she unfurled it, the men cheered.

Staring at the bright yellow square of silk material, Wild Flower asked, "What is that?"

"My banner," Kelda replied and pointed to the brilliantly embroidered red sun. "This is my personal symbol. The Golden Sol. It is also the name of my ship."

"Your *langskip*—the serpent of the water in my dream—is the *Golden Sol?*" Wild Flower murmured disbelievingly.

Kelda nodded. "I wish you could see us when we hoist the sail. It is red and yellow-striped. Truly a glorious sight to behold."

"Aye."

All watched as one of the Vikings raised the banner. In the darkness of early morning, it could be seen as a silhouette fluttering against the sky.

"Thank you for helping us," Kelda said to Wild Flower. "I am going to miss you."

"Nay," the Iroquois answered.

"I will," Kelda said, not far from tears. "I have come to think highly of you."

"That is good," Wild Flower said, "but you will not miss me because I am going to your land with you."

Kelda stared at her in surprise.

Her gaze lifted to the banner. "Thoruald may have sent for his son, but he is going to get his Skrelling bride as well."

Chapter Sixteen

Dawn broke, its light a pearlescent pink. The *Golden Sol* shed smothers of foam and green water, and its scornful gold falcon-head with glowing eyes of amber reared proudly over the bright and broken wastes of the sea. Three tents had been erected on the large vessel.

The one on the stern platform, the *lypting*, was to give Wild Flower privacy. The large one strung over the spar support covered the midsection of the ship, protecting the provisions from water and sun. The third one, on the prow platform, belonged to Kelda.

Standing a few feet away from it, her foot firmly braced against the prow, Kelda held her head high and felt the wonderful sting of the wind and spray against her face. She was proud of her ship and glad to be aboard it again. Here she was mistress.

"It is good to be aboard the *langskip* headed for the shores of Norwegia." Canby sighed, his hands crossed behind his back, his face lifted to catch the salted mist. "We cannot get home quickly enough to suit me."

"Aye," Kelda murmured. She loved the sea and her longship. This was home to her.

"Do you anticipate our having trouble with the Skrelling?" he asked.

Kelda's gaze swept to the gaily colored tent in the midsection of the ship where Brander lay on a pile of soft blankets. Kelda's only comfort was that Hauk had tied him to the breast beam.

"Aye," she replied, "or he would not be the son of the Falcon."

"I think Thoruald is going to rue the day he brought home a Skrelling to be his son, to be the future jarl. Asgaut would be far better than this—this barbarian." He paused, then said, "You should not have permitted the woman to travel with us."

Kelda looked beyond the tent to Wild Flower who stood on the *lypting* with Hauk. In her brightly embroidered buckskin dress, she stood proud and regally. Although she had seen eight and forty winters, she was beautiful.

"Thoruald wants her, too," Kelda said. "Otherwise, he would not have sent the combs to her."

"Bah!" Canby scoffed. "You are putting too much in the etching on them. I know Thoruald better than anyone, and I know he is not a sentimental old fool. Had he been interested in the woman, he would have sailed to Skrellingland many winters ago."

The same thought plagued Kelda, but she refused to give voice to it.

"Thoruald had his position of leadership to think about," she reminded Canby. "His power is dependent on the loyalty of his men and subjects. The journey to Skrellingland was far too long and dangerous for him to make with the promise of no booty. He would have lost his men. This is why Thoruald wants to change the old ways, to convince Norsemen that it is an honor to be a farmer, to build thriving cities and to get their riches through trade."

"That is why Asgaut will make the better leader," Canby muttered. "He is a Norseman who understands our ways. He does not want to change us to be like the Europeans. Asgaut is a proud Viking warrior whom the men will gladly follow. That Skrelling is neither

204

Norse or a Viking warrior. Our men will never volunteer to follow him."

"That remains to be seen," Kelda pointed out.

"Are you soft where this man is concerned?" Canby demanded.

"Nay, but he is much like Thoruald. Remember how Brander swayed the crowd when he spoke at the tournament."

"But that was his own people, not Vikings."

"Nay, Canby, not only the Skrellings. I saw the Vikings. Although they did not understand a word he spoke, they were mesmerized by his speech. He held them captive with only his voice. I believe he is a force to be reckoned with."

Muttering, Canby turned and walked away. Glad to be alone, Kelda soon forgot the old man's words of discontent. She absorbed her environment. She gazed at the red and yellow-striped linsey-woolsey sail taut with the wind; its colors were that of the sun. On the mast her gaily colored banner, embroidered on it her personal symbol—*Sol*, or the sun—fluttered in the wind.

From the right side of the *lypting*, rudder in hand, Hauk shouted commands. With precision born of years of experience, the Vikings—now sailors, the most efficient to sail the seas—dipped the oars into the water, carrying the ship forward. Others worked with the sails and rigging. They talked and laughed among themselves.

The lapping of the waves, the slapping of the sail in the wind, the oars dipping into the water, the talking and laughter of the men, all these were familiar sounds to Kelda, sounds she had wondered if she would ever hear again.

At times she had wondered if she would ever sail the sea again. The silver necklace of the earth, many bards described it.

A various and interesting place, the sea was moving

hills and shifting valleys. It was a solid sheet of blue-green crystal. Its light and color changed quickly from green to purple to blue and silver and back again. This was the sea she knew and loved.

Its lovely sounds filled her ear—the low hum of wind in the rigging, the snap and whisper of the sails above, the rustle of water under the bow, and the high, sweet mewing of the trailing gulls.

To be free again.

She held her shield up high toward the mast and saluted *Sol*. She had won.

Kelda smiled as she thought of the show they would make when they sailed into the village harbor. When the time came she would order the hoisting of the dress sail made of a velvetlike material called *pell*. One side was bright yellow; the other was red. Embroidered on the yellow was a huge, red sun. The Vikings would hang their shields over the sides in alternate colors, her colors, red and yellow. The colors of the sun. What a victorious entry they would make into the harbor!

"Viking!"

Kelda jumped. Brander! The shout she had been expecting since they set sail. Although he was now her prisoner, his shout was a command. Although he was her prisoner, she trembled when he called.

She turned to see Hauk grinning at her from the other end of the ship. She could not help grinning back. The Firebrand was on her grounds now. She was the one to yell the commands not him.

Yet she hastened to the tent where he was bound to the breast beam.

"Viking!"

The tent opening flapped aside, and Kelda was face-to-face with a standing Brander—with a bellowing bull. The wind played against his hair. His handsome countenance was thunderous; his brows drawn into a scowl. Eyes, blacker than a storm-laden sky, as full of

206

potential danger, glared at her. Although not a seasoned sailor, his feet gripped the deck and he stood staunchly, fiercely above her.

"How did you unbind yourself?" she gasped.

They were only four hours at sea; it was far too soon for him to be free. He could yet find his way back to his village. She pulled the dagger from her scabbard. Out of the corner of her eyes, she saw the Vikings arm themselves with swords and battle-axes.

"Put your toy away," he commanded, brushing her hand away from the scabbard and never answering her question. "I am tired of the games."

He rubbed his brow and squinted his eyes several times. An aftereffect of the sleeping herbs, Kelda thought.

"The food and the lovemaking," he said, half-wearily, half-admiringly, "that was all part of your plan to kidnap me. The sleeping herbs that Wild Flower gave you for the tattooing."

"Yes," Kelda answered, but she was telling the partial truth. She had wanted to cook for him; she had wanted to make love to him. She had enjoyed both.

The sleeping herbs had been a necessary evil.

Even now she felt herself growing weak where the barbarian was concerned. His features were strongly chiseled, ruggedly, implacably handsome. Although he wore only his leather breeches and high-cuffed moccasins, he was set apart from all others.

It was more than his dark coloring. He had an aristocratic bearing and needed no fine garments to display his nobility, for his stature and the confidence of his stance made strong men tremble. The very air about him was charged, revealing his vitality.

"I was remiss where you were concerned, Viking. Had I not been so soft, I would have whipped you into subjection when Gray Dawn demanded it," he mused. "I should have."

"You should have," Kelda replied, "because you will not get another opportunity. I am no longer your thrall."

"You did not win your wager fairly," Brander countered.

"The wager matters not, Skrelling," she replied, determined to erase all intimacy from their relationship. "You are now my prisoner. You pointed out to me when I was in your village that I was governed by your laws. Now you are in my domain. You are governed by Viking laws."

"Aye," Brander replied, "but there is one difference. I am not your thrall as you were mine. The jarl claims me as his son, and whether I claim to be his son or not, no one dares to lift a hand to harm me."

Kelda ran the flat side of her dagger blade between two fingers. "Do not push us."

Brander threw back his head and laughed, the sound ringing arrogantly through the air. "Ah, Viking woman, do not think me the fool. The only booty your warriors are getting on this trip will be from your jarl's coffers. And he will not pay an ounce of gold or silver for damaged goods — especially to the son he is expecting to become his heir — especially from the son he expects to produce more heirs for him."

"I promise you, Brander of the Iroquois, my men have been ordered to use force if you should try to escape us. They will not kill you, but we will do whatever is necessary. You are going to Norwegia with us."

"Understand this, Viking, neither you nor your men can keep me if I decide to escape. But I do not wish to."

Swaying slightly, he walked to the prow; Kelda followed.

"Are you eager to see the land of your father?"

"Nay, I am eager to see my son. Wild Flower had dreams about him, and she believes he will regain his memory. If so, I can bring him home to his land and his people."

"What if he does not want to return?" Kelda asked.

"He will," Brander said. "He is an Iroquois warrior, not a Viking."

He leaned against the side of the ship and watched the sea billow below them.

"Would it not be better to leave him in Norwegia if he does not regain his memory?" Kelda asked. "Even if you return to your homeland, you could rest in the knowledge that your son as the grandson of the jarl will have a glorious destiny as a warrior, a better destiny than that which awaits him across the Great Water."

Brander did not reply, and silence stretched between them.

Eventually he said, "Because of your treachery, I no longer have to wait for Asgaut to come to me. I shall go to him."

"To seek your revenge," Kelda murmured.

"Nay, to exact my revenge."

How much sweeter would his revenge be if he knew that the Herred-thing had promised her to Asgaut, that she was his betrothed? If he knew that he had soiled Asgaut's property!

Hauk, having given the rudder to another, joined Brander and Kelda on the prow. "Lord Brander," he said, "I am your servant. It is my pleasure to teach you the way of the sea."

"Pleasure or duty?" Brander asked.

"Pleasure."

"By the jarl's orders?"

"Nay," Hauk replied, "the law of the sea. Everyone who rides in the *langskip* must work, as there is plenty to be done, the most important being the working of the vessel and the constant repairing of worn or damaged gear."

"I obey the laws of nature. I am willing to learn," Brander said. "Also I will need the knowledge when Eirik and I return to our Forestland."

"If you return to your people," Hauk said, "will you teach them how to build such ships as ours?"

"I would teach them," Brander said, "but they are not ready to learn. They have no use for such knowledge. Before someone can learn, he must have a desire to learn, a motivation for doing so."

Brander's gaze ran the full length of the ship, lingering on the warriors who sat mending the sails.

"My people are most unlike the Vikings," he said slowly. "They do not wish to conquer people and lands. They believe the land belongs to the Spirits of Life and is for everyone. Nay, the people of the Great Forestland are not ready for the *langskip*."

Canby arrived in time to hear Brander's comment. He asked disdainfully, "Do you honestly think you will be allowed to leave Norwegia once we get you there?"

With the same disdain Brander looked at him. "I will not ask permission to leave, old man. I do as I please."

"Aye," Canby jeered, "that is why you are on board the *Golden Sol*. You allowed us to take you prisoner."

"You, old man," Brander said, "had nothing to do with my being here. It would take a far better man . . . or woman to do that."

"Come, Canby," Hauk said. "It is time for you to rest. You will have to spell Rollo soon."

When the two men walked away, Kelda and Brander were left alone. They stood together in silence, each staring at the sea in front of them. Although Kelda glowed from the remark Brander had made to Canby, she was also nervous and uncomfortable now they were alone. She wondered what to say to him, she wondered what his thoughts were.

210

"You are a wily warrior, Viking," Brander finally said.

"Did you not suspect I would use the herbs?" Kelda asked, pleased that his anger seemed to have dissipated.

"In truth, I had forgotten about them," he replied.

"Are you yet angry with me?"

"Aye, but I also respect you. I would have done the same had I been you." He turned his head slowly to look at her. "Did you harm any of my villagers in your escape?"

"No."

"How did you manage to do that?"

"I helped her."

Brander whirled around. "Wild Flower!"

"Yes, my son."

"You are going to Thoruald?"

"Yes."

"How can you go to the man who deserted you and who has never made any attempt to see you again, never wanted to know if he had a family or not?"

Wild Flower lifted her head. So did Brander and Kelda. The three of them stared at the banner waving in the wind.

"The golden sun," Brander murmured. "I would you had never seen this banner, my mother."

"The Spirits decreed it," Wild Flower said. "They have directed me through my dreams and visions. But I go for another reason, because I want to go. I loved Thoruald once. I believe I still do. I wish to see him again."

Kelda saw the compassion on Brander's countenance; she heard it in his voice when he spoke.

"I only hope, my mother, that someday I meet a woman who loves me with the same passion and loyalty you have loved Thoruald."

211

"You will, Brander," Wild Flower murmured. "I promise."

"May Thoruald want you with the same passion you want him," he said softly. Turning, he walked away from the women to join Hauk on the *lypting*.

May you want me with the same passion I want you, Kelda thought as she watched Brander retreat out of hearing distance.

Aloud she said, "I was worried that his anger would be far greater. I think perhaps he has adjusted to the idea of going to Norwegia with us."

"Do not be deceived," Wild Flower answered. "He is furious, but he also knows when to vent this fury to his advantage. He will wait for the appropriate time. Patience is a virtue the Iroquois learn when they are young, one that goes with them through life and serves them well."

Hauk's voice floated across the distance to Kelda.

"Aye, 'tis a grand ship, the *Golden Sol*. Kelda's the envy of the village because she owns the largest *langskip*," he said to Brander. "The hull is ninety feet long, sixteen feet wide in the beam, and six feet deep. Made of oak, she is. Strong and durable. The forty-foot mast is made of pine. It is lighter and more easily handled than oak."

"Brander will learn all he can," Wild Flower said, "and use it to his advantage."

Chapter Seventeen

The voyage passed slowly for Kelda. At times she felt as if her freedom from slavery had been ill-gained. Brander ignored her completely, day and night, spending most of his time with Hauk, learning about the ship and sailing. That they had ever been intimate was like a dream. He never spoke to her; anytime she came near him, he moved away. At night he took his leather, fur-lined sleeping bag and slept on the opposite end of the ship from her.

She missed him, his harshness, his softness, his coldness, his warmth.

He did not seem to miss her. He and Hauk forged a friendship as the old warrior taught him the ways of the sea, a friendship that Kelda found herself resenting more with each passing day. As she stood on the prow, or mended sails, or bailed water on a rough day, she heard bits and pieces of their conversation.

"Aye," Hauk would say, "that is the way to hold the tiller. Gently squeeze her like you would a woman, and just like the women the rudder will guide the ship wherever you please."

Kelda remembered Brander holding her and squeezing her gently.

During the passing days, Brander's presence on the ship haunted her. She was so near to him, yet so far. His love was now the ship and the sea.

213

From daylight to the setting of sun, Hauk and Brander rehearsed, moving from one end of the ship to the other and back again. Always around and away from Kelda.

Planking. Ribs. Cross-beams. Stocks. Tar. Keel.

"The *langskip*'s heavy oak planking is riveted together and lashed to the ribs by means of cleats. This construction gives her flexibility in rough seas."

Keelson. Tar. Mast. Prow. Figurehead.

"She has a deep keel," Hauk said, "which makes it strong and easy to steer."

Tiller. Pivot. Rudder. Oars.

"The rudder is a single huge oar, fastened on the right side of the raised stern at a height convenient for the steersman."

Oar ports. Anchors. Ropes.

"The stern platform is called the *lypting*, and from here the captain can keep an eye on whatever is happening aboard the ship and on the surrounding sea."

Sails. Bailers.

"Aye, the small boat is the *faering*."

Gangplanks.

When the wind was high, the men enjoyed the days by fishing and swimming and playing other games. Brander participated in the revelry until Kelda joined in; then he withdrew. When the sea was calm, they rowed by pairs.

One evening the wind was high, the sail taut. All feasted on a meal of smoked herring with crusty dark bread, butter, and cheese, washed down by a beaker of ale. After darkness fell and they could no longer play games, they dragged out their sleeping bags and called for Ulmer to recite a story.

The bard stood on the *lypting* in front of Hauk and began his tale of the flight of the Falcon and his Talon of the Falcon. The Vikings gathered close,

214

their backs to the prow. Although Kelda, like other Vikings, loved to hear a tale recited over and over, especially those about the valor of Thoruald, she had no interest in this telling. She remained on the prow platform close to her tent.

She was lonely, her body yearning for Brander's complete possession. True, he had never placed a visible mark on her, but she wore his brand. If only she had fought off his advances with the same vehemence she fought against a physical branding. She was learning that she could easier live with the mark than without his caresses.

Sitting outside her shelter, she huddled against the hull of the ship, sitting on her sleeping bag, relishing the time to herself.

The blue-black sky was luminous with twinkling stars and a full moon. Silver shadows filled the *langskip*. With the heavens so beautiful, Kelda could hardly believe a storm was imminent. Yet Hauk announced that afternoon that one was in the making. He could smell it in the air.

Kelda rolled the back of her head against the hull and gazed at the silhouetted Vikings who sat close to the stern platform and listened to Ulmer's tale. Although the group was clothed in silvered shadows, she could make out Wild Flower, who also sat by herself on the far end of the *lypting* close to Hauk—who had declared himself to be her champion. However, the men aboard the *Golden Sol* respected the Woman of Dreams and would do nothing to harm her. Although her gods were different from theirs, they believed she had the *sight*.

They were wary of her son but gave him grudging respect. He would be tested before they would completely trust him.

One stood and walked toward her. Brander. She

215

had no doubt it could only be he. Towering in height, broad in the shoulders, lean in the hips, he was a strongly muscled warrior of Valhalla. It was obvious that he was Thoruald's son.

Like all Vikings he rode the tempest of the waves as if he had been born to the sea. Like them his ability was innate. Unlike them his ability was not born of years of experience. It was learned only in a matter of weeks.

Kelda had hated him as her master; she had loved him as her lover. Now she had neither.

Closer he came. Faster her heart beat.

"You are not interested in the bard's tale?" Brander asked when he sat down beside her.

"I have heard it many times before. It is an old story."

Brander laughed softly. "Aye, I have a feeling Hauk requested it for me. It tells of Thoruald's great deeds when he was a young man. The old man would have me respect the jarl even if I do not claim him."

"Aye." She sighed and closed her eyes, wishing Brander had not sat close to her. She did not think she could bear his nearness.

"Why are you up here by yourself?"

"I wanted to be alone."

He chuckled softly. "Why such deep thoughts, Viking?"

She turned her head to gaze into his face. Although the moon shown brightly, his eyes were shadowed. She could see his lips. She could remember the feel of them on hers, on her body. She trembled.

Brander caught her hand in his and held it tightly. "Are you chilled?"

"Nay," she whispered.

He continued to clasp her hand. So softly that

none could hear save her, he asked, "Have you had the bleeding to know if you are with child or not?"

So this was the reason why he had joined her. "Yes."

He was quiet for a while before he said, "I was selfish in wanting to keep you in my land. You were right. The night I first made love to you, I was taking you out of revenge, but soon I had pushed revenge aside. I was making love to you because I wanted you."

"Brander—" Kelda murmured.

"Nay, let me have my say, Viking." He yet spoke softly.

Since they had left Skrellingland, he had not addressed her by her name. He had once again reverted to Viking. As in the village, he always reminded her of her status by referring to her as his slave. Now he separated them and reminded her of their difference by calling her Viking.

"I am the one who persuaded the Council of Elders to burn your ship and to keep you and your men our prisoners."

"Why?" Kelda demanded.

"Because I wanted you to be mine. You pleased me, and I knew that I pleased you."

"But what kind of life could we have had, you the master, me the slave?"

"I was going to marry you."

"You never told me."

Regret stirred in Kelda's heart for what might have been; happiness brushed it away with what might be.

"I intended to," he said, "but we began to make love. Shortly afterwards I fell asleep."

"It is still possible. Even more so now," she said.

Brander twined his fingers through hers; then he turned her hand over and rubbed the callused tip of

217

his thumb slowly over the center of her palm, sending shivers of pleasure through her body.

"Nay," he said. "Had we remained in my land, my claim to you and our children would have been undisputed. They would have been Iroquois. Their heritage would be that which I gave to them. Not so once we are in Norwegia. You are Thoruald's adopted daughter. I am his son by blood. If I place a child in you, it will be his grandchild by blood. It will also be his grandchild by adoption. I will never acknowledge being Thoruald's son, and I will not give him grandchildren to inherit his title. Never."

Kelda's happiness was short-lived.

"So I am still being used as an instrument of your revenge?"

Brander shook his head. "If you were to bear one of my children, I would have to take the child away from you when I leave your land. Because of the way you feel about your homeland and Thoruald, I cannot count on your coming with me. I would not have you hurt when your child is taken from you."

"I would not let you take our child," she replied, then cried softly, "Oh, Brander, why must this great gulf exist between us because you were born Iroquois and I Norse?"

"I have no ready answer," he said.

"Why must I want you so?" she murmured. "Truly it is a sickness."

"Aye, I have felt it too," he confessed. "I have stayed as far away from you as I could, filling all my waking hours with work to rid my body and mind of thoughts of you."

"Have you been successful?"

Before Kelda knew what was happening, she was in his arms. His fingers wound in her hair. He held her. His mouth molded to hers, and his tongue

218

teased her lips, forcing them to part. He pressed her lips even further apart and filled her ever fuller with the hot demand of his mouth and tongue. He was a thirsty man, drinking of her soul.

Kelda felt that he consumed her.

Without moving his mouth from hers, he whispered, "I had not intended to do this, Viking, but I cannot help the wanting within me, a wanting that only your body can satisfy."

"It is so with me," Kelda confessed.

Again his mouth possessed hers.

His hand went to her breasts, curving around the fullness of them. Kelda cried out when he moved his palms over the soft mounds, stroking and kneading her nipples until they hardened and swelled to taut peaks. Kelda softly moaned her ecstasy.

Time hung suspended. Place was their own. The men could not see her and Brander because they were hidden in the darkness of the prow.

"Viking," he murmured.

The word was as soft as the whisper of the sails above, barely spoken. It was not her name, yet it was a caress.

"I have a letching for you. I would that I could invade the sweetness of your body."

" 'Tis nothing more than sexual desire?" Kelda asked.

"Nay, a letching that is all."

Before her disappointment could fully register, he moved his thumbs over her nipples and caressed the full swell of her breasts once more. He opened her shirt and moved a finger down the valley between them.

Kelda knew she should deny his touch. She wanted to, but, unbidden, excitement rushed through her. His callused palm, skimming over her nipples, ignited a slow-building fire within her. It swept down into her, deep into her, into the very center of her being, into the apex of her thighs and her most womanly recesses.

Kelda's hand moved down his chest to touch him. She felt the same fires in him, the hard shaft of his sex. Tension sizzled between them.

His lips parted from hers and touched down upon them again and again, until her mouth was swollen and her breath came raggedly, until she clung to him, never wanting to let him go.

When his lips left hers, they traveled a slow, demanding trail across her cheek to her earlobe, and she felt the hot moisture of his breath there, and then upon her throat.

"Does one ever get over the letching?" Kelda asked, her stomach queasy because she wanted him so much.

"Aye."

Breathing hard, he put her away from him and leaned his head against the hull. He pushed to his feet, braced his hands on the side of the ship and gazed into the distance.

"I should not have touched you," he muttered.

Kelda straightened her shirt and rose also. "Nay, I should not have allowed you to touch me," she said, keeping her voice low so they could not be overheard and hiding her deep-seated hurt. "I was weak this time, but I shall be stronger in the future."

"I wish the doing were as easy as the telling, Viking." There was a weary resignation to this voice.

Her voice teary, Kelda said, "I must be strong, Skrelling. I cannot endure your playing with my emotions like this. I promise I will not be jerked about like a pet animal on a leash."

Brander reached for her, but Kelda dodged him.

220

Turning, she stumbled into her tent and crawled into her sleeping bag. Tears of frustration and anger ran down her cheeks. Her body ached for his possession; her heart cried for his love.

She knew what she must do. Painful though duty was, she would do it.

Chapter Eighteen

The whole world plunged into darkness. A quiet, ominous blackness.

Out of the quietness, out of the blackness, lightning slashed golden across the leaden skies. Thunder cracked through the heavens. Wind whistled and roared. It slapped ruthlessly against the red and yellow sail. It shrieked through the rigging.

The gods were angry!

The *Golden Sol* dipped arrogantly, then crested with the swelling waves, refusing to surrender its sovereignty to the savage sea.

His feet braced against the *lypting*, his arms crossed over his chest, Brander, as arrogant and confident as the ship, rode the tempest. The wind played against his hair and whipped salt spume into his face and against the oiled-skin garments he now wore. It billowed the crimson mantle behind him like a tent. He stared forward into the thunderous clouds and mountainous waves.

" 'Tis Odin riding across the heavens on his eight-legged steed," Hauk murmured. "He is angry this day."

"Pray that our lives will be spared," Canby muttered. "Odin's playing with us. His lightning is pure blazes of fire, likely to touch down upon our ship. 'Tis because of the infidels. We should never have allowed them aboard." He looked around fearfully.

"You have no infidels aboard this ship, old man," Brander said, his gaze fastened on the horizon in front of him. "I do not believe in your Odin or Thor, true, but I believe in myself and in Wild Flower. She believes in the Spirits of Life. Now, begone, else one of the eight hooves of that steed shall dash you in the head."

"By Odin!" Canby cursed, "watch your tongue, Skrelling. You shall have all the gods angry with us."

"I would take great delight in that," Brander admitted. "Even if your gods exist, Canby, you are too inconsequential for their attention."

Hauk laughed. Canby muttered oaths and walked away.

Levity seemed not to please the elements. The wind, out to punish, grimly whipped the sea into a froth. It tossed the *langskip* as if it were no more than a twig or blade of grass. By the minute the water grew more turbulent.

Hauk struggled with the tiller. But even with his strength, he seemed to be fighting a loosing battle. Rushing to his aid, Brander and he together finally lashed the steering oar to the side of the ship. Their task completed, Brander stood for a moment gulping air into his lungs and flexing his aching fingers.

A loud crash sounded. Fire sizzled. Smoke billowed. A cry rang out.

"Odin has hit us!"

Brander spun around in time to see lightning snaking down the sky, its blaze golden and deadly. It and the mast were one until the mast burst into flames and split. Rigging and sail spun crazily in the air. The ship heaved, flinging sailors to the deck, cargo breaking its bonds to slide wildly about.

"Vikings, amidships!" Hauk commanded. "Secure the cargo!"

The ship was their salvation; they must keep her

223

seaworthy. Brander jumped from the stern platform making his way to the toiling Vikings who worked as one to save the ship. From the prow platform Kelda leaped to the floor planking headed amidship.

"Nay, Viking," Brander shouted above the commotion. The wind surrounded him, whipping his words away. "You stay there. I will do this. 'Tis too dangerous for you."

Kelda did not hear him, or perhaps she ignored him. Her blue mantle flying behind her, she raced to the water jar that rolled on its base and teetered precariously. Already its cords were strained to the limit. Should the ship buck once more — and surely it would — the water jar would roll over the deck, spilling the drinking water.

"Kelda, get away from there!" Brander shouted, his words lost to the angry howl of the wind. He moved closer, fighting the wind, twisting through the oarsmen, dodging rolling barrels and trunks of foodstuffs. "Kelda!" he shouted a second time.

Her hair windblown, she looked up at him. "The water jar." She tugged the cords that bound the huge container in place. "We have to save our water."

Yelling orders above the raging storm, Hauk moved across the deck. "We have fought greater battles than this and won, Vikings. We can do it again."

"Aye!" those who heard him cried, redoubling their efforts to save their provisions.

The wind whipped her hair and tore at Kelda's clothes. At times it pressed her mantle against her body. Other times it flared behind her. She groped her way through rolling barrels and sliding cargo. Ulmer joined her, the two of them wading through the water to check on the provisions that so far were secure and dry. A trunk broke, its contents spilling to the deck. Quickly Ulmer hoisted the bag of meal over his shoulder and moved to the *lypting* deck.

224

MORE PASSION AND ADVENTURE AWAIT... YOUR TRIP TO A BIG ADVENTUROUS WORLD BEGINS WHEN YOU ACCEPT YOUR FIRST 4 NOVELS ABSOLUTELY *FREE*
(AN $18.00 VALUE)

Accept your Free gift and start to experience more of the passion and adventure you like in a historical romance novel. Each Zebra novel is filled with proud men, spirited women and tempestuous love that you'll remember long after you turn the last page.

Zebra Historical Romances are the finest novels of their kind. They are written by authors who really know how to weave tales of romance and adventure in the historical settings you love. You'll feel like you've actually gone back in time with the thrilling stories that each Zebra novel offers.

GET YOUR FREE GIFT WITH THE START OF YOUR HOME SUBSCRIPTION

Our readers tell us that these books sell out very fast in book stores and often they miss the newest titles. So Zebra has made arrangements for you to receive the four newest novels published each month.

You'll be guaranteed that you'll never miss a title, and home delivery is so convenient. And to show you just how easy it is to get Zebra Historical Romances, we'll send you your first 4 books absolutely FREE! Our gift to you just for trying our home subscription service.

BIG SAVINGS AND FREE HOME DELIVERY

Each month, you'll receive the four newest titles as soon as they are published. You'll probably receive them even before the bookstores do. What's more, you may preview these exciting novels free for 10 days. If you like them as much as we think you will, just pay the low preferred subscriber's price of just $3.75 each. *You'll save $3.00 each month off the publisher's price.* AND, your savings are even greater because there are never any shipping, handling or other hidden charges—FREE Home Delivery. Of course you can return any shipment within 10 days for full credit, no questions asked. There is no minimum number of books you must buy.

4 FREE BOOKS

TO GET YOUR 4 FREE BOOKS WORTH $18.00 — MAIL IN THE FREE BOOK CERTIFICATE T O D A Y

Fill in the Free Book Certificate below, and we'll send your FREE BOOKS to you as soon as we receive it.

If the certificate is missing below, write to: Zebra Home Subscription Service, Inc., P.O. Box 5214, 120 Brighton Road, Clifton, New Jersey 07015-5214.

FREE BOOK CERTIFICATE

4 FREE BOOKS

ZEBRA HOME SUBSCRIPTION SERVICE, INC.

YES! Please start my subscription to Zebra Historical Romances and send me my first 4 books absolutely FREE. I understand that each month I may preview four new Zebra Historical Romances free for 10 days. If I'm not satisfied with them, I may return the four books within 10 days and owe nothing. Otherwise, I will pay the low preferred subscriber's price of just $3.75 each; a total of $15.00, *a savings off the publisher's price of $3.00.* I may return any shipment and I may cancel this subscription at any time. There is no obligation to buy any shipment and there are no shipping, handling or other hidden charges. Regardless of what I decide, the four free books are mine to keep.

NAME _____

ADDRESS _____ APT _____

CITY _____ STATE ____ ZIP _____

TELEPHONE ( ) _____

SIGNATURE _____
(if under 18, parent or guardian must sign)

Terms, offer and prices subject to change without notice. Subscription subject to acceptance by Zebra Books. Zebra Books reserves the right to reject any order or cancel any subscription.

A careening barrel diverted Brander's attention from Kelda and Ulmer. Thrust against the hull, its rings burst. The staves splintered, flying in several directions, one in the direction of the bard.

"Ulmer!"

The wind caught Brander's words. The lad never slowed in his journey toward the *lypting* deck. Brander leaped forward in hopes of knocking Ulmer to his feet out of harm's way, but Ulmer was too far from him. The jagged point pierced the sack to sink into the bard's back.

Ulmer screamed, and meal sprayed the sky. Swallowing the fine dust, Brander coughed, but he reached the fallen form. Blood already colored the boy's garment, the stain growing larger and larger.

"Am I going to die?" Ulmer gasped, in a pain-laden voice.

"If you do not," Brander replied, grasping the stave with both hands, "you are going to think you are. I have to pull this out, and it is going to hurt, lad."

"Aye." Ulmer's murmur turned into a second full-fledged scream when Brander yanked the missile from his back.

" 'Tis over," he said. "I will take you to Wild Flower. She will tend your wound."

Gently Brander scooped the boy into his arms and made his way to the *lypting*. His mother, her medicine satchel on her shoulders, knelt down to receive him.

"Is it bad?" the boy mumbled.

"Let me look," Wild Flower said softly. She and Brander cut the garment from him, then her fingers began a thorough examination. "Nay, it is a clean wound. It will give you great discomfort, but it will also give you material for another story, *skald.*"

"Aye," Ulmer mumbled weakly. "But at the moment I do not feel like singing or reciting."

"You will," Wild Flower promised.

Brander moved away from the deck, grabbing a loose rigging line to hold onto as he slowly made his way toward Kelda. He stumbled over something and looked down to see Canby. An examination revealed the old man was unconscious, blood running down his face. Brander turned him over to see a nasty bruise and bump in the middle of his forehead. A long cut ran the entire length of his face.

Brander easily tossed him over his shoulder and slowly, carefully retraced his steps to the stern platform where Wild Flower awaited another patient. He laid the man on his back.

He heard the rasp and grating from the sky. His gaze sought and found Kelda as she looked up. He did, too. A slender cord of wood, like a long, thin sewing needle, held the mast to the breast beam. A weapon of death, the mast was a ball of fire on one end, a mass of spiked slivers on the other.

The wind gnashed at it.

Kelda screamed; Brander cursed.

He brushed cargo aside. He pushed through sailors who caught at rigging, who bailed water, who manned the oars.

The ship rolled to the side, tossing the water jug into the air. It landed, splintering into tiny little shards of pottery. Precious drinking water splattered across the floor planking.

The wind caught the rigging to flap it unmercifully through the air. Like sea serpents, ropes coiled about Kelda to choke and suffocate her, to pitch her forward on the deck.

Grasping one of the cords that bound her, she struggled. She rolled over and looked up. The broken mast, truly a torch, spun viciously around the breast beam. It broke. The flaming mass plummeted to the deck, its fall broken by the spar which swayed before it gave way to the added weight of the mast.

226

"Move, Kelda!" Brander shouted, making his way to her.

She rolled over, caught tightly between a sea chest and a wooden cask, the staves broken and jutting out. The fire ball landed on their provisions, the precious provisions, that had been kept dried. Flames greedily conquered the dried bags and barrels, the grains igniting the minute the fire touched them.

All Brander could see was a huddled form hidden by a blue mantle. The ship pitched, the prow reaching for the sky. Angry waves slapped against the sides of the ship. It lunged deep, the stern now moving toward the blackened heavens.

More barrels and chests tore loose from their bindings to slip and slide across the deck. Sailors scrambled to save themselves, to save the provisions, to save the ship itself.

Gripping with her toes and fingers, Kelda crawled from her confinement. She drew in deep gulps of air. She labored, but never moved.

Sails rent. Wood creaked. Waves crested. The spar bounced around, hitting her on the forehead, before it shoved a heavy food chest on her, the spar jamming it and Kelda against the hull.

"The infidels have caused this!" a Viking shouted, his silver hair standing on end, making him look more frenzied than the elements around him. "Because of them, Kelda and Canby and Ulmer are dead!"

Dazed, she lay on the floor planking. Her hand touched her forehead. Blood oozed through her fingers.

"Out of the way!" Brander shoved his way through the Vikings. He fought his way through the flapping sail and falling mast and spar. "Kelda, get up and get out!"

"I cannot," she shouted. "I am caught between the

227

chest and the hull."

The wind howled fiercely around him. The ship, at the mercy of the wind and the waves, reeled, rolled and tossed. Vikings scrambled all about. Hauk shouted orders.

The spar, tangled in the rigging, spun wildly, its jagged end piercing the air. If it fell any lower, it would hit Kelda.

Brander plowed through the flames, his only thought to save her, his progress hampered by the wreckage. He climbed over, beneath, and around. He tugged and shoved.

He prayed. To all the gods, both Iroquois and Norse.

The sail swallowed him. Gasping, he kicked and fought his way out. Flames leaped around Kelda. Greedily they lapped closer and closer to her.

She shoved at the beam that imprisoned her. She twisted her body and wiggled in her bid for freedom. The hem of her mantle caught fire.

"Kelda unfasten your mantle!" Brander shouted.

She clawed at the brooch that drew it closed about her neck.

"I cannot," she yelled and tugged at the material. "The fall bent the pin."

A wall between him and Kelda, the flames danced into the air, higher and higher. They whooshed ever closer to her.

The wind whipping against him, Brander cursed the gods of the Vikings. He scowled at the darkened skies. He defied the lightning bolts. He ignored the drumming of the thunder.

He shouted to the horde of them, then to one in particular, "Odin of the Vikings, if this is the best you can do, you are not worthy to be called the Lord of Viking gods. I, Brander the Firebrand of the Iroquois, defy you. I will save the Viking."

228

Brander pulled the crimson mantle over his head and leaped through the flames. He fell over the broken cask, a stave slashing through his leather garment to pierce his calf. He kicked it aside, leaping over a sea chest. He reached for the water jar to douse her burning mantle, but it was scattered pottery pieces.

The last bit of rigging fell down to coil around Brander's feet. He tripped. The jagged edge of a piece of metal caught his buckskin trousers and tore them a second time. Digging his fingers into the deck wood, tearing the flesh from them, he pulled himself along. The wind whipped a torn section of the sail against him. Time and again it slapped his face, blinding him, stinging him. He had to get to Kelda.

As if reveling in its power, lightning clawed through the air. Thunder rolled.

Finally freeing his feet, Brander crawled to where she lay facedown, her cheek resting against the floor planking in a pool of blood.

"Kelda."

She did not move.

"I am here, Kelda," he assured her. "I will save you."

He scooted closer to catch the mantle in his hands and to rip it from her body, tossing the burning material aside. Still the flames moved in closer on them. Time was against them.

He lowered a trembling hand to her. She had to be alive. She had to be. He brushed her hair from her face, the blood from his lacerated fingers mixing with hers. Tender fingers probed her forehead. The bruise. The cut. It was not so deep, but it would have to be bandaged carefully to keep the scar from being wide and ugly. He ran his fingers gently over the large knot.

"Do not worry, my little Viking, I will free you."

Her lids quivered slowly to open. She licked her lips. "Aye, I know you will," she murmured and gave him a wan smile. "I am caught. I cannot move my legs."

Cannot move her legs!

Fear again coursed through him. "Do you have feeling in them?" he demanded.

She nodded.

"That is good."

Chapter Nineteen

Draping his arm over her shoulders, Brander knelt beside her for a moment to reassure himself she was truly alive. He drew a deep breath and shoved the mast aside, rigging and jagged spar spinning through the air.

"Brander!" she yelled. "Watch out!"

Brander looked up. He ducked. He heard the whine of the deadly piece of wood that swung above his head like a pendulum. Kelda tried to sit up. She cried out and fell back to the deck.

"My legs," she cried out. "I still cannot move them."

Brander twisted her hair into a coil and tucked it into the neck of her shirt. He unfastened her mother's brooch and pressed it into her hand.

"What are you doing?" she asked.

He smiled grimly. "Giving you your talisman for good luck. We are going to need all we can if we are to escape our prison of fire."

On the other side of the flames, sailors were tossing buckets of water. Yet the fire defied them. It danced around the water. Taking off his mantle he swung it over her and lifted her into his arms.

"Nay, Brander," she cried, "save yourself."

"I am. Remember, Viking, I am one with the fire."

He charged through the flames. When he staggered onto the prow, laying Kelda down before he

231

crumbled to her side, his body convulsed with coughing.

On the stern platform he saw his mother tending to Canby and Ulmer. Hauk struggled with the tiller.

Brander rolled close to Kelda, first holding her, then running his hand over her face again and again to reassure himself that her wound was slight. He brushed the soot from her face. He pressed kisses over her face.

"How is she?" one, then another of the Vikings asked.

"Battered and bruised. A deep cut. A bump on the head," he answered as he staggered to her tent on the prow platform.

Lightning tore across the sky and the rain began.

He laughed loudly, triumphantly. Kelda laughed softly, weakly. Both held their faces up to the cleansing drops.

Water streaked her face with soot and blood, but she had never looked more beautiful to Brander. He caught her against himself and held her. It may have been seconds, minutes, hours, he did not know, but it was not nearly long enough.

Then he remembered her legs. He pulled off her boots to begin an examination.

"Has she broken any bones?" Wild Flower knelt beside them.

"I think not," Brander replied. "She is only bruised. How is Canby?"

"He is badly shaken with a slight cut," she answered.

Rain pounded the deck, and the Vikings cheered.

The shaman's knowing hands took over the examination. Brander, not moving from Kelda's side, watched. He held her hand. He stroked her face.

"Thank you for coming to get me," Kelda said, her eyes fastened to his face.

232

Brander smiled and brushed wet tendrils of hair from her cheeks.

"How is she?" Hauk demanded.

"She will live," Wild Flower answered, using the rainwater to cleanse the coagulated blood from Kelda's forehead. Tremors shook her body. "But she will need her cut sewn and bound. Brander, move her inside the tent where it is dry. I will give her an herb."

Picking her up, he carried her to her tent where he stripped off her wet clothes and tossed them aside. He grabbed a discarded shirt and rubbed her trembling body dry. He tucked her into the dry sleeping bag, then opened her trunk and searched until he found a dress made of soft white material.

"Let me help you put this on." He opened the sleeping bag and lifted her up, slipping the dress over her head and shoulders and pulling it below her buttocks.

She felt so fragile in his hands. He had held her in anger and in passion but never had he realized how fragile she was. He had wanted her in revenge, also in desire. Now he wanted to comfort and to soothe her. He simply wanted to hold her, to assure himself that she was all right, to assure her of the same. He covered her up and held the sleeping bag close to himself.

Wild Flower lifted the entrance covering to the tent.

"I want you to chew this root, Kelda," she instructed. "Just swallow the juice. When none is left, spit out the fiber."

Kelda shook her head.

"Take it," Brander commanded gruffly but not unkindly. "You will rest better during the storm."

Kelda took the herb and put it into her mouth, chewing it. When she tasted the vile juice, she

233

gagged and pushed out of his arms.

"Nay." He clamped a hand over her mouth. "Chew and swallow more."

"I will return shortly," Wild Flower said. "Her wound needs to be sewn and bandaged to stop the bleeding and to heal without making an ugly scar."

Kelda glared at him as she continued to chew. She swallowed, again and again. When he was convinced she had taken enough, he removed his hand to allow her to spit out the fiber.

"To think," she said, "I was worried about the tattoo, and now I will probably have worse."

"Perhaps, my little Viking, there is a difference being branded by the sea than by a man."

At the moment Kelda could think of nothing more wonderful than being held by this man. A man who had walked silently in the forest. Who had walked in power as a commanding chief. Who had walked defiantly through the flames to rescue her. A man who now cradled her in his arms as if she were a cherished baby.

She vaguely remembered his calling her Kelda when he was rescuing her. Kelda. Not Viking. Her entire body was in pain, but her heart was light.

"That is the difference between the Viking and the Iroquois woman. The Iroquois would have preferred to be branded by a man than the sea."

"To have you, Brander of the Iroquois," she murmured wearily, her lids growing heavy, "I would have had to accept that I would be possessed and protected, never loved or cherished."

"Cannot they be the same?" he asked softly.

"Nay, possessing is taking. Loving and cherishing is giving."

Neither said more; this was not the time to argue.

"Your breeches," Kelda said, "they are torn. And your mantle is ruined."

"Aye, but you are safe, little Viking."

Kelda squirmed and rested her cheek against his chest, her palm lying next to her face. She was comforted by the steady beat of his heart. At this moment she believed in him with the same confidence she believed in her gods—perhaps even more so. She trusted him with her life.

By the time Wild Flower returned, Kelda was almost asleep. She felt the soft touch of the woman's hands as they moved over her forehead several times to probe the swelling and the bruised skin.

"I will need to sew it," she said.

"Aye." Brander moved to the tent opening.

"Stay with me. I may need you," Wild Flower said. She opened the bag and drew out a needle and sinew. "This will hurt," she told Kelda, "but you will be able to endure the pain. The herb will help you."

"You believe the Vikings are weaker than the Iroquois," Kelda said.

"Nay," Wild Flower answered, and pierced the skin with her needle, drawing the skin together in delicate stitches. "I do not see why anyone—Iroquois or Viking—should have to endure pain unnecessarily. The sleeping herb will not harm your body. The earth gave it to us, and as long as we do not abuse it, it can provide good for us."

Fire, beginning at Kelda's forehead, burned throughout her entire body. She tensed but did not flinch from the agony. She would have a scar on her forehead after all, but at the moment it did not matter.

All that mattered was an easing of the pain and sleep.

She squeezed Brander's hand as another spasm of pain swept through her body.

"It is done," Wild Flower announced.

Kelda smiled grimly, took a deep breath, then

closed her eyes. Before sleep overtook her, she felt gentle fingers massage her scalp.

"She is sleeping," Brander said. He ran his fingers through her wet hair.

"Not for long," his mother informed him. "I do not have enough of the herbs to induce a long sleep. Look in my satchel. I brought you dry clothing."

"I will only get wet again when I leave the tent," he said.

"More surely now that those you are wearing have been torn from your body," Wild Flower retorted. "I have instructed Hauk that you are to stay with Kelda tonight. I want someone with her when she awakens, and I—" she looked at him and smiled "—the infidel, must give aid to the others who are hurt."

Brander took out the clothing. Green cloth shirt and brown trousers, and even darker brown leather boots. Raising a brow, he glanced at Wild Flower.

"We left in such a rush, my son, we did not bring any of your clothing. You will have to wear those."

"What if they do not fit?"

"They will do until I can sew you more. If you had a wife, I would not have to worry about sewing your clothes."

"I had a wife, my mother, and a family." Brander bunched the shirt in his fist. "But thanks to the Vikings, my entire family is gone."

"Save one," Wild Flower reminded him.

"Aye," he muttered, "save one. I hope your Spirits of Life do not fail you, my mother."

"They never do," she replied. "Sometimes we fail ourselves and blame it on them. But they are true, my son. I believe in them."

He smiled. "I believe in you."

Slipping her satchel strap over her shoulder, Wild Flower eased out of the tent. In the cramped quarters Brander changed clothes, glad for the warmth of the

236

dry ones. He enjoyed the feel of the soft material against his skin.

Kelda stirred fitfully. She whimpered in her sleep. She shook and her teeth began to chatter. Brander touched her forehead. She was hot to the touch. He climbed into the sleeping bag with her, holding her shivering body close to his, giving of his warmth, of his strength, willing her to a more peaceful rest.

Lying there, he listened to the rain impinge the deck and the heavy material of the tent. He heard the noises of the men as they cleared up the wreckage, tended the wounded, and settled down. He felt the pitching and rolling and swaying of the ship as it valiantly fought the elements.

Eventually he dozed to be awakened later by Kelda's snuggling. It was yet dark outside the tent, but Brander knew that it was now the darkness of night.

"The storm is over," she whispered.

"Aye."

The ship gently rode the waves. The wind no longer howled and screamed. The thunder had stilled. The lightning had ceased.

"You slept with me?" she said.

"Aye." Brander held her close, cuddling her face against his chest.

"You should not have." She pushed out of his arms.

He should have. This is where she belonged . . . in his arms, in his bed.

"Whatever will Canby think if he discovers this."

"Why should it matter to Canby?" Brander asked.

"He is the reader of the law," she answered. "Second only to Thoruald in the district. He petitioned the Herred-thing for me after Ragnar died and Thoruald was wounded."

"What did you have to petition the Assembly about?" Brander asked.

237

She hesitated, then said, "I wanted a longer period of mourning than that which they had granted. Because the marriage had not been consummated, they wanted to grant me half the seasons. I wanted three winters."

"Did you love Ragnar so deeply, Viking?"

He had reverted to calling her that again.

"I loved him," Kelda admitted, "and if I had lived with him as my husband, I would have come to love him more."

The answer displeased Brander. "Yet he never gave you the fire and excitement that I gave to you."

"No," she murmured, "but there is more to life than letching, Skrelling."

She reverted to calling him that.

"Perhaps," he murmured, "but until this more comes along, I shall be content with the letching."

"Not I." Kelda sat up, taking notice the first time of her clothing. She murmured, "My nightshirt. I do not remember putting it on." Her hand went to the stitches on her forehead. "But there is much about yesterday that I have forgotten."

"You did not put it on," Brander said.

"You?" Her cheeks warmed, and she was glad he could not see their heightened color.

He nodded, tapping his finger against the end of her nose. "Why so maidenly?" he teased. "It is not as if we have not been most intimate with each other."

Kelda turned her back to him. "That was another place, another time."

He combed his fingers through her hair, the tips of them brushing against her back. "But we are the same two people. That will not change, Viking."

"But we are not the same two people," she said. "We have changed since then as have the conditions. Please, do not touch me, Brander." She flexed her shoulders to displace his hand.

"My touch is not pleasing?"

"It is too much so," she answered and reached into her trunk for a small, ornate case. "It is a pleasure I find I can ill afford."

She opened the lid and extracted her comb which she drew through her hair, gently combing out the tangles.

"I am quite confused and do not know how to deal with the emotions that our letching has unleashed in me."

Brander took the comb from her. Without a fight she allowed him to comb her hair.

"You promised that you would create a longing in me that only you could assuage," she said. "I do not know if you are the only man who can assuage it, but I have the longing. And I get no pleasure out of wanting."

He laid the comb aside to curve his hands around her shoulders. He tugged, but she would not look at him.

"When I made that promise, I was filled with bitterness," he said. "I no longer feel the same way. I would that I had not touched you — because I have unleashed the same yearning within me."

The storm was gone, but the tent was filled with tension.

"Viking —"

"When we were in your land," Kelda said, "we had a future together, but not now. You are destined to return to Skrellingland, and I must do my duty to my people."

She paused and drew a deep breath. "Most important, you have already promised that you and I shall never create sons and daughters. You warned that should I have your child, you would try to take it from me. That I would never allow. I would die first."

She smiled bitterly. "Now, if you will leave, I would

239

like to change clothes. I am sure Hauk is looking for land so that we can do repairs on the ship and take on more provisions and fresh water."

Brander was disappointed by Kelda's abrupt change of behavior, but he could not expect her to react any differently. He was responsible for this change. He had been the one to inform her that they had no life together, that he would not marry or give her children.

He crawled out of the tent and straightened, looking about him at the calm beauty of the night. Stars and moon once again graced the heaven. He would never have guessed the sea could be so peaceful after the tempestuous storm of early morning.

A torch burned brightly, casting its flickering light over Brander. Canby walked to where he stood. A long, thin cut stretched from his forehead down his throat. Bruises darkened his face.

"Hauk, tells me you saved my life."

"Aye."

"I wish to thank you."

Brander nodded.

"How is Kelda?"

Dressed in trousers and shirt, she crawled out of the tent. "A cut and a bump and a terrible pounding inside the head," she answered.

Canby looked from Kelda to Brander, back to Kelda. "Did you sleep with him?"

"You are asking what you have no right to know," Brander replied coldly.

Canby's eyes widened in disbelief.

"Canby has a right to know," Kelda answered calmly. "As I told you earlier, he petitioned the Herred-thing for me."

"Not only that," Canby interjected, "I accepted her bride-price for her."

"Because of this you have the right to know the intimacies of Kelda's personal life?" Brander scoffed. "I find that absurd, especially with her husband dead."

"Canby is not talking about Ragnar. He is speaking of my betrothed."

"Your . . . betrothed?"

"Aye. Asgaut."

Chapter Twenty

"Betrothed to Asgaut," Brander repeated, his voice ominously quiet. He crossed his hands over his chest and rocked back on his heels to study Kelda. "A detail you omitted to tell me, Viking."

She returned his gaze with a show of confidence she wished she truly felt.

He asked, "May I inquire what your bride-price was?"

"My *langskip*."

"This *langskip?*"

"Aye. The *Golden Sol.*"

As surely as the moon shined upon them, Kelda knew Brander's thoughts before he expressed them.

"Do you take pleasure, Viking, in delivering me to Norwegia aboard the ship of the man who massacred my family and kidnapped and enslaved my son?"

"Never have I regretted duty more," she replied.

"I would that I had burned your ship that evening instead of playing games with you." Brander snarled the words angrily. "I knew better than to let myself be captivated by you, Viking. You deserve Asgaut; the two of you are very much alike — treacherous and deceitful."

"You would point the finger of blame at me," Kelda exclaimed, "when you, Skrelling, have used me as a weapon of your revenge? While you still do?" She laughed scornfully. "You are angry because I

242

have gotten the best of you, not once but twice."

"Have you?" he murmured softly, a strange glint in his eyes. The torchlight danced across his visage to reveal a face chiseled harshly out of pure ice. "We shall see who wins, Viking."

Brander stepped from the prow platform and moved toward the *lypting* away from Kelda.

"He is a dangerous one, he is. I fear he is going to bring us trouble," Canby muttered. "I only hope Thoruald finds in him what he seeks."

"Aye," Kelda murmured, hurting too badly to discuss Brander and certainly not wanting to discuss him with Canby. "I only wish I were going to find in Asgaut what I seek."

At the moment she grieved because she did not find in Brander what she sought. She fumed because he had awakened a longing in her that no other man could assuage.

"You will," Canby replied quietly. He reached out to lay a comforting hand on Kelda's shoulder. "I know it has been difficult for you, child, with Ragnar's death and possibly Thoruald's, but you have held up quite well. I am proud of you."

"Thank you, Canby." Kelda blinked back the tears. "As Thoruald's adopted daughter, I could have done no less."

"No daughter could have done more," Canby replied.

"Aye, one could have. I promised I would search for his Skrelling spawn," Kelda replied.

"You promised more," the lawreader said.

She nodded, wishing Canby had not reminded her.

The old man seemed dissatisfied to merely point out the promise. He spelled it out for her. "At the adoption ceremony you swore by the sacrificial oxen blood, promising Thoruald that you would marry Asgaut to produce him an heir through you—his adopted child."

243

Vividly Kelda recalled the ceremony. The slaying of the three-year-old oxen. The boot for Thoruald made from the hide of its right leg that sat in the middle of the *stofa* during the ceremonial feast. Because his fever was so high and he too weak to walk, Thoruald had entered the Great Hall leaning on Hauk. He had poured the sacrificial blood on the boot and slipped his foot inside. When he proclaimed his desire to adopt Kelda with the entire village as his witnesses, he withdrew his foot and she inserted hers. Clasping her hand in his, he proclaimed her his daughter by blood, heir to the Talon of the Falcon should Thoruald have no more blood heirs.

"You gave Thoruald the assurance he needed to know that his sword would one day go to one of his grandchildren," Canby added.

"I hope it goes to his blood son or grandson," Kelda said, then added softly, "I pray that Thoruald is alive when we arrive home, Canby. I want to share his happiness when he sees Wild Flower and Brander."

"I wish only happiness for my old friend," the law-reader said, "but I cannot believe it lies in the Skrelling. The gods help us if I am right."

He shook his head and ran his hand down the cut on his face.

"Yet, for all my doubts, Kelda child, you and I owe him a blood debt. He saved our lives."

For what? Kelda wondered, a lifetime of unhappiness with a man whose vision she did not share, whose only ambition was to raid, loot, plunder, and kill. With a man who already had two wives—one of whom was Thoruald's niece—and concubines too numerous to count.

She was Asgaut's legitimate claim to the Talon of the Falcon, his main—not his only—reason for wanting her.

Like Brander, Asgaut was a man who wanted only

to possess not to love or cherish her.

Her head aching, Kelda returned to her tent to rest. Before she lay down, she opened her trunk and pulled out her jewelry casket to stare at the gold collar that had once belonged to Thoruald, then to Brander. Now it was hers . . . hers to give to the one to whom it belonged. Brander or his son? she wondered.

Her attention shifted to the game piece. Clasping it in her hand, she returned the casket to the trunk and lay back on the pallet of soft blankets to ease the aching in her body and the pounding in her head.

Cradled in the ship, rocked by the sea, she finally slept, not awaking until she felt someone touching her forehead. She opened her eyes to gaze into Wild Flower's face. Cool fingers gently examined the area around the wound.

"How is your head?"

"Sore," Kelda mumbled. She licked her lips and closed her eyes to drift in and out of sleep.

"You are fevered," Wild Flower said, "but that is natural with a blow like you received. You will feel better when the sun rises. I will get you some water." Quietly Wild Flower exited from the tent.

Kelda did not know if she would ever feel better. The farther she sailed away from Skrellingland, the closer she was to home . . . the closer she was to Asgaut and marriage.

She squeezed her fist and felt the prick of the game piece. Holding it up, she gazed at the silhouetted hawk. She had been so sure of herself and her destiny when she set sail from Norwegia. Now she was not.

What she wanted most — Brander and his child — was not hers to have.

Fate had played a cruel trick on her.

Fully awake now, she gazed through the opening of the tent. Fine rays of silvered dawn ribboned through the morning-gray sky. Soon the sun would gently rise above the swell of the ocean water. The skies would be purest blue with wispy white clouds. She wondered what the new day held in store for her.

Wild Flower slipped into the tent. "Here," she said, "drink this." She slid one arm behind Kelda and helped her into a sitting position. Then she placed the beaker to her lips to give her small sips of the liquid.

The water dribbled down the corners of Kelda's mouth, cool to her burning skin. When her thirst was slaked, she pushed the vessel away. With a murmured "Thank you," she squirmed into a comfortable sitting position and extended her hand, the game piece sitting on her opened palm.

"I would like for you to have this."

Wild Flower took the game piece and held it delicately. "Thoruald left it with me in hopes that one day it would bring me to him."

"Which it is," Kelda said.

Still looking at the statue of the falcon, Wild Flower asked, "What if he really does not want his Iroquois bride?"

For the first time Kelda witnessed Wild Flower's vulnerability. "He would not have sent you the combs if he had not wanted you."

"Nay, the giving of gifts is easy, Kelda. It is the giving of oneself that is difficult." She trailed the tip of her finger over the statue. "People have a tendency to create their memories. What they dislike, they eventually do away with, leaving only the beautiful. Through the years I am sure Thoruald and I have done that. Seeing each other face to face will shatter the illusion we may have created and make us face reality." She turned her face to gaze out the tent opening.

Kelda laid her hand over Wild Flower's. "My adopted father will be glad to see you." She laughed softly. "A wise woman once told me that I should make sure Brander did not consider me a captive. Now, I say to that wise woman, she must make sure Thoruald sees her only as the beautiful young bride he left behind. It is her responsibility to make him want her with the same passion he felt many years ago."

Softly Wild Flower said, "Passion was not enough for me thirty winters ago. I wonder if it will be enough for me now?"

Understanding only too well what Wild Flower said, Kelda squeezed her hand.

Wild Flower looked at Kelda, brushed a strand of hair from her forehead and smiled sadly. "You have spoken well, Kelda. I will leave you now. Rest until we stop for repairs."

After Wild Flower left, Kelda lay back on the pallet and again gazed out the tent opening. She wondered what her life would be like once she arrived at the village.

A shadow passed over the tent. Footfalls sounded on the platform. Soft leather boots — Norse boots — covered the feet and calves of the muscular legs. Thighs and hips were clad in brown trousers. Brander. She would know him — his physique, his walk — anywhere.

In the soft glow of early morning, he walked to the hull to stand, his back to her. All she saw was broad shoulders covered with a mantle that gently blew in the breeze. For a period of time that Kelda could only measure as the slow passage of winters, she stared at him, hungrily, almost greedily.

As if he knew she was staring at him, wanting him, he slowly turned, his gaze locking with hers. His eyes were cold and bleak, his face closed.

The journey to Norwegia had been long for Kelda. Now it promised to be even longer.

* * *

"The betrothal was not her idea," Hauk whispered softly. "She does not love Asgaut."

Brander made no comment as he and Hauk moved through the deciduous forest, hunting game for the evening meal and the larder while the other Vikings repaired the ship. Brander's gaze skimmed the trees, his eyes squinted against the late afternoon sun that sliced through the leaves.

"Thinking Thoruald was dying, she made a sacred oath, an oath made by a child to her parent," the Viking continued in the low voice.

"One she will have to live with," Brander quipped.

He released the arrow, and in seconds he heard a thwack as his prey fell to the ground.

"And you," Hauk said. "You will have to live with it."

Brander lowered his bow and moved silently over the forest floor, walking in the direction of the sound.

"She did what she had to do. Thoruald formally adopted her."

Brander stopped and turned to face the older man. "I care not to hear the story, Viking."

Hauk gazed into Brander's face. "Aye," he said, "you care, Skrelling. It is gnawing your insides like a fatal disease of the guts."

Brander resumed his walking. At the foot of a large tree, he bent to retrieve the squirrel.

Laying a palm against the trunk, Hauk said, "If you do not claim her as your woman, she will go to Asgaut and in time will produce sons for Thoruald— sons that will be heir to the Talon of the Falcon."

Brander pierced the neck vein of the squirrel and held it up to drain out the blood. "Why should I care about the woman?" he asked.

Hauk shrugged, his arrow nocked in the bow, his gaze skimming through the trees. "I was not thinking about the woman only," he said. "I was thinking about her producing sons for Thoruald, sons according to Norse law who would have legitimate claim to the Talon of the Falcon, as legitimate a claim as you and your sons."

With a deft movement Hauk pushed away from the tree, poised the bow and released the arrow, the whine echoing through the air as it flew toward another squirrel.

"There is a way, you know, to free her from Asgaut." He lowered the bow and moved toward the fallen animal.

Brander concentrated on skinning his kill.

"Ah!" The Viking gave a pleased sigh from a few feet's distance. "I hit it dead center." Looking at Brander, he smiled. "Aye, Chief Brander of the Iroquois, dead center."

Brander did not have to guess at Hauk's meaning. He listened impatiently as the old warrior whistled while he dressed his squirrel.

Hauk was right: this ache for Kelda was like a fatal disease of the guts. It was eating at him, robbing him of coherent thought and restful nights.

He could not understand himself or the conflicting emotions that racked him. Until he had met her, his life had been governed by reason not by emotion; it had been orderly.

Now he felt much like the ship during the storm. One moment he would be riding high toward the heavens; the next he would be plunging into the depths of darkest despair.

All because of a woman? This woman! A Viking woman!

Nay, he was a stronger man than that.

Still he did not want to see Kelda married to Asgaut, to any man for that matter. The thought of any man but himself taking her drove him to distraction. The thought of any man's seed growing within her body filled him with anger.

Kelda belonged to him. Surely she did. He was the one who had awakened her to womanhood. Yet he was not free to love her.

He would not . . . could not . . . sire children for Thoruald.

Brander's words to her had been harsh, but not his heart. He knew Kelda, like him, would not part with her child. Now, he knew another truth about himself. He would not . . . could not . . . allow her to be possessed by another man.

Perhaps if given time, he could convince her she would be happy with him in Forestland. Perhaps come next spring she would return with him.

Aye, perhaps . . .

Chapter Twenty-one

After an exhausting day with ship repairs, the Vikings feasted on roasted game and vegetables. As the sun sank in the western sky, they pulled out their game boards and uncorked the hogshead of beer. A beaker or two of drink and a challenging game promised a good night's sleep.

Preoccupied with thoughts of Brander, Kelda did not wish to participate in the gaming. She walked to the river close by where she sat on a large boulder. Drawing up her legs and propping her chin on her knees, she watched the silvered ripples on the surface of the water. Every so often her gaze would shift to the evening-colored horizon.

"What are you doing out here by yourself?"

Brander. She had not heard his approach, but had sensed his presence.

"Thinking," she replied. "Why are you here?"

"Taking a bath." He ran his hand through his damp hair, then moved closer to her. "How is your wound?"

"My head is sore and hurts a little," she replied. "Otherwise I will soon be fine."

"Aye."

She felt his gaze as it flicked over the sutured cut.

"Why did you not tell me about your betrothal to Asgaut sooner?"

She brushed her hand beneath the weight of her

hair and lifted it from her neck. "It would not have made any difference. You determined to make me your harlot from the beginning."

"Harlot is a harsh word."

"Aye. It was a harsh life you promised me."

"Was it?" His question and his gaze challenged her. "I also planned to make you my wife. Had you not drugged me you would have learned about it."

Although Kelda's heart ached at his confession, she met his gaze and said quietly, "These are but idle words that have no meaning now. You are determined to wreak revenge on your father, your life be damned."

"You and your people have wreaked havoc on my life from its very beginning, Viking."

"Kelda!" she exclaimed in a coarse whisper, balling her hands to her side. Instant pain shot through her head, and she regretted her reaction. "Call me by my name! And you cannot continue to blame me the rest of your life for something you are unable to accept."

"You are truly going to marry this Asgaut?"

"Yes," Kelda answered. "Why should I not?"

"Why? You do not love him. Hauk told me today that he already has two wives and many concubines."

A fact that had plagued Kelda since the Herredthing had solemnized her betrothal to him. Like her mother, she wanted to be one wife to one man, his one and only beloved.

"You speak of marriage now, but only because it suits you to taunt me with what I have lost. Love has never been part of what happened between us," she said sadly, the fight flagging out of her. "Why should it be a factor between Asgaut and me?"

Brander stepped closer to her. In the muted light of sundown, she saw the gleam in his eyes, the hard, tight line of his mouth.

"You belong to me and to me alone."

252

"Nay," she replied softly. "A part of you needs to believe that, Skrelling, but it is not true. I belong to no one but myself."

"Tell yourself that all you want." Brander's voice was soft and caressing, like the brush of silk material against her skin. His hands curling around her shoulders were kind as they drew her to him. He gently touched his lips to the area above her cut. "But I know differently. Furthermore, Asgaut will not want soiled goods."

Kelda laughed shortly. "Asgaut may not want *soiled goods* as you so delicately phrase it, but he will take me any way he can get me. While he desires my body, he desires more the fact that I am Thoruald's adopted daughter. Marriage to me guarantees him a legal claim to the title of jarl. My child insures that he will be the father of the new lineage of the Falcon." She laughed shortly, bitterly. "I will be one possession he has that Brunhild will not abuse."

"Brunhild?" he questioned.

Kelda nodded. "She is the niece of Thoruald's deceased wife and Asgaut's first and oldest wife. Presently she rules with a heavy hand."

"Yet you would marry him?"

"I have sworn a sacred oath to Thoruald," she whispered.

She maneuvered her head to focus her attention on his lips, lips she remembered to be firm and moist and warm. Lips that sent pleasure through her body.

"Aye, Skrelling—" her voice was husky "—Asgaut will take me any way he can get me."

Brander gazed darkly into her face. "I will not let Asgaut have you."

"What will you do to stop him?" she asked. A faint tremor rippled through her body.

"I claimed you as mine when we were under Iroquois law. I will do the same under Norse law."

253

The determined blaze of Brander's eyes as he gazed into her face sent sensations through Kelda's body. He was the sun, she the bud that unfolded to his golden warmth.

"How?" she whispered.

"The *eingigi!*"

"You would fight to the death for me?" Her words were as much an exclamation as a question.

"Aye." He released her shoulder and moved his hand to her chin, his thumb brushing against her lips.

She had known from the first moment she saw Brander of the Iroquois that destiny had brought them together. At times . . . even now . . . she wanted love and wanted to give him the same. While she could and would give it to him, she was not sure that he could give it to her. In the beginning she had thought it possible, but the longer she was with him, the more she realized that his hatred of the Norse had scared him deeply, possibly forever.

Still she wanted him, despite her brave and scornful words. She would take whatever he did offer.

Yearning for more than the tormenting brush of his hand on her lips, she leaned forward. He bent, and with a low sound took the mouth she offered, giving her his own in return. His arms tightened, and he lifted her from the boulder, bringing her whole body into the embrace.

The kiss deepened; his tongue fully, sweetly claimed her mouth. Knowing how to reciprocate, Kelda welcomed him into her mouth and teased him with her tongue. Brander's chest lifted with a deep intake of breath, but his mouth never left hers. He lowered her down until she was standing on her own feet once more. But she was not standing on her own strength. She clung to his shoulders and pressed against him.

Excitement flowed hotly through Kelda, but the kiss was not enough. She craved more of him. As surely as she had received his tongue within her, she wanted to receive him entirely. When he began a retreat, she moaned and clutched him tighter to herself. Her yearnings were not so easily assuaged.

In silent entreaty for him to remain inside her, she gently closed her teeth on his tongue. Again he trembled within her embrace. More daring now, certainly hungry for his possession, she slid her hands to his buttocks and pressured him against her pelvis. She alerted him to her needs, to her desire to receive him altogether.

Brander groaned. His hands shifted on her body, finding and stroking her breasts to send rush after rush of pleasure through her, to create a fevered wanting in the seat of her femininity. She gasped, opened her mouth, and threw back her head in abandonment. The movement thrust her breasts forward, and he took more of her into his mouth. His caresses intensified until her entire body was quaking.

His lips moved in a hot trail over her breasts up her neck, finally to claim hers once more in a hard and searching kiss. His tongue did wonderful things to her as it stroked her mouth inside and out. He had possessed her completely to take her maidenhood from her. Now in a simple kiss he promised to take her soul.

Turning her face from his, yet feeling the heat of his mouth on her cheek, Kelda drew in ragged breaths. She had fought giving up her maidenhood, but that had only been a tiny membrane that separated her from girlhood and womanhood.

Now he asked for her soul. When he took that, she would be his . . . forever.

Brander's lips moved over her cheeks as his hands

255

moved over her breasts, his callused fingers kneading and stroking until her nipples crested. When he rolled them gently between his fingers, Kelda became trembling sensation from the top of her head to the bottom of her feet.

"Brander," Kelda murmured.

"Your defiance is mine," he said, "as is your surrender."

Surrender she would do, but give up her soul? That she could not do.

She opened her eyes and gazed into his. How could she have ever thought them bleak or cold? In their fiery depths she saw her own reflection and knew as surely as he held her, he possessed her. She was his for the taking. Her soul belonged to him. Still she could not confess this to him.

"Never surrender," she whispered and held her head back, her hair flying over his arm. "Mutual need; mutual desire."

His hands moved once more, light, gentle strokes from rounded buttocks to her shoulders and back to the hips. She gladly followed when his hands pressured her hips against the hard heat of his sex. She pressed still closer, wanting to be one with him. She smiled and purred — pure satisfaction from deeply within.

She rotated her hips against his arousal. He groaned, and his arms tightened, locking their bodies together. His hips moving to the rhythm of hers, he joined in this primeval dance of the ages. They moved together, each for himself, each for the other, their pleasure one.

She held her head back, arching toward him. His mouth kissed the column of her throat, beneath her chin, around the bottom of her earlobes. Every time his lips moved to take hers, Kelda laughed and turned her face from him. She felt his kisses on her

256

ears, her temples, the back of her neck.

"Give me your mouth," he commanded hoarsely.

Exhilarated, she laughed. Her laughter seemed to whet the fire within him. His love strokes became more frenzied, more possessive. Yet she kept her mouth from him.

"I want to be inside you again," he said, his tongue trailing fire along the side of her neck.

"I want you inside me."

She arched her hips against him.

"This way." His hands captured her face, and he brought her lips to his. As they slanted toward hers, he murmured, "This is the only way."

She drew back. "Nay, my chief of the Iroquois. You have taught me the most complete way for a man to be inside a woman."

"Your lips, give them to me!" he commanded.

Rising high on the crest of passion, Kelda laughed and gave him what he wanted. The kiss was deep, wet, and passionate. She did not want tenderness this time. She needed the urgent joining as much as he. Her arms locked about his neck, she clung more tightly to him. He held her close and hard even after he lowered her to the soft tuft of grass and deepened the hungry melding of mouths.

When finally he ended the kiss, he raised his head. He touched a fingertip to the bottom of her neck.

"Your body is beating madly, Viking. For me?"

She nodded.

He touched the taut nipples that pressed against her shirt, and again sensations sweetly curled through her body.

"For you," she whispered.

"I promised myself I would stay away from you," he murmured and bent down to her breasts. His mouth touched them, and through the material she could feel the moist warmth of his breath. "I would

257

not touch you, but I find I cannot resist."

"I am glad this is one promise you are unable to keep," she whispered, her words turning into a breathless cry when his teeth closed delicately around one of her nipples. One hand curled around his neck, and she brought him closer to her. She locked his body to hers.

"You promised that I would be obsessed by you, Viking, and I am. I love what you do to me. I despise that you can do it to me."

He was so close she studied the thick black lashes that hooded equally black, smoldering eyes.

"Undress me, Skrelling," she whispered, running her hands through the hair at the nape of his neck. "Make love to me."

"What about your wound?" he asked.

She smiled. "The wanting you have set afire in me needs more attention than my wound. For my yearning to go unattended would cause me far greater pain and distress."

His hands moved to her waist. A few tugs and her clothing was gone to reveal her breasts, swollen and throbbing with her need. His hands possessed them, and again Kelda felt the fiery burst of need. Every touch to her body reminded her how empty she was without him, how much she wanted him.

Before she knew what he was doing, Brander was kneeling at her feet, slipping off her boots. His fingers moved to her waist and he unfastened her trousers, pulling them and her undergarments off. She felt the rush of spring air on her naked and desire-flushed body.

Brander, still at her feet, held one in each hand. How big his hands looked. How small her feet. With his thumb he drew designs on her skin. She cried out with pleasurable surprise, not realizing until this moment that her feet and ankles were so sensitive. The strokes continued, whetting her needs. She whimpered and writhed.

He whispered sweet endearments. When Kelda thought she could endure the pleasurable torment no longer, he brought the foot to his face. He trailed kisses along the bottom, then he lightly rubbed his beard-stubbed cheek and chin against her instep.

She breathed raggedly. She shivered. She arched against him. With the tip of his finger he traced a line of fire beneath her arch. Her pelvic area burned with need. She felt her emptiness, an emptiness that only Brander could fill. Her foot curled, and she moaned lowly.

"Brander," she begged, her hands tangling in his hair. "Please take me. Please . . ."

He released her feet to straighten and to kiss a trail up the length of her legs to her waist, over her breasts and up her neck. He brushed his mouth over her lips, the pulse at the base of her throat, and the tips of her breasts. She moaned softly.

As he claimed her lips in a deep kiss, he pressed his palm over her pelvis. His touch was so wonderful she cried out, the sound lost in the essence of their kiss. He eased his fingers between her legs, and they moved gently, slowly moving higher and higher into her heated body. Sighing, she rotated against him.

He released her lips to press kisses over her face, but she caught his head and brought his mouth to hers once again. She parted her lips to his kiss and felt the hot entry of his tongue and his finger at the same time.

She had called him the sun, herself the opened bud.

He was not. He was the lightning in the blackened sky. He touched her with his fire to send burning pleasure throughout every inch of her body. Newly acquainted with such intense emotion, Kelda was unsure how to handle it. She cried out and rolled her head away from his kiss.

"Brander." Her words were a whimper.

"Aye, little one," he murmured.

She felt the warm bite of tears in her eyes. "I have never known such pleasure."

He kissed each of her eyes, so gently, so wonderfully.

"We have only begun to explore pleasure," he promised.

Twin caresses began again, but this time Brander captured one of her nipples. As he suckled, his fingers began to move deeper and faster within her. They were like delicate bolts of lightning, shooting hot, liquid currents through her body. Any moment she would explode into flames. She would incinerate.

His fingers, touching the hardened hub of her pleasure, pushed her over the edge. She burst into flames, her entire body burning with sheer pleasure. She cried into his mouth and pulled her head away from him. Her body quivered uncontrollably. She was drenched in perspiration, but she knew a peace within and without that she had never known before.

Brander withdrew his touch and gathered her in his arms.

"My woman," he whispered over and over again. "You are mine, Kelda of the Vikings."

As surely as his touch had brought pleasure to Kelda, so did his words. He had called her by her name. He claimed her for his woman—by Norse law this time. He was going to fight to the death for her! No greater honor could a woman have.

"Are you sure you want to claim me as your woman?" she whispered, her hand learning his body more completely.

"Aye." He caught her hand and brought it to his lips.

"Asgaut is a *Jomsviking*," she said, "trained at a highly disciplined warriors' school. None but another *Jomsviking* would challenge him."

Brander laughed quietly. "Are you attempting to frighten me?"

She shook her head.

"I shall not only challenge this *Jomsviking*, but I shall defeat him."

"To the death?"

"To my death, if that be the case," he announced softly, "but I shall not kill this Asgaut. His punishment will be to live in shame."

His lips touched hers, and she cupped her hands behind his head to hold him firmly to her. As his tongue had penetrated her body only moments prior, hers penetrated his now.

She lowered a hand, insinuated it between their bodies to touch his stomach. She felt the brush of crisp hair against her palm as she slid it lower to unfasten the waistband of his breeches and to slip her hands through the folds of material. Her fingertips caressed and traced hot satin skin, that surged within her grasp. As she reacquainted herself with the contours of his hunger, she felt him tremble.

He caught her hand. "Nay," he murmured, gently touching his lips to her cut. "Tonight was for you."

"But what about you?" she questioned.

"Later, I shall be pleased. I have to teach you the many ways a man and woman find pleasure with each other, little Viking." He gently brushed his fingers over her forehead in soothing motion.

"Would you reconsider returning to my land with me come spring?" Brander asked.

Kelda lay still in his arms. "I have pledged a sacred oath to Thoruald," she said.

"If you were released from it?"

"I would think about returning with you," she said,

"but I know deep within my heart that I cannot leave Norwegia. That is my home; that is where I . . . and my children . . . belong."

"What about me?" Brander asked.

"Norwegia is where you belong also, my love."

Brander sighed. "Let us sleep now."

Held close in his arms, protected from the wilds around her, from the nightmares of a future with Asgaut, Kelda smiled and relaxed, drifting into a wondrous sleep, one from which she did not rouse until sunrise.

Not sure what had awakened her, she opened her lids to see Brander bending over her.

"Good morning," he whispered. "It is time for us to return to camp."

"Aye," she murmured, rubbing her palm over his face, loving the rasp of his beard stubble against her flesh.

"I would like for you to wear my totem," Brander said.

"What kind?" she asked and touched the talon necklace that hung about his neck.

"The gold collar," he answered.

Kelda felt as if her heart would burst from happiness. "I would wear it with honor."

"You would wear the collar but not my mark," he murmured.

"The tattoo, like our white uniform and soldered arm and neck bands, was the mark of a slave," she answered.

"Oh, yes," he drawled lowly. Smiling, he added, "It is fitting that you wear the gold collar of the Falcon, the collar that your adopted father, my father by birth, had crafted for himself."

"Yes," she murmured breathlessly.

"Where do you keep it?" he asked.

"In my jewelry casket in the trunk."

262

"While you are bathing and getting dressed," he said, "I will get it."

Later when Kelda had completed her morning toilet, Brander was awaiting her on the shore. Proudly she walked to him. She had always thought him the most handsome man she had ever seen. Now she thought him the bravest. Truly he was Thoruald's son; he was the man to possess Talon of the Falcon. Brander was all a woman could want in her man, in her husband.

Picking up the drying cloth in one hand, he held the other out to assist her from the water. He lifted the large cloth and dried off her body, caressing her in between strokes. When she was fully dressed, he picked up the gold necklace.

Kelda trembled when she felt the cool metal touch her skin and encircle her neck. She trembled at the thought of belonging to Brander. The two of them joint heirs to the Talon of the Falcon. What sons and daughters they would produce!

"Now, my Kelda," Brander bent to plant kisses around the circle of gold, "you are mine."

"Aye," she murmured.

Hand in hand the two of them strolled into camp. Hauk looked up from the plate he held in his hands, his gaze shifting from one to the other and back again. The other men gave them equally curious gazes but said nothing.

Canby stepped into the clearing, his gaze flitting from their clasped hands to the gold collar about Kelda's neck. As if he could not believe what he was seeing, he raised his head and stared at her.

"What are you doing with this infidel?" His voice was hardly above a whisper. His hand shook.

"What does it appear to be?" Brander mocked. "I have claimed her as my woman according to Norse law."

Canby visibly tensed in surprise. "You are going to wed her?"

Kelda choked back laughter. She could hardly wait for Brander to give answer.

"Nay," Brander said.

Kelda's hand went slack in his, and she turned to gape at him.

A strange, sad smile playing around the corners of his mouth, he said, "I claim her as my mistress."

Cold fury swept through Kelda's body. She jerked her hand, but he held it tightly, refusing to unclasp it. She raised the other hand to jerk the collar from her neck, but he caught it, too.

"Your mistress!" Canby hissed the words.

"She wears my mark," Brander said, "the gold collar that once belonged to Thoruald, then to me. Now my mistress wears it."

Hauk dropped his plate and rose. He said nothing, but he gazed incredulously at Brander. Wild Flower, her face drained of color, also looked at them disbelievingly.

"Do you realize that Kelda is Thoruald's adopted daughter, his legal heir?" Canby asked.

"Yes," Kelda answered, surprised that her voice sounded calm, "he knows."

And she also knew the truth, or at least a part of it. In that second she had intuited Brander's intentions as surely as if he had spoken them aloud to her.

"That is why he has claimed me. He fully intends that I shall bear no sons or daughters that are not his issue to inherit the Talon of the Falcon."

"I claim you as my mistress for other reasons," Brander said, gazing at her.

"A slave, a mistress, but not a wife," she said.

"I have explained. You must understand my reasons."

She searched his eyes. "I do not."

264

"Asgaut will kill you," Canby promised Brander. "He will rip you limb from limb."

Brander laughed softly. "He will try."

"Because you have defiled his betrothed," Canby said, "you must give Asgaut the choice of weapons and the method of dueling."

"As long as I have the woman of choice, those two choices may be his," Brander replied. "He will need the advantage."

Tears burned Kelda's eyes, but she blinked them back. While Brander had broken her heart and shattered her dream of being his wife, of presenting him with sons and daughters, he offered her freedom from Asgaut. As Brander's woman, she was safe from Asgaut until such time as he was victorious in the duel to death. With Brander as her champion she did not fear Asgaut's winning the duel.

But she did worry about Thoruald's reaction to her agreeing to be Brander's mistress. Would he understand why she, his adopted daughter, had agreed to such an arrangement? A part of him would, she reasoned. Another would not.

He would want Brander and her to wed so their children, his grandchildren, would be named and would be undisputable heirs to the Talon of the Falcon. But there would be no children between Brander and her! This Thoruald would never understand, certainly never accept.

"Kelda!"

She turned to look at Canby who frowned at her. "This is the third time I have called you. Listen to me and think carefully upon my words. If you gave yourself willingly to this man, you have sinned; you have fornicated against Asgaut. The Herred-thing can have you executed. If he took you against your will, you can throw yourself on Asgaut's and the Herred-thing's mercy."

"Aye, Canby, I know the law," Kelda said.

She looked at Brander, her hurt turning into anger. He was no different from any other man. To him a woman was nothing more than chattel. She was a plaything. She was a means to execute his revenge.

She was no longer his slave; yet she was. In order to be free from Asgaut, she must have Brander for her champion.

She would turn the table on him. She would use him for her plaything.

Looking directly into Brander's ebony eyes, she smiled. "Canby, I have given careful thought to your words of wisdom, and I tell the truth. Last night I lay with this man of my own choice, knowing full well that he may not offer me the bed of marriage. I willingly became his mistress. I willingly remain so."

Kelda's smile widened when she saw the surprise on Brander's countenance. His grip loosened, and she freed her hand to touch the collar about her neck.

"I freely wear the mark of the Skrelling."

His face contorted in anger, Canby stared at her. "Thoruald will hear about this," he threatened.

"Aye," she said softly, "so he will."

Chapter Twenty-two

"Norwegia," Kelda murmured, the one word a litany she had repeated many times during the long voyage to Skrellingland and back.

"Aye," Hauk said. "Home, mistress."

In the silvered gray before dawn Kelda stood on the prow with Hauk, Brander, and Wild Flower, their heads level with the bottom of the prow decoration. Hauk, his feet planted firmly on the platform, held his hands behind his massive body. Wild Flower stood next to him. Brander, the wind playing against his black hair and crimson mantle, braced one hand against the falcon-head; Kelda stood on the other side with an arm hooked about the falcon's neck. All gazed into the distance.

A satisfied smile curled Hauk's lips. "I can smell home in the air, mistress. The gods are granting us a victorious entry to the steading."

"Aye." All signs of the recent storm gone, the turbulent waves had settled into a smooth aquamarine sheet. "When the seas are like this, they remind me of the color of the material Ragnar gave me for my betrothal gown. A beautiful mixture of blue and green."

Brander's head moved slightly in her direction. Catching the movement, Kelda realized what she had said. She lifted her hand to touch the gold neck ring—hard, cold evidence that she was this man's

267

mistress. She a free woman, she the jarl's adopted daughter, was indeed captive to this man.

"Never have I been so eager to see Falcon's Perch," said the seasoned warrior.

Kelda's gaze met with Brander's.

"Aye," she murmured, her mouth going dry, "I shall be glad to see the promontory also."

"What is a steading like?" Wild Flower asked.

"Falconstead is the jarl's estate," Kelda answered. "It is quite large with many workers and people living on it."

"A village?" Wild Flower asked.

"It is a village, but not like the villages of the Iroquois," Kelda explained. "Here the jarl owns the land, and other people work for him. The workers are freemen of Viking birth who are craftsmen and slaves we capture in raids."

Wild Flower gazed upon the Vikings who rowed the vessel into harbor.

"All of these men belong to the jarl?" she asked.

"No, they are free men who have given him their allegiance, much like the Iroquois warriors gave theirs to Brander," Kelda answered. "Many of them own their own land, but their holdings are much smaller than the jarl's. They are dependent on him for providing the ship and plans of plunder."

"Since this was not a raid, and there was no booty for them," Wild Flower asked, "how are they being rewarded?"

With Brander's intent gaze focused on her, Kelda drew in a deep breath. "Thoruald."

"He paid to have his Skrelling issue delivered to him?" the shaman said.

Kelda nodded.

Brander asked, "How much will you get?"

"Much," Kelda answered, refusing to let him make her feel guilty. "Thoruald will be proud that you are here. He will enjoy the songs and poems Ulmer will recite about my cunning in deceiving you. At the welcome feast, I will be honored among the men."

Hauk darted her a warning glance, but Kelda ignored it. At the moment she felt victorious, and she was tired of Brander's callous treatment of her. She wanted to push him to the edge, and she wanted to walk it herself.

"That is important to you?" Brander asked.

"Aye."

Rather hurriedly as if to break the tension between her and Brander, Hauk said, "Once we reach Falcon's Perch, sire, we know we have reached Falcon Fjord, the inlet to the steading. Your new home."

"Your jarl has indeed marked everything along this coast his." Brander turned his attention to the Viking. "Is anything not named after the Falcon?"

Hauk laughed heartily, seeming to take no umbrage at the words. "Nay, Chief Brander. If it is not Falcon, it is Thoruald."

Again Kelda touched the necklace. She was marked by the Falcon's son.

People of Norwegia respected Thoruald as a chieftain. His exploits were so great, *skalds* sang of them in many *stofas* through the land. Many who had been the brunt of his anger feared him.

But none of them had seen the issue of the Falcon.

Both were powerful warriors, august in appearance and action. One was golden, the other dark. One the day, the other night. Both Falcons. One considered to be civilized, the other a barbarian. Both were fearful. Obstinate. Determined to have his own way. Only one could win . . . that was the rule of the game of jarls.

The winner was *not the strongest but the smartest!*

The game would prove interesting, Kelda thought and shivered apprehensively. She only wished she

269

could view it from afar rather than be a player. However, destiny did not grant that desire.

Kelda had known from the beginning that destiny bound her to this darkly handsome barbarian. Where would destiny carry her with him? She could only wonder at the answer.

"I will return to the *lypting* and the steering oar," Hauk said. "I shall be the one to take the *Golden Sol* into the harbor."

"I will go with you," Wild Flower said.

"Will you also join me, Brander?" the Viking invited.

"Nay, I will remain here," he answered, then added, "to have a better view."

Hauk playfully clapped him on the shoulder. "Eager to see your new home, lad?"

Lad. The word leaped out at Kelda. In spite of herself she laughed, thinking the appellation hardly fit Chief Brander of the Iroquois.

Brander smiled kindly at the crusty warrior. "You are determined that I shall accept this as home, are you not, Hauk?"

"Aye. 'Tis your home." Hauk measured Brander with his gaze before he again spoke. "I have taught many a lad how to use his weapons and how to sail the seas on a *langskip*, but you, Brander, had to be taught little. Already you are a seasoned sailor. You took to the sea as if you had been born to it. And, lad, I believe you were."

Kelda observed the knowing glance that passed between mother and son, before the son turned scowling to the front.

Assisting Wild Flower from the platform, Hauk stepped down himself, the two of them leaving Brander and Kelda alone.

Brander asked, "Do you hold the same beliefs as Hauk?"

270

"Concerning what?" Kelda asked, pinning her gaze to the distant horizon.

Brander stepped closer to her, running his hand through her hair. "Do not play the simpleton with me, Kelda."

"I am not playing with you at all, sire," she replied, wishing he would move away from her. "I simply do not have the power to read your mind, nor shall I attempt to answer such a far-sweeping question."

"How long do you intend to sulk?" he asked softly, his hand slipping through the hair to curl about her neck.

"I am not sulking," she replied and slowly turned her head so that she was looking squarely into his face. "At first, I admit your announcement took me by surprise. I had expected more since I believed I meant more to you."

She forced herself not to wince when his grip tightened.

"I care for you, Viking, and I did what I must to save you."

Skeptical, she asked, "From whom or for whom?"

"You care for me also," Brander said. "Given time I am hoping you will wish to return to the Forestland with me. I will protect you until that time."

"Protection. Pooh!" Kelda exclaimed. "You are a cruel, selfish person. You have unleashed the hunger of a woman within my body, yet you promised not to fulfill my needs or desires for fear of giving me a child."

"Part of what you say is true," he replied slowly. "I have promised not to spill my seed within you, but I did not say I would abstain from giving you pleasure, little Viking, or from your giving me pleasure. If you think back, you will remember I said there are many ways a man and a woman can share pleasure. We have only begun to explore the possibilities."

271

"Nay, my lord," Kelda softly said. "Our exploration is at an end. The next man who makes love to me in any form or fashion will be the man of my choosing."

"Spoken bravely," he teased.

"Meant sincerely." She gazed solemnly into the ebony eyes. "Now that I have grown accustomed to the idea of being your mistress, I am quite happy with it. No matter what, I shall always be Thoruald's adopted daughter. Therefore, any child I bear him will be mine and will be a legitimate heir to the Talon of the Falcon."

"You will not bear a child, mine or any other man's."

"Aye, one day." Pleased when a frown drew his brows together, she continued, "As your mistress I enjoy a special position."

"Please explain," he ordered tersely.

Kelda actually smiled. "As long as I am your mistress, I am not worried about you forcing your attention on me."

Brander stared at her for a second, then threw back his head and laughed.

"Nor will anyone else," she said. "I also know you plan to return to Skrellingland as soon as you can, which will be next spring. By that time you will have fought and defeated Asgaut, and I shall be released from my betrothal to him."

Sober-faced now, Brander touched the gold collar with the tip of his finger. "But you will still be my mistress."

"Only until Asgaut releases me from the betrothal through defeat or death."

"What if I change my mind and decide to take you with me?" His eyes narrowed, dark lashes hiding equally dark eyes.

Now Kelda laughed. "I am your mistress by open admission, not your slave. I am a free woman who

272

can do as she chooses with her life, and as soon as you have cleared some of the obstacles out of my life, I shall choose to be free of you."

She paused, searching his face, wanting to see how her words affected him. She was disappointed. He showed no emotion at all.

"Certainly I will not be returning to your homeland with you, Skrelling," she promised. "Thoruald would fight to the death for me. And no matter how much hatred you have for your father, you will not fight him."

"You are so sure?"

"Aye. Once you are gone, I shall choose a mate and present Thoruald with an heir."

"You have pondered the situation well," Brander said.

"I have had plenty of time for thinking," she replied.

Satisfied with her argument but hurting deeply within her heart, she now faced the front, once again to drink in the beauty of the ocean. Rosy-hued dawn came, her blush touching the clouds and the sea, but it did nothing to lighten Kelda's sagging spirits. Rays of sunshine splintered across the sky like tiny golden streamers. Their radiance taunted Kelda.

Brander stood beside her for a long time before he made his way aft. Despite her heavy heart, Kelda smiled. She had the feeling she had said the last word for the first time since he had announced to the Vikings, and to Canby in particular, that she was his mistress.

Being so close to home brought her an assurance and a confidence she had lacked since she met Brander. No matter what the future held, she knew she could handle it . . . she would.

Quickly morning overtook dawn. Sunshine's golden radiance eclipsed the blush of dawn. A squalling sea bird appeared to circle the *langskip.*

Excitement swelled within the men. The sight of the bird—a shore bird—was a portent. Home. Norwegia. The oars clapped the water with a stronger rhythm. Weary faces boasted anticipatory smiles.

"Falconstead," Kelda whispered and pushed forward.

The murmur pulsated through the warriors. Brander remained unmoved.

Morning turned into afternoon.

"There!" Kelda shouted and pointed.

Norwegia. The word ascended from the lips of the Vikings as praise to the gods. On the horizon Kelda could make out the hazy contour of the shoreline. Distance obscured the details; memory painted them in vivid detail.

"Norwegia." Kelda breathed the word.

She saw the landfall. Countless islands. A flock of birds now flew over the *langskip* to escort them home.

Later that afternoon, Hauk put the helm hard over, and the *langskip* passed Falcon's Perch to enter the fjord. Cheers went up from the men. The horn sounded from the Perch to alert the people of Falconstead that a ship approached.

"Hoist the dress sail," Kelda shouted. "Prepare to display the shields."

Once the people saw the colors they would know the *Golden Sol* and its crew were returning home victoriously.

Chapter Twenty-three

Thoruald stood on the summit of the headland above Falconstead where he gazed at the fjord, where he awaited the return of the *Golden Sol* and his offspring. Hopefully a son. But it mattered not if it was a daughter. If Kolby was her son, she had already presented him with an heir. If not, she was young enough to bear many more strapping children. That is, if she accepted him and Norwegia!

He prayed to Odin that he had an offspring or at least that Kelda returned with proof that Kolby was his blood heir. Thoruald knew deep within his heart this was so, but he wanted it to be confirmed.

The boy had to be his grandson! Already Thoruald loved him as if he were.

Only the sound of the water lapping below broke the late-afternoon silence. The sun had several hours left before its setting, yet shadows had already begun to creep down the sides of the sheer cliffs of the fjord.

Thoruald touched his hand to his abdomen gingerly. Although the wound was healing, it was yet tender and sore. More than its not healing properly, it had taken its toll on him. He still ran fevers and tired easily. Pain was his constant companion. He moved more slowly than he had before, and it took all his strength to lift his sword—a fact he confessed to no one.

Sighing, he lowered his head and gazed at the black-haired youngster who stood beside him. Thoruald dared not hope, yet he must. Hope was all that remained for him.

"Is the dragonship coming today, sire?"

"Aye, Kolby," Thoruald murmured, "she will come."

"And we shall see Kelda and Hauk once again?"

Thoruald smiled and gently ruffled the boy's hair. "You will see them in due time. Remember, you are to leave before long with Jarl Gannar to continue your education."

Custom demanded that the boy be raised by foster parents to bond that family to his own in case of war or blood feuds, but Thoruald had another more important reason for whisking Kolby away. He feared losing the boy he had come to love as his own grandson. Kolby, without memory of his former life in Skrellingland, was Thoruald's to mold and fashion into a Norseman. If those memories returned, possibly the boy would distance himself from Thoruald, possibly he would grow to hate him.

If Kelda had returned with his issue, Thoruald did not want to run the risk of the child's memory being jolted back by the surprise of seeing one of his own people—especially if it was his own father or mother. Thoruald must know if his issue—if he had any—was his friend or foe. If foe, Thoruald promised he would protect the boy. He would not let Kolby go.

Kolby was his grandson! The falcon tattoo on his arm proved it. Odin in his wisdom had sent the boy to him. Because of Kolby, Thoruald had a resurgence of life, a determination to live to guide the boy into manhood.

He would not lose the child.

"How are you doing on mastering the *idrottir?*" Thoruald asked, referring to the list of accomplishments a Viking must achieve to be considered an educated man.

Kolby sighed. "Quite well, Grandfather. Already I can defeat most at the game of the jarls." He lifted his head, and his little face lit up in a smile. "I can almost defeat you, sire."

"Almost is not good enough, Kolby. You must learn patience; you must learn to use your mind and not trust in your muscle and strength altogether. Remember, son, the winner of the game of the jarls, or of life, is not the strongest but the smartest."

Kolby sighed. "Aye, Grandfather. You have told me that many times."

"And I shall tell it to you many more times," Thoruald said.

"But to be a fearsome Viking like you, Grandfather, I must be strong."

Thoruald sighed. "I would that you were a fearsome Viking, lad, but you can only become one if you learn your *idrottir* well."

Kolby was silent for a long time, then said pensively, "I much prefer falconry and wrestling and fencing to writing ballads and singing and harp playing."

Thoruald laughed. "Aye, but a leader must be an educated man. You need to learn all these things to be well-rounded, to understand the beauty of life as well as the necessities. You are doing well at reading the runes?"

"Aye," Kolby answered. "Hauk promised, sire, when he returned that he would teach me to wield

277

the sword himself and that he would give me a horse of my own."

Thoruald nodded, his mind drifting back in time. His old friend had been Ragnar's and Kelda's mentor, giving them their first horses.

"It seems to me, sire, that summer will be past by the time Hauk and Kelda return."

"Nay," Thoruald said softly. "They will be here in time for Hauk to take you to the pasture to choose your horse."

Kolby said, "Sire, I know you have already made the plans for me to live with Jarl Gannar, and I want to go to his steading with him. But I would see Kelda and Hauk first. I shall leave after they have arrived."

Thoruald laughed. "Nay, lad, you will not dictate what you will and will not do . . . yet. You will follow my orders. As soon as Gannar's thrall comes for you, you will leave."

Kolby held up his head and stared fearlessly into Thoruald's eyes. "If the Skrelling is aboard the ship, you do not wish me to see him, do you?"

As usual, Thoruald was surprised and pleased by the astuteness of the boy. The longer he was around him, the more Thoruald was convinced that this was indeed his grandson.

"Aye, lad."

Smiling out of the somber face, black eyes enigmatic, Kolby squeezed Thoruald's hand. "I shall do as you say now, sire. But one winter . . . and soon . . . I shall be the one issuing orders, not obeying them."

"Aye," Thoruald grunted, his eyes focusing on the gold arm band that circled the child's upper arm, "but not before you learn many more lessons and my usefulness is spent, my boy, and do not

278

forget that."

The two of them laughed, then stood in silence watching the fjord. Thoruald regretted it when the thrall, on horseback, came to get the boy. He had grown to love him during the past months and would miss his company.

The horn had sounded. Thoruald knew a ship was coming to harbor. He prayed that it was Kelda in the *Golden Sol*. For a long while he continued to squint through the afternoon brilliance.

Then he spotted it. At first it was a mere dot, but the dot grew until it was a brilliant square of color — a large red sun glowing on a background of rich yellow.

The *Golden Sol*.

Kelda had returned.

As the dragonship drew close, Thoruald saw the round shields displayed in a row along the outside of the hull, their colors alternating between red and yellow. The colors of the sun, the god of day. Kelda's colors displayed in victory.

She had returned with the Skrelling? Or news of the offspring? Which? he wondered.

Amid the urging shouts of the Vikings, one of the sailors stripped to his trousers and shirt, climbed over the bulwark and raced around the outside of the ship on the moving oars. This was a favorite pastime of the Vikings and one that demonstrated their agility and dexterity since it required sure-footedness and a good sense of timing.

Thoruald laughed. Many times he had enjoyed such sport himself when he brought his ship successfully into port, showing off for his comrades and for the loved ones who gathered on the docks.

A second raced the oars; he fell. A third and fourth followed to fall also. Loud laughter and

279

good-natured teasing filled the air. Levity made the afternoon even more brilliant.

Hauk slid over the gunwales to begin his walk. Ah, but it was good to see Hauk again, Thoruald thought. To have him and Canby home! As old as Hauk was, he completed his journey without a mishap.

"Aye, Hauk," Thoruald murmured, watching his old friend move to the prow, his shoulders squared, his head held high, "I knew you could do it."

I have yet another task to ask of you, my friend. If I have a Skrelling son, I would have you instruct him in the ways of the Viking. But you already know that, do you not? I will have you become Kolby's mentor as you have been Ragnar's and Kelda's.

Then Thoruald heard another rise of shouts aboard the ship; he saw a crimson mantle swell through the air. Another warrior vaulted over the side. Rays of sunlight glinted on hair as black as the sacred raven's. Through his many years as a Viking and a jarl, Thoruald had learned to curb his emotions, but now unbidden he felt a lump in his throat, the bite of tears in his eyes.

The man was a Skrelling. Was this his son?

As big as the man was, he nimbly jumped from one oar to the other. Those aboard cheered him on. Those on shore who raced to meet the ship at the dock also cheered.

Breathing deeply, elated over his successful run across the oars, Brander returned to the deck. He threw back his head, tossing a shock of black hair back with it.

"How did you learn to do that?" Kelda asked.

" 'Tis no great feat," Brander said. "Just a matter

280

of balance. I was barely walking when I was trained to be a runner. Part of this training was learning to jump hurdles and running down a row of tiny limbs placed across the river. Braves would hold the limbs on each end and would move them in a rippling effect as we ran. When we successfully ran the entire length without falling into the river, we earned a reward."

"That was a good display, lad." Hauk dropped an arm over his shoulder.

"You were not so bad yourself." Brander grinned in warm friendship at the man.

"Aye, but it is taking me a little longer to make the round now."

Kelda laughed. "Watch this one, Brander. He is jesting. He is about to lay a wager with you. He can run the round of oars several times without pausing and losing his balance. He can even juggle three knives in the air at the same time."

"I will challenge you one of these days," Brander said.

"Aye," Hauk said, a serious note to his voice. "You will, lad, and you had better get the best of me, else your future will be bleak."

Brander thought on the Viking's words long after he had returned to his position at the steering oar. True, he had much to learn while he was sojourning in this foreign land. He had much to do.

Eirik. As he had done so many times during the voyage, he wondered about his son. A part of him joyously anticipated the reunion. Another part was afraid.

His gaze brushed past the many islands to the rugged and craggy shoreline. It seemed nothing more than mountains, dropping into the sea. Formidable. Bleak. Compared to the Forestland,

Norwegia was desolate and ugly. He bit back the twinge of homesickness.

"It is beautiful, is it not?" Kelda sighed.

"It is different," he answered.

Brander's heart felt heavier when they finally entered one of the many inlets that cut into the shoreline. Steep bluffs towered on each side.

"Falcon Fjord," Kelda murmured.

After passing more waterfalls, sailing between more craggy bluffs and sheer cliffs, the *langskip* rounded a promontory. People ran down a path cut in the side of the mountain; others waited at the quay.

Brander gazed curiously at the crowd. Almost all of these, men and women, were as fair as the Iroquois were dark. Although most of the women had long, blond hair, none of them were as beautiful as Kelda. Their hair was not as golden, their eyes not the purest of blues. Kelda was the sun; they were pale imitations.

Brander watched the people wave and cheer at the Norsemen who guided the ship around the quay. Activity heightened aboard ship. The unstepping of the mast. The furling, tying, and storing of the sail. Hauk steered the ship against the wooden dock, the landing nothing more than a gentle thud. The Vikings shipped the oars, then began unstrapping their sea chests. All movements were hurried, yet orderly.

The journey was over; they were home.

Brander stepped to the dock, swaying a little until he regained the feel of land beneath his feet. The people crowded around the exiting Vikings. Although exuberant and happy to see their loved ones and friends, they stared at him curiously. He could see the question in their eyes: Was this Jarl

282

Thoruald's Skrelling son?

The whispering crowd fell back. They parted, and a huge Viking—truly a chieftain—regally walked toward Brander. His purple mantle clasped on one shoulder with a large brooch, hung down his back to slap against the ankles of his boots.

He was tall; he was broad. His mere size projected power. It inspired fear. Like the land he claimed as his own, his face was hard and indomitable, yet it seemed to be pinched and drawn as if by pain. It was framed by thick, golden blond hair and an equally thick but neatly trimmed beard. Blue eyes stared at Brander, slowly moving from the top of his head to the bottom of his boots and back up again.

For a moment Brander thought he saw an emotion akin to joy in those eyes, but he must have been mistaken. Now they were as hard as his face, as remote.

"What are you called?" the Viking demanded in a deep voice.

"Who wishes to know?" Brander asked.

The blue eyes narrowed. The mouth drew into a straight line of anger. "Thoruald Eiriksson, jarl of this steading."

Eirik! Brander had named his son after his paternal grandfather. For a moment his hatred of this man and his culture spilled onto Wild Flower. She had been the wise woman who had chosen his son's name. Always she had sacrificed their own culture to give way to the Norse.

All the resolve in the world was not enough for Brander to retain his distance from the Norsemen. Circumstances both here and in the Forestland of the Iroquois conspired to tangle him in his father's

283

heritage.

"Answer me!" Thoruald thundered. "Else I shall have you punished."

"You may try," Brander said, "but you would not be successful, Viking. Perhaps to you, I am a Skrelling, but I am as much a warrior — if not more so — than any you would put up against me, including yourself."

Brander had lived in defiance all his life. One more act would not hurt him. His eyes pinned the Viking chieftain with a contemptuous gaze. He waited until he saw the man's jaws tense, the muscle tick in his temple.

"I will not ask again," Thoruald said. His countenance turned slightly gray, and he grimaced.

Why the grimace? Brander wondered. Anger, disapproval . . . perhaps pain?

"A second asking is sufficient. I am called Brander, War Chief of the Iroquois."

"Aye. The Firebrand. The name suits you." He spoke with grudging respect.

The Viking seemed to relax, but his eyes remained wary. They flicked over the men who climbed out of the longship. They lingered on Kelda. Only then did the face soften, and a smile touch his lips.

"Daughter," he said, holding open his arms. "It is good to have you safely home again."

Kelda went into his embrace. "It is good to be home again, sire, and to see you recovered." When he merely grunted, she pulled back. "You are recovering well, are you not, sire?"

"Aye," he answered briskly and added, "You have returned victorious."

Kelda nodded. "Aye, I brought your son home."

"Aye," Thoruald murmured, nodding his head,

"he is my son."

"Where is my son?" Brander asked.

"Away," Thoruald replied.

"I would see him immediately."

"In time," Thoruald said. "According to our custom he has been entrusted to another jarl for his education and training as a warrior. I told the boy he could return for the welcome celebration."

Brander did not care if the hatred he felt for his father showed in his eyes. He hated even the gods at the moment. He hated fate also because *She* had conspired against him. Had he wanted his child to know the ways of the Norsemen he would have taught him.

But this man—this man who he hated—not only had him and his mother, he had his son and was raising him to be Norse.

Thoruald stared right back into Brander's eyes. Sparks flared between them, but neither intimidated the other.

"When is the welcome celebration?" Brander asked.

"It begins tonight," Thoruald answered, "but I told Gannar to wait until the morrow to bring the child." Then the chieftain spied Hauk.

"Sire," Hauk said, and walked up to Thoruald. The two men hugged. "It is good to see you again."

"Aye, my friend, I am glad to have you home. I have missed you."

"Thoruald!" Dour-faced, Canby pressed through the crowd. "I must speak with you."

"Canby!" Thoruald smiled and dropped an arm about his friend's shoulders. "Why such a long face? Tonight will be a memorable occasion for the house of the Falcon."

Canby cast Brander a contemptuous gaze. "I would talk to you about the Skrelling and Kelda in private, sire. There is much you should know."

"We will talk later," Thoruald said. "Now is a time for happy faces and celebration." He shouted, "People of the steading tonight we feast and celebrate the return of Kelda and the *Golden Sol*. We celebrate the arrival of the jarl's blood son—Brander."

Canby clawed at Thoruald's shirt sleeve. "Sire, a moment of your time, please. I wish to impart words of wisdom."

Brander stood next to his father. Canby eyed him suspiciously.

"In private," Canby said.

"Here," Thoruald instructed.

Canby pulled him aside. "Sire, you will be making a fatal mistake if you claim this Skrelling as your son. He is a barbarian, alien to our customs. He hates us and makes no secret of his hatred. Why he—"

"Nay," Thoruald drawled, interrupting the lawreader, "he is half Norse himself. He cannot hate what he is."

"Thoruald—" desperation caused Canby's voice to escalate to shrillness; his eyes darted madly about "—I fear for the future of our people and of the steading if you allow Brander to become the chieftain."

"Leave the worrying to me, my friend," Thoruald said. "You have done your duty. You have spoken your words of wisdom. I have listened."

"But you choose not to heed them?"

"I do," Thoruald replied.

Canby's gaze raked over Kelda, and he spoke louder. "I have more to tell you, Thoruald, but I would do that in private."

When Brander saw Kelda's face redden, he said, "You are meddling in another's affairs, Canby. I would advise you to make haste to your home and leave me and my affairs alone."

Canby stared at him, his face twisting in absolute fury. He sputtered, then turned to Thoruald to shake a finger in his face.

"I warn you, Thoruald, the people will reject Brander out of hand. They will rebel against you and him. You will lose your position of leadership. He will undermine your authority."

Thoruald's eyes narrowed. His voice hardened, yet a smile continued to touch his mouth. "You are tired, my friend. When you have rested, we will talk more on the subject."

He turned to his men. "Tonight, brave warriors," Thoruald shouted, "to thank the god Thor for the safe return of Kelda and the jarl's son, I will sacrifice an ox and place it on the platform above the entrance door to the Great Hall. I will also give you great reward for bringing home safely the son of the jarl. We will eat and drink in celebration." He then turned to Kelda. "Now, Daughter, we will move to the longhouse and prepare for the feast tonight. I would have you tell me about your voyage."

"I shall be happy to share my adventures with you, sire, and tonight your guests will be entertained by songs and poems from Ulmer," Kelda promised.

"The lad who wants to write poetry and sing songs?" Thoruald teased.

"The lad who *writes* poetry and *sings* songs," Kelda said. "The lad who proved himself a brave warrior on this trip."

287

"I would hear his tale," Thoruald said.

As the dock cleared of people, Brander turned to see his mother standing alone on the prow platform. While Thoruald was speaking with Kelda and Hauk, he returned to the ship and helped her ashore.

"Why is the Woman of Dreams lagging behind?" he asked softly. "Does she now regret she has undertaken this journey to a far land?"

"Nay. She is awaiting her turn. When she speaks, she does not wish to be one lost among the many. She chooses to be one alone, to stand out from all others," Wild Flower answered.

"Even with all the Norse people here," Brander told her, "you would stand out, my mother. You have a dark beauty that far surpasses the paleness of the Norse."

She smiled. "Thank you, my son, but I fear you speak out of prejudice. You love me."

"Aye, lady, I do with all my heart. 'Twas you who held the little boy in your arms and calmed his fears, who soothed his ruffled feathers, who instilled pride and determination into him. Without you there would be no Brander, no war chief of the Iroquois. I owe much to you, lady. May I repay you with the kindness you have given to me."

"Thank you," she whispered.

Brander leaned down and pressed a kiss to his mother's brow.

"Now, my mother, speak to your Viking."

She took several steps and called aloud. "Sire, I have a game piece to return to you."

Thoruald stopped walking.

Wild Flower held out her hand, palm up. The statue was clearly visible. "It is a falcon piece that was entrusted to my keeping thirty winters ago. I

288

believe it will complete a set you had crafted many years ago in a faraway market."

Thoruald turned, a look of disbelief on his countenance as he gazed at Wild Flower. "By the gods," he murmured, "is it you? Can it be?"

Chapter Twenty-four

"Thoruald Eiriksson," Wild Flower murmured.

He was her warrior. Her Viking warrior!

She closed her eyes and breathed deeply to still the trembling of her body. Was this past or present, dream or reality? She was afraid to open her lids again for fear he would be gone. Gone as he had been for the past thirty winters. She was afraid to find herself with memories only. But she had to know. Slowly she lifted her lids.

He was there; he walked toward her.

Tears warmed her eyes. They slid down her cheeks.

His red hair still gleamed like golden fire in the sun. He was yet a big, tall man, but his face was lined with years of responsibility. Behind the mask of hardness, she sensed a vulnerability that he had not had when he was younger. The grayness about his mouth and eyes told her he was in pain. His slightly stooped shoulders and the way he held his arm close to his body, instinctively protecting his abdomen indicated that he gave in to his wound.

" 'Tis you, my lord," she whispered.

"Aye, mistress, 'tis I, Thoruald Eiriksson."

She drank of him, but could not get her fill.

"I dared not hope," he said, the blue eyes as thirsty for her as she was for him. A callused thumb gently wiped a tear from her face.

"You should have known when you sent for your issue that you would also inherit the mother," she said, blinking back more tears of happiness at seeing him again, of sadness for what they had missed through the years.

"I did not know if the mother yet lived."

"Had you visited our village again, you would have known," she chided gently, almost sadly.

"Aye, mistress, 'tis true." The blue eyes shadowed; he pressed his arm closer to his body. "You are yet beautiful."

"As you are handsome." She smiled. "What think you of our son?"

Thoruald grinned, boyishlike. "We produced an obstinate one, lady. I have a feeling my life is going to be miserable with his coming."

"He promises that it will be worse than miserable, lord, and I believe him. You will be well advised to believe also. He has all the attributes of his father . . . many times over."

Thoruald laughed. "War chief of the Iroquois. I am proud of him."

Wild Flower glanced over at her son, who scowled in their direction.

"I am proud of him also, lord. He is much like you."

Thoruald crooked his arm, and she laid her hand on him. Beneath her palm the rock-hardness of his flesh and muscle pulsed to life. Through the shirt, she felt the warmth of his skin. Though his touches were long ago, she remembered them as if they were only yesterday.

As they walked off the dock and up the path to the steading, she said, "I would also see my grandson, lord."

"You will," Thoruald said. "I shall have him

291

brought to the *stofa* on the morrow." He stopped moving and turned to face her. Softly he said, "Your grandson will not know you, lady. He has no memory of life in Skrellingland."

Wild Flower nodded. "Kelda explained, but I have seen in my dreams that he will recover the thoughts which he has lost. He will be whole once again, reunited with his father, as you will never be with your son."

"You speak in riddles?" he asked.

"Nay," she answered. "I would have you know that you cannot breach thirty years with eating and drinking and wishing. Sonship is something that is gained through time, lord, not something that happens simply because a man sires a child."

"I have thought long and hard on that," Thoruald said. "I have no illusions of trying to recapture what is lost between Brander and me. I want to create a relationship between two men, one based on common goals and respect. I want someone to inherit all that I own, someone to carry on my name and blood line."

He paused, then said, "Lady, thirty winters ago I was a young Viking who was setting out to conquer foreign lands and peoples. Today I am a spent old man, waiting to place my sword in my son's hand and to pass on the title of jarl."

Wild Flower smiled tenderly at him. "Both of us have aged, lord, but I would hardly call you spent. I think seasoned or mellow would be a much better choice of word."

Thoruald returned her smile, his eyes twinkling. "Lady, you give me new life . . . a surge of new life, if you follow my meaning."

"I do, lord," she murmured, a flush seeping into her cheeks. "And I wish you well—"

"Thank you," he replied, laughter deepening the color of his eyes.

"With Brander," she finished. Her face was absolutely hot now. "You will find all the qualities you are looking for in him, but he does not wish to be counted your son."

"Are you telling me I have a challenge?"

"Aye, lord, a challenge," she answered. "Not a wife or a son."

Thoruald grimaced, bent and caught at his stomach.

"What is it?" Wild Flower asked.

His face clearing, he tried to smile, but she saw the pinch of pain about his mouth and eyes.

"Your wound," she said. "It is bothering you."

Breathing deeply, he said, "Young men heal quicker than old ones. The healer assures me that the pain will subside in time." He gave her a bigger smile this time and breathed easier. "However, lady, time is a luxury I do not have anymore. I own great wealth, houses, land, cattle, thralls. All this I will leave to my son . . . and my wife."

"All of this land belongs to Thoruald?" Brander asked, his gaze moving across the steading. The one-room homes scattered about that belonged to his karls. The byre for the cattle. Stables for the horses. The pig sty. Storehouses. The forge. The bathhouse.

"Aye," Kelda answered and they walked farther. "He is a wealthy man."

Several women wearing white uniforms of slaves had hides staked to the ground and were hand-tooling them as did the Iroquois women. One thrall was tending to the swine. Another was chopping wood and stacking it against the longhouse. On long racks hung various animal skins and food to dry.

"Thoruald owns many acres of land and slaves. They work in the fields. In the tar pits acquiring tar from resinous woods for daubing ships, treating ropes, and sealing roofs. At the tannery. And at the saltworks where we extract salt from the sea water or by burning seaweed. He employs many craftsmen — metal workers, lumbermen and carpenters, blacksmiths, and has a large army of warriors who are loyal to him."

They moved along a knee-high stone fence. Kelda pushed open the gate and they walked into one of many garden yards to the side of the longhouse.

"This is our vegetable garden," she explained, and pointed to the different plants as she talked. "Turnips, carrots, cabbages, peas, and beans. It is not so different from yours."

He acknowledged with a nod, and she pointed.

"Our meadow is large and partitioned into different fields for rye, barley, wheat, and oats. They will be ready for harvest in the fall. Our dairy barn is quite large and we grind our grain into flour and store it there throughout the winter."

Brander turned to look at the huge building that stood in a separated yard from the longhouse.

With another wave of her hand, Kelda continued, "Our meadow provides enough hay for us to keep hundreds of cattle through the winter. That is why our cow shed is so large. As you can see, Thoruald possesses a large steading. He is one of the richest jarls in Norwegia. The king would like to see his power broken."

"Have you ever wondered if perhaps your king

294

sent the pirates who attacked your village?" Brander asked.

"Thoruald thought there was such a possibility, but it proved to be untrue."

"Kelda! Welcome home. 'Tis good to see that Thor blessed your voyage."

"Aye," Kelda called, waving to the young boy, dressed in a white uniform, who carried two pails of water to the vegetable garden behind the longhouse.

She and Brander passed through the gate.

"How is the planting, Larsen?" she asked.

"Good, mistress."

"Have you been tending your tools while I was away?"

He grinned. "Aye."

She led Brander to a large garden house and walked inside to inspect the tools. He listened as she talked about the farm equipment. The plows that were fitted with soil board for turning the turf, a front wheel, and a sharp plowshare made of iron with an iron blade.

She then walked to the other side of the building and inspected the scythes and hand sickles, spades, hoes, rakes, pitchforks, and sharp pruning knives.

Larsen stood at the door. "What see you, mistress?"

Brander smiled to himself. Although Larsen addressed Kelda, Brander knew that the lad's interest was not in the equipment building or its inspection. The Viking stared openly and curiously at him.

"A sight that pleases me," Kelda said. "You shall be rewarded for doing such a good job."

"Thank you, mistress."

As she and Brander continued to walk through

the steading, they were greeted by the many workers, both the freemen and the slaves. Brander continued to be amused by their reactions. While they pretended an interest in Kelda and news of the voyage, they cast curious glances at him—at the jarl's Skrelling son.

"He is a dark one," Asa, the chief seamstress muttered, her faded blue eyes moving over Brander.

Kelda opened her mouth to speak, no doubt to let them know he spoke Norse, but he laid a hand on her arm and shook his head.

"Aye," the smithy agreed, then said, "I hear tell a Skrelling woman sailed with you, Mistress Kelda. Claims to be the jarl's wife, I heard."

"She was the jarl's wife," Brander replied.

On hearing him speak their language, the man and woman fell back, their jaws slack with surprise.

Quietly Brander continued to speak, "He married her when he sailed to my land thirty years ago. He left her and her unborn babe behind when he returned to his homeland."

Brander gazed at the old couple, then asked, "Are you karls or slaves?"

"Karls," both answered at once. "We are craftsmen the jarl has hired to work on the steading."

"If you wish to continue to work here, good woman and smithy, it would be in your best interest not to be idly discussing the Iroquois woman."

"Aye, sire," both of them answered at the same time, bobbing their heads. "It was a mistake we surely will not make again, sire."

Repeating their apology, they backed away and rushed to their chores, casting worried glances over their shoulders.

"You should not have spoken to them like that," Kelda said. "You are not the jarl yet."

"And probably will never be, but idle talk should be stopped before it becomes hurtful," he replied.

They continued to walk in silence until they stood in front of the largest building on the manor.

"The Great Hall," Kelda said. She pushed open the heavy doors that were located at the far end of the long wall and moved to the interior of the *stofa*.

Brander planted his palm against the door and pushed, feeling the imprint of metal against his hand. He drew back to study the intricate wrought-iron designs that decorated the door.

"The falcon," he muttered.

Kelda nodded. "Thoruald believes his good fortune lies in the power of his talisman."

Brander pushed on through the doors, stepped through an entry hall, and moved into the Great Hall. His gaze slowly, thoroughly moved around the room, finally coming to rest on the large, open fire that burned in the center.

Two men, an older one, and a boy, set up tables in front of benches that lined the walls. A young woman followed to cover the tables with beautifully embroidered linen clothes. The three of them smiled when they saw Kelda.

"Thor brought you home safely," the woman called.

"Aye, Tove," Kelda answered, "he did."

"We remembered to offer sacrifices for your safe journey," the woman added.

The older man stepped forward. "That we did, mistress. We are glad to see your bright and happy face about the steading again."

"I am happy to be home, Sweyn," Kelda answered. "I would like for the three of you to meet

297

Brander, the jarl's son. Brander, these are three of our most trusted house slaves, Sweyn, Tove, and Wray." As Kelda called their names, she pointed and each stepped forward.

"It is an honor to meet you, sire," Sweyn said. "Welcome to Falconstead."

"Thank you," Brander said.

"It is right pleased we are to have the jarl's son home," the young girl said.

Brander paused, his brows drew, but he finally said, "Thank you."

Wray grinned and swiped a shock of hair from his face. "It is right pleased I will be, sire, if you will have me as your personal thrall."

Kelda looked at Brander and shook her head, but he ignored her warning.

"I will fetch and carry for you," Wray said. "Anything you ask of me, sire, I will do for you."

"You belong to one now?"

"I belong to the jarl," Wray answered, "but he has his personal thrall in Sweyn. I want to belong to a young warrior, sire, so I can learn to be one myself. That way, sire, I can earn my freedom, as many of Jarl Thoruald's thralls have done. I have already been trained by Hauk. I am skilled with the bow and the broadax, sire, and I am learning the sword."

Brander contemplated the boy, the sincere eyes, the broad shoulders, the slender firmness of developing muscles. More, he felt the desire and determination emanating from the lad. He smiled and nodded. Hauk was an old man, too old to be with Eirik for many years. The lad would need his own personal companion and mentor. Wray would be ideal for him.

"You may be my personal slave, Wray."

"Thank you, sire," the boy said.

"I—I do not know what Jarl Thoruald will have to say about this," Sweyn sputtered. "He gave this lad to me so my work load would be lightened."

"I will see that the jarl gives you another," Brander promised.

"Aye, sire."

"Now," Kelda said, "it is back to work with you all. Wray, for the present you will continue to work with Sweyn and Tove. We need your help this day with the celebration feast." She cut her eyes at Brander. "Do we have your permission, sire?"

"Aye."

Leaving Kelda to do her instructing and supervising, Brander walked away from them. He pretended to be studying the *stofa*, but he was deep in thought. On the one hand, he hated being here in this country. On the other, he felt as if he had found a missing part of himself. This confused him. Until he had landed in Norwegia, he had never thought of himself as being anything but Iroquois. Now he found himself identifying with these people—with these pale, blond strangers.

His gaze swept over the building. Two of the walls, constructed of beautiful paneled wood, were decorated with colorful tapestries that hung from the ceiling to the floor. The other two were hung with overlapping shields and weapons inlaid with gold and silver that glinted and gleamed in the firelight.

He walked closer to them and studied the craftsmanship and beauty.

"They are a sign of Thoruald's wealth," Kelda said.

"I suspected as much. The tables that are being set up are for the banquet tonight," Brander said.

"Aye, all of his subjects will be here tonight."

"To gawk at his *Skrelling* son," Brander said sarcastically.

"That in part," she answered.

"Thoruald will reward his warriors who went in search of this *seed* and returned with him."

She nodded. "He will pass out the booty, but he could do that without this great celebration. He is having it because he is happy and enjoys company. All Norsemen enjoy entertaining, especially during the long, dark winter months."

Brander walked to an ornately carved chair that sat in the middle of the west wall and faced the rising sun. It stood on a dais and had two large pillars that ran from floor to ceiling behind it. They were as ornately carved, painted, and inlaid with gold as the chair itself.

"The Pillars of the High Seat," Kelda explained. "The jarl's high seat."

Brander ran his hands over the carvings on the pillars—dragons, serpents, vines, and leaves. And falcons. He turned his attention to the chair, again studying the decorations. Then he felt the down pillow, covered in damask, that cushioned the bottom.

"No one sits here but the jarl," Kelda said. "This is his seat of honor. It signifies his exalted rank."

As if her words were an invitation, Brander sat down. Tove gasped and dropped a plate to the floor. Sweyn slumped against the wall as if he expected one of the gods, or at least Thoruald, to appear and immediately execute Brander. Wray's eyes opened so wide, Brander thought surely they would pop out.

"Get out of that chair immediately," Kelda ordered, looking around the room. She could visual-

300

ize Thoruald's reaction should he walk in and discover another sitting in his chair. "I told you no one but the jarl sits in the seat of honor. Is it not enough that you have undermined him by telling Wray he could be your personal slave? Must you flout his authority by sitting in his chair?"

"I have never accorded him any authority to flaunt, and I sit where I choose," Brander answered and laid his arms along the broad armrests. He pushed back in the chair, making himself more comfortable. Again he surveyed the room and pointed to one end. "What is behind that door?"

"The fireroom," Kelda answered, her gaze darting to the entrance door, "where the cooking is done. The door beside it leads outside to the dairy where we keep our cows." She followed his gaze to a third door in the same cluster. "That is the bower or the women's room. There we do our sewing, embroidering, spinning, and weaving."

"The smithy's wife is in there?" he asked. "Asa, she was called."

Kelda nodded. "She is our chief seamstress. She instructs all our women servants in the making of cloth and in sewing. Please, Brander, get out of the chair."

Losing interest in the everyday workings of the steading, Brander rose and walked across the planked floor to the other end of the *stofa*. He wanted to know more about the mistress of the steading, more about Kelda. She followed him. He stopped in front of a door, one of four clustered at this end of the *stofa,* grasped the handle and tugged.

"What are these rooms?"

"The bed chambers," Kelda replied. "This one belongs to Thoruald."

Brander looked around the large room. Against the far wall rested a large frame bed with gaily colored coverlets and large pillows. Two chairs and a round table were grouped together. One trunk sat at the end of the bed; another was shoved against the wall and the head of the bed. A third one, a sea chest, stood beside the wall at the door. Gold wall sconces held torches that had been trimmed and were ready for service.

On one wall he saw a sword and moved inside the room to study it. Never had he beheld such beautiful craftsmanship. Silver and gold glinted in the sunlight that spilled through the open window. He touched it, running his hands over the runes and the inlaid etchings. He touched one of the talons that decorated the hilt.

"The Talon of the Falcon," Kelda murmured.

Brander's gaze moved to the gold and black helmet that sat on top of a trunk. Decorated with the head of a falcon, it was polished to a high sheen.

"If you remain here," Kelda said, "you will inherit the sword and the helmet."

Without a word Brander turned and walked out of the room, shutting the door.

"Where do you sleep?" he asked.

"In the chamber farther down."

He walked the distance to the second door.

"My room is quite small," Kelda said nervously, walking behind him. "There is hardly room in it for one much less two. Beside mine we have Ragnar's chambers, and we have several in the lofts over each end of the *stofa*. They are reached by outside stairs. This is where Hauk and Ulmer sleep."

Brander opened the door and stepped inside the commodious room. The walls were paneled in a

302

rich wood, the window shutters open, a late afternoon breeze blowing into the room. Sweet rushes
strewn over the floor gave the room a fresh, out-
doors odor. As in Thoruald's room, ornate wall
sconces crafted in gold and silver held torches.
Against the inner wall was a large bed, more than
large enough for two people.

Looking at her, he raised a brow and smiled
mockingly. "Pray tell, mistress, what does a large
room look like?"

Chapter Twenty-five

"There is no room in here for more trunks," Kelda said. "You will have need of much more space than my room provides."

"At present," he replied dryly, "I have only the clothes I am wearing."

"But you will have more," Kelda promised. "I will talk with Asa about them. As the jarl's son—"

His gaze caught hers.

"I mean, you will have to dress befitting your rank as war chief of the Iroquois."

Brander grinned. "Aye, Kelda, that I must."

He walked farther into the room, his gaze moving from one of four trunks to the other.

"For my clothes," she murmured.

His glance took in the small table and two chairs that were on either side of it.

"In case I wish to take the morning meal in my room. Like your people," she said, "we only have two, the morning and the evening. 'Tis the evening meal where we socialize the most, the one where we usually have guests and need to dine in the Great Hall."

Brander nodded his head. This much the Vikings had in common with the Iroquois. Not enough to make him feel comfortable, certainly not enough to make him feel as if he were home.

He moved to the center of the room to touch a

piece of furniture that was strange in design and function to him. Beautifully and ornately painted, it was made of metal and was raised from the floor by four legs. The bottom was closed in, but the top was perforated.

"A brazier for heating the room. On one of his many trading trips, Thoruald bought it from an Arab merchant." She opened the bottom of the container. "You put the fuel in here, and it radiates heat throughout the room. It saves us having to build an open fire in the room, and we do not have to have a hole in the ceiling for the smoke to escape. When we close the windows, we can keep the room warmer for sleeping."

Brander moved to the bed and sat down, luxuriating in the softness of the mattress.

"It is softer than the ones we slept on in your lodge," she said, "because the mattress is stuffed with heather."

Brander was not thinking about the stuffing for the mattress. He was thinking about the softness of the woman. Imagining her lying on the bed with her golden hair fanning over the pillow, he ran his hand over the brightly colored bed coverings. He felt a stirring in his body for her and wondered how he would be able to keep his promise to himself. A man could give pleasure to a woman only so many times without taking pleasure himself.

"I shall occupy this chamber with you," he announced, stretching out.

Kelda moved restlessly about the room. Stopping in front of one of the trunks, she said, "This was to be the room that—that—"

"That you and Ragnar shared," Brander said, cupping his hands beneath his head and crossing his legs at the ankles. The only thing that kept him from hating his deceased half-brother was the

305

knowledge that Ragnar had never possessed Kelda. Brander knew that it made no sense, but he was jealous of a dead man. "In order for the two of you to have shared the room comfortably," he said with a hint of sarcasm, "he must have been a much smaller man than I, or either he did not have many clothes."

Kelda glared at him

"Do not be heavy hearted, mistress. Now you will share the room with me. You have traded one son for the other. The fair for the dark."

"The two facets of the Solid Faces," she murmured. "Good and evil."

Brander laughed softly. "Nay, mistress, I did not compare Ragnar to me in terms of one being good, the other evil. I said he was the fair. I am the dark. There is a wealth of difference in the comparisons." He patted the mattress. "Come lie with me."

Kelda spun and walked out of the room, saying over her shoulder. "I have much work to do, sire. I have no time to play."

Brander's feet hit the floor with a thud, and he raced across the floor, his hand banding around her arm. "Nay, mistress, we will have none of this. When I give you an order, I am not playing. I am serious. I would have you lie with me."

Blue eyes stared into his. "I have work to do, sire. I am the mistress of the steading and now that I am returned from my voyage, I must instruct the servants and slaves in their duties."

She yanked her arm out of his clasp.

"That is, sire, if you have no objections?"

He gazed into the blue eyes until he felt that he was losing himself in their depths. He had cared for his wife, but his feelings for her did not begin to compare with what he felt for the Viking. Never was he indifferent where she was concerned. He was

306

either happy or sad; angry or amused; frustrated or at ease.

She had insinuated herself into his life. Now she was penetrating his heart. He had to be wary. He refused to carry an empty and broken heart back to the Forestland with him.

"Take care of your chores," he said.

Kelda gazed at him another second before she walked off. He followed her into the *stofa* and leaned against one of the roof posts. She moved to the table to help Tove place dishes. She glanced at him but said nothing. He continued to watch her for a long while before he pushed away from the post and walked around the room to study the intricately embroidered tapestries that adorned the walls.

"Shall I get more sweet smelling reeds and rushes for the floor, mistress?" Tove's voice drifted over to him.

"Yes," Kelda answered. "I shall be in the fireroom shortly to give instructions for the banquet tonight. How is the cooking going?"

"Fine, mistress," Tove answered, a mischievous smile turning her lips at the corner. "The bake house is quite warm and Olga is complaining loudly."

Kelda laughed. "I do not suppose you have anything to give her that will relieve her crossness?"

Tove laughed with Kelda. "Aye, you have no idea how a tankard or two of ale will improve a cross disposition, mistress."

"Make sure she does not have too many tankards," Kelda admonished.

"I will not," Tove promised. "Now, I will be gone."

As Tove slipped out of the hall through the fireroom, the entrance door opened, and Thoruald and Wild Flower entered the Great Hall. When they joined Kelda, Thoruald spoke.

307

"I see you have assumed your duties, Daughter."
He laughed. "I am glad. The slaves will be glad to
have your soft voice taking them to task rather than
the gruff yelling of the jarl. In fact, after a while, if
things proceeded without mishap, I let them run
the steading."

As Brander had done earlier, Wild Flower moved
curiously about the building, touching the furnish-
ings, appreciating their beauty.

"Take Wild Flower to your chamber," Thoruald
instructed Kelda. "She will share it with you."

"Nay," Brander said. He sat in Thoruald's chair,
his right leg slung carelessly over his left leg.

Thoruald turned. He spied him at the same time
that Kelda did. Brander smiled when his father
gasped and his face twisted in anger. Angry strides
brought Thoruald closer to him. Kelda wanted to
cry.

"Kelda and I will share the room," Brander said.

"You are married?"

"Nay. We are sleeping together." Brander seemed
to take pleasure in pounding Thoruald to the floor
in humiliation.

Shock rooted Thoruald to the spot. Finally he
moved to lean against one of the roof pillars. Wild
Flower joined him, laying a hand on his shoulder.

Kelda's heart went out to this man whom she
loved as a father. When she had become engaged to
Ragnar, she had thought no man as strong as
Thoruald. She had thought surely he would live forever.

"You are sleeping with my adopted daughter
without the marriage vows? You have taken her—
her maidenhood?"

"Aye, Father," Kelda said.

The spirit seemed to seep out of his body, and
she was witness to Thoruald's mortality, to his hu-

manness. Although he was still broad of shoulder, he moved slower and more carefully. Even when he smiled, his face was drawn, and there was a gray tightness about his lips.

"I am his mistress by choice." Kelda's words echoed through the Great Hall.

Brander rose and moved to Kelda, touching the neckline of her shirt. She pulled away from him. Catching the material herself, she tugged it aside.

"I also wear his totem." She had to ease some of Thoruald's pain, to lift some of the humiliation of having his son claim his adopted daughter as his mistress.

"I am sure you recognize it," Brander said. "It is the one you left with my mother when you returned to Norwegia thirty winters ago."

"Slaves are marked," Thoruald shouted, "not mistresses."

"I am not marked, my father," Kelda said softly, although she knew the words were not quite true. Brander had marked her his. "I am only wearing his amulet."

"You are wearing a neck ring that publicly declares you are his mistress," Thoruald exclaimed.

"She is at liberty to take it off any time she pleases," Brander said.

Kelda glared at him.

"But she will not," he continued, "because it pleases her to wear it. It pleases her to have me as her champion. As long as I am that champion, as long as I am going to pit my life against another man's for her, I want every inhabitant of the steading and on those steadings around to know Kelda, adopted daughter of the jarl, is my mistress."

"This is what Canby desires to tell me," Thoruald said.

"Aye," Brander replied.

Thoruald gave Kelda a searching glance, but he spoke to Brander, "When you took her maidenhood, did you know she was betrothed to Asgaut?"

"He did," Kelda answered.

Again Thoruald addressed Brander. "You understand that—"

"I do," Brander interrupted, "and I shall challenge him."

Thoruald nodded. "Aye, there will be a challenge for sure. Who issues it, I am not sure."

"Where is he?" Brander asked.

"He has not yet returned from his search for the raiders. I look for him to arrive home before the winter blows in." Thoruald straightened and paced the *stofa* floor, pensively brushing his hand down his beard. After a while, he stopped and looked at Kelda. "Maybe, this will not be as troublesome as I first thought."

"Nay, my father," she said softly, and looked up to send Brander a silent warning that he should say no more.

The Viking chieftain turned cold blue eyes on Brander. The gaze was frightening in its intensity, and Brander knew that many would cower beneath it. Not he. No Norseman could instill fear into his heart. Certainly not this one.

"Do not mistreat my daughter or you shall reckon with me."

Brander caught Kelda by the upper arm. Her doing her duties was one thing. His being threatened by Thoruald was another. He no longer wanted to remain in the room with the Viking. Nor did he wish to feel guilty when he looked at Kelda or his mother.

"Let us go to our room. I am tired and would rest before we eat tonight."

"Kelda," Thoruald called.

"Do not worry," she said softly, removing her arm from Brander's grasp and moving to her foster father. She laid a hand on Thoruald's forearm. "I am a strong woman, and I can handle the situation. It is really the best. Brander will rid our lives of the threat of Asgaut."

"Aye," Thoruald murmured, "the threat of Asgaut. A man who wants to take my place but does not have the brain to do so." He turned his head to look at Brander. "The man who has the blood, the brain, and the brawn to do so does not want it. The gods do seem to delight in twisting our lives, do they not, Daughter?"

"Perhaps this Asgaut is not nearly as bad as choice for leader as you think," Wild Flower suggested.

"Nay, lady," Thoruald said. "He is far worse. The man has no thoughts that are his own. He is a man directed by others, not one to direct others. As long as Canby is Asgaut's advisor, I do not worry. Canby will give him good advice. But Canby is an old man who does not have many more winters left. I worry about the next man to advise Asgaut."

"Do not worry, my father," Kelda said. "Once Asgaut is removed, I will be able to choose what I wish to do with my life. I will no longer need a champion, and you will not have to worry about Asgaut taking over the steading."

"Come," Brander ordered. He was tired of her explaining his actions. That, too, made him feel guilty. Never before had his actions been so questioned. Never before had he allowed one to question him so.

Kelda moved from her adopted father and followed Brander to the bed chamber. He shut the door and slid the bolt in place.

"Are you afraid, sire?" Kelda mocked.

311

"I wish privacy." He unfastened the mantle from his neck and laid it and the brooch on a nearby chest. He grimaced as he rubbed his hand over his face and chin. "I would have a bath to rid my body of the salt. I have never felt so gritty in my entire life."

"We bathe every Saturday," Kelda said.

"I care not when the Norse bathe," he said. "The Iroquois wishes one now."

Kelda nodded. "You may use the lavatory or I shall have the bathhouse prepared for you, sire."

"The lavatory?" he asked.

She nodded. "It is the farthest room on this side of the *stofa*. Come with me. I will show you."

Brander followed her through the *stofa* to another chamber. On platforms built against the wall were basins—ranging in sizes from small for the washing of the face and hands to large for the washing of an entire person. Above one of the basins was a handle. When turned in one direction, water from a reservoir flowed into the basin. The lavatory boasted two stone-lined drains. One diverted a small stream through the room; another carried the used water out.

Kelda pointed to a large chest. "Bathing and drying clothes are kept in there. Since you wish a full bath, I will have Tove heat you water. Wray will call you when all is ready."

"I am sure you are as gritty as I am," Brander said. "I would have you bathe with me."

"I would follow your bidding," Kelda said, "but as I explained earlier, it is necessary for me to instruct the kitchen staff on the preparation of foods for the banquet tonight. This is an extremely special one for Thoruald. I will take my bath later."

Brander moved to where she stood and ran his hands through her hair. "Viking, it will do you

312

well to obey me and my desires. You no longer belong to Thoruald but to me. My wishes are your wishes, not his."

"Only until you destroy Asgaut's power," Kelda whispered. "Then, *sire*, I will no longer owe you anything."

Brander smiled and traced his finger over her lips. He felt her trembling response to his touch.

"Aye, Kelda, you still owe me a blood-debt for saving your life. You will be in debt to me for a long, long time, mistress."

"If you wish to see the child," Kelda said, "it would be to your advantage to have Thoruald pleased tonight. The happier he is, the sooner he will send for him."

Brander moved his hand and sighed. "Be gone. Have my bath prepared and see to your cooking."

Kelda was moving toward the fireroom, when she heard a noise. She turned to see a robust woman leaning against one of the roof posts.

"Brunhild," she murmured as she gazed at Asgaut's first wife and Thoruald's niece-by-marriage.

A malicious smile curving her lips, the Viking woman pushed away from the post and moved to where Kelda stood. "I have heard the rumors."

Kelda said nothing.

"You and the Skrelling are sleeping together."

"I am his mistress," Kelda affirmed softly.

The woman's face contorted into the ugliness of rage and hatred. "You were Asgaut's betrothed."

"I was."

"You broke your sacred oath."

"Nay, I promised Thoruald that if I could not find his issue or prove that the thrall we call Kolby was his grandson, I would marry Asgaut and give Thoruald an heir."

Brunhild glared at her. "You will not get out of

this so easily. You with your pretty face and hair. I am the one Thoruald should have turned to. Since my mother was his wife's sister, I am his kin. He should have adopted me. But, no, he had to take you, a thrall, into his household. Not only did he give you your freedom, but he legally and formally adopted you."

Her lips twisted as she spoke. "You think because you are no longer a thrall because you are Thoruald's adopted daughter, you are better than us, but you are not. Your day of reckoning will come."

Astounded, Kelda gazed at the woman. "I would think you would be glad that I will be one less woman in Asgaut's life that you will have to worry about, Brunhild," Kelda said.

"I was not worried about you." The woman spat the words at Kelda. "I am more worried about the Irish thrall Asgaut has for his bed-thrall than I am you."

Surprised, Kelda asked, "You wanted me to marry Asgaut?"

"Naturally! Once you had delivered a son for Asgaut, he would have no need of you. Your usefulness would be spent. As the first wife, I rule the house. As first wife and as Thoruald's niece-by-marriage your child—Thoruald's grandchild—would be in my care."

Her hands clenched into fists, and she inched closer to Kelda. "I would have been the most important woman in the steading. Eventually Asgaut and I would have inherited Falconstead. We would have been the lord and lady of the manor. You are trying to ruin that, but you will not."

Kelda had never liked Brunhild, but she had not known the depth of the woman's hatred for her. She wanted to back up and get out of her way, but she would not allow Brunhild to know she was fright-

314

ened of her.

The pale eyes gleamed strangely. "When Asgaut returns, he will challenge your Skrelling. When he wins, you will be his again. Think long and hard upon these words, Kelda."

The woman spun around and marched to the door. Her palm pressed against the heavy wood, she said over her shoulder, "I have sickness in the long-house tonight, so I will not be at the banquet. Please give my apologies to my uncle. I am sure he will understand."

"Aye," Kelda murmured, "I am sure he will."

"Nay, lord," Wild Flower said, laughing softly, "I care not to share your chambers with you. Even if I must climb stairs outside the *stofa* to one of the loft rooms, I will sleep by myself."

"You care not?" Thoruald questioned, hiking a bushy brow.

"Perhaps I should have said, I dare not."

"You are a tease, lady."

Wild Flower laughed a little louder. "Try me, my lord."

Thoruald gave her a puzzled look, then asked, "Would you like to be mistress of the steading?"

"By being mistress do you mean that I am to assume responsibilities such as providing food and supervising the servants and slaves, and cleaning the house?" she asked.

Thoruald nodded. "That is part of it."

"Nay, I will have none of it. Let Kelda do it. As a guest I shall be waited upon, as mistress I must work."

Thoruald threw back his head and guffawed. When his laughing ended, he said, "I am glad you are here. You have brought joy to me that I have

315

not had in thirty winters." He clasped her hands. "I would have you be my lady-wife."

"It is too early for us to be discussing this subject, lord," Wild Flower murmured. "I have much thinking to do. Now, please show me to my chambers. I would rest before the banquet tonight."

"We do have another chamber within the Great Hall," Thoruald said, "but before I show it to you, I will take you to the bower and introduce you to the chief seamstress. She will sew you some dresses while you are here."

He escorted Wild Flower across the hall and knocked on the door. When Kelda answered, he hiked a brow.

"I thought you were with the—Sk—"

"With Brander," Kelda supplied coolly. "I was, but I have chores to do if we are going to have a proper celebration tonight. Also I wanted to see how Asa and the women had progressed on the making of winter clothes."

"Perhaps to see if you had new clothes to wear for the festivities tonight."

"Aye." Asa's cackle of laughter came from behind Kelda. Several garments hanging over her arm, she walked to the center of the room and laid them on the table. " 'Twas for new clothes she came, lord, but not necessarily a new dress for herself. She is looking for clothes for that son of yours."

"Have you any?" Thoruald asked.

"Aye," the old woman replied. "Some that will do quite well. He will look regal enough tonight for your feast, sire. He will do you proud."

She peered through the open door.

"You have a guest with you, sire?"

"Aye, this is Wild Flower," Thoruald said. "I want you to sew her some new dresses while she is staying with us."

316

Asa shuffled to the door and gazed curiously at Wild Flower. "Do you speak Norse also?" she asked.

Wild Flower nodded her head.

Asa caught her hand, tugged her into the room, and shut the door. "Good day, sire," she called loudly enough for him to hear on the other side. "I will need to close the door and be about my work if I have her a dress by dinner tonight."

She led Wild Flower to the window and turned her around several times. Taking a cord from her pocket, she circled Wild Flower's body in different places, murmuring to herself.

"Mistress," she said to Kelda, "I have a dress that I have been sewing for you. With a little work I could have it ready for the — for —"

"Please call me Wild Flower," the Iroquois said.

Asa nodded and smiled. "I could have it ready for Mistress Wild Flower to wear to the banquet." Warming to her subject, she said, " 'Tis that yellow material. I never did think it would be that complimentary on you. It would look better on her with her dark coloring."

"Then alter it for her," Kelda said.

"Aye," Asa mumbled, "this will look beautiful on her. It reminds me of the flowers that bloom in the pasture during early spring." Asa laughed. "Mistress Wild Flower, you will look just like a yellow wildflower."

Wild Flower closed her eyes, but could not close out the vision of the warrior walking toward her, his arms full of dandelions, his eyes full of love. She blinked back the tears.

Where did her dreams end? Where did reality begin?

317

Chapter Twenty-six

"A toast to the jarl's son!"

The shout resounded through the crowded hall. Vikings sat along the benches on the long walls. Their jarl sat in his high seat on a dais, an open chest of treasure beside him. The two seats on either side of him were notably empty, the chairs where Brander and his mother would sit. On the left, on the other side of Wild Flower's vacant chair, sat a glum Canby, muttering in his ale tankard.

"Aye," others echoed, "a toast."

Laughing, Thoruald stood. "Now that you have been rewarded, 'tis time for a toast, but be patient a while longer, my warriors. Wait until the jarl's son and his other guest of honor are present."

"Is the jarl's son going to present himself?" a seasoned warrior bellowed from across the room. "Mayhap he is afraid of us."

"Aye," others shouted, their words finally drowned out by raucous laughter and jokes about the lack of courage possessed by the Skrelling.

Kelda moved to stand behind her adopted father. Grasping the handle of the pitcher, she refilled his glass goblet. He presented a tough face to his men, but he was worried. When she laid her hands on his shoulders, she felt the tenseness that gripped his body, the anger. Brander was pushing Thoruald. Deliberately. She wondered how long Thoruald would be patient, how long he would contain his anger.

She also wondered how long Brander would keep them waiting.

She had been so busy since she arrived home, she had scarcely seen him. While he was bathing she had gone to Asa and gotten clothes for him which she laid out on the bed along with jewelry Hauk had brought to him—his share of the booty from several rich raids with Thoruald. When she had returned to the room later, the clothes and jewelry were still lying on the bed, but Brander was gone. She had not seen him since.

Kelda also wondered what was keeping Brander's mother. When she had stopped by Wild Flower's chamber earlier to offer her assistance in dressing and combing her hair, the woman had assured her that all was well and she would make her appearance shortly.

A loud remark about the Skrelling followed by laughter caught Kelda's attention and brought her thoughts back to the banquet. She filled Thoruald's tankard again, then Canby's. The jesting continued. The taunts grew in intensity.

"I would like to see this Skrelling. This man who Ulmer sings about. Who defies the gods." One of the Vikings pushed away from the table. He dropped his leg of mutton on his plate and wiped his hand down the side of his trousers.

"Aye, Baldur," several shouted.

He drew his arm across his grease-matted beard, then waved a full horn of ale through the air. "I could squash him with my thumb as if he were a pismire."

319

"Would you like the opportunity to try, Viking?"

Kelda lifted her head to see Brander walking into the *stofa*, Hauk behind him. Tension seemed to drain out of Thoruald. He sighed, then lifted his goblet and emptied it in one swallow of ale.

Revelry ceased. The only noise to be heard were the footfalls of Brander and Hauk as they moved through the Great Hall. All eyes were on Brander.

As Kelda had determined to have a victorious display when she sailed into port, Brander was now creating his own grand entrance into the Great Hall. In absolute control of himself, he guided every reaction in the room.

His hair was combed back from his face, the length of it brushing against the cowl of the deep purple mantle that swung loose from his broad shoulders. More elegant than anything she had seen him wearing were the white shirt, decorated with delicate embroidery of purple and gold stitching, tight-fitting black breeches, and black boots of soft leather.

No one had spoken since he asked the question. Yet no one had forgotten the challenge implicit in it. The Viking set the horn tankard down and lifted an arm to wipe his sleeve over his mouth and beard. His eyes narrowed as Brander moved closer to him.

"A toast to Brander, the Firebrand, the jarl's son!" Thoruald rose from his chair and lifted his newly filled goblet in the air.

Several joined in the shout and rose, but Brander waved a silencing hand. "Nay, Thoruald, 'tis not the time for the toast. Your Viking has yet to answer my question." Brander pinned the man to the wall with a dark gaze. "Would you like the

320

opportunity to squash me as you would a pismire?"

The Viking stood his ground, his eyes swiftly running up and down Brander's tall physique.

"I challenge you to sport, Viking," Brander said, "and I choose sport only because this is a grand occasion for the lord of the manor and his lady. I will do nothing to spoil their festivities."

"Mistress Kelda isn't the lady of the manor." Baldur finally spoke.

"I am not speaking of her. I am speaking of Mistress Wild Flower of the Iroquois." Brander turned and held out his hand. "I would escort my mother to her place beside the jarl. Then, Viking, I shall return to this matter at hand."

Wild Flower moved out of the shadows into the light, and Kelda gasped as did Thoruald. Wild Flower's coloring was a perfect foil for the yellow silk that shimmered in the torchlight. Cut low in front, according to Norse fashion, the soft material revealed her breasts and clung to her slender form to accent her height.

Her hair was pulled high in an elaborate coil that was worked around a diadem and held in place with glittering pins. Long, delicate earrings brushed against her bare shoulders and the gold-and-pearl necklace she wore.

Thoruald rose, and Kelda had to step around him to see the spectacular entrance of mother and son, their heads high, their strides regal. Brander led her to his father's side. She placed her hand in Thoruald's.

"Truly you are beautiful, my lady," the Viking chieftain murmured, unable to drink his fill of this woman's beauty.

"Thank you, my lord." Wild Flower laid her

321

hand in his.

Light to her back shone through the material, and Thoruald saw the outline of her slender form. He breathed deeply and remembered all the wonderful secrets of her body. He wanted to know them all again, this time in more detail, this time more leisurely.

"You are more than worth the wait," he murmured.

"I had planned for you to think so, lord."

She laughed, her voice soft and melodious. It teased Thoruald and reminded him how long he had been without a woman, how long since he had truly wanted a woman.

"The Iroquois girl was fascinating," Thoruald confessed, "but the woman is captivating. You are bewitching me."

"I truly hope so," Wild Flower murmured. "Again that is my intention. I want to ensnare you completely, so that you will belong to no one else, Viking, until you journey to the halls of Odin. Even then I want you to be so full of me that you will not even be happy with a Valkyrie, but will wait for me to join you."

"Why would a man want a heavenly maiden when he can have you," Thoruald said. "You build a big fire in me. Can you put it out as quickly, as efficiently as you built it?"

"In due time we shall see." Wild Flower turned her head and smiled at the lawreader. "I am glad to see you again, Canby. How are you faring since we arrived home?"

"I am not faring too well, mistress," he answered absently.

Holding his tankard in both hands, raised and almost to his lips, Canby glowered at Brander

322

who stood in front of the table with his arms crossed over his chest. Rather than drink, Canby contemplated.

Thoruald also turned his attention to his son. He was proud of him, immensely proud that he was independent and rebellious. Only a man secure in himself could lead the robust Vikings. Thoruald's people needed someone strong like Brander.

Yet the lad needed to be whittled down to size. He was far too big for his britches. Humility served a leader well also.

"And you, Skrelling, did you also wish to make a woman's late entrance to gain the attention of the men?" Thoruald shouted.

A twitter of laughter sounded through the hall.

"Unless you wish to be called a derogatory name in front of your warriors and subjects, Jarl Thoruald, never refer to me again as a Skrelling. You may address me as an Iroquois, but not as a barbarian."

Those ebony eyes that held sparks of deep blue pierced Thoruald's. They defied; they challenged.

Brander turned, the purple mantle sweeping dramatically through the air.

"If I hear any of you referring to my mother as a Skrelling or in a derogatory manner, you will answer to me. Know this, Vikings, I have been taught to be both an Iroquois and a Viking warrior. *If I go down* . . . I will not go down easily. I will take many with me."

Now Brander's gaze rested on the Viking who yet stood in the center of the building.

"Have you chosen your sport yet?"

"Aye," Baldur answered with a slight slur as he staggered toward Brander. "Arm wrestling."

323

The words were hardly out of his mouth before the Vikings—their faces lit with grins that told Brander to beware of his opponent—were shuffling around. Hauk directed several of them to bring in a small table and set it in the center of the room. They placed a chair on either side.

When Brander was sitting across the table from Baldur, Hauk recited the rules. Both contestants rolled their sleeves up and braced their elbows on the table, right hand clasping right hand. Their grips tightened. They strained and began to do battle.

Baldur had little trouble swaying Brander's hand to the left. Brander's face turned red; the veins strutted. He clenched his teeth together and grunted, pushing against Baldur's hand with all his might. The Viking was tough. Brander could not budge his arm.

Laughter sounded through the hall. All thought Baldur's victory would be quick and effortless.

With a great surge of power, Brander swung the Viking's arm back up. Baldur grunted, heaved, and pushed Brander's down once again. It swayed dangerously close to the table, but his flesh did not touch down.

Kelda held her breath as did everyone else in the building. All knew Baldur was the champion arm wrestler. No one had the strength in their arms that he did.

The Viking drew in a deep breath, grunted, then snarled, pushing against Brander's hand. Brander held fast. Slowly he pushed until their arms were once again perpendicular to the table.

Hauk moved around the table, monitoring them closely.

With a deep breath and a gasp of pleasure,

324

Brander swept Baldur's hand to the table and held it. Hauk hit the table with his hand.

"The Iroquois chieftain has won!"

Baldur sat for a second, staring at Brander in disbelief. Then he threw back his head and laughed. Finally he said, "Chieftain, I challenge you to another game when I am not so drunk. I promise I will give you a better competition."

"Agreed."

Brander rose amid the cheers of the Vikings. He walked to the vacant chair reserved for him. Before he sat down, he raised the full tankard of ale.

"Brander of the Iroquois would like to make a toast to the jarl and his lady."

Thoruald glared blackly at Brander, but he rose, held out his hand to Wild Flower so that she stood beside him. He lifted his goblet high in the air and echoed the toast.

All drank to it, even Brander who took only a sip of the vile tasting liquid. He wondered how the Vikings could devour so much of it. No wonder he had won a quick victory over his opponent. His senses had been numbed by the drink.

"Now," Thoruald shouted, "we drink to the jarl's son."

All shouted the words time and again. All drank but one. Brander's tankard remained untouched.

Kelda came to stand behind him. "You are determined to make this hard on your father and mother, are you not?"

"Do not attempt to find a soft spot in my heart for the jarl, mistress." Brander caught her hand in his and twined their fingers together. "You are beautiful tonight, but I would rather you wore

325

your hair loose than braided and twisted in that coil."

"I am no longer a maiden," she said. "I wear it this way to let men know I am not for the asking."

Brander's gaze brushed over the low cut gown that revealed her creamy breasts. "If your hair is saying that, mistress, your dress is contradicting it. It truly lets a man know you are his for the taking. In the future, I do not wish you to wear dresses that reveal so much of your body."

Kelda tugged her hand, but he did not turn it loose.

"Where is your chair?" he asked.

"The women do not sit with the men," she answered.

"My mother is sitting with Thoruald."

"She is his guest of honor," Kelda replied. "As mistress of the house, it is my pleasure to wait on Thoruald's guests."

"It is my pleasure that you wait on none but me and that you sit beside me."

"I can sit at your feet," she answered.

"And be hid under the table like a dog," he scoffed. "I want you where I can look upon your beauty, not kick you."

Kelda smiled as if she enjoyed taunting him with their customs. "That cannot be done, *sire.*"

Brander pushed back in his chair, strode across the *stofa,* into their bed chamber. *Cannot be done,* he thought. *Little does the Viking woman know how determined I am to have my own way, or to what lengths I will go to have it.*

Kelda gaped when Brander returned to the Great Hall with one of the chairs from their chamber. As purposefully as he strode out of the *stofa*, he strode back and set the chair down with a loud—deliberately loud—thud beside his. Still standing, he brought her to his side.

"I Brander, War Chief of the Iroquois, have taken Kelda, adopted daughter of the jarl, as my mistress. She is going to sit with me because I desire it. For all to see she wears my gold collar about her neck as a sign that she belongs to me."

Although Kelda knew the rumor had spread through the steading, this was a formal announcement. She noted the surprise that registered on the people's faces, as rumor became fact, as deed became defiance. Heads turned; whispers buzzed; but none spoke aloud.

"I challenge any man who says she does not or should not belong to me," Brander said.

Baldur laughed, his hand once again waving through the air, ale spilling over the brim of his horn tankard. "You may have won in sport, Iroquois, but taking a man's betrothed isn't considered sport in our steading. You aren't going to have to face any of us, since it is yours and Kelda's affair. But you are going to have to face the *Jomsviking*, and he isn't an easy one to defeat. None of us here would challenge him."

Kelda felt Brander's arm slide around her back, his fingers curl around her waist.

"But I am not any of you, and I wanted his betrothed. So I do challenge him."

"What say you, Thoruald?" another Viking called.

Kelda glanced down the table to see Wild Flower gazing sadly at her son. Thoruald was looking straight ahead. He took a long drag of ale, returned his goblet to the table, and gazed around at his subjects.

"I say let the outcome of the challenge be our answer. May the best man win." He turned to his lawreader. "Would you speak, Canby?"

The lawreader rose, recited the laws pertaining to fornication and the challenge. Heaviness settled upon the assemblage at his pronouncements. Again rumblings of discontent could be heard.

As Thoruald had done before him, Canby gazed quietly at the gathering. "I have discussed this with the jarl, and he and I are in agreement. As we settle many things by ordeal, we shall settle this one by the outcome of the challenge. The man who is victorious gets the woman. At his demand the shame can be lifted from her name or he can exact punishment for her—namely death."

"But," Hauk said, rising for the first time, "she is the jarl's daughter. Surely, Canby—"

The lawreader held up his hand for silence. "The law is for all, Viking, not a few."

Kelda rose, her gaze also skimming the crowd. "I have chosen the path I walk. Whatever the consequences, I accept them."

Out of the corner of her eye, she saw Thoruald drop his head and sigh. His wound and the death of his son had aged him. There was a frailty—nay, perhaps a vulnerability—about him that she had never viewed before this last journey. She wanted to run to him and let him know that all would be well.

But she did not have to. Wild Flower laid her hand on his arm, her almond-colored skin in dark contrast with the white material. She touched her head to his and whispered in his ear. Thoruald smiled and nodded. Kelda was glad he had the woman to comfort him.

Thoruald rose and lifted a goblet full of ale into

the air. "Drink up, Vikings. Let us be merry this night."

"Aye," they cried in unison, tankards lifted for another toast . . . and another.

The merrymaking continued, but Brander was not a part of it. He leaned back in the chair and through hooded eyes watched the Norsemen. Finally he leaned over to Kelda.

"Shall we retire?" he asked.

" 'Tis poor manners to leave so early," she pointed out.

"It is better manners to fall asleep in your chair?" he countered.

"I am not falling asleep, sire," she said sweetly, smiling at him. "The most interesting event is about to occur."

Suddenly the shouting and laughter died away. Ulmer, dressed in brightly colored shirt, trousers, and mantle strolled to the center of the *stofa*, his lyre in hand. A large smile on his face, he stopped in front of Kelda and bowed.

"This is the Viking hero of whom I shall sing," he shouted, drawing his fingers across the strings of the musical instrument, the soft, sweet sounds echoing through the room. " 'Tis her valor and cunning that saved the Vikings and captured the jarl's Skrelling son."

Amid the clapping and cheering, Ulmer turned and began to sing about the recent voyage to Skrellingland. In the hush, those assembled listened, spellbound.

"Ulmer is a great poet," Kelda whispered to Brander. "People will remember this for years to come."

Brander gave her a dark look, and she laughed.

"You are not enjoying the poet, sire?"

329

When Ulmer sang about Kelda's giving the sleeping herbs to Brander and kidnapping him, the Vikings—Thoruald included—roared with laughter. Kelda and Wild Flower smiled . . . finally so did Brander. The noise of the laughter was so great Ulmer stopped his singing.

He held his hand up. "Cease your noise!" he shouted. "I have not finished my tale."

He laid his lyre on a nearby table and began to walk to-and-fro looking into the faces of the warriors as if searching for one in particular. He stopped in front of Kelda and Brander.

"I sing this night of another hero, Brander, the war chief of the Iroquois and the jarl's son."

Ulmer tugged his shirt from his trousers. Rolling it up his back, he said, "Look at the scar that runs across my shoulders." Enjoying the attention, he strutted up and down the building, displaying his wound. "Had it not been for the Iroquois chieftain, this *skald* would be doing no singing tonight. You would not be hearing this tale of valor."

He dropped his shirt, moved to the table and picked up his lyre, again strumming it. His voice lifted in song as he told them the brave deeds of the man who defied the gods.

Sitting back in her chair, Kelda watched the expressions of the Vikings as they listened. Truly they were in awe of this man who feared no one.

Ulmer ran his fingers across the strings, waiting until the music quieted to say, "This warrior is the one to challenge a *Jomsviking*. Truly he and Kelda should be together. They are valiant to the death. Although the Iroquois does not believe in the gods, Odin, god of war, sees his great deeds and will take him with Kelda of the Vikings to Val-

330

halla when they enter the Hall of the Slain."

When the last strain of music died out and Ulmer's words no longer sounded through the Great Hall, the Vikings shouted and cheered. To show their pleasure they slapped their hands against the table.

Thoruald reached into his chest and pulled out some jewelry. "Here, *skald*," he said and tossed Ulmer two gold hand rings, a brooch, an arm band, and a necklace. "You have earned your gold tonight. Stay around. Perhaps we will want another tale later."

The Vikings filled their tankards again and toasted the *skald*. They continued to shout and clap their praises. The entrance door to the Great Hall opened with a thud that sounded above the noise, but only served to pause it. A woman dragged another woman in front of Thoruald's table.

"Brunhild," Kelda whispered to Brander.

"Asgaut's first wife?" he asked.

Kelda nodded.

Pushing the white-uniformed captive to the floor, the woman stood, her feet straddled, both hands planted firmly on broad hips. "I demand justice, Jarl Thoruald."

Now the assembly quieted and strained to hear the conversation between jarl and subject. Brander gazed in compassion at the tiny woman who trembled before the jarl. She was beautiful, her darkness setting her apart from the Vikings.

"She is Irish," Kelda informed him. "Asgaut captured her during his last raid. She has since become his bed-thrall. All the men in the steading and the nearby village are jealous of him."

"Aye," Brander replied dryly, "I should imagine

they would be."

Kelda had always thought Lind to be beautiful, but tonight she was seeing her in an altogether different manner, perhaps as a man would see her. Tiny, dark, and voluptuous. Her breasts were large and round, and strained at the confining material of her dress. Never had Kelda seen a slave's white uniform look so seductive.

"The men have bartered for her, wanting her as their bed-thrall, but Asgaut seems to genuinely love her. He refuses to sell her for any weight of gold or silver. Rumor has it that Asgaut will make her his newest bride."

"This Asgaut may not have much of a brain," Brander said, "but he must have a powerful weapon to satisfy so many women."

Kelda laughed softly.

"Brunhild," Thoruald said, "welcome to the banquet. Kelda tells me that you have sickness in your longhouse."

"Aye, lord," she replied. "While I was tending the ones who are ill, this ingrate was up to no good."

Thoruald peered at the slave. "Is this not your thrall, Lind?"

"Aye," the woman answered. "One of my karls caught her trying to escape with Asgaut's favorite steed."

A murmur rumbled through the assembly. Stealing was not looked upon lightly. Stealing a horse called for the death penalty.

After a moment of silence, Thoruald asked, "Lind, what say you."

"I am not guilty, lord." Tears streamed down her face. "I love my master. I would not run away from him, no matter that my mistress mistreats

332

me when he is away a-viking, and I certainly would not steal his favorite steed."

"Stealing a horse is a crime that calls for death," Brunhild shouted.

"But she did not escape with the horse," Thoruald pointed out.

"I demand her life. I want Lind killed for the crime she committed."

Canby leaned forward and spoke quietly. "Brunhild, do you not hate this woman because she is Asgaut's bed-thrall?"

"Aye, 'tis a fact."

"Why not accept *wergild* and allow the thrall to live since she did not escape with the horse?"

"She attempted to steal it," Brunhild insisted. "Our laws are strict and merciless when it comes to a man's horse, sire."

"Asgaut will be angry with you when he returns and finds her dead," Canby pointed out. "So angry he would take it out on you."

"Aye," Brunhild admitted, "that is so. But who would buy a slave who was running away on a stolen horse? Not a Norseman."

With Brunhild's words still resounding throughout the building, the woman turned her gaze to Brander. Everyone else focused on him, too.

"Chieftain," Brunhild said, "it is in your power to save this beautiful child. By taking my husband's betrothed as your mistress, you have already issued a challenge to my husband Asgaut. Why not fight for two women as well as the one?"

Kelda's gaze, as did Lind's, riveted to Brander. The thrall raised tiny hands and wiped tears from her eyes. She moved her body—deliberately, Kelda thought—so that her curves were completely revealed by the clinging material.

333

"Please, my lord," she begged. "I shall be a good thrall for you. I was pleasing to Asgaut, so pleasing he made me his bed-thrall."

"Aye," Brander said, "I can believe that. How much is the *wergild?*"

"While Brunhild is contemplating—" Canby rose and moved to the platform behind the chairs "—I will get the scales."

Angry because Brander was showing public interest in the woman, Kelda leaned over and whispered, "How dare you humiliate me in front of the entire steading."

"How am I humiliating you?" he asked, speaking as softly as she.

"If I am your mistress, why do you have need of a bed-thrall?"

Brander laughed and brushed his hand against her neck. "If I should buy her, Viking, I do not have to make her my bed-thrall."

"Whether you do or not," Kelda said angrily, "everyone here will think so."

"What would you have me do?" he asked. "Let her be killed because her mistress is jealous?"

Kelda leaned closer to him. "I have promised myself that I will be the only wife of my husband. I will not share him with bed-thralls or mistresses. Until I am an only wife, I will be an only mistress. I will not share your chamber with Lind."

Again Brander laughed and leaned over to lightly kiss her lips. Kelda closed her eyes and wished she were stronger when it came to the Iroquois warrior. A part of her wanted to pull away from his touch. Another part—the greater part—wanted to fling herself against him, to have more than a kiss, to prove to him that he had no need of a bed-thrall.

334

"Open your eyes," he commanded.

She did.

"You are beautiful, my little Viking, when your eyes are sparkling with anger."

Not anger, sire. Jealousy. An emotion with which she had been totally unfamiliar until tonight, until she saw the way he was looking at Lind, at the way Lind was looking at him and trying to lure him with her body.

Kelda straightened in the chair and gazed straight ahead. "My words are true."

Chapter Twenty-seven

"How much do you want for the thrall, Brunhild?" the lawreader asked. Never looking at the woman, he placed metal weights to one side of the scales.

Brunhild named her price—an exorbitantly high one, Kelda thought, for such a little woman—and grinned at Brander. Anger surged through Kelda when she saw him finger the jewels he wore. Jewels Hauk had given to him out of his private coffer.

"Well, Skrelling," Brunhild said, her eyes sliding back and forth between him and Kelda, "are you going to buy the thrall?"

Silence, heavy like a blanket in the summer, fell over the banquet hall. The room was suffocating. Kelda could hardly breathe as she awaited Brander's decision.

"Brunhild!" Thoruald spoke, his voice thundering through the quietness. "I will buy the thrall from you."

The woman's eyes opened wide and she stared in shocked surprise at her chieftain.

"Nay, lord," Brunhild cried. "You cannot."

He raised a bushy brow. "I cannot!"

"My dear uncle, Jarl Thoruald, please reconsider. You are a Norseman." Her hand waved to encompass those who sat in the *stofa*. "These are your

336

men. They look up to you and your wisdom."

"All you have said, Brunhild, is fact. I am Norse. I am the jarl. These are my men who respect me." A scowl of displeasure on his face, Thoruald rose and glared down at her. "As long as I am jarl, I shall be the leader and do what I believe is right under the law. If any of these men disagree with my actions, they know what they can do."

Brunhild looked fearfully, yet hopefully, about the building. Not one moved to her defense.

"I am sorry, lord. I did not mean to speak out of turn or to displease you."

"I buy the thrall for Wild Flower. She will need someone to tend to her personal needs. My women thralls already have their duties, and I have no desire to overburden them." Thoruald sat down, reached into his chest and handed several silver rings to Canby. "Weigh these. Brunhild, it is time for you to return to your duties at your longhouse."

"Aye, sire," she mumbled, casting Kelda a venomous gaze before she hastened out of the Great Hall.

Kelda felt a smile begin at the bottom of her heart and blossom throughout her entire body. Brander chuckled softly and brushed his hand through her hair. Lind cast a disappointed glance at Brander, then moved to stand in front of Wild Flower.

"Come," Brander said to Kelda. "I would go to bed. I am exhausted, and do not enjoy this kind of entertainment."

"I would stay longer. The fun has only begun."

"Nay, mistress," Brander mocked. His hand curled around her wrist, and he gently tugged. "The fun has yet to begin, and it will not be in this Great Hall."

"I will stay," Kelda said softly. "Thoruald will be

337

angry if we leave early." She caught Brander's hand. "I know how you feel about your father, but please stay longer."

He shook his head. "I am ready for bed, Kelda. You may come with me or stay here with your father. The choice is yours."

Brander looked over at Lind, who smiled at him. She straightened her back, her breasts thrusting proudly against her bodice. Her nipples hardened. She lowered her lashes until her eyes were hooded and ran her tongue around her lips.

"The thrall wants you," Kelda said.

Brander grinned. "So it seems."

"What are your desires where she is concerned, *sire?*"

The grin broadened. "I find her to be a beautiful and alluring woman," he answered, "but I have the feeling that you are issuing me an ultimatum of some kind."

Kelda touched the gold collar about her neck. "I am your mistress because I have chosen to be, because I wish you to be my champion and to fight for my freedom from Asgaut. But I do not want that enough to share you with another woman. I may not be your wife, but by the gods, Brander, I will not knowingly share you with another. I will take my chances with the Herred-thing or with Asgaut."

Brander played with her hand, rubbing his thumb over her palm. She stared unflinchingly into his eyes.

"You are telling me what I must do, lady?"

"I am dictating the terms by which I shall remain your mistress."

He dropped her hand and rose. "I have to think on this matter, mistress. I am unaccustomed to anyone telling me what I can or cannot do."

Without turning her head, Kelda heard the clip of his boots on the floor as he strode down the *stofa*. She had no compassion in her heart for the Iroquois warrior. At the moment her compassion belonged to herself. She would not weaken her resolve in this instance.

"Sire," Lind called out and raced to join Brander at the end of Thoruald's serving table.

He stopped and waited for her to join him. Kelda gripped the armrests so tightly her fingers hurt and the carvings dug into her flesh. Having seen the way people behaved when they were jealous, Kelda had always scorned the emotion. Now she was eaten up with it and had to restrain herself from leaping to her feet and flying at Lind. She wanted to tear the girl away from Brander and to pull her hair from her head.

Kelda lifted the glass of ale to her lips and drank. She little cared whether she were sober or not. In fact, perhaps a little ale would ease the hurt she felt.

That Asgaut wanted to take Lind as his wife had bothered Kelda when she became betrothed to him, not because she was jealous of Lind but because she did not like sharing her husband with other women. At the time, under the circumstances, she had felt she had no other choice.

Now she seemed to be facing the same situation again, only this time it mattered. She hurt . . . deep inside.

Kelda held the glass to her lips and took long drags of the potent drink. She refilled the glass and drank more, hoping it would lessen the pain. It did not.

Out of the corner of her eye, she saw the thrall

339

fawning over Brander. She leaned against him, brushing her palms over his chest. Brander caught her hands in his and held them still. He said something. Both looked at Kelda. Brander smiled; Lind laughed. Tove joined them, and Brander spoke to her. The two thralls disappeared into the shadowed recesses of the hall.

Brander walked to his mother's chair, leaned over and whispered to her, then returned to where Kelda sat. He stood behind her, his hands on the backrest of the chair.

"Have you thought about my words?" Kelda asked. "Or would you have me demonstrate my charms to you as the thrall did?"

Brander laughed. When she lifted the glass to her lips, he took it from her and set it on the table.

"At the rate you are drinking this," he said, "you will have no sensibilities left. You will be acting as ridiculous as your father's warriors."

"Are you going to answer my question?" She pushed back in her chair.

"I have thought about your words," he murmured, "and although I do wish a display of your charms, I do not want it out here, my sweet. I want them displayed when we are alone in our chamber."

"What about the thrall?"

"She understands that I have a mistress to keep my bed and body warm and that I am in no need of a bed-thrall."

Kelda could not help the smile that tilted the corners of her mouth. Her heart felt lighter than it had since Brander had announced to Canby that she was his mistress.

"I have informed my mother that I sent her to her chamber where she is to await her lady."

Although only a mistress, Kelda knew she meant

340

enough to him that he believed her where Lind was concerned.

"I am ready to retire, sire," she said. Her smile widened when she heard Brander's intake of breath and saw the depth of emotion in his eyes.

They were standing behind Thoruald and Wild Flower bidding them a good night, when the doors to the Great Hall opened a second time and a burly warrior entered the room. Laughing and waving, he walked directly to Thoruald.

"I came as soon as I received word, Thoruald. You have caused me a good day's ride."

"Aye, Gannar, I did inconvenience you," Thoruald said. "For that I apologize, but I am not sorry."

A young boy, walking between two more Vikings, entered the room. His features were dark and appeared even darker in contrast to the fair-colored men who escorted him. His black hair was cut short in Norse fashion.

His crimson mantle, secured about his neck with an amber brooch, swung about his legs and was parted to reveal his white shirt and brown breeches. His boots clipped cadence on the flooring with his escorts. Looking at the high seat, he smiled.

"My lady wanted to see her grandson," Thoruald added.

"He is the one we call Kolby," Kelda said.

Brander stepped forward, his eyes riveted to the boy. The Great Hall quieted. It was closed and stuffy as tension mounted. Kelda kept her gaze fastened to Brander. She wanted to touch him to reassure him, but knew he would reject any public overtures of assurance or comfort—if need be—from her.

"Eirik!" Brander exclaimed, love thick in the one word.

341

"Eirik," Thoruald repeated. "He was named after my father?"

"Aye," Wild Flower said. "Ever powerful. Ever ruler. Like his fathers before him, and his sons after him."

The boy looked at the high seat and smiled. "Sire," he called out and raced to the dais.

"Eirik!" Brander stepped into the boy's path.

The boy stopped short to look curiously at him. Without any sign of recognition, he stepped around Brander and rushed to hug his grandfather first, then Kelda.

"I am so glad you are home, Kelda," the lad said. "I missed you, as did Grandfather."

"I missed you," she said.

Kelda saw the stricken look on Brander's face, and her heart went out to him. At times she had doubted his love for the boy, but now she knew how deep that love was.

Kolby looked from Brander to Wild Flower, then back to Kelda. "You brought two Skrellings home with you?"

"Skrellings!" The word was more ominous than the boom of thunder. It was as deadly as the strike of lightning.

Brander caught the child by the shoulders. "Know you not that you are a Skrelling? That your name is not Kolby but Eirik?"

The lad's eyes darkened. He gazed into Brander's face, then looked over his shoulder at Thoruald. "Sire, is he telling me the truth?"

"Aye," Thoruald said.

"I am Eirik," the boy said, stumbling over the name as if it were unfamiliar to him.

"Aye," the Viking chieftain said. "You were named Eirik after my father, a proud warrior, a valiant leader of the Vikings."

The boy smiled. "I shall be called Eirik." He looked at Brander. "Take your hands off me, Skrelling. I am the grandson of Jarl Thoruald, heir to the Talon of the Falcon."

"Call me not Skrelling," Brander instructed, "or you shall be punished. You may be the grandson of the jarl, but you are my son."

Eirik's eyes rounded. "Grandfather, is he telling the—"

"Do not ask him that one more time, Eirik," Brander said. "I do not lie. The woman sitting next to the jarl is your grandmother, Wild Flower, the Woman of Dreams."

Eirik studied both of them, then said, "I do not remember you."

"Come," Brander said, his hand clasping Eirik's shoulder, "we will go to my chambers. I would talk with you."

Eirik shook his head. "I do not want to go. I want to stay with my grandfather."

"Go with your father," Thoruald said kindly.

Eirik stared at his grandfather a long time before he nodded his head. Brander held out his hand. When the boy refused to take it, Brander stiffened. Kelda laid her hand on his arms.

"Please do not be too disappointed," she whispered. "Give him time to know you again."

"Which chamber are you sleeping in?" Eirik asked.

"Mine," Kelda answered.

The boy turned and walked across the Great Hall. Brander and Kelda followed. When the door closed, Brander turned to Eirik but did not touch him.

"What would you say to me?" Eirik demanded.

343

Gone was the Iroquois boy Brander had known. Standing in front of him was a Viking child.

"On your right upper arm," Brander said, "is the tattoo of a falcon. It is my totem, the one I had marked on you when you became an Iroquois warrior. When you lived in Forestland, you wore a gold arm band on that arm. The arm band matches the necklace that Kelda is now wearing."

"I am not an Iroquois. I am Norse, like my grandfather," Eirik said, but he walked closer to Kelda to peer at the gold collar.

Brander pulled his shirt sleeve up to expose the falcon on his arm. "Roll your sleeve up," he ordered, "and compare the two markings."

Eirik moved closer and peered curiously at the tattoo. He backed away, pushed his sleeve up and removed the arm band to look at his. "I do not remember."

Someone knocked, and Kelda opened the door for Wild Flower. She entered the room with her leather satchel.

Smiling at Eirik, she said, "I brought some of your possessions from the Forestland in hopes they would help you remember."

"You are my grandmother?" he asked.

She nodded and began to pull out personal items that had belonged to Eirik.

"How are you my grandmother?"

"I was married to Thoruald," she answered. "Brander is our son and your father." She laid a necklace on the table. "Your favorite," she said.

He touched it but showed no recognition.

"The small peace pipe that Delling gave you."

Eirik took it, held it in his fingers, turning it over several times. "What does one do with this?"

Item after item she showed him, but he remembered none of them. Kelda looked up at Brander, who leaned a shoulder against the wall and stared at his son. She could see the defeat in his expression.

Wild Flower brought out several game pieces and laid them on the table. She was hunting through her bag when Eirik picked up one and studied it. She brought out the pegged board and set it next to the playing pieces.

He smiled and began to set up the board. All was in place but one figure, and Wild Flower continued to riffle through the bag.

"Do not look for it," Eirik said. "I lost it. I was going to carve another, but—"

"But I promised you that I would do it," Brander said, his voice hopeful. "Do you remember, Eirik? We went hunting together so that we could find—"

Eirik shook his head wildly and backed away from the table. His gaze went from Wild Flower to Brander to Kelda. She saw the fear in the depth of his ebony eyes and reached for him, but Brander moved between her and the child.

He knelt down to catch the boy by the shoulders. "I came to get you, Eirik, to take you back home."

"Nay," Eirik said, "I do not want to go to Skrellingland. This is my home. I am Norse, not Skrelling." He flattened his palms against Brander's chest and shoved. "You are not my father. You are not. I am going to my grandfather."

Eirik ran out the door. Brander went to follow, but Kelda caught him.

"Nay," she said. "Leave him alone, Brander. Do not force him, or he will come to hate you."

"She is right," Wild Flower said. "Only time and love can heal Eirik's memory. He has adopted a new life which with our coming is threatened. He

345

feels lost once again and confused."

Brander moved to the window and stood looking out. The breeze blew strands of hair across his forehead. Kelda joined him.

"He does not recognize me," he muttered.

"Not yet," Wild Flower said.

Kelda placed her hands on his back to rub soothingly. "He remembered the missing game piece. Be patient with him. He will remember you."

"By the time he remembers, he will be more Norse than Iroquois." Brander placed his fist against the window casing. "He has bonded with the Norsemen and has no desire to return home."

Wild Flower, having returned all Eirik's possessions to her leather bag, stood. "My son, whether you have accepted it or not, your destiny also lies on this side of the Great Water."

"Nay, woman."

"I shall go get the boy and ask Thoruald if he may stay at the steading until he gets accustomed to us."

She was standing at the open door when Thoruald approached, Eirik at his side.

"I heard you," he said, "and Eirik may stay with us."

Wild Flower smiled tenderly at the boy and reached out to touch his hair. "If it is all right with you, lord, I would like for him to sleep on the small bed in my room."

Thoruald cast her an enigmatic smile before he said, "He may, lady."

"Come, Eirik," Wild Flower said. "It is late and time for us to retire."

Eirik gazed solemnly at her. "What am I to call you?"

"For now," she said, "call me lady. Perhaps when

346

you know me better you will want to call me Grandmother."

"Yes, lady," he said. "I would like to do that."

When Eirik and Wild Flower had gone, Brander looked at Thoruald, hatred gleaming in his eyes.

"You are responsible for my son not knowing me or his grandmother. At the moment you may think your future is secure because you have your grandson, but do not rest too contentedly. Come next spring, I shall take Eirik and sail again to the Forestland. I shall return him to his land and his people."

"Nay," Thoruald said. "Odin brought the boy to me, and he will see you damned in hell before you take Eirik away from me."

"I have no fear of your gods, Viking," Brander said. "They have not the power to keep my son from me."

"You may not fear my gods," Thoruald said, "but you better fear me, Skrelling. I have the power to keep the boy here, and I will exert it. You will not leave Falconstead. I will give orders that you are not to have a ship, and I will kill the man who lends you a helping hand."

"You will not keep me here by force."

Thoruald gazed at him a long time before he grinned. "Nay, Brander, I will not keep you here by force. We will keep you here the same way we got you here."

Both looked at Kelda.

Thoruald laughed softly and closed the door.

Although merrymaking continued in the *stofa*, the sleeping chamber was quiet. The leaves rustling in the wind could be heard through the open window. His back to Kelda, Brander gazed into the darkness.

347

She walked up to him to encircle his waist with her arms and to press her cheek against his back. She wanted to console him, to assure him that all would be well where Eirik was concerned, but Kelda had no words to relay her thoughts. She knew only that she hurt for the man she held in her arms.

"I hate Thoruald," Brander said, and Kelda felt his tenseness. "He has destroyed my life."

Softly Kelda said, "Nay, Brander." *Nay, my love.* "He is the one who gave you life. He has never meant to harm you. I wish you would attempt to understand your father better."

"As always," Brander said, a bitter bite to his words, "you side with Thoruald."

"No," Kelda replied and straightened from him, "I side with you, Brander."

He turned.

"When I chose to be your mistress, I thought I was doing it because I wanted to be released from my sacred oath, and I did. But the reason why I wanted this was because—"

Kelda paused and gazed with longing into the saddened face of her lover. She traced the outline of thick, black brows and brushed back a strand of hair. She pressed her palm against his cheek, loving the feel of his warm flesh.

"The reason why I wanted this was because I love you," she whispered. "You are my life."

Even as she made her declaration of love, Wild Flower's words returned to haunt her. *Thoruald desires me. I love him.* Kelda knew the same was true for her and Brander, but at the moment he was hurting and hurting deeply. Everything he had ever cared about had been or was being taken away from him. He did not even have the security of being in a country or around people with which he was familiar.

His eyes, at the moment, reminded her of the first time she had seen him. They were that beautiful enigmatic color that hovers between midnight and black. They searched because he wanted to believe but did not dare.

"I love you, Brander, War Chief of the Iroquois." *You are not alone. Not ever.*

Kelda understood loneliness and the grief that comes with having a family snatched away from you. She had been tossed into the alien culture of her aunt and Oscar. In silence she had grieved the loss of her parents and had suffered a sense of humiliation because of Oscar's advances. She had blamed herself because the man kept forcing his attentions on her. She blamed herself because her aunt did, because in youth she was beautiful and desirable and her aunt was not.

The night Ragnar and Hauk had saved Kelda had been the lowest point of her life. She had savored the comfort of Ragnar's caring for her, of his having saved her. What Ragnar had given her was unconditional. He asked for no favors in return.

Tonight she gave pure, unconditional love to Brander.

"I love you, my handsome barbarian."

His lips curled into a smile. His eyes softened.

"I care for you, my beautiful Viking."

These were not the words she wanted or needed to hear, but they were the closest he had ever come to admitting love for her. Care was a beginning. In some cases care was enough.

Brander slipped a hand through her hair and combed it with his fingers. He smiled gently but sadly.

349

Aye, although her circumstances had been different from Brander's, the emotions she had suffered were one and the same. She understood his pain and grief. She identified with his loss. She, too, had felt alone and betrayed. She believed her betrayal was at the hands of the gods. Brander believed his to be human. It mattered not, both sensed the acuteness of betrayal.

Brander needed her support and love now. He needed to hear the words, the promise in them. The hope. She wanted him to know they were freely offered with no conditions.

He laid his hand over hers, and through narrowed lids studied her. "You will return to the Forestland with me and Eirik?"

Kelda could only stare at him through tear-blurred eyes. She had thought the Forestland bountiful with natural resources, but not one time had she contemplated living there. Always she had thought in terms of the Norsemen colonizing the new land or their using the resources.

Now this man whom she loved more than life was asking her to return to this foreign land, to live there as his wife, to adopt his people and his customs as hers.

It would grieve her to leave her people, but it would grieve her even more to lose Brander. She would be happier living in the Forestland with Brander than living in Norwegia without him.

"Aye, lord," she answered, "I will return to the Forestland with you and Eirik."

In the depth of his eyes she saw sadness.

"Lord, if by spring Eirik has not regained his memory, will you consent to leave him here with his grandparents?"

"Are you asking me to take you in exchange for

350

my son?"

Again the somber eyes searched hers.

She shook her head. "If Eirik does not regain his memory, sire, he will be most unhappy in Forestland. As you told me, your people will consider him weak-minded. Here, he will be the jarl's grandson. He will be heir to the Talon of the Falcon. He has a life and a future here, Brander, with a family who wants and needs him."

"You are so sure Wild Flower will remain," he said.

"She loves Thoruald." *As I love you.* "As his wife and as the Woman of Dreams, she will command great respect from our people. If something should happen to Thoruald, she will groom Eirik to be the jarl."

Brander caught her into his arms and held her close. He held her tight, burying his head in the curve of her neck and shoulder.

"Whether Eirik recognizes me or not, Kelda, you cannot know the grief it will cause me to leave him behind."

Her arms slid around him, and she pressed herself against him. She gave to him her warmth, her life, her love. She wanted to assuage his pain and grief.

"Because you are leaving him here in Norwegia with Jarl Thoruald?"

"Nay, because I am parting with my own life. Because I am leaving behind my own."

Kelda tangled her fingers in his hair to lift his head from her shoulder. He resisted, but she tugged all the harder. When she looked at his face, she saw a trace of tears on his cheeks, and she loved him all the more.

He had once confessed to her that the Iroquois

351

never showed emotions to anyone who was not their people. She was his *people*. For the first time since she had known him, Brander had let down the barrier that hid his inner self from her. This moment he was revealing his true vulnerability to her, his capacity to love.

She guided his lips to hers, tasting the salt of his tears as she tasted the hard, firm goodness of his mouth. Their kiss was long and hot and demanding. Brander greedily took her offering. She gave willingly. When he released her lips, she brushed her hand over his face. She felt the dampness of his tears.

"I warrant, the Norse have taken much from you," she whispered, unashamed that she cried with him, "and I can never give your family back to you. I can never replace them in your heart, but I will give you another love and another family. I will never leave you, my darling."

Brander crushed her to him. She thought surely she would suffocate he held her so tightly, but she uttered not a word of protest. Eventually he breathed deeply; he exhaled.

He moved his head slightly and gazed into her face. Laughing softly, the husky sound filling the room, he teased, "If you were planning to seduce me tonight, lady, there is no need."

"No need," she agreed, "but a strong desire to do so." She pulled his shirt from his breeches and brushed her hands up the warm, muscled ridges of his back. She also teased. "I wanted to prove to you, lord, that you have no need of a bed mate but me."

"I needed no proof, my beautiful Viking." He smiled tenderly and slipped his fingers through her hair. "I have been convinced of this ever since the day I saw you on the shores of the Forestland."

Lifting her into his arms as if she were more delicate than the crystal goblet out of which Thoruald drank his ale, he carried and deposited her on the bed. He stood, the torchlight to his back, and gazed down at her.

"Asgaut may have need of many wives and concubines, but I want and need only one." He slid onto the mattress beside her.

Kelda smiled and closed her eyes, feeling the warmth of his body stretched beside her. He had not declared his love for her, but she knew he cared.

"Tonight, my darling Kelda—"

My darling Kelda. He had never called her by an endearment like this before. Happiness seemed to sing through her veins.

"—I am going to show you a new and softer side to making love."

"Nay, lord, tonight I shall show you a new side to making love."

She tugged his shirt up and bent over him to trail her tongue moistly along his heated flesh. Brander groaned his pleasure as her mouth journeyed from his chest to his throat and finally to his ears and cheek. Her mouth teased but never claimed his.

"Kiss me," he murmured, his hands pressuring her back so that she was close to him, her breasts against his chest, her pelvis against the hardness of his arousal. "Kiss me now."

"Aye, lord," she whispered, low and throaty, her mouth covering his to taste his words as she tasted his lips, as her hand slipped into his trousers. "As you gave to me, I now give to you."

353

Chapter Twenty-eight

Not sure what had awakened her, Wild Flower sat up in bed, her long hair hanging loosely about her shoulders. She heard the sound again and knew she had been awakened by a soft knock. Wearing the white nightshirt Asa had provided for her, she hastened to answer the summons before Eirik awakened. She opened the door a crack to gaze at Hauk, the flicker of the torchlight revealing his worried countenance.

"Mistress," he whispered, "the jarl needs you. His body is fevered and he is in great pain. I cannot awaken him from his sleep and fear he is dying."

Wild Flower flung open the door. In the light from Hauk's torch that dimly illuminated the room, she searched for her medicine bag. With it in hand and without taking time to dress, she moved out of the sleeping room. Closing the door, she followed Hauk to Thoruald's chambers.

A torch burning in the sconce above the bed cast its light on the jarl of the steading. He was sprawled across the bed on his back, a coverlet barely across the middle portion of his body. His breathing was labored, his head and one side of his body periodically jerking. One of his hands was bailed into a fist, the other hung limply off the side of the bed.

Wild Flower touched his body; it was burning

with fever. Across his abdomen ran a large, jagged wound, the flesh around it red and proud. She gently probed. The skin was even hotter to the touch than the remainder of his body. He was not healing from the inside.

On one of the trunks was a pitcher and several glasses. She took a small basket out of her pouch and opened it, to pour powder into a glass. She stirred until she had a thick, cloudy solution.

"Help me hold him up," she said. "I want him to drink this. It will help bring his fever down."

Hauk caught Thoruald by the chest and shoulders and gently eased him into a sitting position. Between him and Wild Flower, they forced several swallows of the medicine down his throat.

She returned the glass to the trunk. "I would have many cloths for cleaning and wrapping," she said, "a large bowl of water and many little bowls for mixing."

Hauk nodded and silently disappeared from the room.

Wild Flower sat on the edge of the bed and brushed fever-dampened hair from Thoruald's face. She let her gaze lower to the thick growth of hair on his chest.

He groaned and flailed his arms and legs, kicking the cover from his body, yet he never unclenched his hand. Wild Flower gently replaced the cover, then rose and moved to the table where she opened her medicine pouch to search through her roots and herbs. Even as she laid them out, as she set out her tools, she knew medicine would not be enough to save the warrior's life.

She gazed out the open window into the blackness of night and felt the cool touch of the wind on her cheeks. She focused her eyes on the moon, the

355

beautiful silvered disc that cast its gentle light upon the steading. She took several deep breaths, closed her eyes, and sought the Spirits of Life. She must speak with them to learn what she could do to save Thoruald's life.

Because the Spirits of Life resided in all things, Wild Flower was not accustomed to seeing beings. Rather she saw the herbs she would need to administer to her patients. She envisioned herself opening her pouch and pouring her herbs on the table. She touched each one, her hand getting warm when she touched one that she needed for Thoruald. Although this exercise was mental not literal, Wild Flower trusted it implicitly and was happy that she had brought these herbs with her.

Still meditating, she envisioned Thoruald's wound and asked the Spirits of Life to let her see the area as it looked beneath the surface of the skin. When she beheld the inflammation, she winced and lost her concentration.

This was the first time she had treated one who was so close to her heart and who was so close to death. For the first time since she had become a shaman she feared for her patient's life. She doubted her ability to save him. But she was the only one who could.

Breathing deeper and relaxing, she closed her eyes and again prayed for the *sight* and for guidance. When she felt comfortable with what she knew she must do, she opened her eyes and began to work.

She was going through her herbs for the third or fourth time—she had lost count—when Hauk reentered the room, cloths draped over one arm, a tray full of bowls balanced on one hand, the torch in the other. Wild Flower took the cloths and tray

356

to set them on the table.

"Can you save him?" Hauk asked.

"Aye," Wild Flower said, her hands moving by habit to mix her herbs to create powders and pastes. "I would have a small fire," she said.

Hauk nodded and again departed to carry out her instructions. In a short time he returned with a shallow-bowled pottery dish which he set in the middle of the floor. As quickly, he piled in small pieces of wood, kindled them, and set them on fire. Wild Flower knelt, poured water into several of the bowls, then set them on the fringe of the fire to heat. She held a long, thin awl over the flames.

"Secure Thoruald to the bed," she ordered.

Hauk gave her a questioning gaze. "I do not think the jarl would like that, mistress."

She did not look up. "If he were awake and had his sensibilities about him, I would ask him his preference. I would let him choose to be the warrior. Since he is delirious from the fever, I cannot." She raised her head to gaze steadily into the eyes of the worried warrior. "I cannot take the chance that he will move. I am going to have to drain his wound."

Hauk looked at the awl. "You are going to pierce his belly with that?"

"Aye. The poison must be drained out before healing can take place."

"How do you know this?" Hauk asked. "Have you treated a wound like this before?"

She slowly shook her head. "The Spirits of Life have shown it to me."

"Mistress," Hauk said, fear in his eyes, in his voice, "if Jarl Thoruald should die, your life—"

"Aye," Wild Flower said, "it is the same with the Iroquois. If the patient dies, so does the shaman."

357

After a long, measured look, Hauk rose. "I will secure him."

Wild Flower continued to mix her herbs while Hauk worked behind her. Finally he returned and squatted at the fire with her.

"He is bound."

"Put several torches around the bed," she instructed, "while I move my salves over there."

In silence they worked, Hauk lighting the last of the torches as Wild Flower sat down on the bed next to Thoruald. She had moved the trunks so they formed a semicircle around her, her tools, medicines, and cleaning and binding cloths within hand reach.

Dipping a cloth into the basin of water and wringing it out, she washed Thoruald's face and chest. She gently dabbed around the wound.

" 'Tis bad," Hauk murmured, standing on the other side of the bed, looking down at his jarl.

"I have seen worse," she said. "We can be thankful your jarl is a strong man who will fight for his life. Falconstead needs him as does his son and grandson."

"I will help you," the old warrior said. "Tell me what to do."

"Get the awl," Wild Flower ordered. She bent her head to Thoruald's ear. "My love, I am going to lance the wound. It will hurt, but once the pain is gone, you will rest better. Your fever will break and your wound will heal. Believe in me."

She wrung out another cloth and laid it high across his forehead. Thoruald's lids opened, and fever-glazed blue eyes stared at her.

"Wild Flower," he mumbled, running his tongue around his dried and cracked lips.

She squeezed the rag so that drops of water ran

358

into his mouth. She pressed the cloth tenderly to his lips. "Aye, love, I am taking care of your wound."

"You are going to heal it?"

"Aye. I promise."

His gaze flicked over her, and his lips trembled in a semblance of a smile. Slowly his lids closed. His hand opened and an object dropped to the floor.

Wild Flower pressed her lips to his in a gentle, reassuring kiss.

She prayed to the Spirits of Life, thanking them for their guidance; then she lanced the wound and applied gentle pressure to drain the infection. Thoruald's face twisted in pain, but he never winced or uttered a word of protest, as if he were aware that his cooperation was needed. Wild Flower blotted the seepage of puss, happy when at last she saw the dark stain of pure blood.

"What now, mistress?" Hauk asked, taking the soiled cloths as she handed them to him, in turn handing her clean ones.

"I need the black salve and some material for binding," she said.

Hauk moved to the trunk to select the medication. He held the bowl while Wild Flower swabbed the wound. Then he untied Thoruald so they could bandage him. By the time they were through, Thoruald's body was damp with perspiration.

"His fever is breaking," Hauk said.

"Aye," Wild Flower answered, not deeming to tell Hauk that the crucial hours were yet ahead of them. She brushed her hair from her face. "You go to bed. I will sit with him."

He nodded. "Would you like me to remove some of the torches?"

"Leave the one burning near the door," she said. "That will cast enough light for me to see by."

"Mistress, I will sleep in the Great Hall tonight rather than the loft, in case you need me."

"Thank you, Hauk."

The Viking left the room, softly closing the door. Still tense, Wild Flower straightened her medicines and returned her unused roots and herbs to the leather pouch. Moving back to the bed, she stood, studying the man who lay peacefully beneath the covers.

His face was more relaxed, his breathing less labored. He flung one hand out so that it lay palm up on the bed, the other lay on his chest. She remembered he had dropped something out of his hand earlier. Kneeling beside the bed, she skimmed her hand over the planking. She touched it with the tips of her fingers. She inched nearer. Her hand closed around a small object.

She straightened and opened her hand. In her palm lay the game piece that Thoruald had given to her thirty winters ago. He had gone to sleep holding it.

Her eyes misting with tears, she set the figure on the trunk beside the bed, and wrung out another cloth with which she dabbed Thoruald's body once more. Clasping the game piece in her right hand, she slid into the bed beside him.

Carefully she situated herself close to him, laying her head and her fist on his chest . . . as she had dreamed of doing for thirty winters. She listened to the steady cadence of his heartbeat and prayed to the Spirits of Life that they grant life to him.

"It is true your son and grandson need you, my warrior," she murmured, "but your lady-wife wants you. She has loved you from afar for thirty winters. Now she desires to love you differently. She would replace her dreams and memories with your touches

360

and caresses, with your words of love, with your laughter and happiness. Aye, Jarl Thoruald, your wife loves you."

She closed her eyes and smiled.

Standing in the sunlight corridor of the forest, she heard her warrior, her love say to her, *"I leave this falcon game piece with you, my love, in hopes the falcon shall one day bring you home to me."*

Wild Flower felt the soft movement on her forehead, and she smiled, stretching out. Her feet brushed down hairy legs. She remembered. Her lids flew open, and she stared into sparkling blue eyes.

"Good morrow, lady."

"Good morrow, lord," she whispered, afraid to move for fear of hurting Thoruald.

He brushed hair out of her face. "I see you could not wait to get into bed with me."

She smiled. "Any excuse would have done, lord, but tending your wound seemed the most plausible."

"I only remember seeing you once, love, and hearing you promise that you were going to heal me." He gingerly touched the bandage. "My side is not throbbing today, and I am feeling much better."

His hand strayed to her hips.

"Not that much better, lord. I want to make sure you are healed properly."

"Now that you are here, love, I know I am going to heal properly. You give me added reason for doing so."

Wild Flower pushed up in the bed and opened her hand to show him the game piece. "You were holding this, lord."

"Aye," said he. "I was in great pain both of heart and body, love." He shoved the cover down and started to swing his legs off the bed.

"Nay!" Wild Flower exclaimed at the same time that he grunted and lay back down.

"You are feeling much better, lord, but not strong enough to be jumping about."

"Aye." He sighed.

"Rest today."

Gingerly he lay back down and breathed in deeply several times until his face relaxed. "After I retired last night I began to think over the years."

"We cannot undo them, lord, so think back only in fond memories," Wild Flower said. "Learn from the mistakes, but look only toward the future . . . even when that future seems obscure."

"Brander will never be my son," Thoruald said and repeated his last conversation with their son to her. "And he will one day take Eirik-Kolby from me."

"If the gods take Brander and Eirik away from you," Wild Flower said, "then so be it. They will give you another son to take their place."

His hand curled into a fist, and his voice was emphatic. "A blood son, Wild Flower. A blood heir to inherit the Talon of the Falcon."

Holding his hand to his wound, he slowly pushed up.

"Lord," Wild Flower said. "I would have you—"

"Let me be, lady," he said, biting back the pain. "I am not one to lie about."

He slowly slid his legs over the side of the bed and sat for a moment catching his breath. He walked carefully to where his sword hung on the wall. His body was yet muscle-bound and looked not as if it had been spent with age.

"I do not want another son," he said.

"That is good, lord, because I doubt I can give

362

you another. I fear my childbearing years are past, and I would not like to think you were wooing me on the premise that I could present you with another heir."

"Nay, lady, my feelings are for you alone, not for what you can give to me. This time, my wildflower, I want to give to you."

Wild Flower warmed to his words.

"Would you help me dress, lady?"

"Aye." Wild Flower slid off the bed.

"You will find trousers and undergarments in that trunk," he said and pointed.

With her help he slipped into his clothes and walked to the trunk that sat at the end of the bed. Again pressing his hand to his wound, he unfastened the lid and lifted it.

"I would show you something," he said.

Wild Flower knelt on the floor.

"Look," he pointed at a game board and bent, wincing as he did so, to hold up one of the playing pieces.

"The set you used when you were in the Forestland," she murmured, studying the small statue.

"Aye, I kept it through the years. Remember what I told you?"

She nodded.

"Without you, my heart like the game would be incomplete. Now, both are complete. Thank you for coming, Wild Flower. You have brought me great happiness."

"Thank you, lord."

Sitting down in his chair, he touched her chin and held her face so that he could look into her eyes. "You are more beautiful now than you were then, love. Although I am weak from my wound, my body wants you. Not only to make love to you, but to be near you. I am hungry for your laughter and your conversation. And for your arguments."

"Even my arguments?" Close to tears, Wild Flower smiled at him.

"I may have acted as if you irritated me when you argued, but I enjoyed hearing your opinions. They made me think. They stimulated me, love."

"Aye," she whispered. Both were lost in memories.

Eventually he said, "Dig through the trunk and see what else I have."

"The peace pipe that I gave you."

Holding it in her hands, she turned and slid to the floor. "Why did you never return to the Forestland?" she asked, wanting to know the answer, yet not wanting to know.

Thoruald picked up a strand of her hand and pulled it through his hands. "I thought about it many times, love, but I was a jarl. I had my men and my steading to think about. In order to have the steading I had to have the loyalty of my warriors. To have their loyalty I had to provide them with booty."

"None of which could be found in Forestland."

He sighed and shook his head.

"You desired me," she said, "but never loved me."

"The boy in me thought it was only passion," he replied. "When his ego healed and he matured into manhood, he realized he loved you and only you."

Wild Flower's heart sang.

"By then he was married and had a new family. Yet he kept thinking about you." Thoruald dropped her hair, reached for the pipe and twirled it in his hands. "I kept thinking about next summer. Always next summer until the summer and autumn of my life had passed. So quickly I found myself in the winter of my years."

364

"Did you love your wife?" Wild Flower asked.

"Nay."

He gazed into her eyes and confessed, "I wish I could say I have had no women since you, mistress, but that would be a lie. I have had many, but I have loved none since you. You were always the face and the body I sought. Always I looked for your wisdom when I talked with a woman. I found these qualities in no one else."

"Did your wife know you did not love her?"

Thoruald laughed. "She did not care, love. She married me because I was a wealthy jarl. She wanted to produce a son for me and when that was done, so was her womanly interest in me. Her life was the steading, mine was Ragnar."

"Your son?"

"My second son. He was a good warrior, but he was not as strong as Brander. He had not the qualities from his mother that Brander inherited from you. I am proud of our son, Wild Flower, and I want him to stay here to take over leadership of the steading."

"As Brander must be patient with Eirik, you must be patient with Brander," Wild Flower said.

"What about you?" Thoruald asked. "Are you returning to your home next spring?"

"Nay, lord, I am home."

Their eyes binding them together, Wild Flower went on her knees and gently moved between Thoruald's legs. Gently she kissed him.

"Marry me," he said.

"Not until I have been duly courted."

"Mistress," he promised between kisses, "count yourself as a woman who is being courted."

Wild Flower moved, hitting the trunk causing the lid to land with a resounding bang. He and Wild

Flower laughed. Knocks rapped on the door.

"Mistress, do you need help?"

"Nay, Hauk," Wild Flower called out, the word ending in a breathing sigh as Thoruald's hands slid through the neck opening of her nightshirt to cup her breasts. "I am fine."

"Thoruald," the Viking warrior called.

"Do not worry, my friend," Thoruald shouted. "I have never felt better." He lowered his voice for Wild Flower's ears only. "Or felt anything better."

Chapter Twenty-nine

Warm, golden sunshine spilled into the room. Kelda opened her lids, closed them and slid deeper into the covers. From a distance she could hear the workers talking and laughing. Close by she heard the rustle of the leaves as the morning breeze blew through the trees. Birds chirruped and twittered in the branches. Aye, she thought, she was home in her own sleeping chamber. Smiling, she stretched and ran her hand across the bed.

It was empty, but should not be.

She opened her eyes and bolted up. Fully dressed, Brander sat in one of the chairs watching her.

"Good morrow," he said, a slow smile curving his lips.

"Good morrow," she murmured, the coverlet falling to her waist.

As Brander's eyes caressed her breasts, Kelda remembered his caresses the night before, his ultimate possession. What had started out as her giving to him became a reciprocal giving on the part of both of them.

Still she knew he did not trust her to keep her promise to return to the Forestland with him. They had made love and shared intimate pleasure, but he had not taken her fully as he had when she was his slave. He was yet fearful of spilling his seed inside her.

Although he had given her pleasure and fulfillment, she had been hurt because he did not yet trust her. Still she understood his hesitance to believe her. She would bide her time and gain his confidence. In the meantime, she would love him unconditionally. She had made that promise last night, and it was one she would keep.

"Did you rest well?" he asked.

"Aye," she replied, her gaze hungrily moving over his legs, which rested on the small stool in front of his chair. "And you, lord?"

His smile deepened. "It is possible, lady, that the bed beckons me again." His eyes focused on her breasts.

"Only the bed beckons?" Kelda asked.

"To be honest," he replied, his voice going low and husky, " 'tis the woman on the bed who beckons. I have a hunger for her that cannot be sated."

Unmindful of her nudity, Kelda slipped out of bed and moved to where he sat, kneeling beside him. She touched his face and marveled that his features were no longer harsh and forbidding.

"The lady has a hunger also, lord."

Her lips touched his softly as his hands filled with her breasts. She saw no arrogance in his face now, only the deep enjoyment of a man who had touched something precious and fragile. She wondered how she could have ever thought him a primitive savage without feelings.

"Shall we return to the bed?" Kelda murmured.

"I would enjoy it," Brander replied, "but while you were asleep, I sent word to Tove that we would be taking our morning meal in our chamber."

368

Kelda sighed and slid her arms around Brander's waist, lying her cheek against his chest. "Ah, lord, life has a way of interfering with pleasure, does it not?"

"Aye, but these little interferences make us look forward to our next pleasurable moment," he said.

Smiling, Kelda pushed away from him and stood. She walked to the bed and rummaged through the cover, searching for her nightshirt.

Brander rose and moved to the side of the bed. He leaned down. "Is this what you are looking for?" he asked and held it up.

She reached for it, but he held it from her. Sitting on the side of the bed, he embraced her and captured one of her breasts in his mouth. Gently he kissed it. His tongue laved the nipple until it crested beneath his touch. He drew fiery designs around it, until finally Kelda moaned.

"I never get my fill of you," he murmured. "Each time I see you, you are more beautiful. Each time I taste you, you taste more succulent."

"May this always be the way between us, lord," she murmured and cupped his face with her hands. She drew his head to hers and captured his lips in a long, satisfying kiss. "I would we could stay in this chamber all day, lord, and learn more about each other."

"That is my wish also," he said, "but last night Hauk promised that my training in the use of the sword and the riding of the horse began today."

"Aye," Kelda sighed. "You must be prepared for Asgaut. The choice of weapons is his, and if he chooses the sword, you will be greatly disadvantaged."

A knock sounded.

"Tove with our meal," Brander said and helped

369

Kelda slip into her nightshirt.

He moved across the room and opened the door. Lind, smiling up at him, entered the room, their food on a tray. "Tove asked that I bring this to your chamber for you," she said. "We are right busy this morning in the fireroom and the bake house."

"Are you adjusting well to life at the Falconstead?" Brander asked, his voice friendly.

"Aye," Lind answered. "A thrall always enjoys the pleasure of being at the steading. Jarl Thoruald always treats his thralls fairly and allows them an opportunity to earn their freedom. This is what I shall do since I now belong to him and the mistress."

As Lind talked, her hungry gaze slowly moved over Brander's body, lingering on his crotch. Aware of the woman's thoughts and displeased with them, Kelda slid out of bed.

"Thank you, Lind. Place the tray on the table, and you may go."

"Did you hear about the jarl?" Lind asked, her eyes still on Brander as she followed Kelda's orders. "He almost died during the night."

"What?" Kelda exclaimed.

Lind laughed softly. "No need for worry, mistress. He is much better today. Hauk told us that Mistress Wild Flower has the *sight*. The gods showed her how to save him."

"I must go to him." Kelda pushed past Lind to catch the door handle.

"You need not," the thrall said. "Hauk said the master will recover now. He is yet in his chambers resting. Mistress Wild Flower is with him. And has been all night." A knowing smile played around the pouting lips.

Kelda released the handle.

"That is why Tove was unable to bring your

morning meal," Lind continued. "She took theirs to them."

Leaning against the door, Kelda hoped the news Lind related was true. With Thoruald's recovering completely from his wound, she would not be hesitant to return to the Forestland with Brander. In fact, last night she had been thinking about Thoruald and Wild Flower. Wild Flower was yet a young woman. If she was not past her child bearing years, she could present Thoruald with another child. Such a thought pleased Kelda.

"Master, Hauk said to tell you he will be waiting for you in the *stofa*. Please join him as soon as you have eaten your morning meal. I will be gone now," Lind said. "Please let me know how I can best serve you, master and mistress."

When the door closed behind Lind, Kelda said, "She can best serve me by keeping her distance from you, lord."

Brander grinned. "You are not still jealous, love?"

"A little."

"There is no need to be. You are the woman I care for."

"Thank you, lord."

She moved to the table to sit on the opposite side from Brander. They ate their meal quietly.

"Why are you so pensive this morrow?" she finally asked.

He shrugged, dropped his spoon into the half-empty bowl of porridge, and laved butter on his slice of bread.

"Thinking about your mother and Thoruald?"

"No, my mother has chosen the path she wants to walk. I wish her well."

"Eirik?"

He dropped the buttered bread on his plate and

371

shoved back in the chair. "Neither Eirik nor I chose this path. Both of us were brought to this land forcibly. As a result, my son's memory of his homeland is gone. Falconstead has become his home. I alone want to return to the Forestland."

Kelda laid her hand on his. "I am going to return with you."

He studied her. "I believe you mean to, Kelda, but I do not know if you can return with me or not. You have made a sacred oath—"

"It matters not." She slipped to her knees by him and caught his hands in hers. It was important to her that she convince Brander of her sincerity, that he believe her. "I will ask Thoruald to release me."

"If he does not?" Brander asked.

"I will go with you no matter."

He smiled kindly and caught her face in his hand. "It does matter, my little Viking. I am the infidel, not you. I have defied gods all my life. You have not." His smile turned sad. "Perhaps if I had not been torn between two cultures, I would feel about the gods as you do. Sometimes I wish I could believe in them, in something besides myself."

"Brander—"

"Do not fret, love. We shall find a way for ourselves."

His hand captured hers, and he ran his thumb lightly along the lower ridge of her palm. Sultry black eyes caught and held hers. "Kelda, will you be my lady-wife?"

"Your lady-wife?" she repeated, her entire body going limp with surprise.

"Think upon the subject," he said. "As long as you are my mistress, I will honor and care for you. I will be your champion and fight to the death to release you from your betrothal to Asgaut."

He rose from the chair and tugged her up with him.

"As long as you are my mistress, you have the right to stay here when I return to my homeland. If you marry me, I shall expect you to accompany me. That will be your promise, your commitment that you will journey with me."

"I do not need to think about it," Kelda said. "I will marry you."

"Think on it."

"I have, and I—"

He laid a finger over her mouth. "You have not thought long enough, my little Viking. I do not want to persuade you with an emotional outburst. I will distance myself from you to give you plenty of time to think. After you have thought it through and given me your answer, I shall hold you to it."

He removed his finger to press his lips to hers in a delightful kiss.

"Will you agree to that?"

"Aye."

His arms slipped around her waist, and he tugged her close to him. "I must be going. Hauk is waiting."

Kelda laughed. "What about no emotional persuasion, my lord?"

Brander smiled. "As I once told you, Kelda, the telling is easier than the doing."

After Brander left, Kelda dressed leisurely and moved down the corridor to Thoruald's room. She knocked softly.

"Father, it is I."

"Enter," he called.

Kelda opened the door to see Thoruald and Wild Flower seated at the table. He was wearing only his breeches, and Wild Flower yet wore her nightshirt.

The dishes from their morning meal had been cleared away, and the two of them played the game of the jarls.

"Good morrow, Father," she said. Her eyes focused on the Iroquois woman who had a new and wonderful glow about herself. "And to you, mistress."

Wild Flower smiled. "You are looking lovely, Kelda. Blue is a beautiful color for you. It is the color of your eyes."

"Thank you," Kelda replied, then teased, "The nightshirt looks quite becoming on you."

When Wild Flower's face blossomed with color, Thoruald chuckled quietly.

"What brings you to my chambers so early, Daughter?" he asked.

"From the harrowing tale Lind repeated to me, I expected to find you a-bed," Kelda said, her gaze going to Thoruald's bandage.

"I would be more than a-bed, Daughter, had it not been for Wild Flower."

He leaned across the table to clasp Wild Flower's hand. "She lanced my wound, releasing the poison from my body that was keeping me from recuperating. She has given me new life, new strength." The two exchanged a gaze of love and remembrance that excluded all else.

Kelda waited patiently, and at last, Thoruald turned to her.

"How are you faring on this good morrow?"

Kelda laughed happily. "This is a good day for me. I shall get much of my work done at the steading. Brander and Eirik are with Hauk." *I love Brander, and you and Wild Flower are falling in love all over again.*

"Aye," Thoruald said dryly, "and so is Wray. I understand from Sweyn that Brander has taken the boy as his own. The three of them are training to be Norse warriors."

Kelda nodded. "Wray wishes to earn his freedom."

Thoruald nodded his head and rubbed his hand against his beard. "He will. The lad is resourceful."

"My father, I wish to speak privately with you," Kelda said. "Perhaps you can make some time for me today."

Thoruald gazed pensively and was about to shake his head, when Wild Flower stood.

"Why not now, lord? I must get dressed—"

"Must, my lady?" he teased.

Wild Flower smiled and touched the tips of her fingers to his cheek. "I am going to get dressed, lord, and the two of you can be alone."

"Wild Flower—" he rose.

"I will be in my chambers. Send for me when you have finished your discussion."

Even when Kelda was alone with her adopted father, she was uncertain how to broach the subject. She understood Brander's hesitancy in accepting that she would journey back to the Forestland with him. His arguments had been valid. She had to be the one to show resolve.

Thoruald did not encourage her to speak. Rather he sat in his chair and stared at her.

She finally said, "I wish to marry Brander, my father."

Thoruald drummed his fingers on the ornate armrests. "Knowing that he will be returning to his homeland next spring?"

"Aye."

Once again he lapsed into a pensive silence, finally to say, "Is this a plan of yours to get him to spill his seed within you, so you will carry the child of the Falcon?"

"Nay, lord, I love him."

"This is not good." He furrowed his brow. "What happens to you when he returns to his home next spring?"

"I shall go with him."

"What about your sacred oath?"

"I am asking you to release me from it," she said. "Last night Brander promised me that if by spring Eirik had not regained his memory that he would leave him here at Falconstead with you and Wild Flower."

"I have no doubt Brander is a man of his word," Thoruald said, "but if Wild Flower has seen visions of the child regaining his memory, then I believe he will. If you, Brander, and Eirik return to Skrelling-land, I shall have no heirs."

"Wild Flower is yet a young woman. Perhaps she is not beyond the childbearing years and could bear you another child."

"That is not a chance I am willing to take," Thoruald said, neither confirming nor denying Kelda's words. "You would so easily walk away from your heritage?"

"Nay, lord, it is not an easy walk. I am torn, but I will go with the man of my heart."

"He loves you?"

Wild Flower's words returned to give Kelda confidence. *Do not always believe what the eye sees or the ear hears. Trust in your heart.*

"I believe he loves me, but whether he does or not, my father, I want to be with him for the rest of my life. I want to give him love."

"And sons and daughters."

"Yes."

Thoruald rose. His nostrils flared and his face darkened with fury. His fist came down in a heavy

376

thud on the table. "You are forgetting that I am the one who set you free from thralldom. I took you into my household and made you an adopted blood daughter. You cannot walk out on me, Kelda. I will not let you. I will not release you from your sacred oath. At the adoption ceremony you swore by the sacrificial oxen blood, promising you will marry to produce an heir."

Kelda's heart was heavy. She loved her father and understood his anger. She also knew she had a difficult choice to make, but she had no doubt as to what her decision would be.

"The gods will damn you, Kelda."

"If I do not go with Brander," she said, "I will be damned anyway, my father."

Chapter Thirty

The days quickly turned into weeks, weeks into two months. Thoruald spent most of his time with Wild Flower. Kelda supervised the steading, and during her spare time went to the pasture to watch Hauk as he trained Brander, Eirik, and Wray to ride the horse and to use their weapons.

Brander chose for himself a wild red stallion that he named Firebrand. Hauk helped him gentle and break the horse. Now he taught him how to ride and care for him. Truly Brander and the steed suited one another, Kelda thought, one day when she watched Brander ride him. Both were strong and powerful; they were conquerors.

Each day she and Brander grew closer, yet they had not reached a point where he truly believed she would accompany him to the Forestland. Mostly they did not discuss it. They enjoyed the present and took what it offered them.

Eirik and Wray bonded in trust and friendship. While Eirik was getting friendlier with Brander, he still shied away from him, refusing to accept he was Iroquois, wanting to believe Brander was Norse. Eirik's first allegiance was to his grandfather.

On this particular morning, after her chores were completed and Brander and the boys had been practicing for several hours, Kelda packed a basket with water jar and tankards and headed for the pasture. When she arrived, Brander and Hauk, padding covering their bodies, were dueling with the sword. Had Kelda not known Hauk was the teacher and Brander the student, she would have thought they were battling one another. The impacts were hard and sure. Each had landed hard blows that cut through the protective packing covering their bodies.

"That is it, sire," Hauk yelled, his sword thwacking against Brander's chest, knocking the wind out of him. "You have a way about you when it comes to fighting. You are a champion."

Brander caught his breath, spun around, and using both hands brought his weapon up. With a warrior's yell, he let it slice through the air to land a final blow to Hauk, knocking him off his feet and sending his sword flying through the air.

Kelda clapped. Wray and Eirik crowded around Brander to congratulate him. Smiling, he whipped off the padding and walked to where Kelda waited beneath the sprawling branches of the tree.

"What brings you to the pasture this day, mistress?" he asked, lowering a lid in an audacious wink that she thoroughly enjoyed.

"Need you ask that question, sire?" She opened the basket and poured him a glass of water. "I thought perhaps you were in need of refreshments."

Brander's eyes twinkled. "Indeed I am. While this slakes one thirst, mistress, it does nothing for the other."

"Kelda." Eirik called as he and Wray joined them. Both boys were also bound in padding. "Did you see Brander?"

"Aye," she replied. "He dealt Hauk quite a lick."

"That he did," Hauk added, walking up to them, also pealing out of his protective clothing. "The kind of blows he is going to have to deliver to Asgaut if

379

he plans to win the duel." The Viking pushed his hand through sweat-dampened hair.

"Word has it that Asgaut is on his way home," Kelda said. "A messenger came from Jarl Gannar today, saying his dragonship has been spotted."

Brander took a swallow of the water, rinsed his mouth, and spat it out. "This is good," he murmured. "Autumn promises to be a good season for me. Soon I shall be on my way home."

"Are you taking me to your land with you?" Wray asked, wrinkling his forehead and squinting up at Brander.

"Do you wish to go with me?"

Wray looked down and pushed a pebble with the toe of his boot. Finally he raised his head and said, "If I have any voice in the matter, master, I would like to stay here. But since I am your thrall, I shall obey you faithfully."

"You are my thrall while I am here," Brander said. "When I leave for the Forestland, I shall give you your freedom, if you have not earned it before."

Wray's eyes sparkled.

"You have not begun to earn your freedom," Hauk bellowed. "The way you handle your sword leaves much to be desired, boy."

"I handle it well, Viking," Wray answered. "You said so earlier today."

"I am telling you different now. You and Eirik get out there and show me your mettle."

Draining their tankards and returning them to Kelda, Wray and Eirik laughed. They grabbed their swords and ran to the clearing to begin their practice.

"Did the jarl say how long it would be before Asgaut will arrive?" Hauk asked.

"Within the week, he speculated," Kelda replied.

"Gannar said his ship looked loaded."

"I hardly think Asgaut would bring the pirates home," Hauk surmised. "He probably plundered along the way."

"It seems that he is marking his return to coincide with the *Vetrarblot*," Kelda said, thinking about their harvest festival of the Winter Sacrifice, thinking back to the Harvest Celebration of the Iroquois.

" 'Tis time to be thinking of the coming winter," Hauk said. "We need to send many prayers and sacrifices to the gods in hopes that it will be a mild and short one." He handed his empty glass to Kelda. "Thank you, mistress. I will return to give instruction to the boys."

"Hauk, one moment," Kelda called.

The Viking stopped to look at her.

"Thoruald requested that you come directly to him when you have completed your instruction for the day. He has some news he wishes to give to you personally."

The old warrior smiled. "Aye, mistress, and I believe I know what it is. Thoruald and Mistress Wild Flower are going to be wed at the *Vetrarblot*."

Hauk laughed, his eyes twinkled. "I saw Asa laying out and marking the red velvet material."

Chuckling, he walked away only to stop and return. "Mistress, I believe I saw enough material for two dresses, did I not?"

Kelda felt her face warm beneath her mentor's gaze.

"Enough," Brander answered for her, a gentle smile playing around his mouth. "We shall see how the duel turns out, my friend, before we make an announcement."

"But if you do," Hauk pressed, "it is to be a wedding?"

"Aye," Brander answered, "she has promised to wed me."

"So Asa is to make two red bridal dresses," he murmured. "That is good." He studied them for a second, before he turned and walked to where the boys jousted.

"The smith wishes to see you," Kelda said.

Brander nodded. "He was to send word." He called to Hauk. "The smith has my trappings ready. I shall go view them."

"Be in no rush to return," Hauk called back. "The boys will need much practice this day. I want them ready for the games at the Winter Sacrifice."

Hand in hand Brander and Kelda walked through the steading, finally to reach the smithy.

"Ho, Brander." The apron-clad man looked up to greet them as he laid a red hot piece of iron on his anvil. "Your sword," he said. "I am going to have it ready by the Winter Sacrifice."

"Perhaps you should have it ready sooner," Brander said and moved by the fire, banked in a round, open fireplace of stone in the center of the building. "Jarl Gannar sent word that he has spotted Asgaut's dragonship headed this way."

"Aye, 'tis time for him to return," the smith replied. He nodded his head to a table close by. "Take a look and see if they meet your requirements."

Brander and Kelda moved to the table where Brander inspected the trappings for his horse. As Kelda stared at the bronze, silver, and gold inlay on the saddle and bridle, the whoosh of the billows and the unbearable heat of the fire was forgotten.

The blacksmith came to stand beside them. "The spurs are made of iron, my lord, with thin sheets of silver and gold around them. This guarantees they will be durable as well as beautiful."

382

Kelda ran her fingers over the shining metal. "You have done well, blacksmith."

"Aye," Brander murmured, "Firebrand will be the best ornamented horse in the steading."

"As will his owner, sire."

"How soon can you deliver these to the *stofa*," Brander asked.

"On the morrow." The smith tugged the cord that bound his apron about his waist. "I am not so sure about the sword, sire. That is your life-blood, and it must be well crafted."

" 'Tis true. Take all the time you need, blacksmith." Brander said.

He moved around the building looking at the weapons on display both on tables and on the wall. Kelda followed his gaze, seeing many things afresh. The swords, battle-axes, spears, halberd, throwing axes, scramasaxes, and metal-tipped arrows.

" 'Twas one of my forefathers who crafted the Talon of the Falcon, sire," the craftsman said. "That is a magical weapon. I cringed when I thought it would belong to Asgaut. Never has an unworthy hand clasped it yet. I pray to the gods that one never will."

Kelda ran her hand over one of the frying pans that hung suspended by its handle from the wall.

"Asgaut will not get the Talon of the Falcon," Brander promised. He lightly clasped Kelda by the waist. "Now, good smith, it is time for the mistress and me to be getting to the Great Hall. I shall see you on the morrow."

Brander and Kelda slowly walked to the longhouse and had no sooner entered the building, than a thrall came running in through the fireroom.

"Master!" he screamed. "Master, come quick. Outlaws have struck. Hauk has been attacked."

"Go tell the jarl," Brander ordered. "He is in his chambers."

Grabbing his training sword, Brander rushed through the fireroom out of the house to the far pasture where he and Hauk had been jousting earlier. Kelda ran behind him.

When he arrived, he saw Eirik bending over Hauk. The boy's face and shirt were covered in blood. Groaning, Wray lay to the side.

"Brander!" Eirik shouted, "Hauk and Wray are wounded. I believe they are going to die."

"Are you hurt?"

"Only a cut, sire. Hauk—" his voice broke.

"You see to Hauk," Kelda said to Brander. "I will take care of Wray."

Brander knelt beside Hauk and Eirik, first running his hands over Eirik to make sure he was not seriously harmed, then he turned his attention to the Viking warrior. Blood trickled out of Hauk's mouth, and he breathed heavily.

"We were tricked, sire," he said. "Thought they were friends to the last."

"Do not talk," Brander said, his gaze moving over Hauk's body, resting on the gaping wound to his stomach. "We will get you to the Great Hall where Wild Flower can tend to your wounds."

"Nay, lord, this was my final battle." He clutched his sword in his right hand. "I had The Vindicator with me, and I refused him, sire."

"The thrall said they were outlaws. Did you recognize them?" Brander asked.

"Nay. They were after Eirik," Hauk answered. "Had it not been for Wray, sire, they would have killed your son."

"I have the feeling, my friend, had it not been for you, they would have killed both the boys." Brander

384

clasped the Viking by the shoulder. "How is Wray?"
Hauk asked.

"He is going to be fine," she answered. "Thanks
be to Odin, he was wearing all of his padding."

"What happened to yours?" Brander asked Hauk.

"I had discarded it because it was too hot to wear
and I was through jousting for the day."

Hauk coughed and spat up more blood, then he
curled his hand around Brander's arm.

"Sire, I love Mistress Kelda as if she were my
own daughter. Take care of her."

"I will," Brander promised.

Hauk's voice dropped to a pained whisper. "Love
her."

"Yes," Brander said.

In the distance he heard the murmur of anxious
voices and the opening and closing of the gates.

"What happened?" Thoruald shouted.

Brander lifted his head to see his father holding
his side and moving slowly across the pasture. Wild
Flower walked beside him.

"Grandfather! Lady!" Eirik shouted and ran toward the jarl and Wild Flower.

The boy gasped for breath. "Outlaws attacked us
when Wray and I were jousting." He spoke in a
rush, his words spilling one over the other. "We
fought them off."

"See to Hauk," Kelda called to Wild Flower.
"Wray has only surface wounds. We are stopping
the flow of blood from his arm."

Brander, Thoruald, and Eirik watched as Wild
Flower examined the old warrior. Before Wild
Flower was finished, Wray, his padding stripped
away, a piece of cloth binding the wound he had
received on his arm, moved closer to Hauk, as did
Kelda. Finally Wild Flower removed her hands from

the warrior, and tears ran down her cheeks.

Hauk caught her hands in his. "Do not be concerned, mistress. I know the wound is to the death. I am ready to be gathered by the heavenly maidens and taken to Odin's Hall of the Slain."

"Nay, my old friend," Thoruald said, "Wild Flower can cure you."

"Not this time," Hauk said. "Fate has spoken."

Wild Flower nodded her head.

"No," Kelda cried, "it is not true. Wild Flower, tell him it is not true."

Brander caught Kelda in his arms and held her.

"Mistress," Hauk said, turning his faded eyes to Kelda, "you have been an able student. I am proud to have sailed to Skrellingland with you."

"I am glad you were my teacher and mentor, Hauk." Kelda sniffed back her tears. "You have taught me well."

"The *Golden Sol* is indeed a fine dragonship, mistress," he murmured. "Grateful I am that you allowed me to captain her."

"You shall captain her again," Kelda whispered. "All the way to the Hall of the Slain."

Hauk mustered a grin. "I would like that. Even more, I would like to see Asgaut's face when he learns of it."

He closed his eyes and breathed heavily. Eventually his lids lifted and he looked for Thoruald.

"Sire, this is the first battle I have fought in a long while that you were not with me."

"Aye."

"I have taught your son well. He is skilled enough to meet the *Jomsviking* and to defeat him." Hauk winced in pain, drew a deep breath, then said, "An enemy we can see and recognize is more easily defeated than these whom we are fighting, sire. The

386

men who attacked us were not ordinary outlaws. I say again, they wanted Eirik.

"My family," Thoruald breathed heavily. "Someone is out to get the family of the Falcon. First Ragnar. And now Eirik."

"And you, lord. You were meant to be dead. Be careful, sire. I fought beside you as long as I was alive. Now, you will need another."

Hauk's eyes glazed, and he bolted up, swinging his sword through the air. "Odin, here I am. Send your heavenly maidens to get me."

The Viking warrior sat for a moment, his face illuminated with victory, his eyes glowing. His arm dropped, but he held his sword firmly. A smile on his face, he crumpled to the ground.

Thoruald stared at his friend for a long while, before he lifted his eyes to the small grieving band around him. "He is dead."

Though Hauk's death lay heavy on the chieftain's heart, Thoruald stood and commanded, "Prepare the burial chamber."

He spoke as the jarl.

Chapter Thirty-one

"How could you have allowed this to happen to me?" Asgaut shouted, pacing back and forth in front of the jarl's high seat. "The dragonship was mine."

"You had given it to Kelda as her bride-price," Thoruald said.

"She had no right to bury Hauk in it!" Asgaut's voice throbbed with anger. "Only the wealthiest are buried in *langskips*. Hauk was only a warrior."

"Not *only* a warrior," Kelda said. She sat in a lower chair next to Thoruald. "He was my father's dearest friend and most trusted warrior. He deserved to be carried to the Halls of the Slain in the *Golden Sol*."

Asgaut wagged his finger in Kelda's face. "You will pay for that ship, woman! The loss will not be counted mine."

Brunhild, standing beside her husband, nodded her head.

"Now, sire," the *Jomsviking* said, "I would discuss an important matter with you."

"Can this not wait, Asgaut?" Thoruald asked. On his left side, Wild Flower moved closer to him and laid her hand on his shoulder. "Hauk has scarcely been—"

"Nay, this is a matter you cannot dismiss so easily. Hauk is in Valhalla now, lord, and it is time that we turned our eyes from the dead to the living."

Canby walked out of the shadows to stand behind Thoruald and to whisper in his ear. Thoruald nodded and shifted in the chair. "State your grievance, Asgaut."

The *Jomsviking's* eyes focused on Kelda. "Your daughter made me look like a fool. I have been shamed."

His face a mask of fury, his eyes burning with hatred, Asgaut jabbed his fist at Thoruald. "When I have redeemed my name, I shall take Kelda before the Herred-thing."

"Aye, lord," Brunhild agreed, looking first at Thoruald, then smiling nastily at Kelda.

"That is your right," Canby said. "And you may cease shouting, Asgaut. All of us can hear you quite well."

"Kelda is my betrothed." Asgaut lowered his voice, but what it lost in volume it gained in venom. "The occasion was solemnized before the Herred-thing. I demand you return her to me."

"My daughter does not wish to return," Thoruald answered.

Asgaut's face twisted into an ever uglier frown of fury, and he slung his head, golden blond hair swirling through the air. "I call your son out, Thoruald, and challenge him."

Brander stepped forward. "I accept."

"The *eingigi* or the *holmganga*, Asgaut?" Thoruald asked.

Tensely, Kelda waited for the answer.

"The *holmganga*," the *Jomsviking* answered. "My choice of weapons is the sword. On the fifth morrow."

"Why so long?" Canby demanded.

389

"I would let my warriors have some rest and reveling before the duel."

Asgaut's ice blue eyes fastened on Brander. Like his stance, they projected his hatred and contempt for the Iroquois.

"When I am through with you, Skrelling, you and your son will be crawling back to your land. I will redeem my honor by putting shame on your name."

The blood drained out of Wild Flower's face as Asgaut continued his threat.

"I shall double your shame by letting you live with the knowledge that a *Jomsviking* defeated you and took the woman you claimed as yours from you, yet this *Jomsviking* allowed you to live. I shall give you a wound that will cripple you for life."

"Hope you do all these things, Viking—"

"*Jomsviking!*" Asgaut corrected.

"Viking," Brander repeated, then continued as if he had not been interrupted, "Hope you do all this and more, else your shame will be so great you cannot stay on the steading."

Asgaut again addressed Thoruald. "You have gotten old and soft, Jarl."

"Do not address your jarl in that tone, *Jomsviking!*" Canby snapped. "Show him proper respect."

Asgaut glared at the lawreader. "I am the kind of leader our Vikings need, the kind who will again cause Falconstead to be a name to strike fear in the hearts of the Europeans. I will bring us to glory again even if it means killing your heirs, sire, so that I have claim to the Talon of the Falcon."

Again Thoruald sighed. "This is what I fear, Asgaut."

"I have spoken." The *Jomsviking* spun around, his green mantle flapping against his leggings.

Her maniacal laughter echoing through the Great Hall, Brunhild followed Asgaut.

"Sire," Canby said, "do you suppose the attempts on your life and Eirik and the death of Ragnar are connected with Asgaut?"

"His words today would make me think so," Thoruald said. "I shall have to order more guards around Eirik."

"Perhaps he would be safer with Jarl Gannar," Kelda suggested.

"I do not know this Gannar," Brander said. "If Eirik goes anywhere, I will take him. Only Thoruald and I shall know where he is hidden. I trust no one but Thoruald with Eirik's life."

"This is a wise decision." Thoruald rose and paced back and forth. "Being a mere mortal, I do not understand the way of the gods, but I feel for some reason they are laughing at Thoruald of Falconstead. They have taken my one son and would have the other two."

He spun about. "Will I be left alone with no heirs? With no one to inherit the Talon of the Falcon, but this man who calls being the scourge of Europe glorious?"

"Lord," Wild Flower said, "do not allow the man to get you angry."

"Does no one have a vision for the steading, for Norwegia?" he asked. "The Norse can no longer swoop down on villages, raid, pillage, and loot with impunity. It is time we turned our attention to our people and to progress. It is time we learned to live in peace."

"Sire," Canby said, "I have fought you through the years when you advanced this theory. But I am beginning to see that this is the only way to save our land and our people."

391

"Aye, lawreader." Thoruald playfully clapped Canby on the shoulder. "We must save ourselves from within."

"Sire," Brander said, and Thoruald turned to look at him. "Kelda tells me that the pirates who attacked your village used Viking war tactics."

Thoruald nodded.

"Do you believe they were Norsemen?"

"I thought so at first," Thoruald replied, "but I could find no connection. The only person who seems to have something to gain with the death of my family and me is Asgaut."

"Or Brunhild," Kelda said softly.

After a second of silence, Thoruald nodded. "Or Brunhild."

"She is bitter, lord," Kelda said, "because you released me from thralldom and adopted me as your daughter. She felt that you should have done this for her, so that her children would be heirs to Talon of the Falcon."

"True, Thoruald," Canby said. "Remember the way Brunhild treated Lind, the way she goaded your son to buy her."

"We shall watch both Asgaut and Brunhild," Thoruald said. "One or both of them may be behind the plot to kill all the blood heirs to the House of the Falcon."

"If Asgaut wanted me dead," Brander said, "why did he choose the *holmganga* rather than the duel to the death?"

"He can kill you in either duel," Canby replied. "This one, however, gives either of you an honorable way out. If you were to default, Kelda would be his. You would be alive to see him bring her before the Herred-thing and ask for judgment. Without your death he would be the champion."

Canby stroked his beard. "In fact, he would be more of a champion in this duel than one to the death. People would scorn you and praise him." The lawreader nodded. "He made a wise choice."

"Aye," Brander said reflectively, "a wise choice indeed."

Later that evening, the *stofa* filled with Thoruald's Vikings who had joined him for the evening meal. Brander sat beside the jarl. Kelda and Wild Flower supervised the serving.

"I fear for the life of my son," Brander said.

"Would you entrust the boy with me?" Thoruald asked.

"Aye," Brander answered. "I know you love my mother and him, sire, as much as I do. However, I fear for your life also."

Thoruald slowly lowered his glass tankard to the table. "I would that I knew you better, Brander," the jarl said. "I regret that I did not—"

"Aye, lord, so do I," Brander said and cut him short. "If I should die in the duel, my lord, I would have you take care of Kelda. I do not want her to be at the mercy of either Asgaut or Brunhild."

"I will take care of her," Thoruald promised.

"Will you allow Wray to become Eirik's and her protector, lord?"

"He is young and unseasoned," Thoruald answered.

"But he was trained by Hauk, and he is an intelligent lad."

"Aye," Thoruald replied. "Wray it is."

"Thank you." Brander rose. "If you will excuse me, sire, I would like to have some time to myself to think. I will take the Firebrand and ride into the night."

"Do you know the way to the *saeter?*"

393

"Your pasture in the mountains?"

"Aye, we have a cottage up there."

"Aye, Hauk took me there when he first began to teach me how to use the sword." Brander's hand curled around the back of the chair as he thought of his dead friend and mentor.

"It is a full day's journey, but you will find the solitude you seek there."

"I will go."

"Can you find your way alone?" Thoruald asked.

"Aye."

Without telling Kelda where he was going, Brander ordered Wray to saddle Firebrand. In moments, his weapons strapped to his body, he eased out of the Great Hall through the fireroom where he had Tove pack him a sack of provisions. Food in hand, he made his way to the stables.

"May I go with you, sire?" Wray asked.

Brander lay an arm on the lad's shoulder. "I would appreciate having you accompany me because I trust your sword arm and you," he said, "but I have an even greater need of you here at the steading. I want you to watch Eirik. Where he is concerned, trust no one but Kelda, Wild Flower, and Thoruald. Someone in this village wants to see me and my son dead."

Wray nodded.

In the darkened shadows of the autumn night, Firebrand thundered out of the stables through the steading up into the mountains. Wray stood at the stables door, watching the silhouette of the mantle swelling behind.

Hours later, the serving completed, Kelda walked to where Thoruald sat. The seat next to him was vacant.

"Where is Brander?" she asked.

394

Thoruald ran his hand around the rim of the goblet. "He wanted time to himself," he said. "He rode to the mountains."

"To the *saeter*," she murmured.

"Aye."

He went to the mountain pasture without me.

Hauk's death had numbed Kelda. Her only consolation was Brander. In her grief she had turned to him. As she had cried, he had held her in his arms and brushed her hair, soothing her.

Her heart hurt within her. In his hour of need, he had turned inward by choosing to ride out by himself. Kelda walked out of the Great Hall into her chamber. She stared into the late summer night.

When she heard the soft knock, she called, "Enter." The door opened, but she did not turn.

"Thoruald thought perhaps you were here," Wild Flower said.

"Brander went to the *saeter* without me," she said. "I promised him that I would return to the Forestland with him. I have done all I can to prove to him that I love him, but it is not enough. He does not need me. He needs no one."

Wild Flower quietly crossed the room and took Kelda into her arms. "Brander does need and want you," she said. "But I think he understands you better than you do yourself."

"What do you mean?"

"The other day Brander told me that you reminded him of the alpine flowers, little Viking, that cannot survive away from the mountains. He fears you cannot survive in the Forestland."

"I cannot survive without him," Kelda said. "I love him, and I am not going to give him up."

She moved out of Wild Flower's embrace and rushed to her trunk. Flipping up the lid, she hunted

395

until she found a pair of trousers and shirt.

As she pulled off her dress, she said, "I am going to him, Wild Flower."

Because the journey had taken many hours, Brander did not arrive at the cottage until late the following afternoon. He was glad to have the solitude of the two-room cottage. Small and peaceful, it was like his lodge in the Forestland. During the waning hours of the day, he had chopped firewood and stacked it inside the hut. At nightfall he built a fire in the pit to ward off the evening chill and ate a meal of sausage, bread and butter that he had brought along with him.

He stood at the window and gazed into the darkness for a long time. He had known when he first saw the Viking that she would change his life irrevocably. Now he was not sure which one had done the changing, he or she, but his life had changed.

But the changing was bittersweet.

He loved Kelda more than he had ever loved anyone. He would fight to the death for her freedom from Asgaut gladly. Nothing had meant more to him than her confession of love and her promise that she would accompany him back to Forestland as his wife.

He had exacted the promise from her, knowing that Kelda would not go back on her word, knowing deep within his heart that he would not hold her to the promise. He had needed to hear her say the words, to know that he meant that much to her.

Last night he had left the Great Hall in search of solitude in the *saeter* because he wanted to think, and he had to think unselfishly. He could no longer consider only himself. He had to do what was best for Eirik and Kelda.

Kelda would never be happy in the Forestland. Norwegia, with its mountains and seas, was her home. Only here would she live and flourish. He turned to look at the wilted flower on the table. He had picked it earlier in the day because it reminded him of her, and as surely as it had died when plucked from its natural environment, so would Kelda.

The same was so with Eirik. He was now a Norseman, the true heir to the Talon of the Falcon.

Brander walked into the second room, removed his weapons and his mantle, laying them on a nearby table. He lay down on the bed but could not sleep. His heart ached for Kelda, for what could never be between them. His body ached for her.

He gazed at the dying fire in the other room. The flames were hypnotic and his lids grew heavy. Hoping he could sleep, he closed his eyes.

But sleep eluded him. He was still haunted by the woman who possessed his heart. Minutes later . . . perhaps hours, an unfamiliar noise interrupted his reverie.

He sat up, straining to hear. Quietly he moved across the room to the window, making sure he kept himself out of the moonlight. Twigs cracked. Branches whooshed and popped into place. Whoever approached was not concerned about the sounds they made. Perhaps it was one of the herdsmen. Or it could be a ploy to disarm him, Brander thought. He could take no chances.

A horse and rider emerged from the forest, both silhouetted black. Because of the mantle the rider wore, he could not tell if it was man or woman.

It could be the outlaws who made an attempt on Eirik's life!

Brander's hand tightened on the hilt of his sword, and he moved to the table where his weapons lay. He eased the stiletto into the waistband of his breeches, then slipped into the front room of the cottage.

All was quiet. He heard the door to the horse shed open and after a while close. Using his training as an Iroquois warrior, he strained to hear, his effort finally rewarded when he heard soft footfalls and they neared the cottage.

He heard the knock on the door. "Brander."

Kelda!

His clasp loosened, and he threw open the door to stare into her face.

"What are you doing out here, you little fool!"

In the faint firelight she saw the sword he held and the stiletto at his waist.

"I could have killed you!"

Against all training as a warrior, he dropped his sword to the floor and yanked the stiletto from his waistband to toss it to a nearby table. Slamming the door shut, he captured her in his embrace.

"By the gods, Kelda, I could have killed you."

"Nay, love," she murmured, and surrendered her lips to his.

Chapter Thirty-two

"I had to leave you behind," Brander murmured in between heated kisses.

"I had to come," she answered. Her eyes shining with her love, she leaned back in the circle of his arms to lift her face to his. "We have only now, Brander, no promise of tomorrow. Please let us take what we have."

"Aye," he whispered.

He gently released her from his embrace to shut and bolt the door. Turning, he swung her into his arms as if she weighed no more than the stiletto he had tossed to the table and carried her into the sleeping room to deposit her on the bed. When chilled night air blew into the room, he walked to the window and closed the shutter.

He returned to the bed, bent over it, bracing his body on both palms. Kissing her gently on the lips, he whispered, "Let me tend the fire in the cottage, then I will tend the fire in us, my lady."

Another long, thorough kiss, and her hands tangled in his hair.

He murmured, "I would do it the other way around, but I have no idea how long tending to you will take."

"Forever, lord," she murmured.

"Aye." He gazed at her a long while before he

shoved up and moved into the front room.

He returned to the fire pit and stoked the fire, the wood soon crackling and spitting. Golden light from the flames illuminated the two rooms, its warmth curling seductively around both man and woman. When Brander looked at her, she stood naked beside the bed, her clothing bundled on the floor.

He walked to her. She awaited him proudly.

"I have seen you nude before," he murmured, "but it is as if I am seeing you for the first time. You are beautiful, Kelda."

"I am glad you think so, lord. I would be beautiful for you."

He ran his hands over the pearly curve of shoulders and back, luxuriating in the feel of the texture of her skin. "I have known your body intimately, yet tonight I feel as if this is the first time I have touched you, my first time to make love to you."

His hands cupped her face, and he brought her lips to his in an infinitely sweet kiss, devoid of passion but full of promise.

"It is the first time that I will have made love to you," he whispered. He slid his hands down to her shoulders to her buttocks and felt her tremble.

"I love you, Kelda."

"I have waited long to hear you say those words, lord."

"I have never spoken them to a woman before," he confessed.

"Not to your wife?"

"I cared for her, but our marriage was one arranged by the Council of Elders. We were happy together, but she never aroused in me the depth of feeling that you have, my little Viking."

400

He bent his head to take her lips again, tenderly, but Kelda flung her arms about his neck and pressed herself urgently against him. He felt her hands on his back, stroking and kneading, moving up and down the indentation of his spine. When her breasts swelled and pressed against his chest, passion surged within him. He removed his mouth from hers until it was a mere brush of flesh.

"Nay," she murmured.

Still Brander inched away from her. He bent his face to take one of her breasts into his mouth. He released it and watched the nipple pucker and harden. He captured it a second time with his mouth and ran his tongue over the crested tip, rediscovering its taste and texture. He teased it with the nipping caress of his teeth.

Kelda gasped her pleasure, and her hands cupping his head, she threw her shoulders back and arched to thrust herself more fully into him.

"Please take me," Kelda murmured. "Please."

"I am, my love," Brander replied.

She touched his face, guiding his mouth to hers at the same time that he touched her breasts. He cupped them tenderly, treasuring the feel of her.

Kelda removed her mouth from his and moaned her desires as his hands continued their caress to her breasts. Again her head rolled back as she gave herself to the richness of his touches, to the promise of ultimate possession.

When he lifted his lips from her, he pulled back so that he could look at her. In the golden firelight Brander could see the features of her face filled with passion. Her lashes were dark crescents against her gilded cheeks. Her lips were parted as she took in shallow, quick breaths. He felt himself harden, throb, and thrust urgently against his breeches.

Kelda sat up, captured Brander's head and guided his mouth to her breasts. When his lips closed over the nipple, she moaned anew. He went from one to the other, until Kelda's love cries filled the room, until he thought he could wait no longer to take her.

Kelda became the aggressor, taking Brander's face between her hands. Her head lowered, her mouth claimed his. Her lips urged his to open to receive her tongue. Brander groaned, and he embraced her, knowing her shoulders, her back, and her hips.

When at last Kelda released his lips, Brander was trembling with intense arousal. For the first time since he could remember, he was not afraid to love, to love unconditionally. He wanted to receive love from her; he wanted to give it to her.

"I love you," he whispered, over and over again.

"I love you," she answered as many times. Then, "Take me, lord."

"Nay, my love, my life." He breathed the words. "The time of my taking is over. From this night forward I shall give to you in love."

He stepped away from her and quickly divested himself of clothing. Naked, he returned to the bed and lay down with her so that his chest brushed against her breasts and his legs extended the length of hers. He pulled her into the tight, warm circle of his arms.

Her scent filled his head and the fire of her passion became one with his. Her hands went to his chest, and he trembled as she discovered the sensitive areas. Her hands traced the path of hair that grew down his chest, her fingers moving to

402

his erectness.

Brander caught her hand, removing it and turning her over on her back. He leaned over her, his hands capturing hers and holding them above her head while he explored every inch of her body as if he had never done it before, as if the territory were totally virgin and unclaimed. Her breathing quickened as he ran a hand over her collarbones, down her sides to her waist, over her hipbones, and down each leg to the ankle. She shivered when his hands skimmed up the inside of her legs, brushing lightly over her triangle of soft hair, again and again.

Brander knew he loved Kelda as he had loved no other person and tonight he would give of himself as he had never given before. He would spill his seed within her and hope that she conceived a beautiful child that would be theirs.

"For months I have been yearning for your touch," Kelda murmured.

"And I for yours, my darling." His mouth roved from her breasts down her midriff to her navel, lower to prepare her for his entry.

She writhed beneath his love strokes. She dug her fingers into his scalp. She cried for his fullest touch.

He eased up, lowering his full weight on her. With his knee, he gently urged her legs apart and touched her femininity with firm virility. Kelda opened her legs further and thrust her hips to receive him. As he sank into her, she gasped, opening her eyes to gaze into his face.

Brander moved slowly and deeply, then stopped to let her warm flesh open and pulsate around him. He savored the feel of their sexuality. His lips captured hers in a long, deeply satisfying kiss as he began to stroke gently. Kelda moved with him.

Her passion heightened. He heard her moans and whimpers. His need for release also tightened. Spurred by her cries and by her thrusting, he plunged deeply, rapidly and fiercely. Both of them were an uncontrollable blaze of passion.

Brander's entire body ached with the need to release the burning desire that licked through him. He heard her gasp and felt her tense, then shudder convulsively in his arms. The soft flesh that surrounded him softly quivered. He cried out and buried his face in the sweet scent of her shoulder. She held him close.

They lay together quietly afterwards, both on their backs. Kelda lay her head on Brander's chest. He drew his hands through her hair.

"I love you," she murmured.

"I love you," Brander whispered, his eyes staring through a slit in the window shutter to the black sky outside.

"Are you having doubts about the duel?" she asked.

"Nay, Asgaut's own conceit will be his downfall and my advantage."

"Tell me about life in the Forestland," she said and cuddled to his side.

He laughed softly. "What do you want to know?"

"Everything," she answered. "What is my life going to be like when we return as man and wife?"

Brander talked to her a long while, describing everyday life in the Forestland, but in the telling he realized that he had begun to think less and less of his life across the Great Water. That would change once he had fought Asgaut, once Eirik's memory returned.

"Did you ask Thoruald to release you from your sacred oath?" he asked.

"Aye."

"What answer did he give?"

When Kelda did not speak, he had his answer. "I feared he would not release you, love."

Kelda pushed up on her elbows and gazed into his face. "No matter, Brander, I am going to the Forestland with you. Unlike your mother, I am not going to spend the rest of my life separated from the man I love. I love you, and I want to be with you."

His arms circled her body, and he pressed her cheek against his chest. "Aye, my love, I believe you."

"Else you would not have spilled your seed within me," she murmured sleepily. "Think, my love, we could be creating a baby."

"Aye," he said, brushing her hair from her forehead, "I was thinking of that. Having our child will make you happy?"

"Oh, yes." Again she pushed up, bracing her elbow on the bed, planting her face in her palm. "We shall have many children, girls and boys. They will be strong and healthy."

"All the girls will look like their mother," he said.

"And the boys will look like their father."

Long after Kelda had gone to sleep, Brander lay awake. He had joined in her fantasy, wishing it could be true for him. But he knew in his heart of hearts it could not be so. Again his thoughts went to the wilted flower on the table in the other room. His precious love could not live in the Forestland.

Knowing this he had made love to her. He had given her the issue of his body in hopes that she would have a child, their child. It no longer mattered that his offspring would be Thoruald's grandchild. What mattered was that this child would be his and Kelda's.

Brander also knew that he would not stay in Norwegia. When spring came, he would be returning to Forestland, and he would be returning alone.

He would leave Kelda and Eirik to the life they knew and loved. He had no doubt that Thoruald would take care of both of them, because his father loved them as he did.

Yet he was not ready to confess this to Kelda. He wanted their time together to be beautiful. It would have to last him a lifetime. Like his mother, he was destined to spend the rest of his life separated from his love.

He slipped out of bed and walked into the front room to build the fire. When the flames were dancing into the air, he returned to the sleeping chamber and put on his trousers and boots. He sat in the high seat beside the fire and peered into the crackling blaze.

The Spirits of Life . . . the gods . . . fate . . . whatever it was had dealt him a hard blow. Indeed his fate seemed to be the same as his mother's. She had spent her entire life loving one man. He would spend the remainder of his loving one woman. Both he and his mother loved a Viking, and if fate was kind to him in this one instance, both of them would have been the parent of a half-Norse.

Brander's hand curled around the end of the armrest. He hoped . . . nay, he prayed . . . that he could leave a child with Kelda. Their child.

Kelda and Brander enjoyed their stay at the cottage and were sad when time came to leave. As if loath to turn loose of the memories they had created, they leisurely journeyed from the mountains to the steading. When they arrived, Wray ran out to greet them.

"Come inside, lord, and see what the blacksmith delivered to you today."

"My trappings," Brander said.

"Your trappings and more," the young warrior said.

"My sword!"

"Aye. We placed it on the table in your chamber, sire."

"Ho, Brander," Thoruald called when Brander entered the Great Hall. "Did Wray tell you the news?"

"Aye."

Brander's boots clicked on the planking as he walked toward his chambers. Kelda followed immediately behind him. By the time his hand curled around the hilt of the sword, Thoruald, Wild Flower, Eirik, and Wray crowded into the room.

Brander swung it through the air several times, the gold and silver glinting in the sunlight. He lovingly ran his hand down the blade, the flat side, the cutting edge. He flexed and unflexed his hand. He brandished the sword in the air. He looked at Thoruald, and the two men laughed.

"How does it feel?" Thoruald asked.

"It fits," Brander replied.

"Aye, 'tis an excellent sword. What are you going to call it?" Thoruald asked.

"Retribution."

"With this sword you are going to fight the *Jomsviking?*" Eirik asked.

"With this sword," Brander answered.

"Wagers are being laid, lord," Eirik said. "Many of the people of the steading think you have no chance against Asgaut."

Brander laughed. "If you lay any wagers, Eirik, make sure you count me the winner. Asgaut shall never get the better of me."

"You are sure, sire?"

Brander gazed into Eirik's dark eyes. "I have never been surer."

"Good," Eirik said. "I wagered my gold arm band that you would win, sire."

Brander raised a brow and turned to his father, the two men grinning. In that moment Brander realized that he no longer hated Thoruald. He did not love him as a father, but he no longer had that hatred burning within him.

His gaze shifted, and he looked at his mother. As if she had read his mind, she smiled at him.

Eirik moved closer to his father and touched the sword. "Sire," he said, looking up and brushing the shock of hair out of his eyes, "I—I am proud that you are my father, even though I do not remember our other life."

Brander felt a rush of tears to the back of his eyes. He lowered his head and pretended interest in the sword. "Thank you, Eirik," he replied. "I am proud you are my son."

"I will be your shield man, sire."

Brander lifted his head. "Aye," he said. "I would have you be."

"I hoped you would say this, sire." The boy

408

grinned. "While you and Kelda were at the *saeter* in the mountains, I selected your shields," Eirik said and pointed to the opposite wall. "I hung them for you."

Brander walked closer to gaze at the colorful, round shields. He touched the outer edge of one, remembering the last one he had held. Kelda's white shield of peace.

"This one, sire, belonged to Hauk," Eirik said. "It has much magic and will shield you against Asgaut's blows. And these two." Eirik stepped farther down. "One belongs to Jarl Thoruald."

Brander stared at the falcon that was emblazoned on the center of the shield.

"Our talisman, sire," Eirik said. "The talisman of our family, the House of the Falcon. This one has strong magic also."

The room was unusually quiet, and Brander knew that all awaited his reaction. He turned his head, looking first at Kelda, at his mother, and last at his father. Their eyes caught and held.

"Is this the shield you used in battle?" Brander asked.

"Aye," the Viking jarl replied.

Brander lowered his head and smiled at Eirik. "I will use this one also."

"The last one, sire," Eirik said, "is a new one. It has not been tested in battle, but I designed it for you."

Brander moved closer to study the shield.

"Lady told me about the Forestland, sire, and I painted pictures of it. See the tree with the hawk in it."

"Aye," Brander answered, "I see. It is the tree that was outside our lodge. Did you remember the tree?"

409

Eirik frowned and said, "Nay, sire, I do not remember, but I seem to know the tree, and I know the shield will have special magic for you. Lady told me so. It belongs only to Brander, the Firebrand. You will test it today."

"Aye," Brander said. "Have you decided in what order I shall use them?"

"No, I want to think longer about that. I want you to have good magic throughout the duel. I want you to win, sire."

"I, too, want to win," Brander said.

Chapter Thirty-three

"Hold!" Kelda pushed through the crowd and stepped across the stone border onto the large bear skin that was staked to the ground by metal rods.

Brander, wearing only his black breeches and boots, stood on one side of the skin. On the opposite side stood Asgaut, also wearing only breeches and boots.

Kelda moved to the corner to face Brander. Taking the collar from her neck, she said, "I return your talisman to you, sire. You are the one who should be wearing it, not I."

In the morning sunlight it glimmered golden and felt warm to his skin when she slipped it about his neck.

She pressed her palms against his chest and smiled softly. "I wanted you to have its magic."

"Thank you," he murmured.

He stared into sky blue eyes and saw the hint of tears. He had held her tightly through the night assuring her that all would be well, but he wished for more time. A tear slipped down her cheek, and he wiped it with his thumb.

"Do you remember your mother's instructions concerning the collar?" she asked.

Brander nodded. "You are supposed to return it to its rightful owner."

"I have."

She kissed the outline of the necklace, her lips warm to Brander's skin. He wanted the moment to last forever.

"May you fare as well in this duel as you did in the contest against the Vikings," she whispered.

The morning breeze lifted strands of hair and blew them across her face. Brushing them aside, Brander's fingers grazed her cheek, bringing back memories of that long-ago day when they first met, when they first looked into one another's eyes.

Much had changed since that day. Love and understanding had swept much of his contempt and prejudice of the Norse away.

"I love you, Kelda of the Vikings."

"I love you," she whispered.

"Sire!" Eirik, dressed in brightly colored trousers, shirt and mantle, entered the dueling ring, bringing Brander's attention to center on him. "I have another talisman I wish to give to you." He pulled the arm band from his upper arm and slid it over his father's wrist. "One has good magic. The two of them together have even greater magic."

Brander smiled and wanted to ruffle his son's hair affectionately. But he could not. His son was no longer a child. He was a young warrior, a future leader, a jarl . . . if he remained here in Norwegia. And he would. This was Eirik-Kolby's future. As surely as night followed day, fate had brought Eirik to this land, to his destiny as a Norseman.

"What are you thinking, sire?" Eirik asked.

That I would enjoy hearing you call me Father.

"The bracelet feels good on my wrist."

Brander lifted his arm, looking at the bracelet and flexing his hand. It had been many winters since he had worn it, but he liked the feel of the band on his arm. He liked the idea of his son returning it to him even more.

"You do believe in the magic of the collar and arm band, do you not?" Eirik questioned.

"Aye," Brander answered. "I believe."

While Eirik still did not know him as his father, he was beginning to accept him. A friendship had developed between them.

"I thought you had wagered this," Brander said.

Eirik nodded and grinned. "I had, but as I thought about the order in which you would use your shields, I also reconsidered my wager. Instead, I wagered my peace pipe that lady brought me from the Forestland."

"Get on with the duel!" Asgaut snarled the command.

Brander looked beyond Kelda and Eirik to see the *Jomsviking* strutting arrogantly around the bear skin. He was a brawny man, confident in his ability to win, Brander thought. Perhaps overconfident. If so, that would give the chieftain a slight edge.

"I wish you well, my love," Kelda whispered and gave him a last kiss.

Eirik, holding his head up, brushed a shock of hair from his face. "I also wish you well . . . my father."

Brander's heart constricted, and he had to struggle to keep from flinging his arms around the child and dancing about the fighting arena with him.

Gravely, one man to another, he said, "Thank you, my son."

Vikings clapped their hands and shouted their agreement.

Canby walked to the center of the fighting square and held up his hands for silence. "According to our rules, the fight between the two contestants, Brander and Asgaut, will commence on the dueling cloak. At no time will either contestant be allowed outside the outer square." He pointed to the stones that marked the fighting arena.

"Do you have a shield man, Brander?"

"Aye." Brander pointed to his son. "Eirik."

"Show your shields, Eirik," the lawreader commanded.

Eirik moved to the center of the dueling cloak to hold the three shields aloft one by one.

A murmur of appreciation went up from the crowd as they studied the runes and designs.

"Step aside," Canby ordered. He then went through the same ritual for Asgaut. After the display, the lawreader, said, "When a shield is broken, another can be substituted until all three have been smashed. After this, the shieldless combatant has to continue to fight on the dueling cloak until he is vanquished."

The lawreader paused to let the duelists ponder his words.

"Now that you have seen the six shields to be used by both contestants," he announced, "it is time to display their weapons. Blacksmith, have you examined the swords?"

"Aye, lawreader," he replied moving to the center of the cloak a sword in each hand. "They are of equal weight and length."

Canby nodded. "All standards are met."

The blacksmith handed Asgaut his sword first. When he handed Retribution to Brander, he smiled and said, "No better sword could a man be using. It was forged in fire like you, sire, and will pass the test."

"Enough," Canby ordered.

The blacksmith moved out of the arena, once again leaving the combatants to face each other.

Canby shouted to the crowd, "Can anyone give a reason why the duel should not begin?"

The only sound was the wind blowing through the trees.

"So be it. The challenged man is the first to strike."

Brander raised his shield. The newest one had been chosen for the beginning of the fight because it had not yet been tested and its magic might be the weakest, Eirik had explained, but Brander's strength and stamina would be the strongest.

Holding his new shield protectively over his chest, Brander lifted his sword with his right hand and advanced to the center of the ring for the ceremonial strike. The loud thwack on Asgaut's shield signaled to the crowd that combat had begun.

Amidst the cheers and the taunts, Brander and Asgaut fought, blow for blow. Both were well matched. Although Asgaut's experience far outweighed Brander's, Brander was the quicker, the lighter of the two. Landing several solid blows, he danced out of the way of Asgaut's sword.

He was also the cooler fighter. Asgaut yelled and shouted obscenities. Brander quietly moved about the cloak, his eyes never leaving Asgaut. Always he measured his adversary's moves and calculated his. Brander could have a decided victory if he could outwit, and thus outmaneuver, the *Jomsviking*.

As Brander circled the cloak, he and Asgaut both crouched, their shields in position. As a portent of death, their swords hovered in the air. Brander's gaze brushed by Kelda.

Her face was pale and drawn with worry, but she smiled at him.

His face was covered with perspiration and drawn in thought, but he smiled at her.

415

Kelda could never remember a time when she had been this nervous. Not even when Oscar had put her up for auction. The circling stopped as quickly as it began. Asgaut rushed in, his sword flashing in the sunlight and it rapidly battered against Brander's shield.

Kelda watched Asgaut bring his sword down time and again, beating Brander back until she thought surely he would stumble outside the fighting square. But always he skipped back into the arena.

Time passed, and the sound of steel against steel, sword against shield, and the cries and grunts of battle-weary warriors reverberated through the clearing.

When Brander's first shield broke beneath the assault, Kelda drew in her breath sharply and pressed her fist against her lips. Staggering back, his heel struck the inner edge of the stone border. The first time that he had come this close to disqualifying himself.

Quickly he took his second shield and slid it on his arm. Asgaut, a malicious gleam in his eyes, rushed toward him, but Brander rallied his strength. He deflected the blow and dove back to the center of the dueling cloak, leaving Asgaut behind.

But the *Jomsviking* was quick and sure. Immediately behind Brander, the edge of Asgaut's blade sliced his upper arm. Blood trailed down to drip off his wrist and fingers and to splatter against the ground between the staked skin and the square of stones.

Backing up from Asgaut, Brander hit a stake and tripped. As he fought to regain his balance, he inadvertently lowered his shield. Asgaut came in for a blow that gashed into Brander's other arm and crushed the second shield. Kelda cried out. The

416

broken shield fell to Brander's feet, and blood quickly ran down the wounded arm, this time to drip on the cloak.

"Hold!" Canby shouted, raising a hand.

At the same time that Eirik ran into the arena, so did Canby.

Speaking to Brander, the lawreader said, "You have been wounded so that your blood fell onto the dueling cloak. You may call off the duel without losing your honor."

"My honor is not the issue here," Brander said. "What about Kelda's fate?"

"She will once again be Asgaut's betrothed."

Brander took the cloth Eirik handed him and wiped the blood from his arm. "I will fight to the death before I let Asgaut have her."

"So be it." Canby once again removed himself from the square to shout, "Let the fighting commence once more."

"You are doing well?" Eirik asked.

Brander nodded.

Eirik handed his father the third shield and raced to safety. "This one has the greatest magic, sire," he shouted, "because it unites the family of the Falcon."

"Aye," Brander replied.

Kelda wondered at Brander's thoughts, but her curiosity was quickly brushed aside. He barely had the shield on his arm when Asgaut advanced, his sword swinging to hit hard the right side of the shield, then the left. Right and left. Again and again. Brander reeled from the fast assault before he landed a blow that sent Asgaut backward.

He fell on his back, his legs swinging through the air, his shield breaking. Before Brander could strike him again, the *Jomsviking* rolled over, threw the metal shield-brace from his arm, and took

417

stance for battle.

While Asgaut received his second shield, Kelda watched Brander's chest heave as he dragged air into his lungs. He wiped perspiration from his forehead with the back of his hand. Yet he never took his eyes off Asgaut.

"Odin, god of warriors," Kelda prayed, "protect him."

Thoruald, standing next to her, lay a comforting hand on her shoulder. "Do not worry, Daughter," he said. "Brander will outwit the fool."

"Perhaps," Canby mused, "but I do not think so, sire. Asgaut is far the stronger."

Thoruald laughed softly. "Canby, my friend, have you been with me so long and yet have not learned that the winner is not always the strongest but the smartest? You cannot deny that Brander is the smarter of the two."

On the other side of the fighting square, Kelda saw Brunhild, her face twisted into an ugly smile. When her gaze strayed from Brander, it shifted to Kelda or to Lind, who stood next to Wild Flower. The gaze was so malicious that Kelda dropped her eyes and shivered.

After an hour passed, Brander and Asgaut were slowing down. Their blows were not as heavy, as quick, or as clearly defined. Both had sustained numerous cuts and bruises, and the dueling cloak was heavily stained with blood. Yet neither man would quit. Each determined to have an outright win. Each determined to have Kelda.

She feared the battle would be one to the death.

Asgaut moved forward, Brander stepped backwards. The *Jomsviking* raised his sword and brought it down with all his strength. The blow jarred Brander's wounded arm to send excruciating pain through his body. Thoruald's shield rent in two, the smashing of the wood echoing loudly for all to hear as the piece fell to the bear skin.

His left side numb, Brander fought to keep from losing consciousness. He drew in deep breaths and kept moving backwards, sideways, always away from the pounding blows of Asgaut's sword. In the fray of repeated impacts, the flat side of Asgaut's sword walloped Brander's other arm, hitting him fully on the open, bleeding wound. Again agonizing pain paralyzed Brander. Retribution spun through the air, landing outside the square of stones.

A cry of disappointment went up from those who wanted Brander to win. His third shield, and his sword were gone. He would have to fight the *Jomsviking* without any means of defense other than his wits and resourcefulness.

Asgaut shouted his victory. His sword poised for the kill, purpose etched in the lines of his face and the gleam of his eye, Asgaut slowly advanced toward Brander.

The pain having subsided somewhat, Brander closed his hand around one of the stakes that held the bear skin in place. He rolled over on his side, tugged the metal rod, grunted and tugged again, finally dislodging it from the ground.

"Think you can win now, Skrelling?" Brunhild taunted. "A small stake against a sword? A barbarian against a *Jomsviking?*"

Kelda's heart pounded within her chest, and her breathing was shallow and painful. The stake looked so small and ineffective against Asgaut's sword.

Standing, the sharpened metal in one hand, Brander lowered his arm, so that the useless shield-brace dropped to the dueling skin. Asgaut slowly circled him.

419

"The battle belongs to me, Skrelling," he jeered. "Now you will taste shame."

"Perhaps you have served the meal," Brander replied, "but I have not yet eaten, Viking, and I shall not."

"I thought I would only wound you," Asgaut reflected, still moving in the slow circle, "but as I pondered I realized that you would always be my enemy, Skrelling. And as long as you are alive, Kelda would have soft feelings for you. I cannot allow that."

"Kill him, Asgaut," Brunhild shouted. "Stop talking your nonsense."

If the *Jomsviking* heard his wife, he gave no indication. "If I let you live, it is true I could always take you before the Herred-thing and have you declared an outlaw. Then anyone would have the right to kill you, but I want the pleasure myself."

Asgaut stopped his circling and advanced. He laughed and let his shield slide down fractionally. But enough. Brander had been waiting for this moment. The chieftain drew back his arm and threw the stake, the metal twinging through the air as it headed for Asgaut's shoulder.

Clean like a knife, the rod pierced the *Jomsviking's* flesh, drawing a pained shout from the man as blood spewed over the shield onto the dueling cloak. Asgaut's face registered surprise. The shield slid to the ground and Asgaut stood staring at the wound. He slowly raised his head to look disbelievingly at Brander. He dropped his sword, collapsed to his knees, and pressed a hand against his injury.

His face white, blood oozing between his fingers, he could only stare at Brander.

"He is dying!" someone shouted. "The Skrelling has killed him."

420

"Get off your knees, coward," Brunhild shouted to Asgaut, "and fight to the death."

Asgaut caught the head of the stake and pulled on it, but he could not dislodge it. His face twisted in pain as he tugged a second time.

"Kill the Skrelling!" Brunhild shouted again.

"This cannot be," Canby muttered. "Asgaut is a *Jomsviking.*"

"He is a defeated and shamed one," Thoruald said.

"Will he die?" Kelda murmured.

"Nay," Wild Flower answered. " 'tis not a mortal wound. Brander knows how to maim and to kill. Had he not wanted the *Jomsviking* alive, he would be dead."

No one moved. They stared in disbelief at Asgaut, at Brander.

"Move onto the cloak," Thoruald ordered Canby. "See what Asgaut will do now."

Canby nodded and slowly, as if in a daze, walked to the center of the bear skin. Blood from Asgaut's wound splattered on his trousers and shoes.

"Fighting must commence," Canby said, "or the duel goes to the—the jarl's son."

One hand over his wound, Asgaut reached for his sword. He grimaced, breathed in deeply, then groaned. He fell onto the cloak and cried in a pain-laden voice, "I give, lawreader."

Canby stared at the *Jomsviking* for a long while before he said, "The jarl's son is the champion."

"Get me a healer," Asgaut begged, "before all the blood drains from my body."

Brander held his sword high in the air. "You relinquish your claim to Kelda, Viking?"

"Aye," Asgaut said, "I release her from our betrothal."

"You also make her a gift of her bride-price?"

"Nay," Brunhild shouted. "We can take her to the Herred-thing. She will owe us for the ship. She had no right to allow Hauk to be buried in it."

"Quiet, you fool," Canby replied.

"Aye," Asgaut said, "I made a gift of the dragon-ship to Kelda. She owes me no payment for it. You are the champion."

"Aye, I am." Brander opened his mouth to say more, but shouts, clapping, and whistling drowned him out. He held his hands up for silence. He looked at Kelda. "I, Brander, ask Kelda to be my bride."

"Aye, lord," Kelda answered, unmindful that tears of happiness streaked her cheeks.

"With my lady's permission I announce that we will be wed at the celebration of the Winter Sacrifice."

"Aye, my love," she answered.

Thunderous applause and shouting greeted Brander's announcement. Again he waved his hands for silence.

"One more matter is to be settled. I have fought Asgaut's challenge and won. Now I challenge Asgaut."

The crowd seemed to gasp as one.

"I avenge the death of my family at the hands of this man." The Vikings listened quietly as Brander told them the story of Asgaut's raid on his village and of the subsequent massacre and the deaths of his family.

"After he is healed," Brander announced, "I will fight him to the death."

By the time he stepped off the bear skin, Kelda threw herself against him, uncaring that her clothes would be bloody. Not turning loose of his sword, he

422

held her in one arm.

"I love you, my lord," she murmured over and over.

"And I you," he answered.

"I feared for your life," she cried.

Brander smiled tenderly. "When are you going to learn to believe me, Viking?"

She gave him a puzzled look.

"I told you long ago that I was the best."

"Aye, lord—" she smiled with him "—you did, and you are."

In the commotion that followed, Asgaut was carried from the dueling cloak and Thoruald invited all to the Great Hall for a celebration banquet at the going down of the sun.

"You are truly a great warrior," Wray said, pushing his way to Brander. "One day, sire, I shall be as good as you are."

"Aye," Brander said and smiled wearily at his protégé.

"I will, too, sire," Eirik said.

"That you will," Brander answered.

"When you inherit the Talon of the Falcon, will you give me Retribution?"

Brander looked at the sword, the bronze, silver, and gold inlay glinting in the sunlight, then at his son. "When I am finished with it, you may have it," he answered.

"Sire!" Ulmer shouted. The *skald*'s face wreathed in a smile, he shoved his way to Brander. "I shall be the most sought after *skald* in all of Norwegia. Our steading has a new hero, and soon I shall be singing a new song about his exploits in the Great Hall."

"I hardly think I am a hero, Ulmer," Brander said dryly.

423

Ulmer's eyes twinkled. "You will be, sire, by the time my tale is told. No *skald* in the steading will have the fame that I shall have. Tonight Egil, Asgaut's *skald*, will be hanging his head and weeping in his beer, lord, because his master made such a poor showing. Egil will have to listen to my tale with great envy."

"Aye." Brander laughed and lightly clapped Ulmer on the shoulder. "Now, *skald*, my lady and I would like to be on our way to the *stofa*."

"Mayhap for the mistress to have a fitting for her bridal gown?"

"Mayhap for me to take a bath," Brander returned, joining in the laughter of his family—Wray included—and the *skald*.

His arm still around Kelda, Brander guided her through the throng of people toward Thoruald and Wild Flower. People pressed against him, slapping him on the back, smiling and congratulating him on his victory. He thanked them until finally he reached his parents.

"You fought well," Thoruald said. "Given time and more practice, you will improve."

Brander laughed quietly. "You think you could have done better?"

"I would not say better," Thoruald answered thoughtfully. "I can wield the sword more skillfully than you, but I do not have the dexterity and resilience you have. I noted that the day you walked the oars. You have an uncanny sense of balance that saved you more than once during the duel."

Father and son continued to look at one another with respect.

"Only you could have won against the *Jomsviking*," Thoruald finally admitted.

"Thank you, sire," Brander said, the smile still

424

curving his lips. He was beginning to understand this Viking chieftain, his father. He respected him as a warrior and a leader, and he was beginning to like him as a friend.

"I had no doubt that you would win," Thoruald added. "You are my son."

"Am I?" Brander asked softly, musingly.

"Aye, and when you can admit it, you will be at rest with yourself and the world."

Brander looked at his weapon hand. He tightened his fingers around the hilt and thought how right the sword felt to him. Of all weapons, this one was the one of choice for him.

But the sword was not an Iroquois weapon.

He raised his head to gaze again at his father. As if Thoruald understood Brander's thoughts, he nodded.

Finally he broke the silence to say, "Come. Let us go to the longhouse and celebrate yours and Kelda's engagement."

Chapter Thirty-four

"From the amount of blood that you lost," Wild Flower said as she bandaged the last of Brander's cuts, "I am grateful your wounds are no worse than they are. They should heal quickly."

"Thank you, my mother," Brander said. He scooted off the stool on which he had been sitting in the lavatory while she doctored him and stood.

She looped the strap of her medicine pouch over her shoulder and moved to the door. "Lie down, my son, and rest for a while."

Brander nodded and hitched the bathing cloth around the middle of his body a little higher. He and his mother walked out of the lavatory. She went into Thoruald's chambers. Brander walked to his.

"Sire!" a young male voice called.

Brander saw a young man moving toward him.

"I would speak with you."

"What are you called?" Brander asked.

"Egil," the lad answered. "I am Asgaut's *skald*."

The young man whom Ulmer continually compared himself with, Brander thought. "What would you speak to me about?"

The *skald* turned his head from side to side, looking about. In a low voice, he said, "Please, may we have privacy?"

Puzzled by the boy's visit, Brander opened the door to his chamber and entered, moving directly to his clothes trunk.

h...
cloth...
made...

"Nay, ...
other one.

"You are s...

"In order to ...
the Viking raid ...
you have challenged ...
Egil said.

Slipping into his unde... nodded. "He is responsible for ...

"Nay, my lord."

Brander fastened his breeches a... ...is waist and
walked closer to Egil. "What are yo... saying to me,
skald?"

"Asgaut did not lead that raid, sire."

Brander stared at him.

"Asgaut and his Vikings sailed to Kaupang, sire,
for the purpose of meeting with another group of
Norsemen who had recently returned from a-viking.
They were selling their slaves in the market, and
the boy you call Eirik was among them. Wanting to
impress the people of Falconstead when he returned
and to make them think he had been a-viking also,
Asgaut bought the boy. He ordered me to listen to
the story of this Viking raider until I could recite it
word for word."

"You could be lying to me to protect your lord,"
Brander accused. He returned to the bed, lifted his
shirt, and slipped into it.

"I tell you the truth."

427

ran-

ng, and a good

...ry and also wondering if it
...ucked the shirt into his trousers.
...e meet with this Viking raider?"
...ow not, lord. I only know the night before
...gaut sailed, he and the mistress rode away from
the steading and met with someone. When they returned, it was late, but I was lying awake in my
chamber in the longhouse. I heard them talking
about the message they were to deliver. Being curious, I peeked through the slit in the curtains and
saw them hunched over the table studying a rune
stick in the torchlight."

"Where is this rune stick?"

"Asgaut gave it to the raider in Kaupang."

"A rune stick," Brander murmured. "What was
the message?" .

"I know not," the lad replied. "And I do not believe Asgaut and Brunhild did either, since neither
of them know the *futhark.*"

"They know not the Norwegian alphabet," Brander mused.

"Aye, lord."

"Why are you telling me this?" Brander asked.

Egil lowered his head and gazed at the toes of his
shoes.

"Speak, *skald.* That is why you came to see me,"
Brander commanded.

"My lord has a great fever, sire, and in his delir-
ium he is muttering things about Brunhild. He believes she is going to kill him. Because of what he
has done, he is afraid the lawreader will find out
and take him before the Herred-thing."

428

"What would you have me do?" Brander asked.

"Place Asgaut under the jarl's protective custody, sire, and I will take you to Kaupang where you can find the man who led the raid on your village. I will know him again, sire, if I see him, and if he has sold slaves there before, he will do it again."

"You could be lying to me," Brander accused the boy a second time, "and putting me off to gain time for Asgaut. If he was deceitful in the raid on my village, he would be deceitful in other matters."

"I am not lying," Egil insisted.

Brander believed the boy, but much about the story troubled him. If the story was true, his fight with Asgaut was over. His only interest was in finding the man who wreaked havoc on his village and his family.

"You would recognize this raider if you were to see him again?"

Egil nodded his head. "He had a long scar running across his forehead and the bridge of his nose, sire. He was a fearful-looking man."

"What message did he send back with Asgaut?" Brander asked.

"I know not, sire. We barely returned before Falconstead was hit upon by pirates."

"Did you recognize any of these raiders to be the Vikings whom your master met with in Kaupang?"

"Nay," Egil replied.

"Return to the longhouse," Brander said. "I will speak to the jarl about all you have said."

After the *skald* left, Brander slowly finished his dressing, then walked into the *stofa* to join Thoruald and Canby. During the time that he related Egil's story to the men, Kelda and Wild Flower joined them.

"If this indeed is the truth," Canby said, "Asgaut

429

is correct in assuming I would take the matter to the Herred-thing. But I do not know if I trust the *skald's* story."

Speaking to his father, Brander said, "It would do no harm, sire, to place Asgaut under protective custody and let me sail to Kaupang with Egil."

Contemplating, Thoruald said nothing.

"If Asgaut's life is in danger, this would save him," Brander pushed. "If it is not, we have lost nothing."

"Aye," Thoruald murmured.

"Does this mean that Brander is going to journey to Kaupang?" Kelda asked.

Thoruald smiled. "I have the feeling, Daughter, that he will go whether I give him permission or not."

"Are we, Brander?" she asked.

Brander hiked a brow. "We?"

"I would go with you," she said. "I want to do some bartering in the city."

"I would not think of going without you," he answered. "What think you of taking Eirik with us?"

"He would enjoy that." Kissing him, Kelda said, "I must be back to my work, lord. I have much preparation to do tonight for the celebration of your victory."

"And the formal announcement of our engagement?"

"Aye," she answered.

Asa opened the bower door and walked into the Great Hall, yards of red velvet draped over a bent arm. "If I am to have these dresses sewn by the Winter Sacrifice," she said to Kelda, "you and Mistress Wild Flower are going to have to come in for a fitting."

Brander touched the material. "Such a vibrant color," he murmured.

430

"Aye, the color of the bride."

"A magical color," Brander replied, remembering the discussion they had the night Kelda had painted his face.

"Aye," she murmured, "indeed a magical color, my lord."

Chapter Thirty-five

A garbled and disrupted note sounded on the beacon horn, startling the occupants of the Great Hall. They looked at one another in puzzlement. Again it sounded, this time dying a horrible discordant death.

On his feet, Thoruald shouted to Kelda, "Take the women to a place of safety." He ran to the entrance of the Great Hall.

Brander, Retribution in hand, rushed out of the longhouse beside his father. Wray and Eirik, each of whom had a weapon, followed. They ran to the quay to find pirates pouring out of two raiding ships and pressing their way up the dock and pathway to the steading.

"The ones who attacked us before," Thoruald shouted. "I recognize the pennant. Fight, Vikings."

Brander, as if he were accustomed to fighting with his father, accustomed to taking orders from him, fell into battle formation with the other warriors. Thoruald was always in the lead, barking the orders. Brander fought at his side. Warriors now, Wray and Eirik also battled alongside the jarl and his son.

Again the steading heard the sounds of war. Swords, battle-axes, and spears glinted in the sunlight, their beauty and craftsmanship belying their deadly purpose. Metal-tipped arrows flew from the bows of the defenders as well as the attackers.

During the heat of the battle, Brander saw several of the pirates sneak through their lines up the path toward the *stofa*. His thoughts immediately went to Kelda.

If Egil had told the truth, he lost his wife and family to these raiders. He would not lose another.

His gaze collided with his father's at that moment, and Thoruald nodded. At a lope Brander headed for the longhouse, Eirik at his heels.

"Did you see them, sire?" the boy called.

"Aye," Brander answered.

Brander and Eirik entered the *stofa* through the fireroom. Placing his palm against the door, he said, "Stay by my side and await my orders."

The lad nodded.

Brander entered the far end of the Great Hall cautiously, Eirik following. Hugging the wall, they stayed in the shadows. For the moment they were safe, because the attackers were concentrating on other matters and had their backs to the fireroom.

"Kill them?" a strange male voice exclaimed. "Both of them are beautiful women who will bring a good price if we sell them as slaves in Kaupang or Hedeby."

"I want them dead," Brunhild's voice echoed through the building.

"Brunhild," Eirik whispered. "She is responsible for this, sire?"

Brander shrugged and laid a finger to his mouth for silence. Wild Flower was tied and gagged and being guarded by one of the assailants. A second stood close to Brunhild, and a third held Kelda.

Brander ached for his bow and arrow. If he had it, he could easily, silently disarm one or more of the men before they discovered his presence. He could cause a diversion that would possibly allow

433

Kelda to escape before they bound her. All he had was the weapon of the Vikings, and he must use it to his best advantage.

He had to rely on intelligence along with his skill.

Brunhild, a long stiletto in her hand, sauntered to where Kelda stood. The Viking woman slid the blade down the side of her throat.

"Thoruald made a mistake when he adopted you rather than me," she said. "We planned to kill Ragnar, but we did not plan on Thoruald's adopting you. I was by far the better, certainly the wiser, choice. I shall still rule the House of the Falcon."

"You are going to have to kill us all," Kelda said. She grunted when the man caught a handful of her hair and jerked her head back.

Brunhild laughed. "I intend to, Kelda. That is why *my warriors* are here. I had hoped that Asgaut would win the duel to save me this trouble and expense, but he proved a coward. On the pretense of going to give sacrifice to the gods, I sent word to my men to come."

"They were harbored close by," Kelda said.

Brunhild nodded and slid the tip of the blade so that it rested against the artery in Kelda's throat. Brander winced. One false move and Kelda was dead.

Brunhild spoke again. "I knew this would be the best time to attack, when the men and women were reveling in the aftermath of the duel. They would have lowered their guard somewhat."

"These men obey your orders?"

From the shadows came a male voice. "Not exactly."

"Canby!" Kelda exclaimed.

Intent on the scene in the *stofa*, Brander had not

been aware of the entrance door opening and had been caught off guard by the lawreader's entry.

"I am truly sorry this had to happen, Kelda," the lawreader apologized and materialized. "But you and Thoruald were determined to find the blood heir and bring him back to Norwegia. I tried to dissuade you, but could not."

"I knew you hated Brander," Kelda said, "but I cannot imagine your being part of this, Canby. You are destroying your own steading."

"Not mine, and no longer Thoruald's," Canby hissed. "It belongs to the Skrellings now."

"Aye." Brunhild stepped away from Kelda and returned the stiletto to the sheath at her waist. "Asgaut made sure of that today when he fell. The stupid oaf. But I took care of him. I offered him as sacrifice to the gods."

"You killed Asgaut?" Kelda asked.

Brunhild nodded her head. "Aye. When he returned to the longhouse, he became delirious with the fever and started talking to any who would listen. Although his tale was garbled, one could figure it out if they thought about it. He confessed that Canby and I were the ones who planned the death of Ragnar."

"Brander knows much of the truth," Kelda said. "Egil told him."

A vicious smile possessed Brunhild's lips. "Aye, that *skald* has told his last tale."

"You—you killed him also?"

"Aye. I could not afford for him to identify the men who had raided the village."

"Brunhild and I were afraid that if Brander found these men, he would persuade them to talk and that they would point a finger of blame at us," Canby said. "You see, dear Kelda, men like this offer their

435

loyalty to the highest bidder."

Brunhild let a peal of laughter. "It was time for Asgaut to die. He was no longer effective and was only in the way. In order to rule the House of the Falcon, I needed someone who had the same vision as I for Falconstead."

"Aye," Canby said, slipping his arm around Brunhild's waist and drawing her close to him. "Brunhild and I have always seen matters in much the same light, but until today we did not realize how much so."

Canby and Brunhild! Brander stared disbelievingly at the couple, so oddly paired.

"Why?" Kelda demanded. "Why are you doing this?"

"I really had not bargained for or intended this," Canby said. "I wanted only to kill Ragnar to make sure Asgaut became the jarl with Brunhild at his side."

"You were Thoruald's old friend?"

"Aye," Canby murmured. "That is why I cannot let him lead us to destruction. Falconstead needs a wise man like me to lead it."

"And a woman like me to give you sons," Brunhild added.

"Aye. When all of this destruction is over, we will find your mutilated bodies. All of you will receive a royal burial aboard the *Falcon*'s *Wing*, more spendid than the one you gave to Hauk, and all of Falconstead will mourn. Brunhild and I will rally the people together, and continue with the House of the Falcon."

"You and Brunhild," Kelda said. "Neither of you ever—"

"Nay," Canby said, "necessity drove us together. We need each other."

436

Canby smiled; Brunhild laughed.

"I shall be the leader," she said. "The Talon of the Falcon shall be mine." As the lawreader talked, he sat down in the high seat. "I shall rule from the same chair as Thoruald. Brunhild, go to my longhouse and get the treasure box. We are going to need to pay these Vikings for their day's work."

"Aye, lord." She scurried out of the *stofa*.

Canby waved to the men. "Bind Kelda, then kill her and the Skrelling."

Drawing Eirik close to him, Brander whispered, "While I divert the men's attention, untie your grandmother."

Eirik nodded. With a battle cry, his sword postured for battle, Brander raced deep into the Great Hall.

"The Skrelling," Canby shouted. "Kill him."

The two men who were tying Kelda dropped the ropes and whipped their swords from the scabbards. The man guarding Wild Flower shoved her to the floor to join his friends. The clash of steel resounded throughout the building as Brander attacked the three assailants.

Eirik crept closer to the women. However, before he reached either of them, Canby grabbed Kelda.

"I warn you, Canby," Brander shouted, his attention divided between his battle and the welfare of the women. "Do not harm Kelda."

Twisting one of her arms behind her, Canby held her in front of himself as a human shield. He slowly backed up until he stood beside Wild Flower.

Brander saw what was happening, but blocked by the three men, he could not reach Canby. Renewing his strength, he fought harder and swifter, eventually piercing one of his attackers through the heart. Now he faced two.

437

"Loose Kelda." Brander waved his sword in the air. "She is not a part of this, lawreader."

Sweat pouring down his face, Canby pulled the knife from his waist and held it to Kelda's throat.

"I am the one giving orders," he shouted. "Surrender or I shall kill her!"

Canby pressed the blade into Kelda's flesh, and she gasped for breath. Giving a bloodcurdling Iroquois battle call, Eirik charged out of the shadows and grabbed the hilt of Retribution with both hands.

"The despised Vikings killed my mother," he shouted in Iroquois, charging toward the lawreader, "but you will not kill Kelda. I will stop you this time."

Startled and frightened, Canby released his clasp on Kelda, and she twisted free, falling down and rolling away from him. In the commotion, Canby lost his knife. He looked about wildly, then ran to the wall to jerk loose a battle-ax. He swung it over his head, ready to split Eirik's skull.

Pushing to her feet, Kelda leaped on Canby's back, her nails scratching his face. Cursing, he stumbled and blindly slashed the ax through the air with one arm and tore at her with the other.

Brander saw Eirik and Kelda struggling with Canby, but he could not reach them. He had slain the second man. Yet the third—the better and stronger swordsman—had disarmed and cornered him. Again he felt fear tearing at his heart at the thought of his second family being destroyed by the same men who had killed his first. New strength pouring through his body, new courage, Brander grabbed a spear from the wall, using it to fend off the vicious attack of the man as he backed toward Thoruald's room.

438

"Brander!" Kelda screamed.

"Hold him off, love," Brander shouted. "I will save you."

"You are not going to save them." The man sneered and slowly moved forward, circling his sword menacingly in the air. "I am going to kill you now."

Brander caught the wrought-iron handle and pushed open the door. He rushed into Thoruald's chamber to the far wall and reached for the Talon of the Falcon. When his hand closed about the hilt, he could have sworn an electrical current bolted through his body.

He turned, his stance that of the victor. Two, three, four clashes of metal, and the outlaw lay on the floor in a pool of blood. Brander leaped over the prone body, and raced into the *stofa*. Kelda lay limply on the floor.

She could not be dead!

Canby, holding a battle-ax above his head with both hands, had Eirik cornered.

"Leave him alone, Canby," Brander shouted. "I am the one you want. Settle with me."

Fearfully Canby's gaze darted to Brander as he walked slowly toward him, the Talon of the Falcon in hand. The lawreader's eyes, a hysterical glaze to them, opened wider.

"That is my sword," Canby shouted and turned from Eirik.

"Nay," Brander taunted. " 'Tis mine. I am the next Falcon of the House of the Falcon."

"No," Canby shouted, his eyes focusing on the sword. "No, you cannot have it. The sword is mine. The lineage of the Falcon belongs to me."

His rounded eyes darkened, and he rushed at Brander, tripping on the high seat and falling. Off

439

balance, his slight weight and puny strength could not sustain the weight of the battle-ax. He dropped and fell on top of it, the blade turning to pierce into his stomach.

He cried out in pain, gasped and clawed at his stomach. His fingers curled around the leg of the high seat and he dragged himself across the floor, leaving a trail of blood. His face twisted in death pains, he caught the supporting beam for the seat and pulled himself up.

"Mine." His voice was a ragged whisper.

His hand fell to the floor. His body convulsed, then he lay quietly in his own blood.

"See to your grandmother," Brander ordered Eirik, and he went on his knees beside Kelda.

A quick examination assured him that she was only winded. As he caught her into his arms, she moaned and opened her eyes.

"Eirik?" she whispered.

"He is fine," Brander answered.

"He saved me," she said.

"Aye, he is indeed a warrior."

The entrance door opened, and Thoruald and Wray entered.

"Wild Flower?" Thoruald shouted, quickly moving toward the high seat.

"I am fine, my lord," she answered, rubbing her arms where the cords had dug into her flesh. "Your son and grandson have rescued me."

Thoruald stopped when he reached Canby's body.

"My friend," he murmured. "Dying to save you?"

"Nay, lord, your enemy," Brander said. "The man responsible for the death of your son."

"For the death of my younger son," Thoruald corrected, his gaze swinging to the sword Brander held.

440

"Brunhild," Kelda said. "She went after Canby's treasure box."

"We caught her, mistress," Wray said. "When she saw us, she killed herself with her stiletto. Asgaut and Egil are also dead."

"The other raiders, lord," Wild Flower asked, "where are they?"

"We have them locked in a storage shed," Thoruald answered, "and they shall be held there until we have a trial before the Herred-thing."

He sat down in the nearest chair and pulled his wife onto his lap. "I am saddened about this," he said. "But perhaps the evil that has cast its shadow over the steading is now gone."

"Aye, lord," Brander replied, only now remembering that Eirik had spoken in Iroquois when he attacked Canby. He looked over at his son. "Eirik," he said softly.

"My father!" The boy threw himself against his father and hugged him.

Tears coursing down his face, Brander dropped the sword to embrace his son and to hold him tightly. At the moment he was the boy, his son, not the warrior, not the future jarl.

"I thought perhaps you would never remember me."

"I—I was unable to save my mother and my sisters," the lad cried. "The Vikings were so large and fearful, my father. They swung their swords and battle-axes, slashing skulls and almost halving bodies. Now that my memory has returned, my father, I shall seek to avenge my family's death."

"Nay, Eirik," Brander said. "It is over now. We will leave vengeance to the gods. This day you have proved yourself a brave warrior, and you are needed to lead the people of the steading, even of Norwe-

441

gia, in the paths of peace."

Brander pushed back and took off the gold collar and arm band.

"These rightfully belong to you," he said, slipping them onto Eirik. "My father left them for me. Now I give them to you."

"What about you, my father?" the boy asked.

Brander's eyes flickered over the sword lying on the floor before he gave his father a long, measured look. "I have Talon of the Falcon now," he answered.

Eirik's eyes rounded in pleased surprise. "We are going to stay here, Father!"

"Aye," Brander stood and reached for Kelda, bringing her into the circle of his family. He smiled. "What think you, Eirik-Kolby, of two Iroquois chieftains becoming Viking chieftains?"

"I would like that, my father." He bent to pick up Sword of the Talon. "Does this mean that Retribution becomes my sword now?"

Brander nodded. "Retribution is yours, my son. You have handled it with skill and wisdom."

Eirik handed Sword of the Talon to his father and reached for Retribution. At that moment Wray swaggered to where Brander and Eirik stood.

"Lord," Wray said, "if Eirik is to someday become a Viking chieftain, 'tis time for him to be about his lessons."

"Aye," Brander replied, proud of his charge.

"He did indeed show skill today, but the way he handled his sword leaves much to be desired."

"Aye," Brander nodded, biting back his smile and thinking how much like Hauk Wray sounded. "You will see to his education."

Wray nodded. His arm about Eirik's shoulder, he led him out of the longhouse.

"Now, Brander, what will you be doing until banquet time?" Thoruald asked.

Brander grinned down at Kelda, then looked at Thoruald. "My father, that was not a prudent question. But I think, my lady-love and I shall be doing the same as you and your lady-love."

Wild Flower slid out of Thoruald's lap and moved to her son. Tears sparkled in her ebony eyes. Reaching up, she tousled her son's hair. "You always were arrogant, my son. Now you have become saucy."

"But always truthful, my mother." He swung her around and lightly kissed her forehead when he set her down.

"Aye," she whispered, "always truthful."

"Now, I turn you over to the lord of the manor, and I hope he can control you better than I, my mother." Again Brander addressed his father, "My father, I fear you shall have your hands full with this woman."

Thoruald chuckled and embraced Wild Flower. "I hope so, my son. My hands—nay, my life has been empty far too long."

Brander turned to Kelda and asked softly, "My lady-love, shall we retire to our chamber?"

Her eyes glowing, she murmured, "Aye, my love."

Afterword

When I researched for *Autumn's Fury*, my first historical novel for Zebra, I was impressed with the sophisticated culture of the Algonquin and Iroquois Indians who dominated the northeastern seaboard of the United States. Later for *Satin Secret*, I expanded my research to include the Indians of North and South Carolina, Georgia, and Florida. Equally impressed with their advanced culture, I became intrigued with these first Americans.

I found many similarities between the American Indians and the Vikings. Many of the Algonquins and Iroquois lived in longhouses like the Vikings. The cities of all the American coastal Indians and the Vikings were similarly designed. Surrounded with a palisade, they were planned communities with marked streets; both had military academies, evidenced by those excavated in Denmark and those recorded by the Spanish when they explored South Carolina, Georgia, and Florida in the fifteenth and sixteenth centuries.

Herein was planted the tiny seed that became the basic premise of *Viking Captive*. What if the Vikings sailed southward beyond Newfoundland to the eastern coast of the United States? The more I studied, the more similarities I saw between the two cultures; the more fascinated I became with the idea of an American Indian/Viking hero. Could I create a believable hero? I could.

Now my task fell to finding the location of Brander's home, and a most significant task it proved to be. The answer determined which of the native Americans my hero would be — Algonquin, Iroquois, or Eskimo. I delegated this chore to the scholars who had already established the land sites reached by the Norsemen during their western exploration. These were the Baffin Island, Labrador, and L'Anse aux Meadows, Newfoundland.

While most scholars generally accept L'Anse aux Meadows as Vinland, all accept that it was a Norse encampment. I am one among those who argue that Vinland was even farther south. In the United States every state along the eastern coast has been argued as a site for Vinland with acumen and eloquence.

Yet, I thought, the Icelandic Sagas make mention of another visit to Vinland by the Norsemen in 1009. After a harsh winter, the Norsemen cruised "southward along the coast," looking for a better settlement, and it was "southward" of Vinland they found a most favorable location, which they named Hop, an old Norse name for a land-locked bay or estuary. Here for a second time they encountered Native Americans or Skrellings, as they called them.

According to the Icelandic sagas, the Skrellings made a third and fourth appearance the coming spring. During the last visit, they showered the Vikings with arrows and used a devastating weapon with which the Norse were totally unfamiliar — a ballista. According to historians, the Native Americans constructed this weapon by sewing up a large boulder in a fresh skin to which they attached a long handle. After being painted and hoisted, the ballista had the appearance of a solid globe upon a pole. Several warriors — ballisters — carried it. When

445

slung through the air, it made a frightful noise and on landing killed many.

I found it most interesting and significant that the Skrellings were using arrows. This points to their being Algonquin or Iroquois, since this weapon was unknown to other North American natives of this time. According to the Icelandic sagas, while exploring Vinland, Leif Ericsson's brother Thorvald was killed by an arrow. In 1930, an arrowhead was found in Sandnes, Greenland, that bore the same kind of arrowhead as the one that killed Thorvald. A similar arrowhead was found in the ancient Indian settlement by Northwest River at the extremity of Lake Melville in 1956. The Sandnes arrow is pure Algonquin Indian, made of quartzite identical with that found in Labrador.

Likewise the boats found by the Norsemen on this expedition were made of skin. When traveling, the natives turned them over and used them as shelter at night. We have ample evidence that American Indians on the move slept beneath upturned birch-bark canoes. I, like other scholars, believe these Indians were Iroquois, who at this time held most of the northeastern coast of Canada and the United States.

Many theories have been advanced regarding possible sites of Viking colonization in the United States, but they are based more on wishful thinking than on scientific research. Two sites in New England have characteristics that fit the site of Hop: A rock at Bass River on Cape Cod once bored to receive mooring pins; and Dighton Rock, found in the township of Berkley, Massachusetts, inscribed with mysterious symbols. Most scholars disregard both as a probability; still they remain a possibility.

In an early Indian site at Goddard Point near the

mouth of Penobscot Bay, Maine, a genuine Norwegian coin (the Maine Penny) of 1065-80 vintage was found in reputable circumstances and at an acceptable archaeological setting. Collective opinion considers that the coin passed through the hands of the Dorset Eskimos in northern Labrador to the Algonquin Indians of Maine. I like to believe the Norse left the coin themselves.

Intensive searches have been conducted to determine whether the Norse penetrated America's interior. They were able navigators who knew the winds, tides, and heavens. The Icelandic Sagas mention that Leif Ericsson recorded the sun's position, and the Norse used some kind of primitive astrolabe, forerunner of the sextant, to take sights on celestial bodies. To all of this was added the "sixth sense" that has been attributed to sailors from antiquity and that accounts in part for the Vikings' ability to get from place to place over the wild and uncharted Atlantic.

I believe they did sail into the interior of North America, into what is now the United States by using one or both of two direct sea routes to reach the Great Lakes region. One route is through the Hudson Bay and Sea down the Albany River to Lake Nipigon in Ontario, Canada. On the eastern shore of this lake is Beardmore, a site where legitimate Viking relics—a broken sword, an axehead, and an object that has been called a rattle—were unearthed. It's a straight shot from Lake Nipigon to Lake Superior and Minnesota.

The second route is down the St. Lawrence River directly through Lake Ontario, Lake Erie, Lake Huron, and Lake Superior. Again the sea traveler finds himself in Minnesota. If he chooses to explore the land, he is close to Kensington, the site where a rune stone was unearthed by a Minnesota farmer in 1898. This stone bears a runic inscription telling of a western journey of Vikings from Vinland in 1362. Most condemn it as a forgery; others defend it as genuine.

The whole story of the Viking voyages to America may never be known, but it is positive they came. Who's to say they did not travel into North America before 1000 A.D.? Even to the interior? After all, the Norse "discovered" Greenland almost one hundred years before they explored it.

Certainly it's within the realm of possibility that goldenhaired Kelda and her Viking warriors sailed into a New England harbor where she met a dark and brooding Iroquois chieftain who stole her heart and in return gave her his.